Keeper of the Light

DIANE CHAMBERLAIN

Keeper of the Light

MIRA®

Recycling programs
for this product may
not exist in your area.

ISBN-13: 978-0-7783-2954-1

KEEPER OF THE LIGHT

For questions and comments about the quality of this book please contact us
at Customer_eCare@Harlequin.ca.

www.MIRABooks.com

Printed in U.S.A.

First Printing: December 2002
10 9 8 7 6 5 4 3 2 1

Dear Reader,

I'm so pleased that *Keeper of the Light* is once again available for you to enjoy. Originally published in 1992, *Keeper* quickly became one of my most popular books—so popular that readers pleaded with me to write a sequel. I finally did so eleven years later, turning the story of the O'Neill family into a trilogy. The second book, *Kiss River,* will be reissued later this year, and *Her Mother's Shadow* next spring.

I took certain liberties with the geography of North Carolina's Outer Banks to make room for Kiss River and its lighthouse. Kiss River and the people who love it are purely works of fiction, but the unique and beautiful Outer Banks are very real and hold a special place in my heart. I hope they will in yours, as well.

Diane Chamberlain

CHAPTER ONE

Christmas 1990

It rained the entire day. It rained with such force that the shrubs next to the emergency room parking lot lay flat to the ground and the new roof sprang a leak. One of the nurses set a bucket on the floor of the waiting room to catch the water, and within an hour the rain had filled it to the brim.

Olivia Simon watched the downpour through the broad windows of her office. The rain sapped her concentration, and the journal on her desk was still open to the article she'd started hours before. There was something unnatural about this rain. It sucked the oxygen from the air and made it hard to breathe, and it pounded above her head like marbles falling on a sheet of tin. Just when she thought she could no longer tolerate the noise, it stopped. In the silence, Olivia watched the sky turn light and shiny, like the inside of an eggshell. Then suddenly, it was snowing.

She walked into the reception area, where Kathy Brash and Lynn Wilkes had been playing pinochle for the last abysmally quiet two hours.

"It's snowing," Olivia said.

They lifted their rained-dazed eyes to hers, then turned their heads toward the windows.

"Unreal." Lynn stood for a better look, her white coat scraping a few cards from the table.

"It's beginning to be an annual tradition on the Outer Banks," Kathy said. "Last Christmas we actually got snowed in."

Olivia looked at her watch. Five-thirty. She couldn't afford to get stuck here tonight.

Lynn took her seat again. "Want us to deal you in, Olivia?"

Olivia declined, and returned to her office. She couldn't make herself join them tonight. She was too antsy, too preoccupied. She needed to get home.

She sat behind her desk and dialed her home number.

"It's snowing," she said when Paul answered.

"Yeah, I know." He sounded irritated. She was getting accustomed to the curt tone he used with her these days. "When are you getting out of there?"

"Soon. Just a half hour more." She'd had no choice but to work today. Of the four emergency room physicians, she had the least seniority. She wished she could tell Paul that it had been worth her while coming in today, worth their being apart when, God knows, they needed the time together. But all she had seen in eleven long hours was a scraped knee and a case of severe post-turkey indigestion. On days like this, she found herself missing the chaos of Washington General, where she'd worked for the past ten years, where her seniority had given her some control over her schedule. It scared her these days, being away from Paul. When she wasn't close enough to touch him, she was afraid he might disappear.

They'd spent last Christmas with his family in Philadelphia.

Paul had written a poem about her and stitched it into a sampler sometime during the long hours she was at work and he was not. The sampler hung in the study, and now each time she looked at it she wondered how the warmth Paul had felt for her one short year ago could have disintegrated so quickly.

"Turkey's falling off the bone," he said now. "Should I take it out?"

Olivia started to answer, but just then the police radio in the hall outside her office coughed to life.

"Hold on, Paul." She held the receiver away from her ear and listened as Kathy sat down in front of the radio.

"Kill Devil Hills Emergency Room," Kathy said.

"We've got a gunshot wound to the chest." A male voice broke through the static. "Female. Mid to late thirties. Pulse one-fifty and thready. B.P. seventy-five over forty."

"What's your ETA?" Kathy asked.

"Fifteen minutes. Maybe twenty. It's fucking snowing out here."

Olivia stood up. "Paul, I've got to go." She hung up the phone and raced to the treatment room. "Call Jonathan," she said as she passed Kathy. Jonathan Cramer was not Olivia's favorite physician to work with, but he was the back-up physician tonight and he lived closest. He could be here in seconds.

She was soaping her hands and wrists at the treatment room sink when Jonathan arrived. "Gunshot, huh?" he said as he rolled his shirtsleeves over his beefy forearms. "We'll stabilize her and fly her up to Emerson."

Olivia turned on the EKG monitor. "We haven't even seen her yet."

"She's going to need a trauma unit."

Olivia began setting up the intubation tray. Jonathan had

last worked in a sleepy Louisiana hospital. Gunshot wounds were probably not his area of greatest confidence. He had been here a little over a year, the first physician hired by the new free-standing emergency room, the only emergency facility serving North Carolina's Outer Banks. She'd been told she'd be on an equal plane with him, with equal say in all decisions made. Yet she often wondered if someone had neglected to pass that information on to Jonathan.

"Let's see her first," she said.

They had the treatment room ready by the time the two paramedics wheeled the woman into the ER. Her shirt and bra had been cut off. The bullet hole in her left breast was deceptively small and bloodless. That could mean only one thing—the bullet had penetrated the heart. Olivia felt a rush of adrenaline. Surgery was the only possible course of action and they had no time to waste.

"Get the surgical tray," she said to Kathy.

"What?" Jonathan was helping one of the paramedics fit the inflatable MAST trousers on the woman's legs. "Forget it, Olivia. Let's get her out of here and up to Emerson."

"Get me two units of O-negative packed cells," she said to Lynn as she checked the woman's vital signs. It would take the helicopter forty minutes to fly her to Emerson, probably longer in the snow, and at least another fifteen minutes before she could get into surgery.

"She won't make it," she said.

Kathy produced the surgical tray. The instruments rattled against one another in her trembling hands. She had pinned her dark hair up, and Olivia wished she'd thought to do the same. Her fine brown hair was a little longer than chin-length, and each time she lowered her head it slipped forward, like blinders.

"You can't be serious," Jonathan said. "We're not set up for anything like this."

"Fifty over thirty," Lynn said. "I can't get a radial pulse."

"Hang normal saline wide open. And do a cutdown, please, Jonathan," Olivia said. This woman needed blood fast.

"Olivia, this isn't the goddamned District of Columbia. She needs a trauma unit."

"Start a bicarb bolus," she said to Lynn. "And epinephrine. And get that blood hung." Then she turned to Jonathan. "Look. We can ship her up to Emerson and you and I both know she'll die on the way. Working on her here might not be ideal, but it's the only chance she has." She turned back to the table and did the cut-down herself, slipping the scalpel into the blue vein in the woman's groin. She picked up the large bore needle.

"I can do it." Kathy took the needle from her and fit it into the vein. Her hands no longer trembled and Olivia admired her for getting her fear under control so quickly.

Jonathan glowered at her. "I won't be a part of this. I'm calling the helicopter." He turned on his heel and walked out of the room.

Olivia stared after him, dumbfounded. "I don't believe it." She turned to one of the paramedics. "Call Dr. Shelley," she said. "Tell him to get over here stat." She began swabbing Betadine on the woman's chest and side. Then she slipped her hands into the sterile gloves Lynn held out to her.

"Maybe we *should* send her up," Lynn said quietly. Perspiration glowed on her forehead.

"We're going to do our best for her, Lynn." Olivia picked up a second scalpel from the tray and noticed the tremor in her own hand. She was suddenly aware of being the only physician in the room. *Steady, come on, steady.* She set the scalpel between the woman's ribs and felt all her concentration flow into the task ahead of her. She bore down. No blood at all. She cut deeper, through the layers of muscle, until she reached the heart cavity. Blood suddenly gushed from the wound she'd created. It poured down the front of her scrubs and onto the floor, and the paramedic standing nearest her let out a moan.

"No BP," Lynn said. "And no pulse."

Olivia looked up at the flat green line on the monitor behind the patient's head. She felt a film of sweat break out across her own forehead. They were losing her. She had to widen the incision. She looked at the tray of instruments. "No rib spreader?"

Kathy shook her head.

Of course they had no rib spreader. Olivia set the scalpel again and forced it through the woman's fifth rib. Once the wound was wide enough, she slipped her hand inside. She cautiously curved her fingers around the woman's heart, then slid her thumb over the surface, hunting for the bullet hole. She found it quickly—a little dimple in the heart's smooth surface—and held her thumb over it to block the flow of blood. Then she found the exit wound in the back of the heart. She covered it with her middle finger and felt the heart contract in her palm. She looked at the monitor as a cheer went up in the room.

"We've got a pulse!" Kathy said.

Olivia smiled and let out her breath. There was little they could do now except wait for Mike Shelley, the director of the ER, to get over here. She wasn't sure how long she could hold her position. It was painfully awkward. She was nearly crouching, her spine twisted to keep her hand in the right position on the heart. If she moved her fingers, the woman would die. It was that simple. The muscles in her thighs began to quiver, and her shoulder ached.

She could hear the helicopter making its approach, the familiar *thud* as it landed on the roof. She hoped they would need it, hoped they could repair the damage to this woman's heart and stabilize her well enough to make the trip.

For the first time she looked at the woman's face. Her skin was white and lightly freckled. She wore no makeup. Her hair was cherry-wood red, long and full. It fell over the edge of the table in a mass of corkscrew curls. She looked like an advertisement for Ivory soap.

"Who shot her?" She raised her eyes to the younger of the two paramedics, trying to get her mind off her own discomfort.

The paramedic's face was as white as the patient's, his brown eyes wide. "She was a volunteer at the Battered Women's Shelter in Manteo," he said. "Some guy came in, threatening his wife and kid, and this lady got in the way."

The Battered Women's Shelter. Olivia felt a spasm of pain in her own chest. She had to force herself to ask the next question. "Does anyone know her name?"

"Annie somebody," said the paramedic. "O'Brien. O'Something."

"O'Neill," Olivia whispered, so quietly none of them heard her. She let her eyes run over the body in front of her, over the creamy white, freckled breasts, the softly sloping waistline. She closed her eyes. Her shoulder burned; the tips of her fingers were numb. She was no longer certain they were in exactly the right place. She lifted her eyes back to the monitor. She would be able to tell by any change in the heartbeat if her fingers were slipping.

Had it only been a month since Paul had written that article for *Seascape Magazine?* She remembered the pictures of the stained glass in Annie Chase O'Neill's studio. The women in silk, the sleek blue heron, the sunset on the sound. Paul had changed after that story. *Everything* had changed.

Mike Shelley arrived and she saw in his dark eyes his shock at the scene. But he scrubbed quickly and was at her side in seconds. "Where's Jonathan?" he asked.

"He thought she should go up and I thought she should stay. So he left to call the helicopter and he hasn't come back."

Mike threaded the curved needle with his gloved hands. "Maybe she *should* have gone up." He spoke very quietly, very softly, his lips close to her ear. "This way her blood's on your hands."

Olivia's eyes stung. Had she made the wrong decision? No, this woman would never have survived the trip. Never.

Mike had to work around her fingers. If she moved just a fraction of an inch, the blood poured from the bullet holes. The pain in Olivia's shoulder became a steady fire and the shaking in her legs spread to the rest of her body. Still she held her position while Mike slipped a tiny piece of felt beneath her thumb and stitched it into place. But the exit hole was not so easy to close. It was large and nearly impossible to reach without damaging the heart in the process.

She watched the lines deepen in Mike's forehead as he struggled with the needle.

"Please, Mike," she whispered.

He finally shook his head. The felt refused to hold, and the blood seeped, then poured from the back of the heart. Olivia felt the heat of it on her fingers as the green line of the monitor shivered and flattened, and the room grew hushed with failure.

For a moment no one moved. No one spoke. Olivia could hear Mike's breathing, rapid and deep, keeping time with her own. She straightened up slowly, gritting her teeth against the pain in her back, and looked at Kathy. "Is any of her family here?"

Kathy nodded. "Yes, and we called Kevin in. He's with them in the little waiting room."

"I'll tell them," Mike said.

Olivia shook her head. "I should do it. I was with her from the start." She turned and started walking toward the door.

"Whoa." Mike caught her arm. "Better change first."

She looked down at her blood-soaked scrubs and felt a ripple of doubt. She was not thinking clearly.

She changed in the lounge and then walked to the small, private waiting room. Through the high window in the hallway she caught a glimpse of snowflakes dancing in the darkness. She wished she could step outside for a second. Her muscles still burned. And she hated what lay ahead of her. She hoped Kevin Rickert, the social worker, had prepared them for what she had to say.

Kevin looked relieved to see her. "This is Dr. Simon," he said.

There were three of them—a girl about thirteen who looked strikingly like the woman she had just left on the table, a boy a few years older. And a man. Annie's husband, Alec O'Neill. He was dark-haired, tall and thin, with an athletic tightness to his body. He wore jeans and a blue sweater, and he held his hand toward her, tentatively, his pale blue eyes asking her what his future held.

She shook his hand quickly. "Mr. O'Neill." She would make the words come out very slowly. "I'm so sorry. The bullet went straight through her heart. The damage was too extensive."

There was still hope in his eyes. It was always that way. Until you said it clearly, until you stopped mincing words, that hope would be there. The son understood, though. He looked like a younger version of his father—the same black hair, striking pale blue eyes beneath dark brows. He turned to face the wall, his shoulders heaving, although he made no sound.

"Do you understand what Dr. Simon is saying?" Kevin asked.

The man stared at her. "Are you saying Annie's dead?"

Olivia nodded. "I'm sorry. We worked on her for over an hour but there was..."

"No!" The girl threw herself at Olivia, knocking her into the wooden arm of one of the chairs. She flailed at her with closed fists, but Kevin wrapped his arms around her from behind before she could cause any real harm. "She can't be dead!" the girl screamed. "There wasn't any blood."

Alec O'Neill extracted the girl from Kevin's grip and pulled her into a hug. "Shh, Lacey."

Olivia regained her balance and set a hand on the girl's back. How did she know about the blood? "She was bleeding inside, honey," Olivia said.

The girl pushed Olivia's arm away. "Don't call me honey."

Alec O'Neill pulled Lacey closer to him and she began to weep against his chest. Olivia looked at Kevin. She felt helpless.

"I'll stay with them," Kevin said.

Olivia walked to the door but turned back to face the family once more. "If you have any questions, please call me."

Alec O'Neill looked across the room at her and Olivia stood fast, forcing herself to face the hurt in his eyes. She'd taken something from him. She needed to give him something back.

"She was very beautiful," she said.

Jonathan and the helicopter pilot were standing in the hallway, and she had to pass them to get to her office.

"Nice job," Jonathan said, his tone mocking.

She ignored him and walked into her office, where she cranked open her windows to let in the cold air. The snow was still falling, so silently that when she held her breath she could hear the thunder of the ocean two blocks away.

After a while, Kevin poked his head in her door. "You okay, Olivia?"

She turned away from the window, sat down behind her desk. "Yes. How's her family?"

Kevin stepped into the room. "Dad and the son went in to see her," he said as he sat down across the desk from her. "Daughter didn't want to. I think they'll be okay. Pretty solid family. Mom was the hub, though, you know, so it's hard to say." He shook his head. "Life sucks sometimes, doesn't it?"

"Yes."

"Looks like this one was pretty rough on you."

She felt a tear hit her cheek and Kevin plucked a tissue from the box on her desk and handed it to her.

"Cramer's an asshole," he said.

"I'm all right." She sat up straight, blew her nose. "So, do you ever have to comfort Jonathan or Mike? Hand them tissues?"

Kevin smiled. "You think women have exclusive rights on feeling like shit?"

She thought of Alec O'Neill's eyes when she'd left the waiting room. Those eyes were going to haunt her for a long time. "No, I guess not," she said. "Thanks for stopping in, Kevin."

It was after seven. Her shift was long over. She could leave now, anytime she wanted. She would drive to her house on the sound where she would have to tell Paul what had happened tonight, and for the second time that night she would watch a man crumble. What was it about Annie O'Neill?

Olivia looked down at her hand where it rested in her lap. She turned it palm side up and thought she could still feel it—the life, the warmth of Annie's heart.

CHAPTER TWO

Paul Macelli turned off the Christmas tree lights at seven forty-five and returned to the dining room table, where the turkey, the sweet potatoes, the green beans had grown cold. The gravy had formed a skin and he dabbed at it with his knife, watching the pale brown film coat the silver. He'd lit candles, poured wine. He was trying, wasn't he? But damn Olivia. She gave his anger justification at every turn. Her work was more important than her marriage. Even on Christmas she couldn't get out of the emergency room on time.

He looked up at the darkened tree. He probably wouldn't have bothered with one this year, but Olivia had bought it on her own a week earlier, a mountainous blue pine that she set up herself in front of the window facing Roanoke Sound. She decorated it with the ornaments they'd collected over the nine years of their marriage and strung it with tiny white lights. Last year he had dropped the crystal star they'd always put on top, and so, he thought nobly, it was up to him to find a replacement. He knew exactly what he wanted, had seen it weeks earlier in Annie's studio. He'd been excited by the prospect of having a legitimate reason to go back, a legitimate reason to see her and feel himself surrounded by her stained glass and photographs. But she hadn't been there on that particular morning, and he struggled to mask his disappointment as Tom Nestor, the ponytailed artist who shared her studio, wrapped the ornament in tissue paper for him.

"I feel bad charging you for this," Tom said. "Annie'd probably just give it to you."

Paul had smiled. "Annie would give everything away if she could," he said, and Tom smiled back, as though they shared a secret, as though they both had the privilege of knowing Annie's true nature.

He'd brought the ornament home and set it on top of the pine. It was a stylized stained glass angel in an oval frame with a light behind it. The angel's silver-white robe had that look of liquid silk that was Annie's trademark. How she was able to do that in glass he would never understand.

The first time Olivia saw the angel, her face paled and a look of utter defeat came into her eyes.

"Do you mind?" he'd asked her.

"Of course not," she said, with a truly admirable attempt at sincerity. "It's lovely."

He heard Olivia's car pull into the garage, directly below the dining room table. Paul felt the scowl grow on his face as the engine sputtered to a stop, and in a moment Olivia came in the front door, pulling her gray scarf from her neck. She glanced into the dining room and shook her head quickly, as if to rid her sleek brown hair of the clingy snowflakes.

"Hi," she said quietly. She took off her coat and hung it in the closet by the front door.

Paul slouched in his chair and let his scowl speak for him, not liking himself much at that moment.

"Why don't you have the lights on?" Olivia asked. She hit

the wall switch and Annie's angel sprang to life, the silvery robe seeming to swirl in the glass.

He didn't answer, and Olivia moved to the table and sat down across from him. Sylvie, their gray Persian cat, leaped softly to her lap. "I'm sorry to be so late," Olivia said, her white hands absently stroking Sylvie's back. "We had a terrible case come in."

"Everything's cold."

She glanced at the food, then back at him. Her eyes were beautiful. Green. Dark-lashed. A striking contrast to her white skin. "Paul," she said, "the case that came in—it was Annie O'Neill."

He drew himself up straight in the chair. *"What?"* he said. *"Why?"*

"She was working at the women's shelter in Manteo tonight and she got in the middle of some gunfire."

"Is she all right?"

Olivia shook her head. "I'm sorry, Paul. She died."

He stood up so quickly she jumped, and the silverware shivered on the table. "Is this some kind of sick joke?" he asked, although he knew Olivia was not the type for jokes, sick or otherwise.

"The bullet went straight through her heart."

The glowing angel taunted him from high above Olivia's head. "Please tell me you're lying. *Please,* Olivia."

"I'm sorry."

She was so calm. So cool. He hated her just then. "Excuse me," he said. He turned and started up the stairs, Olivia close on his heels. He pulled his suitcase from the hall closet and carried it into their bedroom, where he tossed it on the bed. Olivia hung back in the doorway as he pulled some of the neatly pressed clothes from his closet and threw them into the suitcase still on their hangers.

"What are you doing?" Olivia asked.

"I have to get out of here." He felt trapped by her voice, by her presence. She could never understand.

"Paul." She took a step toward him and then seemed to think better of it, retreating once more to the doorway, gripping the jamb with her fingers. "This is crazy, Paul. You barely knew her. You were *infatuated* with her. That was your own word, remember? You said it was one-sided, that she was happily married. I met her husband tonight. I had to tell him..."

Paul leaned toward her. *"Shut up,"* he said. She took a step back into the hall and he knew he had scared her. He was scaring himself. This was a new and alien Paul Macelli, not the person he'd been for the past thirty-nine years.

Olivia clasped her hands in front of her, the fingers of her right hand playing with the diamond-studded wedding ring on her left. When she spoke this time, her voice was small. "You can talk about her if you like. I know I said I didn't want to hear it anymore, but this is different. I'll listen. Just please don't leave, Paul. *Please.*" Her voice cracked and he winced. He wanted to put his hands over his ears to shut her out.

He stepped into the bathroom and gathered up his toothbrush, his razor, the case for his eyeglasses. He walked back into the bedroom and dumped them on top of the clothes in the suitcase and zipped it closed. Then he looked up at Olivia. Her lips and cheeks were still red from the cold, her eyes blurry behind tears he had no desire to watch her spill. He looked past her, into the hall where he could see the faint light from the tree downstairs.

"I'm sorry, Olivia." He pushed past her, moving as quickly as he could, letting his shoes pound the hardwood stairs so he would not be able to hear her if she cried.

He was usually cautious on the road, but tonight he drove recklessly. The few other cars on the long wide highway that ran the length of the Outer Banks crept along the slick road, but he bore down on the gas pedal of the gray Honda, feeling the car slip out of his control over and over again and not caring. He didn't even slow down when he passed Annie's studio in Kill Devil Hills, although he did look over. Sometimes the lights inside the studio would be on at night, creating a vivid montage of stained glass in the front windows. Tonight, though, the glass walls in the front of the building were black and opaque-looking, like pieces of slate.

The snow silently battered his windshield, and he nearly missed the turn into the parking lot of the *Beach Gazette.* There was one other car—a blue station wagon—in the lot, and he wasn't surprised to see it. Gabe Forrester, the *Gazette*'s police reporter, was already here, probably delighted to have a meaty story to liven up his job.

Paul didn't bother to stop in his own office before knocking on Gabe's door. Gabe was just getting off the phone. "Macelli!" he said. "You look like hell, fella. What are you doing here this time of night?"

"I heard about that murder over in Manteo and thought maybe I could help you out. Do a color piece on her." He tensed, hoping that Gabe would look puzzled and tell him he had no idea what he was talking about. Maybe Olivia had made it up after all.

"Yeah, a big one." Gabe leaned back in his chair, his broad, square face sober. "Annie O'Neill. You probably don't know her, being new here and all."

"I did a story on her in *Seascape.*"

"That's *right.* Well, you're the perfect fella for the color stuff then, I guess." He shook his head with a rueful smile. "She was one of a kind, I'll say that. I have to call my wife to tell her and I keep putting it off. There'll be one of the biggest funerals you've ever seen around here." Gabe looked out the window. The snow was slowing down, the flakes small specks of glitter beneath the streetlight. "I don't know how I'm gonna break it to my kids," Gabe continued. "She was Jane's softball coach last year and Jimmy's den mother years ago. Crazy lady. Good heart, but a little wacky." He pursed his thin lips, flattened his palms on the top of his desk. "Poor Alec. Do you know her husband, the vet over at the animal hospital in Kill Devil Hills?"

Paul shook his head and sat down across the desk from Gabe because his knees were giving out. He rested his hands on his lap. "How did it happen?" he asked.

Gabe sighed. "She was serving food to the women and kids over at that Battered Women's Shelter in Manteo when this guy—" Gabe lifted a notepad from his desk and read the name "—Zachary Pointer, came in and started threatening his wife. He had a gun and he was aiming it at her, talking about how it was Christmas, how could she keep the kids from him on Christmas, et cetera, et cetera. Annie stepped between them to protect the wife. She talked to the guy, you know, trying to reason with him, and the bastard fired. That was Annie for you. It happened just that fast." Gabe snapped his fingers. "Pointer's in custody. Hope they fry him."

Paul shivered inside his coat. He worked at keeping his face calm and unreadable. "I'd better get started on the article," he said, standing up. At Gabe's door, he turned back. "Uh, are you going to be talking to the family?"

"I was planning on it. You want that part?"

"No, no. I was going to say, it's probably best if just one of us does it. You know, not make them go through it twice. So I'll let you handle that, okay?" There was no way he could talk to Alec O'Neill. He'd never met him, never wanted to meet the man Annie slept with night after night, although he had seen him a few times. The last time had been at Annie's studio. Paul had pretended to be absorbed in the stained glass when Alec walked in for a word with his wife. There was a mirror in the piece Paul was looking at, and in it he watched Annie and Alec speak to one another, their backs to Paul, their voices soft, intent, their heads together. As Alec started to leave, Annie slipped her hand to the seat of his jeans, and Alec kissed her temple. Paul had shut his eyes, trying to block that display of intimacy from his mind. No, he could not talk with Alec O'Neill.

He stopped in the file room and pulled the thick folder on Annie. He was familiar with it, having looked through it numerous times while he was writing the freelance article about her for *Seascape*. He carried the folder into his office and settled down at his desk, not bothering to take off his coat.

There were dozens of articles. Annie as community leader. Annie as stained glass artist. As photographer. As president of the Animal Welfare League. Many of the articles referred to her as *Saint Anne,* a nickname that had made her giggle. The oldest article, nearly brown with age, was from 1975. The headline read: Artist Heads Fight to Save Keeper from Eviction. Ah, yes. Annie's first claim to fame in the Outer Banks. Paul spread the article flat on his desk and scanned it. In 1975, the Park Service had planned to take over operation of the Kiss River Lighthouse site. They wanted to use half of the keeper's house as their headquarters, the other half as a museum of sorts for the tourists. Annie had met old Mary Poor, the keeper who was then in her seventies and who had lived in the house most of her life. Annie thought the eviction was an incredible injustice. She gathered public support for Mary's cause and the Park Service relented, allowing the old woman to retain one half of the large keeper's house for her own use.

There was a picture of Annie with the article that, for a moment, made the muscles in Paul's chest contract to the point of pain. He stared hard at the picture, then closed his eyes. *An infatuation.* Go to hell, Olivia.

He'd been told by the editor of the *Gazette* that he wrote in an "overly emotional" style, a complaint he'd also heard during his years on the *Washington Post*. How he would avoid that in writing Annie's color piece, he didn't know. "You could romanticize a flu epidemic," the *Post* editor once told him. "Forget you're a poet when you walk through your office door."

Paul spent the next hour putting together the bare bones of the article on Annie and then made a list of who he would interview in the morning. Tom Nestor, of course, and the director of the Battered Women's Shelter. He jotted down a few more names. He had time. The *Gazette* was only published three times a week. This issue wouldn't be out until the day after tomorrow.

He left his office and got back in his car. The suitcase taunted him from the back seat. *So, where are we going now, huh, Paul?* He knew a few places he could find a room, but that could wait. He pulled onto Croatan Highway again and started driving north, turning off after a couple of miles into the parking lot near Jockey's Ridge. He got out of his car and began walking through the sand toward the enormous dunes. The snow had stopped while he'd been in his office, and now the sky was cloudless and alive with stars. The dunes quickly surrounded him on all sides, like an eerie moonscape, and he relished the quiet, the solitude. His heavy breathing was the only sound as he hiked up the slope of the largest, snow-dusted dune, swinging his arms back and forth to stay warm.

His breath fogged up his glasses, and he took them off to finish the climb.

The muscles in his thighs were stiff by the time he reached the summit. He slipped his glasses back on and turned to face north. A bitter cold wind blew stinging particles of sand against his cheeks, and he rammed his ungloved hands deep into his coat pockets. He was above everything here. He studied the horizon, waiting.

Yes. There it was. The pinpoint of light. It disappeared, and he counted. *One, one-hundred, two, one-hundred, three, one-hundred, four, one-hundred.* There it was again. The Kiss River Lighthouse. He watched the light glow and vanish in the distance, setting its languorous, hypnotic pace. A clear white light. Annie had told him during one of the interviews that she saw no point to clear, uncolored glass. "It's like being alive without being in love," she'd said, and then she'd told him about her fantasy of putting stained glass in the windows of the Kiss River Lighthouse.

"Women," she'd said, "in long, flowing gowns. Roses, mauves. Icy blues."

He hadn't written any of that in the *Seascape* article. There were many things she'd said to him that he'd kept entirely for himself.

A gust of cold air tore through his coat and stung his eyes.

Annie.

An infatuation.

One-sided.

Paul sat down on the cold sand and buried his head in his arms, finally allowing himself to cry, for what he'd lost, for what he'd never had.

CHAPTER THREE

June 1991

Alec O'Neill's favorite memory of Annie was also his first.
He had been standing right where he stood now, on this same
beach, and it was as moonless a night then as it was now, the
night air black and sticky like tar. The lighthouse high above
him flashed one long glare every four and a half seconds. The
wait between those light flashes seemed an eternity in the
darkness, and in one of those blasts of light he saw a young
woman walking toward him. At first he thought she was a
figment of his imagination. It did something to your head,
standing out here alone, waiting for the beacon to swing
around again and ignite the sand. But it *was* a woman. In the
next flash of light, he saw her long, wild red hair, a yellow
knapsack slung over her right shoulder. She was probably a
year or two younger than him, twenty or so. She started
speaking as she drew near him, while he stood mesmerized. Her name was Annie Chase, she said, her husky voice
a surprise. She was hitchhiking down the coast, from Mas-
sachusetts to Florida, staying close to the water all the way.

She wanted to touch the ocean in every state. She wanted to feel the water grow warmer as she moved south. He was intrigued. Speechless. In the beacon of light he watched her pull a Mexican serape from her knapsack and spread it on the ground.

"I haven't made love in *days,*" she said, taking his hand in the darkness. He let her pull him down to the blanket and fought a sudden prudishness as she reached for the snap on his jeans. It was, after all, 1971, and he was twenty-two and five years beyond his first time. Still, she was a complete stranger.

He could barely concentrate on the sensations in his own body, he was so enchanted by hers. The beacon teased him with glimpses of it, delivered in four-and-one-half second intervals. In the tarry blackness between light flashes, he would never have known she was there except for the feel of her beneath his hands. It threw off their rhythm, those lambent pulses of light, made them giggle at first, then groan with the effort of matching his pace to hers, hers to his.

He took her back to the cottage he shared with three friends from Virginia Tech. They had just graduated and were spending the summer working for a construction company on the Outer Banks before going on to graduate school. For the past couple of weeks, they'd been painting the Kiss River Lighthouse and doing some repair work on the old keeper's house. Usually they spent the evenings drinking too much and looking for women, but tonight the four of them and Annie sat together in the small, sandy living room, eating the pomegranates she had produced from her knapsack and playing games she seemed to have invented on the spot.

"Sentence completion," she announced in her alien-sounding Boston accent, and she immediately had their attention. "I treasure..." She looked encouragingly at Roger Tucker.

"My surfboard," Roger said, honestly.

"My Harley," said Roger's brother, Jim.

"My cock," said Bill Larkin, with a laugh.

Annie rolled her eyes in mock disgust and turned to Alec. "I treasure..."

"Tonight," he said.

"Tonight," she agreed, smiling.

He watched her as she plucked another red kernel from her pomegranate and slipped it into her mouth. She set the next kernel in her outstretched palm, and she continued to eat that way as they played—one kernel in her mouth, the next in her palm—until her hand had filled with the juicy red fruit. Once the shell of her pomegranate lay empty on her plate, she held her handful of kernels up to the light, admiring them as if they were a pile of rubies.

He was amazed that his friends were sitting here, stone cold sober, playing her games, but he understood. They were under her spell. She had instantly become the red-hot core of the cottage. Of the universe.

"I need..." Annie said.

"A woman." Roger groaned.

"A beer," said Jim.

"To get laid," said Bill, predictably.

"You," Alec said, surprising himself.

Annie took a bloodred ruby from the pile in her hand and leaned forward to slip it into Alec's mouth. "I need to be held," she said, and there was a question in her eyes. *Are you up to it?* her eyes asked him. *Because it's not a need to be taken lightly.*

In his bed later that night he understood what she meant. She could not seem to get close enough to him. "I could love a man who had no legs, or no brain, or no heart," she said. "But I could never love a man who had no arms."

She moved in with him, abandoning her idea of hitchhiking down the coast. It was as though she had found him and fully expected to be with him forever, no discussion needed. She loved that he was studying to be a veterinarian and she would bring him injured animals to heal. Seagulls with broken wings, underfed cats with abscessed paws or torn ears. In the course of a week, Annie came across as many hurt animals as the average person encountered in a lifetime. She did not actively seek them out, yet they found her. He understood later that they were drawn to her because she was one of them. Her injuries were not physical. No, physically she was perfect. Her pain was hidden, and over the course of that summer he realized she had given him the task of making her whole.

He stood now in the thick black air, a prickly tension in him as he waited out the seconds between the light. Twenty years had passed since that first night. Twenty excellent years, until this last one. Until Christmas night, a little more than five months ago. He still came out here three, maybe four nights a week because more than any other place, it reminded him of Annie. Was it peace he felt here? Not exactly. Just close to her. As close as he could...

There was a rustling sound behind him. Alec turned his head, listening. Maybe it was one of the wild mustangs that roamed Kiss River? No. He could hear the steady footsteps of someone coming through the field of sea oats, up from the road. He stared in their direction, waiting for the light.

"Dad?"

The beacon caught his son's black hair, red T-shirt. Clay must have followed him. He walked through the sand to stand at his father's side. He was seventeen, and this past year had grown to Alec's height. Alec still had not adjusted to standing eye-to-eye with his son.

"What are you doing out here?" Clay asked.

"Just watching the light."

Clay didn't respond, and the beacon swung around once, then twice, before he spoke again. "Is this where you come at night?" he asked, his voice hushed. Both he and Lacey had taken on this careful tone when they spoke to him.

"Reminds me of your mother out here," Alec said.

Clay was quiet for another minute. "Why don't you come home? We can rent a movie or something."

It was Saturday night and Clay was two weeks away from his high school graduation. Surely he had things he'd rather do than spend the night watching movies with his father. In the next flash of light Alec thought he saw fear in Clay's blue eyes. He rested his hand on his son's shoulder.

"I'm all right, Clay. Go on now. You must have plans for tonight."

Clay hesitated. "Well, I'll be over at Terri's."

"Fine."

Alec listened to the sound of Clay's footsteps retreat across the field. He listened until he could hear nothing other than the waves breaking against the shore. Then he sat down on the beach, his elbows resting on bent knees, and stared out at a small yellow light on the black horizon.

"Remember, Annie, the night we saw the boat on fire?" He spoke out loud, but his voice was a whisper. So long ago—a decade, maybe more. They'd been sitting right where he sat now and probably they had made love, or were about to, when they spotted the ball of gold light on the horizon, shooting yellow tendrils into the sky and spreading shimmery waves of liquid gold into the water. The keeper's house was locked tight and dark, Mary Poor asleep for the night, so Alec had driven out to the road to call the Coast Guard from a pay phone. They were already on the scene, he was told. Everyone was off the boat and safe. But by the time he'd returned to Annie she was weeping, having created her own scenario. There were children on board, she told him, old people too feeble to save themselves. He comforted her with the truth, but it was many minutes before she could let go of her own catastrophic vision. They watched the fire burn itself out, until the black smudge of smoke against the night sky was all that remained.

They'd made love on this beach as recently as last summer. The park was closed at dusk, but over the years they had never felt the chain across the road was meant for them. No one had ever disturbed them, not once, although until two years ago they'd known that Mary was sleeping close by.

They'd swim at night, too, when the water was calm enough. Alec was always first back to the beach because he liked to watch her lift up from the black water, a glittering specter in the stark white bursts of light. Her hair was darkened and tamed by the water, sleek and shiny over her shoulders and breasts. Once last year she'd stood in the water, wringing it from her hair and looking up at the beacon. She said something about the lighthouse, about its being as much a comfort to those on land as on sea. "It's a touchstone," she said. "It keeps you safe the same time it helps you chart your course." He'd felt a lump in his throat, as though he knew what lay ahead, what he was going to lose. He'd thought it would be the lighthouse. He hadn't known it would be Annie.

The lighthouse had been the only real source of friction between them. It stood close to the water, unlike its neighboring lighthouses at Currituck Beach to the north and Bodie Island to the south, which sat, secure, farther inland. Each year the ocean crept closer to the foundation of the

Kiss River Light, and Alec joined the desperate battle for its preservation, while Annie distanced herself from that work.

"If it's time for the sea to take it, we should just let it go." Every time she'd say those words Alec would picture the graceful white brick lighthouse crumbling into the ocean and feel nearly overwhelmed with sadness.

He closed his eyes now as he sat on the beach, waiting for the next blast of light to shine red through his eyelids. If you stayed with the lighthouse long enough, your heartbeat slowed almost to the rhythm of the light, until it barely seemed to beat at all.

CHAPTER FOUR

Olivia was obsessed with Annie Chase O'Neill. It was getting worse instead of better, and now as she sat in her living room watching Paul and the tanned young boy he'd hired carry boxes and furniture out to the rented U-Haul, she felt the obsession crystallize inside her.

She hadn't wanted to be here when Paul moved his things out. She hadn't expected him to do it this soon, this abruptly, but he'd called early this morning to say he had the truck, did she mind? She said no, because she wanted to see him. She would take any opportunity to see him, even though every meeting left her bruised. A little more than five months had passed since he walked out, yet she still ached at the sight of him. Even now that he'd met with a lawyer and signed a long-term lease on a cottage in South Nags Head, she still clung to the hope that he would take a good look at her and realize his mistake.

He stopped now in the arched doorway between the living room and dining room, pulling a handkerchief from the pocket of his khaki shorts to wipe his forehead.

"Are you sure about the dining room set?" he asked.

He'd taken his shirt off sometime in the last hour and his skin glistened. His dark blond hair was damp and pushed back from his forehead, and his glasses caught the light from the windows behind her head. She felt a futile wave of desire, and looked past him into the dining room.

"It's yours," she said, holding a finger to mark her place in the journal on her lap. "It's been in your family for years."

"But I know you love it."

He was not without guilt, she thought.

"It should stay in your family."

He looked at her a moment longer. "I'm sorry, Liv."

She'd heard those words from him so often these past few months they no longer had any meaning. She watched him lift the two chairs from one side of the table and head toward the door.

She sat glued to the sofa, afraid to see the rest of the house and the gaps he had left her. Once he and the boy were gone she would brace herself and walk through. Slowly. It would be good for her. Maybe reality would sink in. Maybe she would stop hoping.

Paul walked back into the house, into the dining room. Olivia rose and stood in the arched doorway as he and the boy turned the table upside down and unbolted the legs. When the last screw was removed, Paul stood up to look at her. He adjusted his gold wire-rimmed glasses on his nose and gave her a quick grin that meant nothing. A nervous gesture. He still had that slightly gawky, appealingly academic look that had attracted her ten years earlier, when he worked at the *Washington Post* and she was a resident at Washington General. She thought now of how quickly she could change this scene. With just a few words she could have him back. She let the fantasy unfold in her mind. *"I'm pregnant,"* she would say, and he'd drop the table leg and stare at her. *"My*

God, Liv, why didn't you tell me?" Maybe the news would snap him out of the crazy stupor he'd been mired in all these months. But she would say nothing. She didn't want the baby to be his reason for coming home. If he came back to her it would have to be because he still loved her. She could accept nothing less.

She poured herself a glass of ginger ale and took her seat again in the living room while they carried the table out to the truck. She listened to Paul's voice rising up from the driveway and through the open front door as he told the boy to get himself some lunch. "I'll meet you at the new house at two," Paul said. Then he came back into the house, walking slowly through the kitchen, the study, the bedrooms, to see if there was anything else he could take from her. When he was finished, he sat down in the rattan chair on the opposite side of the living room from Olivia. He was holding *Sweet Arrival,* the slim volume of poetry he'd published a few years earlier, and one of the copies of the book they'd written together, *The Wreck of the Eastern Spirit,* and he rested them in his lap.

"So," he said. "How have you been?"

She sipped her ginger ale. "Busy."

"What else is new?" His voice bit her with its sarcasm, but then he softened. "That's good, though, I guess. Good to keep yourself occupied."

"I've started doing some volunteer work at the Battered Women's Shelter." She watched his face closely. The change in his features was abrupt. The color left his cheeks and his eyes widened behind his glasses. He leaned forward.

"Why?"

She shrugged. "To fill the time. I work there a couple of evenings a week. They really need the help. Infections pass like wildfire through a place like that." It had been hard at first, working there. Everyone spoke of Annie in the same reverent tone Paul had used. Her photographs adorned the walls, and her stained glass seemed to fill every window, bathing the broken women and restless children with color.

"It's a rough place, Liv."

She laughed. "I used to work in D.C., remember?"

"You can't predict what'll happen in a place like that."

"It's fine."

He sat back, letting out a sigh. Olivia knew he had spent the last few weeks covering Zachary Pointer's trial. She had not read the articles he'd written. She didn't want to know how he would allude to Annie, didn't want to read of his delight in seeing Pointer locked up for life.

"Look," Paul said to her now. "There's something I've been wanting to ask you for a long time. Don't get mad, okay? I mean, whatever your answer is, I won't hold it against you. I know you're human." That quick, nervous grin again. He fanned absently through the pages of *Sweet Arrival,* while she waited for him to speak again. "When you realized it was Annie in the emergency room that night—did that affect how you treated her?" he asked. "I mean, did you try as hard to save her as you would have if she were just some..." He must have seen the look on her face, because the words froze on his lips.

Olivia tightened her fingers around the glass of ginger ale. She stood up. "You bastard."

He set the books on the end table and walked toward her, rested his hand on her elbow. "I'm sorry, Liv. That was out of line. It's just that...I've always wondered. I mean, if it had been me in your position, I don't know if I could have..."

She jerked her arm away from him. "You'd better go, Paul."

He walked back to the end table, not looking at her, not speaking to her, and she watched as he gathered his things together and left the house. When he was gone, she sat down again, her legs too weak to carry her through the house. How far they were from a reconciliation if he could think that of her. Hadn't she wondered about it herself, though? In her bleakest moments, hadn't she asked herself the same question? She knew the answer. She had tried—with every ounce of strength in her—to save Annie O'Neill's life. That night had been the hardest she'd ever endured in an emergency room and she was certain she had done her best, although the irony of the situation had not been lost on her for a moment. She had, quite literally, held the life of the woman her husband loved in her hands.

Paul had not hidden his infatuation with Annie from her, and at first that had made Olivia feel safe. If Annie had been a threat, she thought, he would never have been so open about his feelings. It started with the spread he did on her in *Seascape*. He spoke admiringly of her, but the admiration quickly turned to adulation. It was like a sickness in him. It was one-sided, he assured her—Annie barely knew he was alive. Yet he could speak of nothing else. Olivia heard lengthy descriptions of Annie's physical beauty, limitless generosity, charming quirkiness, boundless energy and extraordinary artistic talent. She listened, feigned interest. It was a phase, she told herself. It would pass. When it didn't, she carefully, tactfully suggested he was going a little overboard. No, he said. She didn't understand.

It wasn't until Paul mentioned Annie's two children that Olivia began to feel truly threatened. Paul was one of six children in a closely knit family. He was hungry for a family of his own, and all the medical tests had pointed the finger at Olivia as the reason they had none. She'd finally had surgery this past fall to improve her chance of conceiving, but

by then it was too late. Even at the hospital, while holding
Olivia's hand after the operation, Paul spoke of Annie. She
had once donated her bone marrow, Paul said. "Can you
imagine that? Undergoing surgery to save the life of a total
stranger?"

"Yes, Paul, you've convinced me." Olivia spoke in anger
for the first time. "She's a saint."

After that, he stopped talking to her about Annie, which
worried Olivia even more because she knew by his brood-
ing silence that Annie was still much on his mind. He was
restless in his sleep. Losing weight. At the breakfast table he
pushed his food from one side of the plate to the other. He
lost track of their conversations, misplaced his car keys, his
wallet. When they made love—their futile attempts at con-
ception—his fingertips felt as dry as ash on her skin, and no
matter how close their bodies were she felt the gulf between
them that she couldn't narrow with her words or her touch.

She had asked him outright if he and Annie were lovers,
and he hadn't bothered to mask his disappointment when he
told her they were not. "She's completely in love with her
husband and committed to her marriage," he'd said gloom-
ily, in a way that let Olivia know he no longer felt any such
commitment himself. Obviously, the platonic nature of his
relationship with Annie had been dictated by Annie herself
and not by Paul.

After walking out on her the night Annie died, Paul had
taken an apartment close to his office. He'd written her a
long letter, filled with his apology and confusion. He knew
he couldn't possibly have Annie now, he wrote, but knowing her made him realize what he was missing with Olivia.
Olivia's self-esteem, which had taken a lifetime to construct
from the scrappiest raw materials, disintegrated in the few
minutes it took her to read his words.

She saw him from time to time over the next few months when he needed things from the house. Clothes. Tools. The computer. She watched his hands as he folded, lifted, packed. She missed his touch—she'd started getting massages once a week just to feel another human being's hands on her skin. Paul was no longer cool when he spoke to her, and there was occasionally a smile in his eyes when he saw her. She clung to the hope that the smile meant there was something left between them, something she could build on, but he never gave her the chance. He never stayed in the house longer than he had to, except for that one night in April when she'd shamelessly begged him to stay and he relented, only to kill her with the regret she saw later in his eyes.

What had become of the man she'd married, the man who had written an entire volume of poetry about her, who had helped her put her past aside and made her feel safe for the first time in her life? Who made love to her as though she were the only woman he could ever imagine loving? The man who had not yet met Annie O'Neill.

She wanted him back. She *needed* him back.

Olivia stood now at her living room window, the room behind her taunting her with new empty spaces to fill, as she watched the U-Haul disappear behind a dune. Out of the hundreds of times they'd made love, why had the forces of nature picked that particular night to leave her pregnant?

She felt a sudden determination replace her dejection. Like the room behind her, she had empty places to fill, and she would fill them with the qualities that had drawn her husband to Annie. But first she would need to learn what they were, and as her impulsive decision to work at the shelter had shown her, she would do whatever it took to find out. She had to admit the truth to herself: Paul's obsession with Annie had become her own.

CHAPTER FIVE

Alec woke up with Annie's old green sweatshirt beneath his cheek. He'd taken to sleeping with it, a practice which seemed absurd to him during daylight hours but to which he surrendered at night. The sweatshirt was little more than a rag Annie used to throw on for her early morning runs. When he'd come home from the emergency room that Christmas night, he'd found it lying on her side of the four-poster bed, a crumpled patch of green on the old, faded double wedding ring quilt. He'd slept with it that night, except that, of course, he hadn't slept at all.

He'd given all her other clothes away after offering them to Lacey, who'd cringed at the thought of wearing them. The sweatshirt, though, he couldn't part with. He hadn't washed it and surely after all these months it had taken on more his scent than hers, but it comforted him all the same.

He had a Save the Lighthouse Committee meeting this morning, and he shaved for the occasion, quickly, avoiding a long look in the bathroom mirror. He did not like to see the toll these last few months had taken on his face.

Clay and Lacey were already at the breakfast table when

he came downstairs. They were arguing, which was typical of them lately, but they fell silent when he walked into the room.

"Morning," he said, pouring himself a cup of coffee.

"Morning, Dad," Clay said, while Lacey mumbled something under her breath.

Tripod walked over to Alec with his jaunty, three-legged gait, and Alec bent low to scratch the German shepherd's head. "Anybody feed the animals?" he asked.

"Mmm," Lacey said, and he took her reply to mean yes.

Alec poured himself a bowl of raisin bran, picked up a stack of photographs from the counter, and took his seat at the table. He looked through the pictures while he ate, holding them in one of the few patches of clear light that flowed through the kitchen windows. Annie's stained glass colored nearly all the light in the room, splashing greens and blues and reds against the white cupboards and countertops.

Alec studied the photograph he'd taken from the base of the lighthouse, looking up at the black iron gallery. "Your pictures are getting stranger and stranger, Alec," Tom Nestor had told him when Alec stopped by Annie's old studio to use the darkroom. Alec propped the picture up against his coffee cup as he dipped his spoon into the raisin bran. It *was* a weird picture. He liked it.

"Dad?" Lacey asked.

"Hmm?" He turned the photograph on its side to see how it looked from that angle.

"Miss Green is going to call you this morning."

"Who's Miss Green?" He raised his head to look at his daughter and she quickly dropped her gaze to her cereal bowl. Why did she do that? "Lace? Look at me."

She raised her eyes, dark blue and wide like her mother's, and he had to struggle not to look away himself.

"Who's Miss Green?" he repeated his question.

"My counselor at school."

He frowned. "Are you having problems?"

Lacey shrugged and looked down at her bowl again. She played with her spoon, her fingertips stubby and sore-looking. She'd always bitten her nails, but this raw look, this biting them down to the quick, was new. "She's on my case about my grades."

Clay laughed. "What do you expect, O'Neill? You haven't opened a book all semester."

Alec set a quieting hand on Clay's arm. "I thought you were getting all A's, Lace."

"Not this year."

"Why didn't you tell me sooner so I could have helped you?"

She shrugged again, a little spasm of her slender shoulders. "I didn't want to bother you."

"*Bother* me." He felt his face cloud over. "You're my *daughter,* Lacey."

The phone rang on the wall behind him.

"That's probably her," Lacey said. Her face had gone white beneath her freckles.

"You're in deep shit now, O'Neill," Clay said as Alec stood up to answer the phone.

"Dr. O'Neill?" the woman said, her tone formal, removed.

"Yes."

"This is Janet Green, Lacey's counselor."

He had an immediate image of her: dark hair sprayed into place, too-pink lipstick, a smile wide and false. Someone too cold, too rigid to be working with teenagers.

"Lacey mentioned you'd be calling." Lacey had certainly waited until the last minute. He watched his daughter pick at her raisin bran, her head bowed, her long red hair falling like curtains on either side of the bowl.

"I live near you," Janet Green continued. "I'd like to stop by this afternoon and talk with you about Lacey. Save you a trip in."

Alec looked around him. Last night's dishes, streaked red with tomato sauce, cluttered the counter next to the sink. The spaghetti pot was still on the stove, one long strand of spaghetti stuck to its side in the shape of a question mark. Pieces of mail and old newspapers littered the countertops, and his pictures of the lighthouse were strewn everywhere.

"Let's just talk on the phone," he said.

"Well, did she tell you why I want to see you?"

"She said her grades aren't very good."

"No, they're not. She's really plummeted, I'm afraid. She has nothing above a C and she's failing biology and algebra."

"Failing?" He shot Lacey a look. She leaped from her chair as though he'd touched her with a live wire, swung her book bag from the counter to her shoulder, and flew out the door. He lowered the receiver to his chest. "Lace!" he called after her, but he saw the red blur of her hair as she ran past the kitchen window and out to the street. Alec lifted the phone back to his ear. "She took off," he said.

"Well, I know she's upset. She'll have to take biology and algebra in summer school if she wants to pass the year."

Alec shook his head. "I don't get it. She's always been a straight-A student. Shouldn't I have known about this sooner? What about her last report card? I would have noticed if she was slipping."

"Straight C's."

He frowned into the phone. "She must not have shown

it to me. That's so unlike her." He'd never seen a C out of either of his children. For that matter, he'd never seen a *B*.

"Your son's kept up with things quite well despite losing his mother, hasn't he? I hear he's going to be class valedictorian."

"Yes." Alec sat down again at the table, suddenly exhausted. If it were not for the lighthouse meeting, he would go back to bed.

"And he's going to Duke next year?"

"Yes." He watched his son get up from the table. Clay took a peach from the fruit bowl and waved as he walked out the door.

"I think Lacey's a little concerned about what that'll be like, having her brother gone, just the two of you in the house."

Alec frowned again. "Did she say that?"

"It's just a feeling I got. She seems to have had a very difficult time adjusting to her mother's death."

"I—well, I guess if her grades are down..." She was *failing*. He'd had no idea. "I haven't picked up on anything unusual." He hadn't *looked* for anything. He'd let his children fend for themselves these past few months.

"You're a veterinarian, right, Dr. O'Neill?"

"Yes."

"Lacey said you're not working right now."

He wanted to tell her it was none of her business, but he held his tongue for Lacey's sake. "I've taken some time off." He'd thought he'd take a few weeks off after Annie died. The weeks turned into months, the months accumulated at breakneck speed, and he still had no intention of returning to work.

"I see," Janet Green said, her voice dropping a degree or two to the level of pure condescension. "By the way, are you aware Lacey's had two detentions in the last few months for smoking on school grounds?"

He started to tell her that Lacey didn't smoke, but obviously this woman knew his daughter better than he did. "No, I didn't know that," he said. "Thank you for telling me."

He got off the phone and sat down at the table again, drained. This weariness was new for him. He was known for his energy, for his inability to sit idly for more than a minute or two. Now he was too tired to wash the spaghetti pot.

They ate spaghetti a few times a week. It was easy. Boil water, open a jar of sauce. Every once in a while one of the kids would cook, but they were not much more inventive than he was.

Annie used to make everything from scratch. Even bread. Two loaves of honey whole wheat every Saturday. The house would fill with the smell. This kitchen had been alive back then. She'd leave certain items on the countertops—a row of fruit along the backsplash, or colorful packages of exotic teas on the windowsills—so she could admire them while she worked.

Back in those days, Annie would usually get home ahead of him and create something wonderful in the kitchen, and often—in his memory, it was every other day or so—he'd come home and invite her into the bedroom and she would hand the spoon over to one of the kids, who would groan and resign themselves to another late dinner. Annie, the flush of longing already burning in her cheeks, would tell them, "Remember, loves, it's *elegant* to dine late."

That was the way this house operated back then. Annie had been a firm believer in spontaneity. "This is a house without rules," she'd say. "We have to trust ourselves and our bodies to tell us when to sleep, to eat, to get up in the morning. To make love."

It had only been in the last couple of years that the kids realized there were plenty of rules in this house—they were just not the same rules their friends lived by, but rather the peculiar rules of Annie's creation. She allowed no clocks in the house, although Alec always wore a watch. Lacey and Clay were free to make their own decisions in the matter, both of them following their mother's example until last year, when Clay began wearing a watch identical to Alec's. Before that, Clay and Lacey were often late for the school bus, or on a few bizarre occasions, extremely early. They had never had a curfew, which made them the envy of their friends. Even when they were small, they were allowed to go to bed anytime they pleased. They regulated themselves quite well, actually, which probably had something to do with the fact that the O'Neills did not own a TV.

Lacey and Clay were never punished for their few misdeeds, but were rewarded frequently, just for existing. When they were young, Alec had often felt like a spectator in all of this, Annie setting the tone for the way they were raised. He caught on quickly, though, discovering that if you treated kids with respect they behaved responsibly. Lacey and Clay had always been a testimony to their methods. "The most important thing is that you're having fun and you're safe," Alec would tell them before they went out. He took delight in that, in trusting them when the parents of their friends weighed their kids down with warnings, threats, and reprimands.

On a whim, Alec got up from the table and went upstairs to Lacey's room. He opened the door and shook his head with a smile. The room was a wreck, the bed unmade, clothes heaped everywhere, the hamper in her corner overflowing. Her desk was stacked with books and tapes and papers, and the walls were covered with posters of decadent, noxious-looking musicians. On the shelf that ran around three sides of her room, at the level of his shoulders, sat her antique dolls, providing a weird contrast to the depraved young men. There were thirteen of the dolls, neatly spaced on the shelves he'd built five years ago. Annie had given her a doll for each birthday. Right now they looked out at Alec with placid smiles on their haunting, small-toothed mouths.

She's smoking, damn it. Should he talk to her about it? What would Annie have done? An open discussion at the dinner table, most likely, with no accusations, no expectations, no demands. Alec let out a long sigh. He wasn't up to it.

Tripod hobbled into the doorway and leaned heavily against Alec's leg. Alec gave the dog a perfunctory scratch behind one ear as they stared together into the disaster that was Lacey's room. Annie had been no sterling housekeeper— she was notoriously disorganized—but she'd been a master at cramming things into closets and cupboards, and the house always had the appearance of neatness. Lacey's room had certainly never looked like this when Annie was alive, but Alec could hardly hold his daughter responsible for the mess in this room when it only reflected what was going on in every other room in the house.

He leaned against the door jamb and shut his eyes to block out the reproachful, saucer-eyed stares of the dolls. "I'm screwing up, Annie," he said, and he felt Tripod turn his head to look up at him at the defeated tone of his voice.

At ten-twenty that morning, Alec pulled into the parking lot of the Sea Tern and slipped into the space between Nola Dillard's BMW and Brian Cass's old station wagon. He was late again, but he was loaded with excuses this time. First the call from Lacey's counselor, which admittedly had not taken that long but which had forced him to spend a good hour thinking about his life. Then there was the call from Randi, begging him to come back to work. She was handling just about everything since he'd left, and she'd been tolerant at first. Very understanding—a quality of Randi's he had always criticized her for. She let people walk on her, and now he was doing the walking. Well, she was starting to fight back. This was the third phone call this week, but he wasn't about to bend. He told her once again he wasn't ready to return to work. He wasn't sure he would ever be ready.

"Here he is." Nola Dillard stepped toward him as he walked into the meeting room at the back of the restaurant. Her jaw had a peculiar set to it. She clutched his arm, her heavy, flowery perfume filling the air between them, and whispered close to his ear. "We've got problems, hon."

"Thought you got lost, Alec." Walter Liscott stood up and pulled out the chair at the head of the table for him.

"Sorry I'm late." He took the seat Walter offered him.

The entire Save the Lighthouse Committee was assembled in front of him. Two men in addition to himself and two women, already well into their coffee and doughnuts. They had undoubtedly grown accustomed to his tardiness by now. Sondra Carter, the second woman on the committee and the owner of a small boutique in Duck, had suggested it was his little tribute to Annie, who had never been on time for anything in her life.

The waitress appeared in the room and poured Alec a cup of coffee. "Help yourself to a doughnut, Dr. O'Neill," she said.

Alec nodded and set his notebook on the table. He looked at Nola, wondering what she had been trying to tell him.

"Okay," he said. "This morning we're brainstorming fund-raising ideas."

Walter ran his hand over his thinning gray hair. He cleared

his throat and began speaking in a deep, syrupy voice. "We were talking before you came in, Alec. And the truth is, we're not altogether in agreement on something."

Alec tensed. "What are you saying, Walter?" he asked. He would have to come on time from now on. Didn't want to invite a mutiny.

"Well..." Walter cleared his throat again and glanced at the others. He'd obviously been selected as their spokesperson. "While we're all in agreement on the goal of this committee—raising funds to save the lighthouse—we're not in agreement on how the lighthouse ought to be saved. Me for one, I don't want to bust my tail raising money and then have them screw the whole thing up by trying to move the damn thing and topple it over in the process."

"I agree," Sondra said. "Either our money goes to building a sea wall around the lighthouse, or they get none of it."

"Hold it." Alec raised his hand. "You all know the choice on how the lighthouse is saved is not ours to make."

"That's right," Nola said. Her white-blond hair was pinned up as usual and she wore her gray power suit this morning, a blue Dorsett Realty pin attached to the lapel. She pointed a long red fingernail at Walter. "The Park Service wants to save the lighthouse as much as we do, Walter. They won't agree to something they're not absolutely certain will work. Come on, folks," she pleaded. "We've worked so hard and the money's starting to come in. Now that it's getting close, y'all are chickening out."

"I'm just afraid they'll make the wrong choice."

Walter sounded close to tears, and Alec understood his concern. Everyone in this room loved the Kiss River Lighthouse and understood its fragility. Up until a few weeks ago, the plan had been to build a sea wall around it. Within a few years, the lighthouse would be on its own small island in the sea. An aesthetically appealing solution. Now, quite suddenly, the Park Service had changed its mind and was speaking very seriously about moving it—building a track, lifting it up, and sliding it 600 yards inland, all at the cost of several million dollars. It was a frightening and impossible concept to comprehend. Not only did he understand Walter's fears; he shared them.

"Nola's right," Alec said. "We have to trust the engineers to come up with the best solution. We can't second-guess them."

Nola winked at him. "I move we get on with the meeting."

"I second the motion," Brian said.

There was some grumbling, but no one left the table, and Alec led them through an hour of ideas. A silent auction. An educational brochure to generate interest. More talk shows and speaking engagements. It wasn't until he was driving home that he let his own fears surface. Engineers were human. Fallible. What if they destroyed the lighthouse by trying to save it?

He was at his desk in the den when Lacey got home from school. He spotted her through the window. She was out on the sidewalk talking to Jessica Dillard, Nola's daughter and Lacey's best friend. Jessica was grinning, but there was a meanness in the grin, an ugly superior quality that surprised him and made his heart ache for his daughter. Jessica stood with one hand on her hip. Her sleek blond hair rested on her shoulders and she had a cigarette elegantly balanced between her fingers. She looked very much like her mother.

Alec leaned closer to the open window.

"You should try it, Lacey," Jessica was saying. "You're so lame this year. You've forgotten how to have fun."

Lacey said something he couldn't hear before turning toward the house. Try what, he wondered? Alcohol? Marijuana? Sex? He shuddered and turned to face the door, his chair creaking. "Lacey?"

She stepped into the den, folding her arms across her chest.

"Things okay with you and Jessica?"

"Yes." Lacey let a wall of red hair fall over her left eye, cutting him out. He wouldn't push her. Not now.

"I signed you up for summer school. Biology and Algebra."

"Only losers go to summer school."

"I'm afraid you don't have much choice."

She looked up at him with her one exposed eye. "Are you going to ground me?"

"*Ground* you? Of course not." He'd never grounded his kids. "But I want you to promise me that if you start having that much trouble with school again, you'll let me know."

"Okay." She swept her hair back over her shoulder and turned to leave the room. In the doorway, she hesitated and looked back at him. "I'm sorry, Dad. I just haven't been able to do my work this year."

"I know what you mean, Lacey," he said. "I haven't been able to do mine, either."

CHAPTER SIX

Paul was still in bed when he heard the interview on the radio. They were talking about the Kiss River Lighthouse. At first he thought he was dreaming, but the voice began to make sense, to clear his head. He opened his eyes to the blue and gold light streaming through the stained glass panel hanging in his bedroom window. He lay very still, listening.

The woman's name was Nola Dillard and she was talking about the Save the Lighthouse Committee. "We're going to lose the Kiss River Lighthouse within three years if erosion continues at its current rate," she said.

Paul rolled onto his side and turned up the sound as Nola Dillard continued to speak of the disaster facing the tallest lighthouse in the country. When she was finished, Paul pulled his phone book out of the nightstand and dialed the number of the radio station.

"How can I reach the woman who was just interviewed about the lighthouse?" he asked, propping himself up against the headboard of his bed.

"She's still here," the male voice on the other end of the phone told him. "Hold on."

There was a thirty-second wait. He could hear voices in the background. Laughter.

"This is Nola Dillard," a woman said.

"Yes, Ms. Dillard. My name is Paul Macelli and I just heard you talk about the Kiss River Lighthouse. I'd like to help."

"Great!" she said. "The bottom line is money, Mr....?"

"Macelli. I'm afraid there's not much I can do for you financially, but I have some spare time and energy. I'd be happy to help in some other way. I didn't realize the lighthouse was in jeopardy."

There was a silence. He had somehow stumbled, said something wrong.

When she spoke again, her voice had developed a barely perceptible chill. "Are you a new resident of the Outer Banks, Mr. Macelli?"

So that was it. He was an outsider. He thought of telling her about the summer he'd lived here long ago, the summer after he got his masters degree, but he stopped himself. He had told no one about those few months in the Outer Banks, not even Olivia.

"Yes," he said, "I'm new here, but I work for the *Beach Gazette*. Surely there's some way I can help."

Nola Dillard sighed. "Well, I tell you what, hon. We're having a committee meeting Thursday night at the Sea Tern Inn. Do you know where that is?"

"Yes." Oh, yes. Two of his interviews with Annie had been in that restaurant. He'd avoided it since her death.

"Meet me out front about seven forty-five. I'll talk to the committee first and clear the way for you a bit, all right?"

He thanked her and got off the phone. At least she hadn't

asked him what his interest was in the lighthouse. He would have said something about being a history fanatic, someone who couldn't bear to lose the past. It would have been the truth.

Nola Dillard was a striking woman. Early forties, probably. Pale-blond hair pinned up in back, enormous gray eyes, and skin a little too lined from a tan she probably nurtured year-round.

She reached her hand toward him and he shook it. "We're all set, Mr....Paul, is it? I'm Nola. Come on in."

He followed her through the familiar main room of the restaurant, with its heavy wooden tables and sea-lore accents, to a small room in the back. The committee members sat around one long table, and they looked up when he entered. There were three men and one woman besides Nola. He glanced at their faces and was startled when his eyes found Alec O'Neill at the head of the table. He recognized him immediately, from the glimpse he'd had of him with Annie, and more so, from the photograph of him in her studio—the black and white picture that had frightened him a little with its dark, unsmiling countenance and a threat in his pale eyes. Those eyes were on him now as Nola guided Paul toward the head of the table. He glanced quickly at the exit. Should he take off, make an absolute fool of himself? Nola's hand was soft at his elbow, pushing him forward, as Alec rose from his chair.

"Paul, this is Alec O'Neill, our venerable leader. Alec, Paul Macelli."

Alec O'Neill raised his dark eyebrows in Paul's direction. Paul shook his hand, mumbling a greeting, his tongue suddenly too big for his mouth. He nodded his way around the rest of the group and took a seat next to Nola. A waitress came into the room and asked him what he'd like to drink.

His first thought was something stiff and fiery, but a quick look around the room told him alcohol was out. Alec himself was drinking what looked like lemonade.

Paul ordered iced tea. He leaned back in the chair, loosening the collar of his shirt.

Alec looked at him with those riveting eyes and Paul felt totally exposed. Could he possibly know? Perhaps he recognized Paul's name as the man who'd written the article about Annie in *Seascape.*

"Nola says you're a journalist," Alec said.

"Yes. I work for the *Gazette,* but I freelance too. So, if there's any way you think I can help, just let me know." He laughed nervously, the color rising in his cheeks.

Alec took a swallow of his lemonade. "Well, I think there probably is a way you can help us. We need to educate the public. I handle speaking engagements locally and around the state, but we need to shift our publicity to the national level. The Kiss River Lighthouse is a national monument, so it shouldn't be up to the locals to support the preservation effort. We're talking about putting together a brochure of some sort on the history of the lighthouse, something that would have wide distribution." Alec leaned back in his chair. "Do you think you could help with that?"

"Of course." Paul had dropped his eyes to Alec's hands sometime during the last few minutes. Alec's fingers were long, tanned, and angular. Paul thought of him touching Annie with those hands, pulling her close to him in their bed. Hands she welcomed on her body. Alec still wore his wedding ring. From this distance it looked like a plain gold band, but he knew that up close it would be inlaid with the same gold braid that had graced Annie's ring. What had Alec done with her ring? She'd been cremated. What did they do...

"So, paper and printing will be donated," Alec was saying, and Paul quickly returned his gaze to Alec's face, to his eyes, ice-blue and unavoidable. "It's the compilation of the facts and the actual writing that we need."

"Is there a historical collection I can use?" Paul asked, and then he had a sudden, disconcerting thought. What if the old lighthouse keeper, Mary Poor, was still alive? She couldn't be, he reassured himself. She'd been an old woman the last time he had seen her, and that had been many long years ago.

"There's a private collection," Alec said. "I'll check into getting you permission to look at it. But for now, how about just covering our efforts in the *Gazette?*"

"Fine," Paul said, and he sat back, glad to have the attention of the room off him as Alec shifted the topic to a silent auction. He would leave the moment the meeting was over.

CHAPTER SEVEN

It was Mary Poor's ninetieth birthday and she was quite content. She sat on the porch of the blue, two-story house that had been her home for the past two years and watched the early morning sunlight turn the boats on the waterfront purple, then pink, then yellow. She had gotten used to this view, to the gentle rhythm of the rocker, to sharing her porch with others her age. She had expected to live out her life at Kiss River, but she knew she was luckier than most to have had sixty-five years under the warmth of the beacon.

She still spoke of the lighthouse to anyone who would listen. Over and over again, she recounted tales of the storms, the wrecks, the sea. She knew she sounded like the others when she rambled on that way, trapped in the past, but she didn't care. It was a conscious decision she made to allow herself to babble, a privilege that came with age.

The doctor who examined her yesterday had marveled at her keen vision, her fine hearing, and her strength, despite the tortured bone in her hip. Mary had talked politics with the man, showing off. "You're sharper than I am, Mrs. Poor," the doctor had said, and Mary was certain he had not been patronizing her.

"So, if I'm in such good shape, why can't I have a cigarette?" she'd asked him, but he'd only laughed, and slipped his stethoscope into his bag.

Mary rarely let others know just how capable she still was. She wanted to enjoy some of the pleasures of old age, of being taken care of, pampered. She even let Sandy, one of the girls on the staff, cut her short, snow-white hair now, although she could still do it perfectly well herself if she had to.

She tried to keep up with things. She watched the news, television still an amazement to her. She'd had one at Kiss River, but all it ever brought into her house there was static and splintery gray lines. She kept up with the newspaper, too. Right now the *Beach Gazette* rested on her lap, and when the boats on the waterfront finally lost their color and the show of the sunrise was over, she picked up the paper and began to read. Her favorite part was the crossword puzzle, but she always saved that until last, until she'd read everything else and needed something to work on as she waited for Trudy or Jane to get up and join her on the porch.

She read the front page and then opened the paper. She was folding the page back when she saw the picture: the tall, glittering white brick lighthouse against a dark sky. A little well of pain surfaced briefly in her chest, then subsided. In the corner of the picture she could just make out the northern tip of her old house, her husband Caleb's family home, the house the Park Service now owned. The headline read, *Erosion Threatens Kiss River Lighthouse.* There was a byline. Paul Macelli. Mary narrowed her eyes. Paul Macelli? They'd let anybody write about Kiss River these days. She read the article through. A committee had been formed to save the lighthouse. Alec O'Neill was chairman. Mary smiled when she read that. It fit.

She rested the paper on her lap again and thought about Alec O'Neill. She had learned of Annie's death too late to get to her funeral, and she'd wept, unable to remember the last time she'd cried over a loss. But *Annie*. A kindred spirit. Like a daughter in a way, although Mary's own daughter, Elizabeth, had never listened to her with such interest. Mary could tell Annie anything, and Annie had told her all, hadn't she? "Mary," she'd said one night, after the fire had burned out and they'd drunk brandy, coffee, "you know me better than anyone in the world."

Mary had loved her, fiercely, with a lay-down-her-life-for-her sort of love. She thought of that after Annie died. Why couldn't it have been her instead? She'd lived long enough, while Annie was just beginning, really. In more ways than one. Mary felt that blind sort of love that led her to do the things she did for Annie, to see to Annie's happiness without bothering to think through the consequences, without stopping to think that what she did might be wrong.

For a while after Annie died, Mary couldn't imagine going on without her visits to look forward to. She'd seen Annie less since moving here to the old folks' home, but the younger woman had still come once or twice a week, with gifts more often than not. Things Mary didn't need, but that was Annie, and Mary would never tell her not to bother. Annie's visits were shorter here. There were always people around; she watched her words.

It was her last visit that haunted Mary, that stayed in her mind. She told herself Annie was gone now, what did it matter? But Annie had been so distressed that afternoon as she sat with Mary in the living room, surrounded by the other residents of the home. The dimpled smile was gone, and she struggled to hold back tears. Mary had finally taken her up to her bedroom and let her weep, let her talk about what she'd done. Mary had absolved her, like a priest in a confessional. She actually thought of that later, that Annie had died forgiven.

Mary had sent a card to Alec and her children. Sandy took her out to buy it, and she made that girl drive her to four or five card stores before she found one with a white lighthouse on it. She lay awake for one full night trying to decide what to write. She composed long dissertations in her mind on how extraordinary Annie was, how terribly she would miss her, but in the end she wrote something simple, something anyone might write, and sent the card off.

Alec O'Neill. She had never been able to look that man in the eye. "I won't hurt him," Annie had said, too many times to count. "I'll never hurt him."

Mary looked down at the article again, reading it through once more. They needed historical information on the lighthouse. Incidents. Anecdotes. Soon they would be looking for her. Who would come? Alec O'Neill? Paul Macelli? Or maybe someone from the Park Service. That would be best. If she saw Alec or Paul—well, she sometimes said too much these days. She might tell them more than they wanted to hear.

CHAPTER EIGHT

Olivia bought a strawberry ice cream cone at the deli and sat on a bench across the street from the cedar-sided building that housed Annie's studio. The front wall of the building was composed of ten large windows. She could see that stained glass panels hung inside them, but from her seat directly under the midday sun, she could not make out their shapes or designs.

She'd done this one other time, sat on this bench and stared at the studio. It was just a month or so after Paul started talking about Annie, back when she was alive. Already Annie had assumed a larger-than-life dimension in Olivia's mind, and she'd sat here hoping for a glimpse of the woman that never came. She'd lacked the courage to go inside the studio. She couldn't be certain of her reactions if she came face to face with her. Paul was very bright, very attractive. If he were trying to seduce Annie, it could only be a matter of time until she gave in. Olivia imagined letting Annie see her, get to know her. If the woman had a shred of decency, she wouldn't want to hurt her.

Her reasons for sitting on this bench today were different.

Now she just wanted to understand the pull Annie'd had over Paul. She already felt herself changing. She was beginning to enjoy her volunteer work at the shelter, although she had never simply given her skills away before. Her medical training had always included an unspoken focus on pulling in a hefty income.

At first she had found the work at the shelter painful. She'd take the stories of the shelter residents home with her and lie sleepless in her bed, the tired faces of the women filling the empty darkness of her bedroom. The plight of those women and their children opened old wounds in Olivia she thought had healed long ago. She understood too well how it felt to be a victim, how it felt to be poor and desperate, and she had to continually remind herself that she was strong now. She was skilled. *The consummate professional,* Paul had once said of her, and she'd thought at the time that he'd meant it as a compliment. Still, seeing the hungry, battered children at the shelter triggered memories of snowy winters spent with one pair of thin-soled shoes, or meals of canned beans and a single hot dog, to be split between herself and her brothers, Clint and Avery.

She swallowed the last of her ice cream cone and stood up. The beach traffic was heavier now that some schools were out for the summer, and she crossed the street carefully. She was cautious these days, aware that every move she made affected the tiny life forming inside her as well as her own.

The small wooden sign next to the door read simply, STAINED GLASS AND PHOTOGRAPHY. She stepped inside, closing the door behind her and shutting out the street sounds. It took her a moment to adjust to the quiet, cool, multicolored beauty of the room. A man sat at a broad work table directly in front of her and he looked up when she walked in. Smoke curled in the air above him as he stubbed out a half-smoked cigarette in the ashtray on the table. He was a large man, with hair the color of shredded wheat tied back in a ponytail, and a ragged mustache above generous lips. His thick hand held some sort of tool, and he raised it from the piece of glass on which he was working.

"Let me know if you have any questions." His voice was deep, raspy.

Olivia nodded, and walked to the right, away from his eyes. She was moving in slow motion, it seemed. She felt drugged, hypnotized, by the sunlit colors on either side of her. The studio was small and high-ceilinged, and the glass walls in the front and back were covered from floor to ceiling with stained glass panels in all sizes. Overwhelming. At first she could barely separate one piece from the next, but then her eye was drawn to a long panel, perhaps five feet by two, of a woman in Victorian garb. Her white dress seemed to flow and sway on the glass, and Olivia was reminded of the small angel Paul had bought for their Christmas tree. The woman peered out, coy-eyed, from beneath the brim of her flowered hat.

The man at the work table caught her staring. "That one's not for sale," he said.

"It's beautiful," Olivia said. "Did Annie O'Neill make it?"

"Uh-huh. I kept it for myself when she died." He laughed, a soft, guttural chuckle. "Told myself she would've wanted me to have it, since it was my favorite. The ones on the right side there were all Annie's. Not too much of hers left. Most of it's been sold."

Much of it, she guessed, to Paul.

"The rest I made," the man continued. He gestured toward the east end of the studio, where a maze of white temporary walls were covered with framed photographs. "Photographs are mostly mine, too, although Annie was an accomplished photographer in her own right."

Olivia walked toward the photographs. The first few walls were covered with color prints—seascapes, sunsets, nature shots—most of them with Tom Nestor's signature in the lower right-hand corner. There was a surprising delicacy to the pictures for such a large man.

She turned a corner and found photographs of three people she remembered all too well—Annie's husband and two children. The shot of the girl was from her shoulders up. She grinned mischievously, deep dimples carved into her lightly freckled cheeks, her full red hair blowing wildly around her face.

The photograph of the boy had been taken on the beach. He stood shirtless next to his surfboard, his dark hair slicked back and droplets of water sparkling starlike on his chest.

Between those pictures was a black and white portrait of Alec O'Neill. Olivia was drawn to his eyes, pale beneath his dark brows, the pupils little black daggers that made her shiver. He wore a black cardigan sweater and a white T-shirt, the dark hair on his chest just visible at the neckline. His head was tilted, one hand against his temple, as though his elbow rested on his raised knee, perhaps, or on a table out of the camera's range. There was no smile. His lips were flattened, tight, the perfect match for the cold accusation she saw in his eyes.

She stepped away, his eyes following her as she turned the corner to come face to face with a huge black and white portrait of Annie herself. Olivia stared. Annie looked familiar in her creamy-skinned beauty, but like a stranger in the lively contours of her face. Her hair was an untamed halo of pale silk against the glossy black background.

"They broke the mold after they made Annie." The man had come up behind her, and Olivia turned to face him.

"Did you take it?"

"Yes." He seemed to have difficulty shifting his gaze from Annie to Olivia, but he finally reached forward to shake her hand. "I'm Tom Nestor," he said. He smelled like smoke.

"Olivia Simon." She looked back at the portrait. "She must have been a wonderful subject for a photographer."

"Oh, yeah." He dug his hands into the pockets of his denim overalls. The sleeves of his blue-striped shirt were rolled up to his elbows, and thick blond hair covered his meaty forearms. "You know, you hear about people dying, you think, I can't believe it, but then you start facing up to it. It took me months to believe it with Annie, though. Sometimes I still think she's going to walk through that door and tell me it was all a gag, she just needed some time away. I love the idea that she might..." His voice drifted off and he shrugged and smiled. "Oh, well."

Olivia remembered the woman on the table in the Emergency Room, the flat line of the monitor, the life slipping out of her hand.

"I should really get another artist in here," Tom continued. "I can't pay the rent on this place myself. Alec—Annie's husband—he's been helping me out. But I just can't imagine working with someone else. I worked with Annie for fifteen years."

Olivia turned to face him. "My husband did a story on her in *Seascape Magazine*."

Tom looked surprised. "Paul Macelli's your husband? I didn't realize he was married."

No, she imagined he hadn't spoken of her much. Maybe he'd never even told Annie he was married. "Well, he's... we're separated," she said.

"Oh." Tom fixed his gaze on Annie's picture again. "He still comes in here from time to time. Said he's fixing up a new house. He bought a lot of her stained glass. He wanted that Victorian lady you were looking at, but I'm not parting with her."

Olivia glanced at the rest of the photographs and then walked back to the center of the studio. She touched the corner of a stained glass panel hanging from the ceiling. "How do you do this?" she asked, running her fingers over the dark lines between the segments of blue glass. "This is lead, right?"

Tom sat down behind the work table. "No, actually that's copper foil covered with solder. Come over here."

She sat down on the chair next to him. He was working on a panel of white irises against a blue and black background. For the next ten minutes, she watched in fascination as he melted ropes of silvery solder onto the copper-wrapped edges of the glass, while the colors from the panels in the windows played on his hands, his cheeks, his pale blond eyelashes.

"Do you give lessons?" she asked, surprising Tom no more than herself.

"Not usually." He looked up at her and grinned. "You interested?"

"Well, yes, I'd like to try. I'm not very creative, though." She had never done anything like this. She'd never had the time, never taken the time, to learn a skill so thoroughly unrelated to her profession.

"You might surprise yourself," Tom said. He named a price and she agreed; she would have agreed to any amount.

Tom glanced down at her sandaled feet. "Wear closed-toed shoes," he said. "And you'll need safety glasses, but I think

I've got an old pair of Annie's somewhere around here. You can use them."

Before she left she bought a small, oval-shaped panel Annie had made—the delicate, iridescent detail of a peacock feather. She was leaving the studio when she nearly tripped over a stack of magazines piled close to the door.

Tom sighed. "I've got to do something about this mess." He waved a hand toward the magazines and a few piles of paperback books stacked next to them. "People have been bringing in their books and magazines for years. Annie would take them to the old folks' home in Manteo. I haven't wanted to tell people to stop, 'cause Annie would have had my head, but I just don't feel like driving over there."

"I can take them sometime," Olivia said. When? she wondered. Her impulsivity was beginning to worry her.

"Hey, would you? That'd be great. You just tell me when you're headed out that way and I'll load you up."

She arrived at the studio at exactly eleven the following Saturday. Tom fitted her with Annie's green safety glasses, Annie's old green apron. He drew a pattern of squares and rectangles on a sheet of graph paper, laid a piece of clear glass over it, and showed her how to use the glass cutter to score the glass. Her first cut was perfect, he said, as were her second and third.

"You have a natural feel for this."

She smiled, pleased. She had a steady hand; she was used to a scalpel. She only needed to adjust her pressure to the fragile glass.

Her head was bowed low over her work when she heard someone enter the studio.

"Morning, Tom."

She looked up to see Alec O'Neill, and her hand froze above the glass.

"Howdy, Alec," Tom said.

Alec barely seemed to notice her. He was carrying a camera case, and he stepped through a side door in the studio, closing it behind him.

"What's in there?" Olivia asked.

"Darkroom," said Tom. "That's Annie's husband, Alec. He comes in a couple of times a week to develop film or make prints or whatever."

She glanced at the closed darkroom door, and returned her attention to her work. Her next cut splintered a little, and she jerked her hands quickly away from the glass. "Shouldn't I be wearing some sort of gloves?"

"No." Tom looked offended. "You want to *feel* what you're doing."

She worked a while longer, glancing at her watch from time to time, hoping she would be finished before Alec O'Neill came out of the darkroom. Her next cut was crooked. This was not as easy as she'd thought. She had hung the peacock feather in her kitchen window, and now that she had a better sense of the work that had gone into it, she was anxious to see it again, to study it from a new perspective.

She was using pliers to break apart a scored piece of glass when the darkroom door squeaked open, and she kept her eyes riveted on her work as Alec O'Neill walked back into the studio.

"I left the negatives in there," he said to Tom.

"Those closeups you made of the brick came out good," Tom said.

Alec didn't respond, and she felt his eyes on her. She lifted her face, slipped off the glasses.

"This is Olivia Simon," Tom said. "Olivia, Alec O'Neill."

Olivia nodded, and Alec frowned. "I've met you somewhere."

She set down the pliers and lowered her hands to her lap. "Yes, you have," she said, "but not under very good circumstances, I'm afraid. I was the physician on duty the night your wife was brought to the emergency room."

"Oh." Alec nodded slightly. "Yes."

"You were *what?*" Tom leaned back to look at her.

"I stopped in to take a look at your wife's work, and I liked it so much that I asked Tom to give me lessons."

Alec cocked his head at her, as though he were not quite certain he believed her. "Well," he said after a moment. "You came to the right guy." He looked as though he wanted to say something more, and Olivia held her breath, aware of the still, colorful air surrounding the three of them. Then he gave a slight wave of his hand. "I'll see you in a couple of days, Tom," he said, and he turned and left the studio.

"You were there the night Annie died?" Tom asked, once the door had closed behind Alec.

"Yes."

"Why didn't you tell me that?"

"It wasn't a night I particularly want to remember."

"But, Christ, I mean that's weird, don't you think? We stood right over there," he pointed to the photographs, "and talked about her, and you never said a word."

She looked over at him. His heavy blond eyebrows were knitted together in a frown, and his eyes had reddened.

"Aren't there things you just can't talk about?" she asked.

He drew back from her, and she knew that, unwittingly, she had struck a nerve in him.

"Yeah. Right." He shook his head to whisk away whatever emotions had been stirred loose in him over the past few minutes. "Didn't mean to jump on you. Let's get back to work here."

She returned to her work, but as she cut, as she measured, she was aware of Tom's troubled silence, and she knew that this was yet another man who had loved Annie Chase O'Neill.

CHAPTER NINE

"You're coming to graduation tonight, aren't you?" Clay looked across the table at his father, while Lacey drowned her frozen waffle in maple syrup.

"Of course," Alec said. "I wouldn't miss it." He wondered how Clay could have thought anything else, but he guessed his actions hadn't been too predictable lately.

"How's the speech coming?" he asked. Clay had seemed uncharacteristically nervous the past few days, and right now he was tapping his foot on the floor beneath the table. He'd been carrying his notecards around with him, wedged into his shirt pocket or clutched in his hand. Even now the cards were perched, dog-eared and smudged, in front of his orange juice glass. Alec felt a little sorry for his son. He wished there was some way he could make it easier for him.

"It's fine," Clay said. "By the way, is it okay if I have a few people over after?"

"Sure," Alec said, pleased. "It's been a while since you've done that. I'll disappear."

"Well, no, you don't have to disappear," Clay said quickly.

Alec reached into his back pocket and pulled out his wallet. He set it on the table next to Clay's cereal bowl. "Take what you need for food and whatever."

Clay stared at the wallet for a moment. He glanced at Lacey before he opened it and pulled out a twenty.

"Can't get much with that," Alec said. He took his wallet back and handed Clay a couple more twenties. "You only graduate once."

Clay held the bills on the table. "You act like money's nothing these days," he said, carefully. Alec had the feeling both his kids thought he was losing his mind. He was not working; he was spending freely. But he wasn't quite ready to tell them about the insurance policy. He needed to keep it to himself a while longer—a sweet, tender secret he shared with Annie.

"You don't need to concern yourself with finances other than your own," Alec said.

Clay looked around the room. "I'd better get home early today to get this place cleaned up."

"I'll do it," Lacey volunteered, surprising them both. "It'll be your graduation present."

Alec spent the day with his camera on the beach at Kiss River. He was taking slides for a change, pictures he would use when he spoke to the Rotary Club in Elizabeth City next week.

He and Clay arrived home at the same time and they barely recognized the house they walked into. It smelled of lemon oil, and whatever it was Annie used to put in the bag of the vacuum cleaner. The living room was spotless, the kitchen scrubbed and sparkling and full of color from the stained glass at the windows.

"God," Clay said, looking around him. "Seems a shame to have a party here. I hate to wreck the place."

Lacey walked into the kitchen from the laundry room, a basket of clean clothes in her arms.

"The house looks fantastic, Lace," Alec said.

She set the laundry basket down and wrinkled her freckled, sunburned nose at her father. "It was getting to me," she said.

Alec smiled. "Yeah, it was getting to me, too. I just didn't have the energy to do anything about it."

"Thanks, O'Neill," Clay said. "You can always get a job as a maid if you flunk out of high school."

Alec was staring at the laundry basket. There on top, neatly folded, was Annie's old green sweatshirt. He picked it up, the folds coming undone, the worn fabric falling over his arm.

"You washed this?" He asked the obvious.

Lacey nodded. "It was on your bed."

Alec lifted the sweatshirt to his nose and breathed in the scent of detergent. Lacey and Clay looked at one another, and he lowered the shirt to his side.

"Your mother wore this a lot, you know?" he explained. "So when I threw her things out, I kept it as a remembrance. It still smelled like her, like that stuff she used on her hair. I should have set it aside so you didn't get it mixed up with the dirty clothes." He tried to laugh. "I guess I can finally get rid of it." He looked over at the trash can in the corner of the kitchen, but slipped the sweatshirt under his arm instead.

"It was right there with your dirty sheets," Lacey said, her voice high. Scared and defensive. "How was I supposed to know it wasn't laundry?"

"It's all right, Annie," he said, "it's..."

Lacey stamped her foot, her face crimson. "I am *not* Annie!"

Alec quickly played his words back to himself. Yes, he'd just called her Annie. He reached for her shoulder.

"I'm sorry, sweetheart."

Lacey dodged his hand. "Next time you can do your own fucking laundry!"

Alec watched as she ran out of the room, and in a moment they heard her light, quick steps on the stairs, followed by the slamming of her bedroom door.

"You've done that a lot, you know," Clay said quietly.

Alec looked at his son. "Done what? Called her Annie?" He frowned, trying to think. "No, I haven't."

"Ask *her*." Clay nodded in the direction of the stairs. "I bet she could tell you how many times you've done it."

Alec struggled out of his suit jacket and pressed his back against the car seat. He felt perspiration on his neck, across his chest. He tried to slow down his breathing. Keep it even. Stop gulping air.

He'd parked a little bit away from the rest of the cars in Cafferty High's parking lot. He needed a few minutes to pull himself together before he could face people. Parents of Clay's friends, he hadn't seen in months. His teachers. Everyone who was going to want to talk to him and say wonderful things about his son. If he could just keep a smile on his face, say the appropriate thing at the appropriate moment. God, he was never going to make it through the next couple of hours. *Damn it, Annie.*

She used to talk about seeing her kids graduate. As much as she tried to pretend that Lacey's and Clay's accomplishments were immaterial, she took pride in everything they did. She would have thrown a huge celebration for Clay's graduation. She would have hooted and hollered her way through the ceremony to make sure Clay knew she was there. *Annie is one intense mother,* Tom Nestor had said to him once, and he was right. Annie always tried to give her children the things she had never received from her own parents.

Her parents did not go to her graduation from the exclusive high school she'd attended in Boston. "We would have been proud to come if you'd kept your grades up," her father had told her. "But losing your membership in the National Honor Society during your last semester of school is inexcusable."

Her parents had been very wealthy. They'd groomed Annie to fit into their social circle, to date the sons of their well-connected friends and acquaintances. When she failed to meet their expectations, which she did often, either by accident or design, they punished her by withholding their love. When Alec pictured her childhood, he saw a little girl with unruly red hair sitting alone in the corner of her room, teary-eyed, hugging a teddy bear. Annie had never described that scene to him, yet it had been vivid in his mind from the night he first met her and learned how desperately she needed to be loved.

Annie's response to her upbringing was to criticize nothing in her children, to love them unequivocally. "I wouldn't care if they were so ugly people couldn't look at them without getting sick, or so dumb they could never learn to count to ten," she'd said. "They'd still be my precious babies."

Alec could see her making that little speech as she kneaded bread dough in the kitchen, and in his memory she was wearing the green sweatshirt, sleeves pushed up high on her arms, the fabric over her left breast smudged with flour.

The sweatshirt. Why had that hit him so hard? It was only his imagination that it still smelled like her, but when he saw it lying on the pile of laundry he'd felt as if he'd lost her all over again.

"Grow up." He said the words out loud to himself as he picked up his camera and stepped from the car. The air was sticky hot, with a breeze that ballooned the sleeves of his shirt. He would think about the lighthouse. Or windsurfing. He had to get through this for Clay's sake.

"Alec?"

He turned to see Lee and Peter Hazleton walking toward him. The parents of Clay's girlfriend, Terri. He hadn't seen them since the memorial service for Annie.

"Hi!" He manufactured what he hoped was a great smile.

Peter slapped his back. "Big day, huh? My camera's out of commission. Take a few of Terri for us, okay?"

"Clay would never forgive me if I didn't." He spotted Lacey on the lawn with a group of girls. "I'm going to get my daughter and find a seat," he said, pleased for the escape.

It shocked him every time he saw Lacey these days. He wished he could see Annie again to compare their faces and mark the differences. Maybe it would put an end to this jolt he felt every time he saw his daughter. She looked more like Annie than Annie had. He felt awkward with her. He could no longer look at her for more than a few seconds without feeling an overwhelming sadness.

He called to her and she walked over to him, looking alternately at the ground or the sky, steadfastly avoiding his eyes. He hadn't seen her since the explosion in the kitchen that afternoon. "Let's find our seats," he said to her now, and she followed him without speaking.

Clay had reserved two seats for them in the front row. Alec sat between Lacey and a heavyset woman who was perspiring profusely and who squeezed his thigh with her own. He shifted a little closer to Lacey and could smell smoke in her long hair. She was only thirteen. Damn.

He pulled his camera out of the case and started to change the lens. Lacey stared straight ahead at the empty wooden platform, and Alec knew it was up to him to break the silence.

"I'm sorry I called you Annie, Lace," he said.

She shrugged, her response to the world. "Doesn't matter."

"Well, yeah, it does. Clay says that's not the first time I've done it."

She shrugged again, her gaze dropping to the dry patch of lawn in front of their chairs.

"I overreacted about the sweatshirt."

She turned her head away from him. She was rocking slightly, as though she heard a beat he couldn't hear.

"When does summer school start?" he asked, struggling to engage her, but just then Clay appeared in front of them. He was already in his blue cap and gown, and a film of perspiration lined his forehead. "Aren't these great seats?" He held out his hand and Alec shook it, the gesture making him feel old. Clay reached inside his gown and took the battered notecards from his pants pocket. He handed them to Alec. "Hold these for me. I don't want to rely on them." He tugged a long strand of his sister's hair. "How're ya doin', O'Neill?"

Lacey shrugged. "'Kay."

Clay glanced behind him. "Better get to work," he said, and he turned and walked back toward the stage.

The band began playing "Pomp and Circumstance," and the graduates filed into their seats. Alec and Lacey turned to watch them. Alec tried to tune out the familiar, stirring music, imagining himself sailing across the sound, working with the wind.

The graduates were finally seated and the speeches began. He felt Lacey tense next to him as Clay walked up to the podium. He wanted to put his arm around her, pull her close, but he kept his hands in his lap as he watched his son. Clay looked for all the world like a man up there. His voice seemed deeper as it poured through the loudspeaker; his smile was genuine. There was nothing at all to betray his nervousness. Anyone would think he was making up the speech on the spot, he seemed so comfortable with the words. He talked about his class and its accomplishments. Then he hesitated briefly, and when he spoke again his voice quivered, almost imperceptibly.

"I'm grateful to my parents, who, through their love and respect, taught me to believe in myself and think for myself." Clay looked at Alec for a moment and then back up to the crowd. "My mother died in December and my only regret is that she can't be here to share this moment with me."

Alec's eyes filled. He felt a shifting in the audience behind him as people turned to look at him and Lacey. He would not fall apart here.

Windsurfing. Cutting through the water, far out in the sound, far from the shore. Far from the joyless reality that had become his life.

A woman leaned forward from the front row to get a look at him. For a moment he thought it was the doctor he'd met at the studio. Olivia. He leaned forward himself to see her more clearly, and felt some disappointment that the woman was a stranger.

Tomorrow was Saturday. He would go to the studio about the time she'd be done with her lesson. He would buy her lunch. He would finally ask the questions that had been haunting him for the last few long and lonely months.

CHAPTER TEN

The glass was cool beneath her fingertips. Olivia drew the glass cutter cleanly across the surface, mesmerized by the changing color of her hands. Tinted sunlight flooded the studio and fell across the work table in violet and teal and bloodred, at first making concentration on her task impossible.

"You'll get used to it," Tom said.

He was right. After a while, the colors seemed essential. Intoxicating.

Tom handed her another glass cutter, this one with a beveled, oil-filled handle. "Try this one on that piece," he said.

She took the cutter from his hand and scored a perfectly straight line down the center of the glass.

"You've been practicing," he said.

She beamed. "Nothing to it." She *had* been practicing, setting up the glass at her kitchen table each evening after work. She'd had to force herself the first time—there were several articles she should have been reading in *The Journal of Emergency Medicine*—but then she got into a pattern, and she began to look forward to getting home in the evening, sitting down with the glass. She'd drawn her own geometric design on graph paper last night, and now she was cutting shapes to fit the design from scraps of colored glass.

She had nearly finished scoring the third piece when Alec O'Neill arrived. He nodded to Tom before his eyes settled on her.

"I'd like to talk with you," he said. "Do you have some time after your lesson?"

She took off the green safety glasses and glanced at her watch, although she had no other plans for the day. "Yes," she said, looking up at him. He was wearing acid-washed jeans and a faded blue polo shirt, but at that moment he was bathed in a vermilion light from head to toe.

"Twelve?" he suggested. "I'll meet you across the street at the deli."

He disappeared briefly into the darkroom and then left again after telling her he'd see her soon. The stained glass panel on the door swayed for a moment after he closed it, and Olivia watched the wall near the darkroom change from blue to rose, then blue again.

She reached for another scrap of glass, a piece she'd been eyeing since her arrival at the studio that morning. It was a deep green, with a light, rippled texture.

"No," said Tom. "Not that piece. It's hand-rolled. Too delicate."

"But it's so beautiful." She ran her fingers over the cool, wavy surface. "I haven't broken anything yet, Tom. Couldn't I try it?"

"All right." Tom reluctantly let her set the glass in front of her on the table. "But pretend this piece of glass is Alec, all right? He's about as fragile as a person can get. I don't know what it is he wants to talk to you about, but keep in mind you need a light touch, okay?"

She looked at Tom's dark blue eyes. "Okay," she said, and the word came out in a whisper. She slipped on the safety glasses again, then carefully set the cutter to the glass, licking her lips, holding her breath. But despite her caution, despite the lightness of her touch, the glass splintered raggedly in pieces beneath her multicolored hands.

The tiny deli was crowded. People in bathing suits pressed up against the counter, and the smell of cold cuts and pickles mingled with the scent of sunscreen. Olivia felt overdressed in her flowered skirt and green blouse. She stood against the wall by the door, searching the crowd for Alec's face.

"Dr. Simon."

She followed the voice with her eyes, peering around the back of a woman standing next to her to see Alec at one of the four small tables near the windows. She squeezed her way through the crowd. Alec stood up and leaned across the little table to pull the chair out for her.

"Thanks." She sat down, catching her reflection in the window. Her straight, dark hair brushed the tops of her shoulders, and her bangs had grown long enough to sweep to the side. She remembered the black and white photograph of Annie, with her wide smile and glittering hair.

"It's crowded, but they're fast here." Alec turned to look up at the menu, written in chalk on a black slate board hanging above the counter. "What would you like?"

"Turkey on whole wheat," she said. "And lemonade."

Alec got up—*sprang* up—and walked behind the counter where he spoke to one of the young women who was making sandwiches, his hand on her shoulder. Olivia studied him from the safety of her chair by the window. He looked about forty and a little too thin, thinner than he had been that night in the ER. He was tan, but there were circles beneath his eyes she did not remember from that night, and hollows in his cheeks. His hair was very dark, yet even from this distance she could see the gray creeping into it at his temples. He moved with an athletic grace and she imagined he worked construction, something that put him outside all the time, that allowed him to use up his wired energy and kept him in shape.

The woman behind the counter handed him their drinks and he nodded his thanks to her before turning to work his way back to the table. Olivia wondered if he ever smiled.

He put her lemonade in front of her and took a long drink from his own cup before sitting down again. She had the feeling he did not sit often.

He looked at her across the table. The sunlight hit his eyes and sharpened the contrast between the translucent blue and the small black pupils. "I asked you to meet me because I need some answers about what happened to my wife that night," he said. She felt his denim-covered knees touch her bare ones and drew her chair back a little. "It didn't seem important then, but I can't seem to... I keep wondering..." He rubbed his temples with his long tanned fingers. "There are these gaps for me. I mean, I said good-bye to her on Christmas morning and that was it." He dropped his eyes and leaned back as the waitress set their sandwiches down in front of them. His Adam's apple bobbed in his throat and Olivia knew he was very close to the edge.

"Mr. O'Neill," she said after the waitress had left.

"Alec."

"Alec. I'll answer any questions you have to the best of my ability, but some of the answers might be hard to hear. Maybe this isn't the right place."

He looked around him at the press of bodies. "I have an office near here," he said. "I'm not working these days, but it's open. We could take our sandwiches over there. Would you mind? Do you have time?"

She nodded. "That would be fine."

Alec got a bag for their sandwiches, and they walked outside and across the street to the studio parking lot.

"You can follow me," he said, opening the door of a navy-blue Bronco.

She got into her Volvo and followed him out to Croatan Highway, where he turned left towards Nags Head. He had an office, he'd said. Maybe he *managed* a construction crew. What did he mean he wasn't working? She realized she knew nothing about him, other than the fact that he'd been married to the woman she both idolized and detested.

They pulled into the parking lot of the Beacon Animal Hospital and she frowned when she saw the shingles hanging below the sign: *Alec O'Neill, DVM* and *Randall Allwood, DVM.* He was a *vet.* She had to quickly reorganize her thinking about him.

Alec got out of his car, carrying the bag with their sandwiches. "Let's sneak in the back way," he said.

Olivia felt oddly criminal, as though she should tiptoe across the pea gravel that crunched beneath their feet as they walked around to the back of the building. Alec opened the door and they stepped into a cool, vinyl-tiled hallway. Frantic yapping filled the air. He unlocked the first door on the left and let Olivia in ahead of him. It was a small office, the walls paneled a pale, ashy color. The air was warm and stale, and Alec reached up to turn the knob of the air conditioning vent in the ceiling.

"Sorry it's so stuffy," he said. "Should be better in a minute."

"You're a vet," she said, taking a seat in the red leather chair he gestured toward.

"Uh-huh." He handed her the wrapped turkey sandwich and sat down behind his desk. The paneling was covered with photographs, many of the Kiss River Lighthouse. There were also a few pictures of windsurfers, and a portrait of a tawny-colored cocker puppy sitting next to a gray Persian cat that reminded her of Sylvie. She considered mentioning that to him, but he seemed so preoccupied with his own thoughts that she let it go.

Hanging in the window above his desk was a stained glass panel, the letters *DVM* in blue nestled between the tail of a black cat and the outstretched wings of a gull. Olivia had a sudden image of Annie presenting it to him—a surprise, a symbol of her pride in him.

He opened the wrapping on his sandwich and pressed the paper flat against his desk. "I can't say that I feel much like a vet these days, though. I was going to take a month off when Annie died, but..." He shrugged. "It's been a little longer than a month."

Olivia nodded. She knew exactly how long it had been. The night he'd lost his wife was the night she'd lost her husband.

"So." He looked up at her expectantly.

"What do you want to know?" she asked.

"Exactly what happened in the emergency room that night. You said you worked on her. I understand in *general* what you mean by that, but in her case, specifically, what happened?" He drew in his breath and glanced at a photograph on his desk. It was set at an angle so she couldn't quite make it out, but she was certain it was Annie and their children. She could see a patch of red that was most likely Annie's hair. "I guess more than anything I want to know if she was ever conscious," he continued. "If she felt anything. Suffered."

"No," she said. "She didn't suffer, and she never regained consciousness. I honestly don't think she ever knew what hit her. She probably felt a sharp stinging pain from the bullet—just enough to surprise her—and then immediately lost consciousness."

He licked his lips, nodded. "Good," he said.

"When they brought her in she was in very bad shape, and I could tell from her symptoms that the bullet had entered her heart and surgery was the only option."

"Was it you who performed the surgery?"

"Yes. Along with Mike Shelley. He's the director of the ER, and he got there about halfway through."

"Shouldn't she have been sent up to Emerson Memorial— to a trauma unit—for that sort of injury?"

Olivia stiffened. She heard Mike Shelley's voice in the back of her mind. *Maybe she should have been sent up. This way her blood's on your hands.* "Ideally, she should have had a trauma unit, yes. But it would have taken far too long to transport her to Emerson. She would have died on the way. Immediate surgery was her only chance."

"So you had to...open her up right there?"

"Yes. Then I... Do you really want to hear more?"

He set his sandwich down. "I want to know everything."

"We'd lost her heartbeat. I was able to get my hand around her heart and hold my finger and thumb over the holes the bullet had made, and then her heart began to contract again." Olivia had lifted her hand involuntarily. Alec stared at it and something contracted in *him*. She saw him start, saw his breathing quicken, and she rushed on, dropping her hand to the arm of the chair. "I was very hopeful then. I thought if we could just close those holes we'd be all right." She explained about Mike Shelley trying to sew the hole in the back of Annie's heart. She remembered feeling the blood seeping over her fingers. Sometimes still she woke up at night, winded, and had to turn the light on to be certain her hand was not warm and sticky with blood. Suddenly she was afraid of crying herself. The tears were so close. Her nose burned with the effort of holding them back.

"Well," said Alec. There was no feeling at all in his voice. "It sounds as though everything that could have been done was done."

"Yes."

He sank lower in his chair. "I've forgotten most of that night," he said. He was not looking at her. His eyes were focused on some invisible point in the air between them. "Someone must have called my neighbor, Nola, because I know she drove us home. I couldn't tell you a thing about that ride, though. My kids were with me, but I don't remember them being there at all." He looked over at her. "I get the feeling it was a difficult night for you too."

"Yes." She wondered what she was giving away in her face.

"Even talking about it now isn't easy."

"You have a right to know."

He nodded. "Well, thank you. For everything you did that night, and for taking the time to talk with me now." He gestured toward the sandwich in her lap. "You haven't touched your lunch."

She glanced down at the tightly wrapped sandwich. "I'll save it for dinner," she said, but he wasn't listening. He was staring at the photograph on his desk.

"I just wish I'd had one extra minute with her to say good-bye," he said. Then he looked at Olivia's hand, where her wedding ring circled her finger. "You're married?"

"Yes."

"Be sure to treat every minute with your husband as though it's your last."

"Well, actually, we're separated." She squirmed, feeling somehow guilty that she and Paul were alive and healthy, yet apart.

"Oh," Alec said. "Is that good or bad?"

"Horrible."

"I'm sorry. How long has it been?"

"Six months." If he made any connection between his six months without his wife and hers without her husband, he gave no sign.

"His idea or yours?"

"Entirely his." She looked down at her hand, where she was twisting the diamond ring around on her finger. "There was another woman," she said, wondering how far she would take this. "It wasn't an affair, exactly. They weren't...it was platonic. He barely knew her. I think it was more of a fantasy, and anyway, she's no longer around. She...moved away, but he's still upset about it, I guess."

"Is there any chance you two will get back together?"

"I hope so. I'm pregnant."

He dropped his puzzled gaze to her stomach.

"Just eleven weeks," she said.

Alec raised his dark eyebrows in a question. "I thought you said...?"

"Oh." She felt herself blush. "He...stopped by one night."

For the first time, Alec smiled, and she could see the handsomeness hiding behind his haggard demeanor. She laughed herself.

The door to his office opened a crack and a woman stuck her head in. "Alec?" She stepped into the room. She wore a white lab coat over jeans, and her dark hair was braided down her back. She glanced at Olivia, then back at Alec.

"I'm sorry," she said. "I didn't know you were with someone. Are you working?"

"You wish." Alec actually grinned. He stood up and walked around his desk to kiss the woman's cheek. Then he gestured in Olivia's direction. "This is Olivia Simon. She was the doctor in the ER the night Annie died."

"Oh." The woman's expression sobered and she turned toward Olivia. "I'm Randi Allwood."

"Randi's my partner," Alec said.

"Can't prove it by me," said Randi. "I seem to be running this place singlehandedly these days."

Alec nodded toward Olivia as a signal it was time to leave, and she rose from her seat.

"I need to talk to you, Alec," Randi said as Alec started for the door.

"All right," Alec held the door open for Olivia. "I'll be back in a minute."

He walked Olivia to her car. "Thanks again for doing this," he said, "and good luck with your husband."

"Thank you." Olivia turned to face him.

"Does he know about—" Alec dropped his hand between them, nearly touching her stomach with the back of his fingers "—what happened the last time he...stopped by?"

Olivia shook her head. "No."

"Does he know you still love him?"

"I think so." Did he? There had been so much unpleasantness between them lately that perhaps he didn't.

Alec opened her car door. "Make sure he knows that, okay?"

Olivia got into her car and waved to him before pulling out onto Croatan Highway. She could not recall the last time she'd told Paul she loved him. What about that night in April? She must have, but she couldn't remember. She'd avoided the memory of that night for the past few months.

It had been a Thursday night, early in April, and he'd stopped by the house, looking for something. Software for his computer? She didn't remember. It wasn't important. She was already in bed, but she was not quite asleep when she heard him let himself in. Her first thought was angry, bitter—what *gall,* marching into the house as though he still lived there— but it was quickly replaced by relief, that she could see him, talk with him. She lay still as he walked through the living room and up the stairs. He came into the bedroom and sat down on the edge of the queen-size bed.

"I'm sorry to disturb you this late," he said. "I just need to pick something up and then I'll be out of here."

She looked up at him. It was dark in the room, but she thought she saw something tender in his eyes. He was actually sitting on their bed, next to her, the warm length of his thigh against her hip. She reached for his hand and held it softly on his knee, grateful that he didn't try to pull away from her.

"You don't have to rush off," she said.

He lightly ran his thumb across the back of her fingers, encouraging her, and she brazenly drew his hand beneath the sheet to her bare breast.

He said nothing, but she felt the tips of his fingers graze over her nipple, once, then a second time. She wrapped her hand around the buckle of his belt, worried she was pushing him too far, too fast, but unable to stop herself. She had gone without him far too long.

He gently withdrew his hand from under the sheet and took off his glasses, folding the wire arms before setting them on the night table, close to the lamp. He lowered his head to her lips and kissed her softly. Then he began undressing, slowly, folding his shirt, his pants, and Olivia's heart pumped with anticipation, not just of making love to him but of the possibilities wrapped up in this moment. The hope. When he slipped into the bed next to her, she was smiling. She wanted to welcome him home.

He touched her woodenly at first, as though he did not quite remember who she was, what she liked. His penis lay limp and cool against her thigh, and she bit her lip in disappointment. She was doing something wrong; he was not aroused. The old uncertainty washed over her. Insecurities she had thought were long gone.

His touch grew more certain, though, as he stroked her body, and when she finally straddled him, reaching down to draw him inside her, he was more than ready. They made love with an exquisite slowness that Olivia knew she was controlling with her own body. She did not want it to end. While they were locked together she could pretend that everything was all right, that they would be together not just at this moment, but tomorrow as well, and next week, next year.

She cried when it was over, bathing his shoulder with her tears, and he ran his hand over her hair. "I'm so sorry, Liv," he said.

She raised herself to her elbow to look at him, not certain why he was apologizing. "Please stay," she said.

He shook his head. "We should never have made love. It just makes it harder for you."

"You still think about her." She tried to keep the accusation out of her voice.

"Yes." He rolled out from under her and sat up on the side of the bed, reaching for his glasses. "I know it's sick," he said. "I know she's dead, but it's as though she's taken over my mind. I've stopped trying to fight it. I've just given in."

Olivia sat up and moved next to him, resting her chin on

his shoulder, her hand on his back. "Maybe if you moved back in," she said. "If we tried to build a life together again. Maybe then you could forget her."

"It's no use, and it wouldn't be fair to you."

"Let that be my choice. I'd like to try, Paul. It was so wonderful making love just now. That's what we need to do to—" the word *exorcize* slipped into her mind "—to help you forget her."

"It won't work, Liv." He pulled on his shorts and stood up, staring at the dark sound through the window. "When we made love just now, I couldn't get into it until I imagined you were Annie." He turned to face her. "Is that what you want?"

Her tears were immediate. She pulled the blanket around her to cover her nakedness. "What was so extraordinary about her?" she asked. "What did she have that I'm so horribly deficient in?"

"Shh, nothing." He bent down, patronizing her with a quick hug. "Don't cry, Liv. Please."

She looked up at him. "Was it ever any good for you with me? Have you just been pretending it was good all these years so you didn't hurt my feelings?" He had been her first and only lover, and although she'd been far past the age when most women first made love, she'd been terrified. Paul's patient encouragement had made it easy for her, though. He'd fed her confidence with loving praise, tender compliments, and he'd told her, in the most flattering tone, that she had become an animal in bed. It relieved her to know she was capable of passion and desire when she'd long thought those emotions were impossible for her.

"Of course it was good," he said. "This has nothing at all to do with sex." He turned his head to the window, letting out a long sigh and rubbing his hands tiredly over his face.

"I'm sorry I said that about Annie, Liv." He shook his head, and when he spoke again, his voice was thick. "You didn't deserve that. I'm really sorry."

She did not know what to say. She had no idea what words she could use to save the little scraps of whatever they had left together. And so she watched in silence as he finished dressing, as he bent low to kiss the top of her head, as he left the room. She listened to him hunting in the study for whatever it was he needed. Then she heard him leave the house, closing the door quietly behind him, but closing it all the same. She listened to him pull the car out of the driveway, and she could still hear it as he turned the corner onto Mallard Run. It was another hour before she shut her eyes, and an hour after that before she slept. And it was just a few short weeks before she knew that the seed Paul had imagined himself planting in Annie had started a new life in her.

Alec wasn't surprised to find Randi still waiting for him in his office. He had avoided seeing her these past six months. He'd bumped into her a couple of times, once in the grocery store, once at the Sea Tern, but he'd kept those meetings brief, shifting away from her when he saw impatience replace the sympathy in her eyes. Now, though, he was cornered.

"Sit down, Alec." She was sitting in the chair Olivia had vacated, and he sat down once again behind his desk.

"It was so great to walk in here and see you in that chair," she said.

"Look, Randi, I was here because we were talking about something too heavy for a restaurant. This was the best place to meet. Don't read so much into it."

"When are you coming back, Alec?"

He hated being asked that question so directly. It made it impossible to dodge. "I don't know," he said.

She sighed, exasperated, and leaned forward in the chair. "What the hell are you living on? How are you keeping your kids fed? How do you plan to get Clay through four years at Duke?"

"It's not a problem."

"Isn't your brain disintegrating?"

"I *like* the time off, Randi. It gives me loads of time to work on the lighthouse committee."

She sat back, scowling. "Alec, you're pissing me off."

He smiled.

"Don't give me that condescending smile," she said, but she was smiling herself. "Oh, Alec, the bottom line is I *miss* you, and I *worry* about you. But you just dumped everything on me. You said it would be one month, and here I am nearly a year later doing it all."

"It hasn't even been six months, and you're not alone. Isn't Steve Matthews working out?"

She waved her hand impatiently through the air. "That's not the point."

He stood up and walked around to the front of his desk, leaning back against it, working his way toward the door. "Randi, if it's really too much for you, tell me and we'll get someone else in to help out. I don't want you to be overextended."

She sighed and seemed to deflate in the chair. "I'm all right. I just thought playing on your guilt might work." She stood up too, and he was pleased to see she was surrendering. She walked over to him for a hug, which he provided, stunned for a moment by the way her breasts felt against his chest, by the way her hair lay warm and fragrant next to his cheek.

He pulled away from her, gently. "Wow, do you feel good. It's been a while since I hugged a woman."

There was a sudden glint in Randi's eyes. "I've been dying to fix you up with this friend of mine," she said.

He shook his head.

"You'd love her, Alec, and it's time you went out. There's a world full of single women out there, and you're a free man."

He was irritated by the word *free*. "It's way too soon," he said.

"What about that doctor? She's pretty and..."

"And married and pregnant."

"Don't you miss sex?" she asked bluntly.

"I miss *everything*," he snapped, suddenly angry, and Randi took a step backward. "This is not some high school game, here, Randi. I've lost my wife. My right arm, you know? Annie wasn't replaceable."

"I know that," Randi said in a small voice. There were tears in her eyes.

"Let me do things at my own pace, okay?" He picked up his keys from the desk and started for the door.

"Alec," she said. "Please don't be angry."

"I'm not." He opened the door and looked back at her. "I shouldn't expect you to understand, Randi. Don't worry about it."

He was sweating by the time he reached the Bronco. He sat for a moment with the door open, letting the air conditioner blow the heat from the car. Then he pulled onto the road, heading north, his car practically operating on autopilot. In a short time, he had reached Kiss River. There might be tourists at the lighthouse this time of day, but he knew how to escape them.

He turned onto the winding, wooded road that led out to the lighthouse. He had to stop for a minute as one of the wild mustangs—the black stallion he had treated for an infection

last fall—leisurely crossed the road in front of him. He drove
on until he reached the small parking lot, surrounded on all
sides by thick, scrubby bayberry bushes. He got out of the
Bronco and took the footpath that led to the lighthouse.

The ocean was rough today. It broke wildly over the jetty,
and he felt the spray against his face as he neared the lighthouse. It rose above him, the white brick sun-drenched and
blinding. There were a couple of kids on the crescent of sand
that made up the small, ever-shrinking Kiss River beach,
and a few tourists milling around, some of them reading the
plaques, others shading their eyes as they looked skyward
toward the black iron gallery high above them.

Alec tried to make himself invisible as he approached the
door in the white brick foundation. He glanced over at the
old keeper's house. It looked as though no one from the Park
Service was around today. Good. He slipped a key from his
pocket and into the lock, jiggling it a little before the door
opened. Mary Poor had given the key to Annie years ago,
and she had cherished it. Controlled it jealously.

He disappeared inside, locking the door behind him. It was
cool, almost chilly. There were birds somewhere in the tower.
He couldn't see them, but he heard the echoing flap of their
wings, the occasional chirp that ricocheted off the rounded
brick walls. The brick was white in here as well, although the
paint was crumbling, flaking onto the floor in a coarse white
powder.

Alec began the long climb to the top up the steel circular
staircase, not bothering to stop at the six rectangular windows that marked the landings along the way, and by the
time he reached the claustrophobic room below the lantern,
he was winded. He was not getting enough exercise these
days.

He opened the door and stepped into the sunlight on the

gallery. He sat down, close to the tower so he could not be seen from below, and breathed in the damp, salty air.

Glassy blue water stretched out in front of him for as far as he could see. He had a clear view of the jetty, and it made him remember the funeral and the welcome numbness that had befriended him back then. From the moment Olivia Simon told him Annie was dead, he'd felt nothing. He didn't cry, didn't even feel close to crying. Nola helped him make the arrangements, weeping most of the time and talking about how Annie usually did that sort of thing, how good she was at rallying people together at a time of crisis, and he'd muttered some form of agreement from inside the comforting protective capsule that had formed around him.

The funeral was held in the largest church in the northern Outer Banks, but even it was not big enough to hold everyone who wanted to come. Someone told him later that people stood in the vestibule and spilled out onto the front steps and into the parking lot.

Alec sat between Clay and Nola. Lacey had refused to come and he didn't press the issue with her, although person after person wanted to know where she was. He was too dazed to realize that his response "—she didn't want to come—" was not enough.

Even Annie's mother was there, and Alec let her sit in the back of the church, although Nola begged him to try to make peace with the woman.

"Annie would never have let her sit back there, Alec." She spoke quietly in his ear.

"I don't want her near me," he said, and he wished he could stop Clay from turning around to get a glimpse of the grandmother he had never known.

Alec listened as people recounted how Annie had touched their lives. They walked up to the podium in the front of the church, one after another, ending finally with the county commissioner, who spoke of how Annie had been "woman of the year" for four years in a row, how she'd donated stained glass panels to the library and the community center, how she'd fought for the rights of people who could not fight for themselves. "She was our Saint Anne," he said. "You always knew you could turn to her for help. The word 'no' was simply not in her vocabulary."

Alec listened to it all from behind the wall he'd built around himself. He did not like it, this recitation of her generosity. It was her generosity that killed her.

Nearly everyone met on the cold beach at Kiss River afterward to watch Alec and Clay walk out on the windy jetty with Annie's ashes. It wasn't until Alec let them fly, until he watched in horror as the wind caught them and carried them away from him with cruel speed, that the numbness gave way to a searing pain. The ashes had been all that was left of her and he'd cast them away. He stared after them, stunned, until Clay tugged at his arm.

"Let's go back, Dad," he said. By the time they reached the beach once again, Alec was weeping freely and leaning on his son. Arms reached for him, and he was quickly pulled into a loving circle. Clay, Nola, Tom, Randi. Everyone. They moved closer to him until they formed one black mass with Alec at its core, completely surrounded, completely alone.

Alec leaned forward and looked directly down from the gallery. The ocean was closer to the lighthouse than the last time he was up here, or perhaps that was his imagination. Whatever the Park Service decided to do to save it, he wished they would hurry up.

He patted his pocket for the illicit key. *Mary!* Alec had a sudden brainstorm. He would call that journalist, Paul Macelli, as soon as he got home and tell him to get in touch with Mary Poor. He hoped the old woman was still alive, still thinking clearly. She would be loaded with anecdotes. Paul might not even need the historical collection if Mary was lucid enough to help him out.

Alec stood up and drew in a long breath of salty air. He felt better, although he could still hear Randi's voice, telling him about the joys of being "free." He shook his head. Randi couldn't possibly understand, he told himself. He shouldn't hold it against her.

He thought of the doctor. Olivia. The woman whose husband had left her for an illusion. *She* knew how he felt. He could tell by the way she spoke to him, by the empathy in her eyes. She had understood completely.

CHAPTER ELEVEN

Paul lay on his bed, staring at the colors in his ceiling. It was six in the evening, his favorite time in this room. The slant of the sun was just right to lift the tropical fish from the stained glass panel at his window and transpose them onto his ceiling, a bit distorted perhaps, but shimmering with blue and green and gold. He could easily lie here watching them until darkness fell. He had spent many evenings in this house watching his room grow dark, and this evening in particular he was anxious for darkness, for sleep. He wanted to sleep away the call from Alec O'Neill. He wanted to pretend he had not picked up the phone in the kitchen an hour earlier to hear the enthusiasm in Alec's voice. How could he sound so content, so pleased with life? He had an idea, Alec told him. He couldn't understand why he hadn't thought of it sooner. Paul could interview the old lighthouse keeper, Mary Poor, for the brochure on the lighthouse.

Paul had said nothing, stunned. *Oh sure,* he thought. *Why don't I just lie down on a bed of nails?*

"She's living at the Manteo Retirement Home," Alec continued. "My wife used to visit her there, and as of the last time she saw her—about six months ago—Mary was very lucid."

Paul could see no way out of it. He'd set his own trap the morning he'd called Nola Dillard and begged to be on the committee. But maybe Mary Poor would not remember him. Regardless of how lucid she was, she was a very old woman and she had not seen him in many years. He thought of telling Alec that something had come up and he would not be able to serve on the committee after all, but the pull of the lighthouse was too strong. He would be happy to meet with the old keeper, he said. He'd get on it as soon as he could. Then he'd hung up the phone, walked into his bedroom, and lay down to let the colors soothe him.

The phone rang again, and Paul reached over to his night table to pick it up.

"Am I interrupting something?" Olivia asked.

"No." He lay back again, phone to his ear. The colors were beginning to blend, melting onto the far wall.

"I just called to see how you're doing."

"I'm all right," he said. "You?"

"Okay. I'm working at the shelter tonight."

"Still doing that, huh?" He hated her working there. Annie had worked at the shelter out of a genuine desire to help others, but he did not understand Olivia's motivation. Occasionally he'd pictured something happening to her there, something horrible. Another crazed husband, perhaps. The thought of her being hurt terrified him in a way he hadn't expected.

"Yes. Just one night a week." She hesitated. "But the real reason I'm calling is to let you know I still love you."

He closed his eyes. "Don't, Olivia," he said. "I'm not worth it."

"I haven't forgotten the way things used to be between us."

He felt villainous. This was so hard for her. She'd counted on him, been *dependent* on him. She could be tough and self-assured in the ER, but once she took off her stethoscope, she was far frailer, far softer than anyone would guess.

"Paul?"

"I'm here."

"I'm sorry. I don't want to make you uncomfortable. I just needed to let you know that."

"All right. Thank you."

She hesitated a moment before saying good-bye. Once she'd hung up, he squeezed his face into a grimace. *Damn.* What was he supposed to say? She kept setting herself up to be hurt again.

He thought of telling her the truth. It would upset her at first, but then she'd understand. She'd know that what he'd felt for Annie had been no infatuation. It burned him every time he thought of that word coming out of Olivia's mouth, although it was hardly her fault for thinking that. He had let her believe it.

He had done countless interviews with Annie, dragging them out, putting off the inevitable writing of the article when he would no longer have any legitimate reason to see her. Those interviews had been torture for him. He'd had to keep his distance from her, hanging on every word across the vast plane of a restaurant table, when what he longed to do was touch her cheek or curl a strand of her phenomenal hair around his finger. He knew better than to try to get that close. He could tell by the little light of warning in her eyes to deal with her in a businesslike manner.

He'd taped the interviews, despite her reluctance. *"Promise you'll interview me as though we've never met before, Paul. As though we're total strangers to each other,"* she'd pleaded, and he had done his utmost to comply. He was afraid to listen to those tapes now, to actually hear her husky voice and her Boston accent and her crazy giggle.

She'd filled the tapes with talk about Alec. Paul hated listening to her talk about him, always with warmth, always a softening in her tone when she mentioned his name. He didn't need to hear about Alec, he told her. Her husband was not a necessary part of the article. She persisted, though, stubbornly reciting anecdotes of her marriage, drawing the words around herself like armor. He allowed her the armor, the distance. Until the night he could allow it no longer.

On that bitter cold night, five days before Christmas, he drove to her studio. He had not planned it, not in any conscious way, but he knew exactly what he would do. He parked in the little lot and looked up at the studio windows. The lights were on inside, and the colors of the stained glass in the windows were vibrant. He approached the front door, dizzy from the array of multihued designs mapped out on either side of him. Or perhaps from nerves.

Through the front door, he could see Annie leaning over the worktable, her hand moving slowly above a stained glass lampshade. The door was unlocked, and she looked up as he stepped inside. Her mouth was open, her eyes surprised and, he knew, a little frightened. She was alone, at night, in the cozy, colorful warmth of her studio. There was no safe restaurant table here, and she must have known he would not allow her to weave little stories about Alec and her marriage to deter him. He understood the fear in her eyes. He was just not certain if it was him she was afraid of or herself.

"Paul." She leaned back in her chair, making an effort to smile.

"Keep working," he said. "I just want to watch."

She made no move to lift the ball of cotton she was

holding. He pulled a second chair close to the end of the table and sat down.

"Go on," he said.

She dipped the cotton into a bowl of black liquid. Then she carefully smoothed it over the lead veins in the stained glass lampshade. She was wearing green corduroy pants and a heavy, off-white fisherman knit sweater. Her hair fell over her arm, spilling onto the table, onto the glass.

He watched her work for several minutes before he spoke again.

"I love you, Annie," he said, the words crackling in the silence.

She looked up, brushing her hair back over her shoulder. "I know," she said. She returned to her work but within a minute or two raised her head again. "Maybe you should go, Paul."

"Do you really want me to?"

She dropped her eyes quickly to the lampshade. Then she set down the ball of cotton and knotted her fingers together on the table. "Paul," she said, "*please* don't make this so hard."

"If you can honestly tell me you want me to go, I will."

She shut her eyes and he reached over to rest his hand on hers. Her fingers were cold and stiff. "Annie," he said.

She looked over at him. "I was so grateful to you for the way you handled the interviews," she said. "For not bringing up the past, for not trying to...take advantage of the situation when I knew that was what you really wanted to do."

"It was so hard to be with you and not..."

"But you *made* it," she interrupted, leaning toward him. "We both did. So why come here now and undo three months of willpower?"

"Because I'm going crazy, Annie," he said. "You're all I think about."

She withdrew her hand from his and lowered it to her lap. "You have a wife to think about," she said. "And I have a husband."

Paul shook his head. "I've treated Olivia terribly since we've been here."

"You need to put your energy into *her*, not me. Here." She pulled open a drawer in the worktable and took out a rubber band, which she slipped onto his wrist. "Every time you think of me, do this." She pulled back hard on the elastic and let it snap against the inside of his wrist. He actually winced at the sting. "You'll forget about me in no time," she said.

He smiled at her. "It's that simple, huh?" He looked down at his wrist, running his fingers over the reddened skin. "Will you wear one too?"

"I don't have to," she said. "When I think of you, I remind myself about Alec. My marriage comes first. I'm nearly forty now and my priorities are very clear in my mind. Forget about me, Paul. Walk out that door and forget I exist."

He stood up. "I won't ever be able to forget you," he said. He took off the rubber band and set it on the work table. "And I don't need this. Thinking about you is already painful enough. But I'll leave. The last thing I'd ever want to do is hurt you."

He bent over to kiss the top of her head, her hair soft beneath his lips. Then he walked slowly to the door, determined that he would leave without taking one last look at her.

"Paul?"

He turned around. She had stood up. She folded her arms stiffly, tightly, beneath her breasts, and he could almost see the battle going on inside her. "I don't want you to go," she said. "Could you just...hold me?"

He walked back to her and pulled her gently into his arms. She fit snugly against him, her hair smelling like sunshine. She sighed, letting her arms circle his back, and he felt a shiver run through her body.

"Oh, God, Paul."

He raised his hand to her throat. Her pulse was warm and rapid beneath his fingers. "I want to make love to you," he said.

She drew her head back to look at him, a crease between her brows. "This is a dangerous place to make love," she said. "There's glass everywhere. It gets into the carpet. It..."

"Shhh." He pressed his finger to her lips. "I don't care." He leaned forward to kiss her, and he was not surprised when she tipped her head back and opened her mouth for him.

She stepped away from him and reached for the wall switch to turn out the light, but he caught her hand.

"Leave it on," he said. "I want to see you."

"This is a glass house, Paul." She extracted her hand from his.

She was right, of course. On either side of them the glass walls were filled with the black night outside, but everything that went on in here would be visible from the parking lot, filtered through the multicolored images in the glass.

Annie hit the switch and took his hand, suddenly the leader. "Come with me," she said.

She led him to the far end of the studio, where photographs were displayed on a maze of white walls. She walked among the pictures, turning on the little light above each one to create a soft white glow around herself and Paul. Then she sat down on the floor, her back against the wall.

He was about to drop down beside her when he glanced at

the photograph closest to his head and found himself looking directly into the unsmiling eyes of Alec O'Neill. A chill ran up his spine, and he was a bit shaken as he lowered himself next to Annie. But she pulled him toward her, and his anxiety disappeared.

He watched her face as he undressed her. There was a need in her eyes, a need she had masked during the interviews that was open in her now. "I just want you to hold me," she said, but she did not try to stop him as he unfastened her bra. She rose to her knees to unzip her corduroy pants, and he helped her take them off. There was a softness, a fullness to her body he had not expected, a fullness he wanted to drown in.

He laid her back on the carpet and kissed her again before lowering his head to her breast. She caught his chin, drawing his face up until their eyes met. "Couldn't you be satisfied just lying here with me?" she asked.

He shook his head slowly, and as he touched her, as he moved his hands over her body, her resistance fell away.

He felt a sort of joy when it was over, when he lay holding her close to him and felt their hearts pounding in harmony. It seemed that they had lain that way for a very long time before he realized she was crying.

"What is it?" he asked, kissing her eyes.

She pulled away from him abruptly, covering her face with her hands. "I'm such a fool," she said.

"No, Annie, don't say that. Don't think it."

She sat up and drew herself into a corner, grabbing her clothes and holding them in a bundle against her breasts. She sobbed, her face lowered into her sweater, her shoulders tightening up when he tried to touch her. In the white light he could see silver in her hair, dozens of pale strands battling with the red, making her seem even more vulnerable.

He smoothed his hand over her hair. He didn't know what

to say, other than that he loved her, and he said that over and over again while she wept, her face buried in her arms.

"Annie, talk to me," he pleaded. "Tell me you're angry with me. Tell me *anything*."

She didn't respond, and after a few minutes he began to dress. He stood up, switching off the light above Alec's picture before lowering himself to her side again. Her crying had stopped, but she didn't raise her head and an occasional tremor still shook her shoulders.

"Let me help you get dressed," he said.

She shook her head. "No. Please just go home."

"I don't want to leave you like this."

"Please."

He stood again and reluctantly walked to the door.

"Paul?"

He looked back at her. She had raised her head and in the dim light he could see the terrible glistening red of her cheeks.

"Can you leave the Outer Banks?" she asked. "Can you move away? Please, Paul, I'm begging you."

The desperation in her voice made him cringe. He walked back to the maze of pictures and knelt down in front of her, resting his hands on her bare knees. It suddenly felt very cold in the studio, and she didn't try to stop him as he pulled the fisherman knit sweater from the bundle in her shivering arms. He fit it over her head, and she put her hands into the sleeves he held out for her. Then he lifted her thick hair out of the collar and leaned forward to kiss her forehead. "I would do anything I could for you, Annie," he said. "But I can't move away. This is my home too, now."

Olivia was asleep when he arrived home. He had called her to say he'd be late, not to wait up. He showered in the downstairs bathroom so he wouldn't wake her, and it was then that he found the slivers of glass. In his knee. His shoulder. His palm.

He went upstairs to the bathroom they shared and picked quietly through Olivia's side of the medicine cabinet for her tweezers. He sat down on the edge of the tub, struggling to remove the crystal thorns in the waxy light of the bathroom. The shard in his palm came out easily; the one in his knee slightly less so, and the cut bled each time he bent his leg. He would have to bandage it or there would be blood to explain on the sheets in the morning.

The glass in his shoulder was the most difficult to remove, the hardest to reach with the tweezers. When he was finished and in bed, when he was thinking back to the night, he wondered if Annie had them too, those slivers of glass. He hoped not. He could not bear to think of her in pain, or to remember her tears.

What if Alec was still awake when she got home? Maybe he would question her lateness, or catch her struggling to remove bits of glass from her shoulders. What would she tell him? What words would she use to explain away the evidence of her deception?

CHAPTER TWELVE

The young man was nervous, as well he should be. Mary could see it in his cautious smile, in the way his eyes refused to rest on her face. He wore round wire-rimmed glasses, and the glass looked very thin, almost as though it offered no correction. As though he wore them for show, to make himself look smarter than he actually was. He tapped the tip of his pen against his briefcase as he launched into an elaborate explanation of what he wanted, and Mary assumed the watery-eyed blank look of the elderly to make him wonder just how much she was following, to make him talk more, to watch him squirm.

She had not immediately known who he was. People change, yes. Plus he mumbled when he introduced himself. *Pawmasell,* he'd said. But now Mary knew. Now she had it all figured out.

"So we want to put together an educational brochure with anecdotes from your years in the lighthouse. You know, how the keeper would spend the day, or anything unusual that might have happened back then." He looked directly at Mary for the first time. "Does this make sense to you?"

"Yes, Mr. Macelli," Mary said, clearly startling him.

"Uh." A grin came quickly to his lips. "I guess you remember me," he said. "It's been so long, I figured..."

"I don't forget people."

"Well." He fumbled with the latch on his briefcase. "Do you mind if I record our conversation?" He pulled a notepad and a small black tape recorder from the briefcase. Apparently he did not want to talk about the past, which was fine with Mary.

"Not at all, not at all," she said. She had developed this habit of repeating things, which seemed to irritate no one more than it did herself.

Paul set the recorder on the broad flat arm of Mary's rocker, and his fingers shook as he turned it on. "Just begin anywhere," he said.

Mary rested her hands in the lap of her cotton dress and crossed her sneakered feet one over the other. She looked toward the waterfront, where the boats glistened in the sun. How Caleb would have loved this—this invitation to speak for as long as he chose about Kiss River! He would have known right where to begin his story. But Mary had some uncertainty these days about what came when, what was truth and what was legend. It didn't matter, though. No one would know.

She leaned back in the rocker and closed her eyes for a few seconds, listening to the faint hum of the recorder as it took in her silence. Then she opened her eyes and began to speak.

"The Kiss River Lighthouse was illuminated for the first time the night my husband Caleb's father was born," she said. "He came into the world in the downstairs bedroom of the keeper's house. Caleb's grandfather was the first keeper, and he and his wife had been in the house just a week when my father-in-law made his appearance—several weeks early, I should add. Everybody said it was the light that did it, that brought on his mother's labor. The midwife timed her contractions by the rotation of the beacon. That was September thirtieth, 1874. Twenty-seven years later, in 1901, Caleb himself was born in the very same room, right about the same time of night, brought into the world by the same midwife, who they say was old as the stars by then."

Mary was quiet for a moment. She looked toward the waterfront again and suddenly felt the limitations of the view, as she had when she first moved here. She missed the panorama from the tower and the endless expanse of sea rolled out beneath her.

"It's inborn, Caleb used to say." Mary nodded to herself. "All of it. Inborn."

"What is?" Paul asked.

Mary looked at him. His pupils were mere specks in the center of his dust-colored eyes. "When you're born under the light, you're born with a need to protect people from the sea and the storms. From their own mistakes in navigation. Your first breath is filled with the sea; your first vision is a pure white light. And you know right from the start what your life work is—no one has to tell you. That light must never go out and so everything you do, day and night, is toward that end." Mary paused a minute, cleared her throat. "It's the same when you marry into it," she said. "I knew from the day I first set foot in Kiss River that I would be Caleb's partner in that task.

"You can't grow up the son and grandson of a lighthouse keeper and not respect the sea, Caleb used to say. It's beautiful and it's dangerous, all at once, like some women." Mary looked again at Paul Macelli, who began writing feverishly on his notepad even though the recorder was picking up every word. His fingers were white from squeezing the pen, and in spite of herself, she felt some sympathy for him.

She continued quickly. "There was supposed to be a minimum of two keepers at Kiss River. The assistant keepers came and went, but Caleb's family never left. It was home to all of us."

She talked about what it had been like for Caleb growing up at Kiss River, how his mother had carried him across the sound in a boat every morning so he would attend school in Deweytown. "That's where Caleb and I met," Mary said. "We were married in 1923, and that's when I became the assistant keeper. But I'm getting ahead of myself, here."

Her mouth was dry. She would have liked something to drink. A beer would be just right, but alcohol was taboo here at the home. She sighed, drawing her mind back to her visitor.

"So how did the keeper spend the day, you ask? Climbing stairs, that's how." Mary smiled to herself. "I still climb those steps in my sleep, all two hundred and seventy of them, and when I wake up in the morning my legs ache and I could swear the smell of kerosene is on my pillow. I guess you could say it was a monotonous life, but looking back it was anything but. It's the adventures that stand out. The storms. The wrecks that washed up on the beach. How about the night the mosquitoes put the light out? Would you like to hear about that?"

"I'd like to hear anything you're willing to tell me."

"You don't happen to have a cigarette, do you?"

"Uh, no." He looked surprised. "Sorry."

Mary shook her head in disappointment and then told him about the summer after she and Caleb were married, how the mosquitoes were as big as mayflies and how they were drawn to the light to such an extent that it could barely be seen from the sea. She told him about the time when Caleb was just ten years old and the clockworks that turned the lens failed. His father had broken his leg and couldn't climb the steps to the lantern room, and they were between assistant keepers, so Caleb and his mother took turns for two entire nights, cranking the lens at the proper speed so that ships out at sea would know which light they were seeing and would not be driven off course. Mary could still remember worrying when Caleb did not show up for school those few days. When he finally made it in, he could hardly move from the stiffness in his arms, and he said his mother cried all night long from the pain in her shoulders. It was only the physical labor that was difficult, he claimed in later years. The timing of the rotations had posed no challenge, because their bodies had long existed in perfect harmony with the rhythm of the light.

Mary told him about the first wreck Caleb ever remembered being witness to. She could tell the story easily, she'd heard it so often from her husband. The wreck occurred one morning in 1907 when the four-masted schooner, the *Agnes Lowrie,* stranded on a bar off the coast of Kiss River. "She'd been sitting there quite a while by the time Caleb and his father got to her, along with the men from the lifesaving station," Mary said. "They could see the people on the deck, waving at them, thinking they were finally about to be rescued. But everything went wrong." She described the futile attempts to reach the schooner with the breeches buoy, dragging the story out, enjoying herself. "As she broke apart, people started jumping in the water, swimming toward the beach for all they were worth, but they didn't know how mean the sea could be. By the time they got close to Caleb and the others, they were floating dead men." Mary shuddered, remembering how Caleb's voice had grown hushed when he recounted that tale.

Someone inside the retirement home turned on the television. It blasted loudly onto the porch for a few seconds before someone else turned it down.

"Well," Mary said, "Caleb's father died right before we got married, and seeing as how Caleb had plenty of experience, he was made the new keeper. He had to apply for it. They didn't just pass the job on down, father to son, but it was no problem for him to get it. He was without an assistant for a few weeks before we got married, so it was just him and his crippled mother at the station one night when he was struck by a bolt of lightning."

"Really?" Paul Macelli looked impressed.

"Yes, indeed. Indeed. Frightening thing, and I can tell you I was glad I wasn't there to see it. He was standing on the steps inside the lighthouse when a bolt hit the tower and sent an electrical charge right through those two hundred and seventy steel steps. Caleb's legs went numb, but he wasn't about to let the light go out. No, sir. He dragged himself up to the lantern room right after he was hit and did a full night's watch." Mary looked out at the boats, thinking how typical that was of Caleb. Always steady and true. "That's the way it was in the old days," she said. "People had a sense of responsibility. They took pride in a job. It's not like it is with young people today."

Mary closed her eyes and was quiet for a full minute or two, long enough for Paul Macelli to ask her if she was through talking for the day. She looked over at him.

"No," she said. "I have one more story for you. Let me tell you about the *Mirage.*"

"Pardon?"

"The *Mirage.* It was a ship. A trawler." Mary's voice was so low that Paul had to lift the recorder close to her mouth to catch her words. "It was March of 1942. You know what was happening then, don't you?"

"The war?" Paul asked.

"The war indeed," Mary nodded. "The lighthouse had electricity by then, so we didn't have to worry about winding the clockworks or taking care of the lanterns. The only reason we were still there was that *someone* needed to be, so the Coast Guard let Caleb stay on as a civilian keeper. Thank the Lord. Don't know where we would've gone. Anyway, seems like back then most of the war was being fought right here off the coast. The lights were blacked out all up and down the Outer Banks and the lighthouse light was dimmed. You couldn't have any lights on shore because the German U-boats might see our ships silhouetted against them. Didn't seem to make much difference, though. Those subs were picking off our ships one a day back then. One a day."

Mary paused to let her words sink in. "Well, one morning, just before first light, Caleb was up in the lantern room and he spotted a small boat drifting way out to sea, bobbing up and down in rough water, most likely broken down. He could just make out two men in her. So he got in his little power boat and went out to them. The breakers were mean and cold, and Caleb wasn't sure he'd make it, but he did. By the time he reached the men, they were half froze. Caleb towed them in, and once up on the beach, they told him they'd been on an English trawler called the *Mirage* which had been torpedoed by the Germans sometime during the night. They were the only ones who managed to get off before she went down." Mary looked out toward the street. "When Caleb told me the name of the trawler, I remembered way back to when I was a girl and saw the word 'mirage' somewhere and asked my father what it meant. He told me how on a hot day, the beach can look like it has water on it when it doesn't. 'Sometimes, Mary,' he said, 'things are not what they seem.' I should have paid better attention to what he was trying to tell me." Mary looked at Paul Macelli to be sure *he* was paying attention himself.

"So Caleb brought these two British sailors up to the house. They spoke English with a kind of uppity accent. My daughter Elizabeth—she was about fourteen then—and I fed them three good meals that day, while they told us about being torpedoed and losing their friends and all.

"I bedded those boys down in the spare room upstairs that night. About eleven or so Caleb and I heard a scream coming from Elizabeth's room, so Caleb quick grabbed his shotgun and went up there. One of the boys was in Elizabeth's room, trying to talk her into some indecency. Caleb let him have it with the gun—killed him right there in the upstairs hall-way. The other fella took off when he heard Caleb shoot his friend, so we quick called the Coast Guard and they caught up with him." Mary smiled at the memory. "Found him tangling with a wild boar—a fate no man deserves. It turns out they weren't Brits at all. They were German spies. The Coast Guard had been getting reports of them for weeks and hadn't been able to track them down. Caleb got a medal for it, even though he was kicking himself for not just letting the two of them freeze to death out in the ocean. The *Mirage* didn't exist, of course."

Mary took in a long breath, suddenly exhausted. She pointed her thin, straight finger at her interviewer. "Sometimes, Mr. Macelli, things are not what they seem," she said. "Not what they seem at all."

Paul Macelli stared at her for a moment. Then he clicked off the recorder and lifted his briefcase to his lap. "You've been very helpful," he said. "May I come back sometime to hear more?"

"Of course, of course," Mary said.

Paul put the recorder in the briefcase and stood up. He looked out toward the waterfront for a moment and then down at Mary. "They tried to get you off lighthouse property in the early seventies, didn't they?" he asked.

Mary stared up at him. He was a fool. He could have simply left, not tempting fate and her ire any more than he already had. Obviously, though, he couldn't help himself.

"Yes, that's right," she said.

"Wasn't it Annie O'Neill who helped you out back then?" he asked, and Mary wanted to say, *You and I both know it was Annie, now, don't we, Mr. Macelli?* but she wanted this young man to come back. She wanted to tell him more stories of the lighthouse. She wanted to speak for hours into that little black recorder.

"Yes," she said. "Annie O'Neill."

She watched him walk down the sidewalk and get into his car. Then Mary leaned her head back against the rocker and closed her eyes. There was a burning pain in her belly that didn't subside until she heard the sound of Paul Macelli's car fade into the air.

Mary had met Annie in May of 1974, when she was seventy-three years old, practically a young woman. She'd been cleaning the windows in the lantern room of the lighthouse when she spotted a young girl down on the beach. *Her* beach, for the road leading out to the lighthouse was unpaved then and not too many people were willing to risk it. So at first Mary thought Annie was an apparition, and she stood at the window of the lantern room to see if the girl moved, if she was real. From that height, Annie was a tiny, doll-like figure, her dark skirt and red hair whipping out behind her as she stared out to sea.

Mary climbed down the stairs and walked out to the beach.

"Hello, there!" she called as she neared the girl, and Annie turned, shading her eyes with her hand and smiling broadly.

"Hi!" she said, her voice surprising Mary with its huskiness. So deep for such a young girl. Then she asked, as though Mary were the interloper here, "Who are you?"

"The keeper," Mary replied. "I live here."

"The *keeper*," Annie exclaimed. "Well, you must be the luckiest woman in the world."

Mary had smiled herself then, because that was exactly how she felt.

"I wanted to come out here by the lighthouse." Annie looked down at the sand beneath her bare feet. "I met the man I married right here on this spot."

"Here?" Mary asked, incredulous. "There's never anyone around here."

"He was painting and doing some repair work on the house."

Ah, yes. Mary remembered. A few summers ago the place had swarmed with young men, half-naked and bronzed and beautiful, scarves tied around their foreheads to keep the sweat from their eyes. She must mean one of them.

"It was nighttime when I met Alec, though. It was very dark, but every time the lighthouse flashed I could see him. He was standing right here, just enjoying the evening. The closer I got, the better he looked." She smiled, blushing, and turned her face back to the water. Her hair blew in long tufts up and around her head, and she lifted her hands to draw it back to her shoulders.

"Well." Mary was startled to know this had gone on

within a short distance of her home. "So this spot's special for you."

"Uh-huh. Now we've got a little boy. We've been living in Atlanta while Alec finished his training—he's a veterinarian—but all the while we knew this was where we wanted to settle down. So, now we're finally here." She looked puzzled and glanced up at the lighthouse. "You're the keeper?" she asked. "I didn't think they still had keepers. Aren't all the lighthouses run by electricity now?"

Mary nodded. "Yes, and this one's had electricity since 1939. Most of them are maintained by the Coast Guard these days. My husband was the last keeper on the North Carolina coast, and when he died, I took over." She studied Annie, who was shading her eyes to stare up at the tower. "Would you like to go up?" she asked, surprising herself with the question. She never invited anyone up with her. The tower had been closed to the public for many years.

Annie clapped her hands together. "Oh, I'd *love* to."

They walked toward the door in the lighthouse, Mary stopping for the bucket of wild blackberries she'd picked earlier that morning.

She could still climb to the top of the tower with only one or two stops along the way to catch her breath and rest her legs. Annie had to stop too, or maybe she just pretended she needed to so Mary didn't feel too old. Mary led her right up to the lantern room, where the enormous honeycomb lens took up so much space there was barely room to walk around it.

"Oh, my God," Annie said, awestruck. "I've never seen so much glass in one place in my entire life." She looked at Mary. "I love glass," she said. "This is fantastic."

Mary let her slip inside the lens, through the opening made when one segment of glass had to be removed a few years earlier after being damaged in a storm. Annie turned slowly in a circle, taking in all of the landscape, which Mary knew would appear upside down to her through the curved glass of the lens.

It took her a while to lure Annie away from the lens and down to the next level, where they stepped out onto the gallery. They sat on the warm iron floor, and Mary pointed out landmarks in the distance. Annie was quiet at first, overwhelmed, it seemed, and Mary watched her eyes fill with tears at the beauty spread out below them. She learned right then that nearly everything made this girl cry.

They spent a good two hours up there, eating berries and talking, the windows Mary had been cleaning in the lantern room forgotten.

Mary told her a little about Caleb, how she used to love to sit up here with him, how after decades of living at Kiss River they had never tired of the view. Caleb had been dead ten long years then, and having Annie to talk with, having someone listen to her so attentively, made her depressingly aware of how few friends she'd been able to make over the years, how hungry she was for companionship. For some reason, she told Annie about Elizabeth. "She hated living in such an isolated place, and she resented her father and me for making her live here. She just took off when she was fifteen years old. Quit school and married a man from Charlotte who was ten years older than her. She moved there and never sent us her address. I went there once to try to find her but without any luck." Mary looked out at the blue horizon. "That child broke our hearts." Why was she telling all this to a stranger? She no longer discussed these things even with herself. "She'd be forty-five now, Elizabeth." Mary shook her head. "It's hard for me to believe I've got a daughter who's forty-five years old."

"Maybe it's not too late to make things right with her," Annie said. "Do you know where she is now?"

She nodded. "I have an address I got from a friend of hers. I heard her husband died a few years back, so she must be living alone now. I write her letters a couple times a year, but I've never once heard back from her."

Annie frowned. "She doesn't know how lucky she is to have a mother who cares about her. Who loves her," she said. "She doesn't know what she's thrown away."

Mary felt a little choked up. She took a pack of cigarettes from the pocket of her brown work pants, pulled one out and lit it in her cupped hand, drawing the smoke deep into her lungs. It had been a long, long time since she'd let herself think about Elizabeth, and she could not bear how much it hurt, so she changed the topic to the young woman sharing her balcony. Annie's hands and lips were stained with the juice of the berries, the color clashing wildly with the red of her hair.

"Where are you from?" Mary asked. "Where did you pick up that accent?"

"Boston." Annie smiled.

"Ah, yes," Mary said. She sounded like one of the Kennedys, the way she strangled most of her words.

"My family has a lot of money." Annie rolled a berry between her thumb and forefinger. "My father is a heart surgeon. People come from all over the world to see him."

There was pride in her voice. And something else. A wistfulness, perhaps.

"I haven't seen him or my mother for a while, though."

"Why is that?"

Annie shrugged. "Well, they're incredibly busy. My father with his practice, my mother with her volunteer stuff and garden club and things. They never had much time for a kid. I was the only one, but even so, I think I was an after-thought. They just threw money my way from time to time. They had so much money they didn't know what to do with it. I could have anything I wanted. Anything material, at any rate." She looked out at the horizon. "I'm not going to raise my son that way. Not on your life."

Annie visited Mary often after that first meeting, some-times bringing her adorable baby son along with her, some-times not. Mary looked forward to her visits, and she found herself listening for the sound of Annie's little red Volks-wagen out on the dirt road, or searching for it when she was high up in the tower. Annie brought her things—bread or cookies she'd baked, or sometimes full meals that she'd make for Mary while cooking for her own family. Mary chided her. "You shouldn't spend your money on me, child," she'd say, but Annie said it wasn't polite to turn down a gift or mention what it might have cost the giver. Although Annie had come from money, she didn't seem to have it now. Her husband had to work long hours, she said, often at night, driving out to the mainland farms to doctor cows and horses and goats. There was little work to keep him gainfully em-ployed on the Outer Banks themselves.

It was only a few weeks after Mary first met Annie that the Park Service started talking about taking over the op-eration of the Kiss River Lighthouse. Rumors flew around Kiss River. They would pave the little sand road, people said. They would turn the keeper's house into a tourist attraction.

For the first time in her life, Mary had trouble sleeping. She knew what was coming, and she wasn't surprised when someone from the Park Service came to tell her that her ser-vices would no longer be needed. As a matter of fact, the man said, Mary would have to leave. They would help her relocate, he continued, but by that time Mary had shut the door in his face.

Annie got wind of it and was off and running before Mary knew she was involved. She had petitions signed, and dragged the newspapers into the fracas. She even showed up on Mary's doorstep one day with a television crew. She left no stone unturned, no politician unharassed in her rigorous, though often disorganized, crusade. By the time it was all over and Mary was granted permission to stay in one half of the keeper's house, everyone in the Outer Banks knew Annie's name as well as hers.

"Come on, now, Mary. Into your chair. Time for dinner."

Mary felt someone tugging at her arm. She opened her eyes to see Gale, one of the young girls on the retirement home staff, holding her cane in front of her. She looked out at the street.

"Is the young man still here?" she asked. Then she remembered watching him get into his car and drive away.

"No, Mary. Your visitor left an hour ago."

"He'll be back," Mary said, rising to her feet, wincing as her left foot hit the floor and sent the pain up into her hip. "He'll be back, all right."

Chapter Thirteen

Alec could have taken his film into the studio anytime that week, but he waited until Saturday. It wasn't until he'd pulled into the parking lot that he admitted to himself the reason for his delay: he wanted to see Olivia Simon again. He'd found himself talking to her in his head all week, telling her things about Annie other people were no longer interested in hearing. He could always talk to Tom Nestor, but Tom's grief was still as real as his own, and that bothered Alec. He had never particularly liked sharing Annie with Tom.

Olivia was at the work table where he was accustomed to seeing Annie. Her head was bent low, and she was wearing Annie's old green safety glasses. It had given him something of a jolt, seeing her in those glasses for the first time last week, but he could think of no good reason why she shouldn't use them.

She was holding the soldering iron and a coil of solder. Tom leaned close to her, guiding her fingers, giving her encouragement. Cigarette smoke snaked into the air above Tom's head. He had never smoked in here when Annie was alive.

Tom looked up as Alec closed the front door.

"Howdy, Alec," he said.

Olivia lifted her head from her work and smiled.

"Hi." Alec walked over to the table and peered down at the pieces of glass. "What are you working on?" he asked Olivia.

She handed him a sheet of graph paper, and he studied the design drawn in felt tip pen—a rectangle with a crazy quilt of shapes inside it, each labeled a different color. He smiled at its simplicity, and at the pleasure in her face.

"She's a natural," Tom said, nodding toward her, as Alec placed the paper on the table again.

"I'm a *novice*," Olivia corrected him, and neither Tom nor Alec was about to argue the point.

Alec tapped her lightly on the shoulder and she looked up at him, the green of the oversized glasses a near match for her eyes. "Let me buy you lunch," he said. "A real one. No indigestion this time."

She seemed to weigh the invitation for a moment, then nodded. "All right."

Alec went into the darkroom and began developing the black and white film he'd used the Sunday before. He thought of the little stained glass panel Olivia was working on. Annie's first panel had been large and elaborate—two sheep standing in a meadow composed of five different greens. She had always refused to waste her time on anything just for the practice. If her first effort didn't produce something she could display with pride, there would be no second attempt.

He met Olivia in the parking lot at noon. "Are you in a hurry?" he asked as she got into his Bronco. "We can drive up to Duck and eat on the sound if you have the time."

"That's fine." She buckled her seat belt across the lap of her white cotton pants, and for a few seconds he was mesmerized by the delicacy of her hands, the whiteness of her fingers, and the smooth, rounded tips of her short nails. He remembered what she'd told him about holding Annie's heart in her hand, and he could barely tear his eyes away as he started the Bronco and pulled it out onto the road.

"I haven't been up this far," she said when he took the right fork in the road, heading toward Duck.

"Really?" That seemed ridiculous. "It's just a few miles from where you live, and you've been down here...how long?"

"Nearly a year," she admitted. "I started working the day after we moved here. We had a new house to fix up, and there simply hasn't been any time for us to explore the area."

She spoke as though she and her husband were still together. Maybe in the week since he'd seen her things had changed. Maybe he'd moved back in.

They got a table on the deck outside the tiny restaurant. They were directly over the water, and a few fat geese looked up at them expectantly as he and Olivia took their seats.

They both ordered crab salad. Alec was relaxed, a different person than he'd been a week earlier. He remembered ordering their sandwiches in the deli, his body coiled and tense, ready to bolt. He'd been afraid to hear Olivia talk about the night Annie died, but it had helped him immeasurably to listen to her describe what happened, to hear her talk about feeling the same desperate need to keep Annie alive that he had felt.

He ordered wine, but Olivia did not, patting her stomach by way of explanation, and he remembered the baby.

"How are you feeling?" he asked. She looked healthy,

except for the nearly translucent whiteness of her skin, which he assumed was natural for her.

"I'm all right," she said. "A little tired. I worry about how the baby's being affected by the stress I'm under."

"You husband's still gone?"

"Yes." She looked down at her hands in her lap, probably playing with her ring as she had the week before. "I never imagined going through a pregnancy alone, much less raising a child by myself." She smiled up at him. "I have nightmares that it might be twins. That's all I'd need."

"Are there twins in your family?"

"I'm one."

"Really? Identical?" He tried to picture two of her.

"No. He was a boy."

"Was?"

"He died a few years ago." Olivia brushed her hand through the air, obviously whisking that topic away. "Anyway, I'd get this feeling every once in a while that there were two of them in here and it made me panicky. But I heard the heartbeat at my doctor's appointment this week, and there was just one."

They were quiet while their food was set in front of them. A ray of sunlight shimmered in Olivia's dark, arrow-straight hair.

"How are things with your husband?" he asked when the waitress had left their table.

Olivia lifted her fork. "Not good," she said. "He seems completely disinterested in me. I called to tell him I love him—as you suggested—and he said I shouldn't bother, that he's not worth it." She tried to smile, but didn't quite succeed.

"Maybe he feels guilty about the affair."

He saw her start. "He didn't have an affair. I *told* you it was more of a fantasy."

"Sorry," he said.

She took a bite of her crab salad, chewing and swallowing before she spoke again. "He worked with her, and then he became obsessed with her, talking about her all the time. He'd compare me to her, and I didn't compare too well."

"I find that hard to believe."

"She was married and not the least bit interested in him. He admitted that it was completely one-sided." She spoke forcefully, as if she were trying to convince herself as much as she was him. Maybe more. "Nevertheless," she continued, "I didn't measure up to his image of this woman, so when she... so even though he couldn't have her, he still left me."

Alec frowned. Her husband sounded like a jerk.

"She was all he'd talk about, and I put up with it. I thought I shouldn't overreact, I should let him talk and get it out of his system, but he never did."

"Did he leave so he could get closer to her? I mean, forgive me, Olivia, but maybe he *wanted* to have an affair with her and didn't feel right about it while he was still with you. So he..."

Olivia shook her head. "She moved away before he moved out."

"Where did she go? Could he still be in touch with her?"

She suddenly laughed, then covered her mouth with her hand. "No, I'm sure he isn't." She picked at the crab salad with her fork. "She's in California."

"California's not on another planet. What makes you so sure he's not still communicating with her?"

"He would have told me. He never hid his feelings from me, although at times I wished he had." She looked across the table at him. "She was a better person than me in some ways," she said. "Ways that were important to my husband."

Alec sat back in his chair. "Hey, listen," he said, "the man's obsessed. Irrational. Don't get sucked into thinking he's right. He never really knew her. If he'd ever had the chance he probably would have figured out she was a shrew."

She lowered her head, and he saw a small, glistening teardrop on her lower lashes, watched as it fell to her lavender blouse, where it made a dark round spot above her breast.

He leaned toward her. "Olivia?"

She raised her napkin to her eyes, glancing at the other diners. "I'm sorry," she said softly, "I'm sure you didn't invite me to lunch so that I could embarrass you."

He pulled his chair closer to the table. "I didn't invite you to lunch to upset you, either." His knees touched hers beneath the table, and she pulled back slightly.

She began slowly shredding her napkin into long, ragged strips. "I just don't understand it," she said. "He was so wonderful before he met her. Our marriage was really good, excellent, and then suddenly it fell apart. I keep waiting for the old Paul to come back, but it's as if he died."

Alec shook his head. "Probably just hibernating. Stay in his life until he wakes up, Olivia. Remind him how good things used to be."

She had stopped crying, but her nose was still red and it made her look helpless. Nothing like the woman he'd met the week before, the woman who had meticulously described her attempt to save Annie's life.

"I've been trying to be a little more like her," she said. "Like the other woman."

Alec frowned again. "It's *Olivia* he fell in love with, right? It's Olivia he had the healthy relationship with, not this—" he wanted to say *bitch,* but he did not quite feel comfortable using that word in front of her "—this woman who brings out the craziness in him."

She folded her arms across her chest, her hands balled into tight, white fists. "I was infertile," she said. "I think that's when it changed. When his *feelings* changed. I had surgery, but it was too late to snap him out of it."

"Maybe if you told him about the baby?"

"Then I'd never be sure if it was me or the baby he wanted."

There was a sudden bleating sound from her purse, and she reached in to turn off her beeper. "Is there a phone here?" she asked.

"I'm sure they'll let you use the one inside."

She stood up, straightening her spine and giving a slight toss to her shimmery dark hair as she walked into the restaurant, once again the competent doctor.

He picked apart his uneaten slice of bread and was feeding chunks of it to the geese by the time Olivia returned to the table and took her seat again.

"Do you have to go?" he asked.

She shook her head. "They can handle it without me." She looked down at her shredded napkin, frowning, as though she had no idea how it had gotten there. She scooped the shreds and deposited them on her plate, giving him a rueful smile. "I'm sorry, Alec," she said. "Next time I start babbling about my problems, shove a cork in my mouth, okay?"

"I don't mind listening," he said, dropping the last piece of bread into the water. The geese fought over it, noisily. "Your circumstances are very different from mine, but the bottom line is that we're both alone. I know how that feels."

She played with the straw in her iced tea, now that her napkin was no longer available. "When I start missing Paul, I think about you without Annie—without the *possibility* of

Annie—and I..." She hesitated, shook her head. "I miss *touching*. I don't mean sex, exactly, but just...holding hands, just that *intimacy* with another person. You don't know how good you've got it till it's gone."

He nodded, and she leaned back in her chair and dropped her hands to her lap again.

"I've started getting massages just so I can feel someone *touching* me," she said.

He smiled at her candor, and he understood what she meant. He wondered if she went to a man or a woman, or if it would matter, or if he should get a massage himself. How would it feel, paying someone to ease the pain of a body suffering from neglect?

They stopped for the light at the corner of Croatan and Ash on the way back to the studio, and Alec pointed down Ash toward the sound. "See the third cottage on the right?" he asked. "That was where Annie and I first lived when we moved here." The small cottage stood on stilts above the sand. It was blackened with age; it had been black even when he and Annie lived there. "We didn't have much money, as you can tell."

Olivia was quiet as the Bronco began moving again, slowly, through the heavy summer traffic. "I started working at the shelter after the night Annie died," she said finally.

He glanced over at her. *"Why?"* He hated that place.

She shrugged. "Well that was the first I'd become aware of its existence. My husband was gone and I had the time." She looked over at him. "The staff still talk about Annie."

He smiled. "Do they?"

"They adored her. They talk about how she was always full of ideas and how everyone depended on her creativity.

The place is falling apart without her. At least that's what they say."

"Like my house," he said, almost to himself.

He pulled into the studio parking lot. Olivia unbuckled her belt, but turned in her seat to face him. "What was she really like, Alec? When they talk about her at the shelter she sounds like she should be canonized."

He laughed. "I doubt they canonize atheists." He turned the air conditioner up another notch. "She had very strong values and she put her money where her mouth was, literally. She donated practically all the money she made to various causes. Animal rights, AIDS, the homeless, the right-to-lifers."

"The right-to-lifers?"

"Oh, yeah. She was a rabid antiabortionist. I made donations to Planned Parenthood to try to nullify her effort." He smiled at the memory. "Made her mad as hell."

"I'm surprised she'd be antiabortion. She sounds so liberal."

"She was about most things, but she was also very pro-family." He looked up at the studio windows. "People talk about her like she was perfect, but she wasn't. She was human. She'd get moody sometimes." He felt a little guilty, tarnishing Annie's image in Olivia's mind, but those strange periods of melancholy were as much a part of Annie as her altruism. It was a moodiness that came and went in waves. He never understood it, and she never seemed able to explain it to him. She would withdraw from him, from everyone. *It's my dark side,* she'd tell him, and he could almost see the black shroud settling over her shoulders, over her head. He learned quickly there was nothing he could do to turn the tide of those moods. All he could do was wait for them to pass on their own. It bothered him enormously that she had died in the midst of one, that she had died troubled.

"I've come to admire her." Olivia sounded almost shy. "Now that I know how challenging it is to work in stained glass, I look at her things and I'm in awe."

He was touched. He looked up at the studio and could just make out one of Annie's few remaining stained glass panels, a design of beveled glass. "She was an extremely talented artist," he said. "I think she could have gone a lot further if I hadn't dragged her out of school to get married."

"Where was she going?"

"Boston College."

"Really?" Olivia looked slightly stunned. "That's where my husband went. He graduated in seventy-three."

"That would have been Annie's class," Alec said. "Next time you speak to him, ask him if he knew her. Her maiden name was Chase."

Olivia was quiet for a moment. "Well," she said finally, reaching for the handle of the door. "Thank you for lunch."

He stopped her with his hand on her arm. "Do you have many friends here?" he asked.

She shook her head. "Just at work."

He pulled out his wallet and removed a business card. He turned it over and wrote down his home phone number. "Keep me posted on how things go with your husband," he said, handing it to her.

"Thanks." She started to step out of the car.

"Olivia?"

She turned to look at him.

"I want you to know how glad I am that you were the doctor in the emergency room that night."

She smiled. "Thank you," she said. She got out of the

car and closed the door softly behind her. He watched her step around the front of the Bronco, brushing a strand of her sleek, dark hair from her face.

Her husband was a fool.

Chapter Fourteen

It was the fourth time Olivia had stopped in to look at the crib. She'd intended to go directly home after Alec dropped her off, but the little shop was right across the parking lot from the studio and it had a lure on her she could feel from a mile away.

The crib was a white Jenny Lind, and she could picture it in the small third bedroom of the house. It would look wonderful, that clean white against the sunny yellow wallpaper she had already picked out. She wished she could buy the crib now, today, but there was still the chance that Paul might stop by the house for something. She didn't want him to learn he was going to be a father from the sudden appearance of a crib rather than from her.

She was still clutching Alec's business card when she returned to her car. It was soft as felt from months of being carried in his wallet. She slipped it into the back of her own wallet, gnawing on her lip. She had lied to him. Omitted things. She hadn't told him that Paul was the author of that article on Annie in *Seascape*. What choice did she have? She couldn't take the chance of telling him, of having him realize it had been Annie that Paul worshiped.

When she got home, she made a batch of cookies—she couldn't remember the last time she'd baked—and changed into a blue flowered blouse Paul had always loved on her. She studied her map at the kitchen table, checking it against the address he'd given her, while the house filled with the smell of oats and brown sugar. She carried the cookies out to the car and drove the ten miles to South Nag's Head.

It was close to six when she pulled up in front of his house, a small gray cottage one block from the ocean, in the midst of the tourists and their summer rentals. It was new. She could smell the cedar siding as she stepped onto the front deck and knocked at the door. She had to knock a second time before Paul opened it.

"*Olivia,*" he said, not bothering to mask his surprise.

She smiled. "I wanted to see your new house." Her tone was that of an intimate friend. Curious. Caring. "And I made some cookies for you."

He stepped aside to let her in. "You *baked?* I didn't think you knew how to operate an oven."

His house felt like a shrine to Annie. Each of the four large windows in the living room was adorned with a stained glass panel—two of the silk-clad women, and two underwater scenes filled with tropical fish and fluid strips of blue and green in that distinctive Annie O'Neill style. Tom Nestor had explained that technique to her at length—twice—and she still could not begin to understand how it was done.

"Your house is very nice, Paul," she said.

There were four skylights in the cathedral ceiling above them and they let in a welcome pool of clear white sunlight.

"Thanks." He walked over to the dining area and began straightening the already neat piles of paper on the dining room table, the table she had long considered her own. He seemed flustered at having her there, and she felt as though she'd walked in on him with another woman. In a way, she had.

"I'm interrupting your work," she said. His portable computer was also on the table, and it was apparent he'd been in the throes of something when she arrived.

"No, that's all right. I'm ready for a break. Have a seat."

She lowered herself into one of the familiar dining room chairs.

"I've got some iced tea. Or would you rather have wine?"

"Tea would be great," she said. She watched him disappear into the kitchen, knowing she was keeping things from him as well. She could hardly tell him she'd had lunch with Alec, and she certainly wouldn't ask him if he'd known Annie went to Boston College. She could imagine his reaction if that was something he hadn't known. He'd torment himself over what might have been. She didn't want to feed his fantasy of Annie any further.

He returned to the dining room and set her iced tea on the table, but he didn't sit down, and he had brought nothing to drink for himself. He stood near the computer, hands in his pockets.

"Have a cookie." Olivia gestured toward the plate.

Paul lifted the foil and raised a cookie to his mouth. "No arsenic in them I hope." He smiled, and for a moment she was struck by his hazel eyes, by the warmth his smile gave them. Seeing that charm in his face made her realize how long it had been since she'd felt any affection at all from him. She wished she knew how to seduce. She had never learned—had steadfastly avoided learning—those skills.

She forced her eyes back to the table. "What are you working on?"

Paul glanced at one of the stacks of paper. "I joined the Save the Kiss River Lighthouse Committee. We're putting together an educational brochure to generate interest in saving the lighthouse."

He had always had a weird fascination with that lighthouse. The day they arrived in the Outer Banks, before they had even gotten all the boxes in the house, he went to see it. Olivia stayed home and unpacked, a little annoyed at being left to do the work by herself and disconcerted by the fact that he hadn't invited her to come along. That day had been the beginning of the end.

"It was bizarre, Olivia," he said now. "I walked into this meeting and who should be the chairman of the committee but Annie's husband." He looked at her and she knew he was checking to see if this was a safe topic. She could not be sure of her own expression. Alec was chairman of the lighthouse committee? Paul was working shoulder to shoulder with him? She thought quickly. Should she tell Paul that she knew Alec? Then she'd have to tell him about the stained glass lessons, the two lunch dates. She felt herself getting wrapped more tightly in the web of lies.

"I wanted to get up and leave," he continued, waving the cookie in the air, "but I was trapped. I'd practically begged to be allowed to join, but the last thing I expected was to find Alec O'..." He stopped and grimaced. "I'm sorry. I'm sure you don't want to hear any more of my Annie crap."

"It's all right," she said. "You can talk about her. I know you need to. I know there isn't anyone else you can talk to about her." He probably felt the way she had earlier that afternoon when she'd bent Alec's ear about *him*. She finally understood Paul's need to spill it all out.

He sat down across the table from her, staring at her, and his eyes had reddened. "Why would you do that?" he asked. "Why would you sit here and let me ramble on about someone who destroyed your marriage?"

"Because I still love and care about you."

He turned his face away from her. "I can't talk about her to you anymore. It was never fair of me to do that."

Olivia stood up and walked over to his chair. She knelt next to him, resting her hand on top of his, but he stiffened and drew his hand away.

"Don't," he said.

She sat back on the carpet. "Do you remember when we used to take those long walks together early in the morning?"

He frowned at her. "Why are you bringing that up?"

"It's one of my favorite memories, walking with you through Rock Creek Park, holding hands. Buying bagels with cream cheese and scallions at Joe's little deli and..."

"And your beeper going off half the time."

She leaned back against the wall, defeated. "Did it seem like that often?"

"At least."

"I'm sorry. If I'd known what it would cost me, I would have done something about it." She had thought he'd admired her for her diligence. A *workaholic,* he used to call her, although he had always made it sound like a term of endearment rather than a complaint. Certainly he understood the forces that had made her that way. He understood them better than anyone. Even in high school and college, she'd intentionally lost herself in work, leaving herself no time for a social life. Work had kept her safe from the flirting she had never been able to master, the casual sex that was entirely out of the question. By the time she met Paul and discovered she felt safe with him, her work pattern was firmly in place and there seemed to be no reason to change it. Now she could see her mistake. She'd taken him for granted. She had given Paul so little of herself that he needed to turn to a fantasy to feel whole, and he'd found the fantasy superior to his marriage.

"It's my fault." She rested her head on her arms. "It's my fault everything fell apart. I miss you so much, Paul. I would do anything if you'd come back. I'd quit my job. I'd work as a waitress. I'd shell shrimp. Shuck oysters. Just weekdays. No evenings or weekends."

She heard him laugh and when she looked up he had taken off his glasses. His eyes were still rimmed with red, but there was a smile on his face.

"Liv," he said, a tenderness in his voice she had not heard in many months. "I'm the one who's screwed up here, not you."

"Nine years," she said. "You seemed happy. You seemed content."

He nodded. "I was *very* content. It was good. It was nearly perfect. I've changed, Liv, and I'm sorry."

She thought of the crib, of the heartbeat that had filled the examining room in her doctor's office. "We could see a counselor," she said. "There must be a way we can work it out."

He shook his head and stood up, holding out his hand to help her up from the floor. He let go as soon as she'd reached her feet, and he started walking in the direction of the door, obviously telling her she had stayed long enough.

"Thank you for the cookies," he said, opening the door.

She felt a wave of desperation as she stepped out onto the deck. She turned back to look at him. "I meant what I said,

Paul. About changing. About quitting my job if that's what it takes. Maybe I..."

He stopped her with another shake of his head. "You should have your own lawyer, Olivia," he said, and then he closed the door softly between them.

CHAPTER FIFTEEN

July 1991

"Where did you get that?" Clay looked across the breakfast table at his sister. Alec glanced up from the newspaper to see what he was talking about. Lacey wore a headset attached to a small red transistor radio which rested next to her plate. It was the first time he'd seen it.

"Jessica gave it to me for my birthday," Lacey said, her voice flat. She picked up the radio from the table and attached it to the waistband of her shorts as she stood up, leaving half of her frozen waffle on the plate.

Alec frowned. "For your *birthday?* Which birthday?"

"Doesn't matter." Lacey grabbed her book bag from the counter. "I've gotta go."

"Lacey, wait a second." Alec stood up as Lacey slipped out the screen door. He heard the slap of her tennis shoes on the driveway as she ran out to the street to wait for the bus. It was her first day of summer school.

He looked at Clay, who stared back at him, his fork poised in the air. "We missed her birthday," Clay said.

"We couldn't have. It's the first, right?"

"Right. And today's the second."

Alec felt as though someone had socked him in the gut. *"Damn."* He sat down again, closing his eyes, pressing his fingers to his suddenly aching temples as he thought back to the day before. Lacey had been quiet at breakfast, and he'd been absorbed in a report on the erosion at Kiss River. He'd barely taken his eyes off it during the entire meal. She'd been up in her room when he got home last night. She said she wasn't hungry, so he and Clay ordered a pizza and ate it by themselves in the kitchen. Lacey didn't come out of her room the entire evening. He'd been surprised by that. She spent a lot of time in her room these days, but it was odd for her to completely disappear for the night.

"Dad?"

Alec opened his eyes at the sound of his son's new, adult-sounding voice. He sat back in his chair with a sigh. "I don't believe I did that," he said. "Did I miss yours too?"

Clay smiled. "No, Dad, I'm October, remember?"

Alec ran his hand over his chin. He needed a shave. "We'll have to celebrate it today," he said. "I'll pick up a gift for her. Will you have time to get her something, too?"

Clay nodded.

"What can I get?" He looked helplessly at his son. "What does she want these days?"

"Mom always got her an antique doll."

"Yeah, but she's fourteen now." He had no idea where he could find one, anyway. Annie usually picked up the dolls sometime during the year and tucked them away for Lacey's birthday. Besides, they were Annie's special gifts. Annie died when Lacey was thirteen, so Lacey should have thirteen dolls.

After Clay left, he stopped by Lacey's room. It was not

nearly as messy as it had been before her whirlwind cleaning spree on the day of Clay's graduation, but the clothes
and papers were starting to mount up again. This room had
become her refuge.

She'd come home late the other night, rushing past him to
get to her room. But the glimpse he got of her was enough to
tell him something was wrong: her blouse was misbuttoned,
her face tear-streaked. He stood outside her door for several
minutes, listening to her crying, before he knocked and went
in. The room was very dark and he had to feel his way to her
bed. He sat down on the edge and as his eyes adjusted to the
darkness, he saw that she was on her side, facing the wall. She
was sniffling as quietly as she could, trying to hide her tears
from him.

"What's wrong, Lace?" he asked.

"Nothing." He had to lean close to hear her.

"Has someone hurt you?"

She made a sound of disgust. "God, you are so *warped.*"

Alec pressed his hands together in his lap. "Maybe it would
help if you saw a counselor, Lace," he said. "Would you like
that? You'd be able to talk about whatever's on your mind."

She didn't answer.

"Would you like to see a counselor, Lace?" he repeated.

"No."

"Could you tell *me* what's bothering you then?"

"I already told you, *nothing.*"

"Sweetheart." He touched her arm and she snapped her
shoulder away from him, a wounded sound escaping her
lips.

"Would you please go away?" she asked.

He stood up and walked to the door. "I love you, Lace,"
he said, before closing the door on her silence. He waited in
the hall outside her room, and sure enough, her tears started

again, worse this time, as though he had somehow increased her pain.

Now as he stood in the doorway of her room, he wondered how he could make everything up to her. The dolls stared back at him reproachfully, and the leather-clad, bare-chested young men on the walls leered. Well, he'd really given her something to cry about now.

He bought her a cake, chocolate with white frosting. He had the woman in the supermarket bakery write *Happy Birthday Lacey,* in blue letters amidst the sugar flowers on the top. He looked in the clothing store she used to shop in with Annie. The racks of shorts and T-shirts, skirts and dresses, overwhelmed him. He did not know her size. He no longer knew her taste. He finally settled on a gift certificate from the record store—he didn't even know what kind of music she liked anymore—and feeling reasonably satisfied with himself, drove home to make her favorite chicken enchiladas for dinner.

The notecard in Annie's recipe box offered him little guidance. Annie had obviously made up most of the enchilada recipe as she went along, and the little that was there was in her scratchy handwriting. He'd become good at deciphering it over the years, but just about all he could make out on this particular card was down in the lower right hand corner. *Lacey's fave!* she'd written.

He called Nola. "Would you believe I forgot Lacey's birthday?"

"I know, hon. Jessica told me."

"I should have written it on the calendar. My memory's not the greatest these days."

"Don't beat up on yourself, Alec. She'll get over it."

"I wanted to make those enchiladas Annie used to make.

Lacey loves them, but Annie's recipe is illegible. Do you have it?"

"Sure do. Let me come on over and help you."

"Well, no, please. Don't do that. Could you just read it to me?" Nola lived on the other side of the cul-de-sac and it would take her only a minute to come over, but that was the last thing he wanted. He wondered if she was aware of how carefully he avoided being alone with her.

There were more steps than he'd anticipated in making the enchiladas. He burned his fingers shredding the chicken, and destroyed four of the tortillas before he managed to get a system going for dipping them in the sauce and folding them quickly around the filling.

Lacey came in the back door at five-thirty and he wrapped his arms around her, hugging her close to him before she had a chance to object. She felt thin and stiff. The headset she wore was cool against his cheek and he could hear the faint rocking beat of the music. "I'm so sorry, Lacey," he said. "The days just got away from me."

She pulled away without looking at him. "It's no big deal." She took the headset off and set it on the counter.

"Call Clay for dinner, okay?" he asked. "I made your favorite. Enchiladas."

She glanced at the oven and headed toward the stairs.

"These are good, Dad," Clay said, digging into the cheesy mass on his plate. The enchiladas did not taste like Annie's and he wondered what he'd done wrong. Lacey hung her head over her plate, twisting her fork in the cheese, making a mess.

"Not like Mom's, though," Alec said, acknowledging his failure before either of them could.

"Mom put those little cans of green chilies in them." Lacey didn't lift her head.

"Ah," Alec said. "I'll know better next time."

"Don't bother," she said, her voice sarcastic. Cruel.

Clay raised his eyes to Alec, incredulous. "You're a bitch," he said to Lacey, and Alec quickly shook his head at him.

"Let's just get on with dessert," he said. "I didn't make it so maybe it'll be a little better than dinner."

The cake was waiting for him on the dining room table, and as he lit the fourteen candles it occurred to him that Annie would never have had a birthday celebration in the kitchen as he was doing. He hadn't given it a thought. He and the kids had not eaten dinner in the dining room once since Annie died.

He carried the cake and its flaming candles into the kitchen, singing.

"Please don't sing," Lacey said as Clay joined in, prompting Clay and Alec to sing louder. Lacey clamped her hands over her ears. "Don't!" she said. "I hate it!"

Alec saw the tears in her eyes and stopped singing, signaling to Clay to do the same. "Okay," he said. "Enough of the entertainment." He set the cake on the table and handed Clay the knife while he got the wrapped gifts from one of the cupboards. He placed them on the table in front of Lacey and felt suddenly mortified. There was a box from Clay—water shoes—and the thin envelope from himself. That was it. Annie always had dozens of things for her, for any of them. The table would be piled high with gifts wrapped in paper she had made herself. A day late and he still had not managed to do this right.

Lacey went through the motions. She genuinely liked the water shoes; he could see that in her face, and he was grateful to Clay for knowing his sister as well as he did. She thanked

Alec for the gift certificate and then began idly poking at her cake. He felt desperate to make her happy.

"I have a check for you too, Lace," he said, although he had not thought of one until this minute. "Fifty bucks. You can spend it on whatever you want." Annie would have killed him. She would have laid him right out on the kitchen floor and kicked the life out of him.

All I ever got growing up was money, she'd said to him once, when he'd suggested giving money to the kids as a Christmas gift. *That's absolutely all I ever got, when what I really wanted was my parents. I would have traded everything I owned, every cent they ever gave me, if they'd just once said, "We love you, Annie. No matter what you do, no matter what you look like, you're our child and we love you."*

"This is the first birthday in my entire life that I didn't get a doll," Lacey said. She was not looking at either of them. She poked her fork up and down in a pink sugar flower.

"Well, I figured you're fourteen now," Alec said. "Pretty old for a doll."

She shrugged. "Mom said she'd get me one each year till I was twenty-one."

"She did?" Alec asked, truly surprised.

Lacey looked up at him, meeting his eyes for the first time in what seemed like months, and he cringed at the hurt in her face. "When I have kids, I'll never forget their birthdays."

"I didn't actually forget it, Lacey. I know your birthday's July first. I just didn't realize that it was already July."

"So you thought maybe it was just June twenty-ninth or thirtieth, then, right? You must have been planning what you would get me. I just bet you were." She got up from the table. She was starting to cry and trying to hide her face from him, letting her hair fall forward to cover her eyes.

Alec stood up too and reached for her shoulder. "Sweetheart..."

She jerked away from him. "I bet you know the exact date your stupid lighthouse was built, don't you? I bet you have some gigantic anniversary celebration planned." She took off out the back door.

"You have school tomorrow, Lace," he called through the screen. "I don't want..."

"Fuck you!" she shouted over her shoulder, words that shut him up, that sent a pain into his chest where the enchiladas lay like concrete behind his breastbone. He wanted to go after her, tell her he wouldn't stand for her to talk to him that way, but Annie would never have made an issue out of it. Besides, Lacey had come entirely too close to the truth. The construction of the Kiss River Lighthouse began on April 5, 1869, and was completed five years later. The lantern was lit for the first time on September 30, 1874, and for this year's anniversary of the first illumination they were indeed planning an enormous celebration. He had already ordered the cake.

Chapter Sixteen

It was not exactly impulse that made Alec stop by the Kill Devil Hills Emergency Room. He'd been planning to do it for a few days now, but it wasn't until he pulled into the parking lot, his heart rocketing a little from the memory of the last time he'd been there, that he knew today was the day.

The waiting room was packed, and he wondered if Olivia would be able to get away. He was pleased to see all those people, though. They gave the emergency room an entirely different appearance from the night Annie died. He would hardly know he was in the same place.

He approached the reception desk, where a balding, barrel-chested man was bullying the frightened young receptionist.

"I've been waiting a goddamn hour!" The man pressed against the desk, jutting his chin toward her. He held a blood-smeared rag to his forearm. "You could *bleed* to death waiting to be seen here."

The receptionist stuttered as she tried to explain the reason for the delay, and the man interrupted her with expletives and threats. Alec thought, unhappily, that he should probably intervene. He was trying to figure the best course of action when Olivia appeared at the young woman's side. For a second, Alec didn't recognize her. She looked different here. It was not just the white coat. She seemed taller, her eyes greener, the lashes long and black. She didn't notice him as she leaned across the reception desk toward the man.

"I'm sorry you've had to wait," she said. "But this isn't McDonald's."

Alec grinned, and the man opened his mouth to say something, but Olivia cut him off.

"There are people ahead of you with injuries more serious than yours," she said. "We'll get to you as soon as we can."

Something in her voice shut the man up. He turned, grumbling to himself, and took his seat again, and then Olivia noticed Alec. She frowned. "Are you all right?"

He was surprised by the question. "Oh, yeah, I'm fine." He leaned across the desk to speak without being overheard. "Are you free for dinner?"

She smiled. "You really want to take me to a restaurant after I cried in my crab salad?"

"Yes," he said. "I do."

"Well, why don't we pick up some Chinese and take it over to my house? I get off at seven."

Obviously her husband had not moved back in. "Fine," he said. "I'll get it and meet you there. What would you like?"

"You choose." She jotted down directions on a piece of paper and handed it to him.

He walked back to his car. She was in her element in there. There was a confidence in her that had been entirely absent in the restaurant in Duck. He wished he could watch her work. He wanted to see how she would treat that man's bleeding arm, how she would talk to him while she worked. He wanted to watch her brain and her body work in harmony. He knew how that felt—he could still remember—although it had been so long now. Suddenly, he missed the sensation of touching a living being, of using his hands to heal. He was healing the lighthouse, he told himself, working to save it, but he knew it was not the same. No matter how warm the day, how intense the sun, the lighthouse still felt cool and lifeless beneath his hands.

As soon as she left the ER, Olivia regretted her impulsive decision to ask Alec over. She wanted to see him, she wanted to talk to him again, but at her house? The house Paul still paid half the mortgage on? Paul might even be there. Not likely, but not impossible either. This was the first time she had driven home from work with the hope that he had not decided to stop over.

Alec was waiting on the front deck of her house, a paper bag cradled in his right arm. She parked next to his Bronco in the driveway and got out of her car.

"Smells good," she said, reaching past him to unlock the door. She stepped into the living room. "Come in."

Sylvie meowed at them as they crossed the room to the kitchen. Alec set the bag on the table and reached down to pick her up. "She's a pretty one." He held Sylvie in the air in front of him and she batted at his nose with her paw. "How old is she?" He cuddled the cat against his chest. Olivia could hear her purring.

"Six," Olivia said. "Her name's Sylvie, and ordinarily she hates strangers."

"Mmm." Alec smiled and set Sylvie down on the floor again. "Just don't tell her I'm a vet and we'll get along fine."

Olivia took two plates out of the cupboard, wishing she could shake her uneasiness. She busied herself with silverware, napkins, watching him out of the corner of her eye as he removed the cartons from the bag. He had on jeans and a white and blue striped short-sleeved shirt. His arms were tan and tightly muscled, and they were covered with smooth, dark hair. He smelled subtly of aftershave, and his hair was damp from a shower, or maybe the sound. He was an undeniably masculine presence in her house, and she could not remember the last time she'd been alone with a man other than her husband. What if Paul walked in right now? She listened for the sound of his car in the driveway as she set the plates on a tray. What if he walked in and found her entertaining Annie O'Neill's husband?

"This is Annie's." Alec touched the stained glass peacock feather hanging in the window over the sink.

"Yes," she said. "I bought it the first time I stopped in the studio." If Alec knew it was Annie's, Paul would certainly know as well. She would have to move it someplace where he would be unlikely to see it if he came over. "Let's eat out on the deck," she said, lifting the tray. She led him out the sliding glass doors to the covered back deck overlooking the sound.

"This is very nice," Alec said, setting the cartons down on the glass-topped table. He stood up straight and put his hands on his hips as he took in the view. "My house is on the sound, too."

Olivia sat down and started opening cartons. "I was shocked when we came down here and discovered we could afford something like this, right on the water. I felt as though I'd found my spiritual home." She smiled ruefully. "I was so optimistic that this was where we would settle down and raise our family."

Alec sat down across from her. "How are the twins?" he asked.

"*What?*" Olivia had not heard anyone ask that question in

a very long time, and yet immediately she was transported back to the tiny, one-bedroom house she grew up in. She could hear people asking her mother, *how are the twins,* and her mother's slurred reply.

Alec nodded toward her middle.

"Oh." Olivia laughed. "*Please,* Alec. Twins I don't need." She opened the carton of rice, her fingers shaking.

"Are you okay?" Alec asked. "Or are you just hungry?"

He had graciously given her an out for her nervousness and she opted not to take it. "It feels strange having you here," she said. "Like I'm doing something wrong."

"Oh." He stopped a spoonful of rice midway to his plate. "Would you like me to go?"

"*No,*" she said quickly. "I was just wondering how I would ever explain this to my husband if he decided to pick tonight to stop over."

Alec shrugged and passed her the carton of rice. "We'd just tell him that we're two lonely people who get together from time to time to ruminate over our losses. Does he come over often?"

"Hardly ever." She spooned rice onto her own plate. "There's something I have to tell you about him."

"What's that?"

"Well, first of all, you've met him. His name is Paul Macelli and he's working on your lighthouse committee, although I didn't know that the last time I saw you."

Alec set his fork down and stared at her. "Paul? The journalist? He's your *husband?* God, I didn't picture your husband anything like Paul."

"What do you mean?"

"I figured your husband would be someone...I don't know, *brawny.* Dark-haired. In need of a shave. A Neanderthal type.

A little mean-spirited and thick-skulled. Someone stupid enough to leave someone like you for a fantasy."

Olivia laughed.

"Paul seems very...*cerebral*."

"Yes, he is."

"Very sensitive. He interviewed the old lighthouse keeper and sent me an essay of sorts on what he'd learned. It's...I don't know...*moving*. Captivating. I expected something interesting, but dry, you know, just a few paragraphs to get the facts across. He's very talented."

She smiled. "I know."

"He's quiet, though. Reserved."

"Not always." She could imagine, though, how reserved Paul would be around Annie's husband. "There's something else," Olivia said. She would say this carefully. She did not want Alec to be able to put the pieces of this puzzle together. "Did you know he wrote that article on Annie in *Seascape Magazine*?"

"He *did*? I never even noticed the guy's name. I know Annie had a few interviews with him...that was Paul?"

"Yes." She tensed. *Please don't figure this out.*

"It was a terrific article. I was a little worried about how it would come out, because Annie just wasn't herself last fall. She was in one of her down moods." Alec shuddered. "I hadn't seen her quite that withdrawn in a long time, so I was relieved when I read the article and saw that he'd managed to capture the real Annie." He took a swallow of tea, then looked up at her, a puzzled expression on his face. "Why didn't he tell me he wrote it?"

"Well, it's like you said. He's reserved. Modest." She ate a little of the spicy hot Hunan chicken. "He and I wrote a book together," she said. "Do you remember that terrible train wreck in Washington back in 1981?"

"When most of the cars went into the Potomac?"

She nodded. "That was how we met. Paul worked for the *Washington Post* and he was covering the story in the ER at the hospital where I was a resident."

She hadn't even noticed Paul, but he had certainly noticed her. He'd introduced himself to her when the crisis was over, two full days after it had begun. He was in love with her, he said. She was so coolly confident, so skillful with the patients, yet compassionate with the families. He showed her the articles about the crash in the *Post,* the factual articles other reporters had written, and the articles he'd written himself about the amazing young female doctor in the ER. She was taken aback by his romantic idealism, but she could not deny the thrill of knowing he had observed her being herself and had fallen in love with her.

"So, a few years later we decided to write a book about it," Olivia continued. "We followed the wreck from different perspectives—the passengers and the rescue workers and the hospital staff. It turned out pretty well. We did the talk show circuit and won a couple of awards."

"I'd like to read it."

She got up and walked into the living room, where she pulled her worn copy of *The Wreck of the Eastern Spirit* from the bookshelf. She carried it back to the deck and handed it to Alec.

"Oh, my God," he said as he studied the cover. It was an aerial view of the wreck, taken from a great height so that at first it was difficult to see that between the two cherry blossom-covered banks of the river lay a wreck that had taken forty-two lives. He opened the book and read the jacket, then turned to the back page to read the little blurb about her and Paul.

"He's had a book of poetry published?" Alec asked.

"Yes. It's called *Sweet Arrival*."

"*Sweet Arrival*." Alec smiled. "What's that refer to?"

"Me." Olivia blushed. "He said his whole life fell into place when I came into it."

Alec looked at her sympathetically. He reached across the table and softly squeezed her hand, his gold-braided wedding band catching the light from the kitchen. Then he returned his eyes to the book jacket. The small black and white picture of her and Paul was upside down from Olivia's perspective. Their smiles looked like frowns.

Alec shook his head. "That must have been a nightmare. How do you do that kind of work without falling apart?"

"You get used to it. Hardened a little, I guess. I cry at sad movies and that sort of thing. And sometimes in restaurants over lunch, but I almost never cry at work." She looked down at the book cover where it rested next to Alec's plate. "I did cry a little the night Annie died, though."

"Why?" Alec asked. "With all the horrendous things you've seen in emergency rooms, why would that get to you?"

"It was you," she said, telling him only half the truth. "Your eyes. You were so devastated. I was just losing Paul, and...I don't mean to compare what I was going through to what you went through...but I felt your sadness. For the longest time I couldn't get your face out of my mind."

Alec looked down at his plate. He started to lift his fork to his mouth, then rested it on the table, raising his eyes once more to Olivia's. "Do you remember my daughter?" he asked.

Olivia smiled. "She tried to beat me up."

"Did she? I don't remember that." He turned his head to look out at the sound. "She's changing. I didn't notice it because I've just tuned my kids out since Annie died. My son's done all right. He's working and getting ready to go to Duke in the fall. But Lacey..." He shook his head. "She's started smoking—I guess that's no big deal. Most kids her age try it. But she cries so easily now. The other night she came home in tears with her blouse buttoned wrong. I don't want to read too much into..."

"How old is she?" Olivia interrupted him.

"Thir—fourteen. Just."

Olivia set her own fork down and folded her arms across her chest. "It's a vulnerable age for a girl," she said. "Especially one without a mother."

"Well, I'm trying not to be too naive. She's always been a very good kid, very responsible, and I'm sure she's not having sex or anything but..."

"Maybe against her will." She spoke carefully.

"What do you mean?"

"Well, she was crying. Disheveled. Maybe someone...I don't mean she was raped out on the street, but you know how boys can be and maybe she was at a party, and someone...took advantage of her."

Alec's eyes had widened. "You're certainly reassuring."

"Sorry. Working in an ER gives you a warped view of the world. Why don't you talk to her about it? Be straightforward."

"She won't talk to me. I tell myself it's typical adolescent stuff, but Clay never acted this way and I'm not sure how to handle it. Annie and I just let them be. There were no rules they had to follow. We trusted them, and they were basically perfect."

"What do you mean, no rules?"

"No curfew, no restrictions. They made their own decisions about where they wanted to go and what they wanted to do." He pushed his plate to the center of the table. "Even when they were little, we let them decide what to wear and what to eat. Annie was big on making them take responsibility for themselves, and they did a good job of it. But now Lacey sits at the table with a radio headset on. I want to say, take that radio off and listen to me, damn it." He struck the table with his fist. "And don't curse at me. *Talk* to me. But Annie would never have made those kinds of demands on her. I can't figure out what Annie would have done if Lacey had acted up like this when she was alive."

Olivia sat back in her chair. "Maybe it doesn't matter what Annie would have done," she said. "Do what *Alec* wants to do. Tell her she can't listen to the radio at the table. Tell her..."

"I *can't.* I'm afraid of losing her, too. I..." He shut his eyes for a second, and then stood up. "Excuse me." He set his napkin on the table and walked into the house.

Olivia closed up the cartons and moved them to the tray, thinking just as he had done: what would Annie do now? Annie would never have let a distraught guest leave the room without following him to make sure he was all right. She left the food on the tray and walked into the kitchen. Alec was at the window, staring out at the sound. She rested her hand on his bare arm. "Alec?"

"I'm afraid of my daughter," he said. The sound was reflected in his eyes, turning the pale blue a milky gray. "I'm afraid to look at her because every time I do I see Annie." He glanced down at Olivia, and she lowered her hand self-consciously to her side. "She was with Annie that night at the shelter," he said.

"I didn't know that."

"She was helping in the food line. She was right next to Annie when she was shot. She saw it happen."

"That's how she knew there was so little blood," Olivia

said. "I always wondered about that. How horrible for her, Alec."

"I could have lost her, too. I'm so aware now of how quickly you can lose someone. If I get too close to her or to Clay and something happened to them...I couldn't go through it again. And if I try to figure out a way to discipline her, I'm afraid she'll hate me. She already seems to." He lifted his hands to the counter, and looked once more at Olivia. "I completely forgot her birthday. One hell of a dad, right?"

She felt a sudden, wrenching twist of sympathy for Lacey. Most of her childhood birthdays had been forgotten, but at least she'd had Clint to share the hurt with. "Well," she said. "I guess she's learning that you're human."

Alec turned away from the window and leaned back against the counter. "What were you like at her age?" he asked.

"Oh." She felt herself color. "You can't use me as a comparison. I wasn't particularly...normal."

He laughed. "You want to explain that?"

"Just being a twin and all." She knew it was the *"and all"* that told the story, that had made her unlike other girls her age. She wanted to tell him. She had the feeling he would understand, and her heartbeat quickened at the thought of sharing her past with him. She opened her mouth to speak, but just then he sighed and stretched, shaking away the last few minutes, and Olivia quickly pulled herself back to the present.

"I'd better go," he said. "Let me get the book." He walked back to the deck and returned with the copy of *The Eastern Spirit* she'd given him. She walked him to the door, a little shaken at how close she'd come to telling him things about herself no one knew. No one except Paul.

Exactly what would Alec say to Paul at the next lighthouse committee meeting?

"Alec," she said, "I'd rather Paul didn't know about us being friends."

He raised his eyebrows.

"I don't want to complicate things." They were complicated enough as it was. "Can we just say that you and I met to talk about what happened in the emergency room that night? Let him think that's all there was to it?"

He frowned. "I'm a terrible liar, Olivia. It's not like we're having an affair."

"I'd just rather he didn't view you as a rival. The two of you have to work together, remember?"

He nodded. "All right."

After he left, Olivia loaded the dishwasher and began sweeping the deck. She had to keep busy or the memories would seep in. They would stay for days once they started, and already the memory of her tenth birthday was taking shape in her mind. That was when she finally came to the realization that her mother was incapable of keeping the days straight. She couldn't stay sober long enough to cook a meal, much less to remember a birthday.

Clint had made Olivia a card in school during the morning of their tenth birthday, and when he brought it over to her on the playground at recess, some of the kids starting taunting him, as they always did when one of the "slow-learners" stopped by. One of the boys, Tim Anderson, grabbed the card from his hand.

"Look at what the retard brought Livvie," he said, waving it in the air. A few other boys gathered around Tim to read the card as Clint stood nearby, his face open and trusting. Olivia ached for her brother. She knew what the card would look like: the *p*'s in *happy* would be backwards; *birthday* would be misspelled. He'd probably drawn a picture of a cake as he'd done the year before. It would look like the drawing of a five-year-old.

She tried to grab the card from Tim's hand.

"Love," Tim mocked. "He signed it *love* Clint. Is he your boyfriend, Livvie? He's a retard." With that the boys jumped on Clint, four of them, pinning him to the ground and pounding on him with their fists while Clint struggled helplessly to get free. Olivia watched the ineffectual flailing of his hands around the heads of his assailants. She beat at their backs with her fists, screaming for them to leave him alone. She kicked at their legs, their sides, until Mrs. Jasper came out of the building. She walked toward them briskly, clapping her hands, crying "Children! Stop it this instant!" Upon hearing her voice, Tim and his cohorts immediately scattered and Olivia dropped to the ground next to her brother. His nose was bleeding and his face was red and streaked with tears.

Mrs. Jasper smoothed her skirt over her legs and knelt down on the other side of Clint. She pulled a lacy handkerchief from her skirt pocket and pressed it to his nose. "There, dear," Mrs. Jasper said. "Are you all right?"

"Yeth," Clint answered, with his little lisp.

Olivia spotted the card he'd made for her a few yards away and ran over to pick it up. It was crushed almost beyond recognition, but she could still make out the birthday cake with its ten candles. Clint had colored it green.

"They're such bullies," Mrs. Jasper was saying to Clint, as Olivia knelt beside them again.

"Avery'll beat 'em up." Clint sat up, still holding the bloody handkerchief to his nose.

Olivia looked toward the corner of the playground where the older kids were playing dodgeball. Her brother Avery had the ball, and she watched as he threw it hard at one of the girls who jumped out of the way just in time. Yes, Avery would take great pleasure in beating up Tim Anderson. He would use any excuse at all for a fight.

Mrs. Jasper looked at Olivia. "Maybe Clint should go home for the rest of the day. Shall I call your mother?"

Olivia shook her head, aware that Mrs. Jasper knew the futility of calling Mrs. Simon. "I'll walk him." Olivia held out her hand to her brother and he locked his blue-stained fingers with hers. Blueberry season was long over, and the few dollars the Simon children had earned picking the berries had already been spent. Still, it would be weeks before the stain left their fingers.

She walked Clint home, hoping their mother had passed out on the sofa by now, because Olivia knew what she would say when she heard Clint had gotten beaten up again. She'd shake her head, her thin, uncombed hair sticking up in dark tufts from her head. "God must've screwed up the day he made you two, Livvie," she'd say, as though Clint couldn't understand how she was insulting him. "Gave you Clint's brains on top of your own, so it's up to you to take care of him."

Their mother was on the sofa, her doughy face pressed into the soft cushions. The bottle lay on its side on the floor next to her. Olivia tucked Clint into his bed, one of three in the cramped bedroom she shared with her brothers. Clint was worn out from his ordeal and fell asleep quickly, the blood scabbed and scratchy-looking around his nose. Back in the living room, Olivia picked up the bottle from the floor next to the sofa and put it as high as she could reach in the kitchen cupboard so her mother would have to hunt for it when she woke up. Then she left the house, thinking she would have to make Clint a card, too, when she got back to school. She knew it was all either of them would get.

Olivia stopped sweeping the deck to listen. Someone was in the house. She peered through the sliding glass doors into the living room, but it was too dark to see. Had she forgotten to lock the front door after Alec left?

"Olivia?"

Paul. She let out her breath as he stepped onto the deck. She was annoyed he thought he could simply walk into this house at any time, but she was too relieved to see him to say anything that might put him on the defensive. "You startled me," she said. If he had come over twenty minutes earlier he would have gotten quite a surprise himself. She thought of the peacock feather in the kitchen. She would have to keep him from seeing it.

"Sorry. I knocked, but you probably couldn't hear me out here." He sat down at the table and looked up at her. "I wanted to talk to you," he said. "If you're willing."

"Of *course* I'm willing." She rested the broom against the house and sat down across from him.

"Did you mean it when you said I could talk to you about Annie?"

She didn't let the disappointment show in her face. "Yes."

"I need to. You were right when you said there was no one else I could talk to. No one who cares about me as much as you do." He tapped his fingers nervously on the table. "This isn't easy, but ever since you stopped over and you were so...kind, I just thought maybe I should try telling you the truth."

Olivia locked her hands together in her lap. "I thought I knew the truth."

He shook his head. "You know most of it. You know I fell in love with someone I couldn't have, and that I sort of got crazed in that process. But what you don't know is..." He looked up at the wooden ceiling and took in a deep breath. "Oh, Liv." He shook his head at her. "I'm so sorry. When we got married I couldn't imagine doing anything like this. Anything that would hurt you."

"You slept with her."

Paul licked his lips. "It was just one time," he said. "Right before Christmas. I felt as though I had to, as though..."

"More than you had to honor your vows to me?" She thought the pain in her chest might kill her. He'd made love to both of them. He'd compared them, and Annie had emerged victorious.

"I should have left you earlier," he said. "I didn't feel good about it, but I convinced myself that you were somehow to blame, with your late hours and..." He stopped talking and looked out into the darkness again.

"And what?"

"Just the kind of person you are. A little rigid, while Annie was so free-spirited and full of life and..."

"Stop it!" Olivia stood up. "You must think I have no feelings at all."

He looked up at her and continued as if she hadn't spoken. "I just got swept up into it. She was such a good person."

"Oh yes, she sounds wonderful. She was cheating on her *husband,* Paul. How good is that?"

"It was my idea, not hers. I pushed her. I mean, I didn't *rape* her, she wanted to do it, but..."

"Paul, I said I'd listen, but I can't. It just hurts too much."

He stood up and, to her surprise, took her in his arms. She didn't fight him. She couldn't. It had been too long.

"I still care about you, Liv," he said. "But she destroyed me. I wish to hell that we never moved here. I wish I'd never met her."

He smelled warm and familiar, yet all she could see when she closed her eyes was the image of him in bed with Annie. She pulled away from him with a whimper. "Go home, Paul," she said. "Go back to your little shrine."

He hesitated for a moment before turning to leave. Olivia waited until she heard his car pull out of the driveway. Then she walked into the kitchen and removed the peacock feather from the window. She took it outside to the end of the pier, lifted it over her head in the darkness, and brought it down hard on the piling, listening with enormous satisfaction to the breaking of the glass.

CHAPTER SEVENTEEN

Paul ran into Alec in the supermarket—literally—their carts colliding as he turned the corner by the dairy case. Alec broke into a smile when he saw him, and Paul nearly groaned with dismay. He was trapped.

"Paul!" Alec gave him a hearty handshake. "You've been on my mind a lot lately."

"I have?"

Alec leaned on his cart as though he was settling in for a long discussion. "The lighthouse material you sent me is terrific. I talked to Nola about it, and with a little more information we can put together a booklet rather than a brochure. The printer's agreed, and we've figured out a way to distribute it nationally."

"Fantastic," Paul said. He rearranged the packages in his cart to avoid looking at Alec.

"I have an idea for your next interview with Mary Poor," Alec said. "Get her to talk about *herself*. People used to call her the 'Angel of the Light.' I have a few old articles about her I can send you so you'll know what to ask her, in case she turns out to be the modest type. Then maybe later in

the summer we can get her to give a few of us a tour of the
keeper's house. Does she seem up to it?"

"A tour of the house?" Paul moved his carton of vanilla ice
cream from one side of his cart to the other. "I'm not sure,"
he said. "She was sitting in a rocking chair when I spoke
with her, so I don't know how well she gets around." He was
not at all certain he could handle another interview with the
old woman, much less a tour of the house. How much could
his nerves take? He had gotten sick after the first interview,
had to pull off on a side street in Manteo to throw up in the
gutter.

"Well, we'll see," Alec said. "By the way, why didn't you
tell me you did that article in *Seascape* on my wife?"

Paul tried to read his tone. Alec was smiling; there was
nothing accusatory in his face. It was more that he thought
Paul was being modest. "Oh, well. I didn't know what kind
of memory that would be for you."

"It was a very nice tribute to her. She loved it."

Paul smiled himself. He'd never known that. She had
never said that to him. "Thanks," he said. "That means a lot.
How did you figure it out?"

"Your wife was the doctor on duty the night Annie died.
I guess you knew that, huh?"

Paul froze. "Yes."

"So, I've spoken with her—with Olivia—a few times to
understand exactly what happened that night. You know, I
just needed to sort it out in my head."

"Right." How much had Olivia told him? Paul's palms
began to sweat on the bar of the shopping cart.

"Olivia's been very helpful to me," Alec said. "It helps
knowing she was the one treating Annie."

"Yes, I...it must."

"Did you know that you and Annie were in the same class at Boston College?"

How the hell did Alec know that? "Uh, yes. It came out during the interviews."

"You didn't remember her from back then?"

"There were a lot of students in that class."

Alec looked down at his grocery cart and Paul followed his eyes to the frozen foods, cans of vegetables. "Annie would have a fit if she could see this," Alec said, nodding toward the cart.

"Well, I've gotten into the frozen stuff myself, lately," Paul said. "Speaking of which, we'd better get going before everything thaws." He started to push his cart past Alec.

"Right," Alec agreed. "Oh, by the way, I'm reading *The Wreck of the Eastern Spirit*."

Paul turned back to look at him. "How...?"

"I'd mentioned something about how well you wrote to Olivia, and she thought I might like to take a look at it. That's when you two met, huh? It must have been something, watching her in action."

"Olivia?" he asked, stupidly, the memory jarring him. She had been young and pretty, caring and efficient, and he had been genuinely smitten. He had seen something in her that made him think, *yes,* she could be the one to help him forget, and for the longest time she had unwittingly done exactly that.

Alec rested his elbows on the bar of the shopping cart again. "As I'm reading about the train wreck, though, it makes me realize how poorly equipped our little emergency room is to handle a major trauma," he said. "Like a gunshot to the heart."

Paul was disturbed by Alec's candor. Did he think they were friends? "I guess that's true." He glanced toward the inviting open aisle behind Alec's head, then looked at his watch. "Well, I've got to get this stuff home," he said. "I'll see you at the next lighthouse meeting." He pushed his cart away, cringing, knowing that his exit had been totally graceless.

Something seized him as he pushed the cart past the meat aisle. A sort of panic. He could not focus his eyes on the list he'd written an hour earlier. He stared down at the steaks and chops and bloody roasts. He abruptly took his hands from the cart, did an about-face, and walked out of the store, picturing his ice cream melting through the seams of the carton, dripping into a pool on the floor.

He got in his car and drove the two blocks to the beach at Nags Head. It was still early, just seven-thirty in the evening, and the beach was nearly empty. A few fishermen stood close to the water and occasionally a couple walked past him, hand in hand. He sat down in the sand and waited for the tension to leave his body.

Alec had spoken to Olivia. At length. Obviously, though, she had not told him anything earth-shattering or he never would have treated Paul with such goodwill, such respect. God. He had spent so much of his time and energy hating that man. Half his life.

A young couple and their dog ran along the water's edge, laughing. The woman's long hair was a true brown, and yet in the fading sunlight Paul could almost kid himself into thinking it was red.

Boston College. *There were a lot of students in that class.* Alec had bought it. Paul shook his head. How could Alec believe that anyone could have been on the same campus with Annie Chase and not have known her?

CHAPTER EIGHTEEN

Paul had been cast as the lead in Boston College's freshman production of *Angel Street*. He had been an average student in high school, disdaining math and science in favor of literature and poetry and the endless melodrama of his own imagination. He'd also been president of the drama club, and he had a natural talent for which he was awarded a scholarship to B.C. His family would not have been able to afford to send him to a good school any other way, although his father's Philadelphia fireworks business had done well during Paul's high school years, and his mother had tucked away nearly every cent she'd earned as a maid. Still, there were six Macelli children—Paul and his five sisters—and they were all bright, all ambitious. They would all want to go to school.

His was the first role to be cast in *Angel Street*. He could tell, as Harry Saunders watched him read for the part of Jack Manningham, that no one else would have to bother reading. So he sat, relaxed and relieved, next to Harry in the front row of the auditorium, while other anxious freshmen read for their parts.

Annie Chase auditioned for the part of the flirtatious maid

on a whim. She'd come with a girlfriend and had agreed to try out in order to give her friend courage. She skittered up the stairs when it was her turn, and her hair seemed to fill the stage. Harry, who'd been slouching in his seat, leaned forward and rested his hands on his knees.

"Go ahead, please," he said, and she read a line or two in a throaty voice before she began to laugh. It was a giggle, really, a sound only Annie Chase could make, and its rippling, ringing tone was a surprise given the huskiness of her voice. Everyone in the theater turned to look at her, their own faces slowly breaking into grins. Paul smiled himself. He glanced at Harry, who was nearly laughing.

"Do you want to try that again, Miss Chase?"

"Sure." She read again, this time making it nearly to the end of her soliloquy before the giggles got her, and although she seemed like a young girl clearly out of control, and although the reading itself had not been anything outstanding, Paul was not surprised when Harry cast her in the role. Neither was he displeased.

"She'll grab the audience," Harry said, speaking to Paul as though he were a colleague. "She'll grab them and she won't let go. We just have to get her—and that hair—under a little bit of control without taking the life out of her."

Harry needn't have worried about that. It was impossible to sap the life out of Annie Chase. She sparkled, she bubbled, she drew people to her like a minstrel on a busy street.

He fell in love on that stage at Boston College. Annie came late to rehearsals and no one seemed to mind. It was as if they were all waiting, holding their breath for her arrival, letting the smiles spread across their faces when she finally bounded onto the stage.

He had to kiss her. It was in the script, and for several nights before the first time, he lay awake imagining that kiss.

He wished he didn't have to do it in front of Harry Saunders and the rest of the cast. He wanted to kiss her in private.

When the afternoon of the kiss finally arrived, he made it quick and light.

"Again," Harry said from the front row. "Longer this time, Macelli."

He kissed her longer, trying to keep his wits about him, and when he pulled away from her she was grinning.

"You're not supposed to smile, Annie," Harry said. "You're supposed to look *seductive*."

She giggled. "Sorry."

"You two better practice on your own till you get it right." Harry gave Paul a knowing nod.

So they practiced. They met in his dorm room or hers, reading their lines, working up to the kiss and away from it, the rest of their lines anticlimactic. When they had finished rehearsing for the day, he would read her his poetry if they were in his room, or look at the jewelry she was making if they were in hers. She'd form gold and silver into intricate shapes for earrings and pendants and bracelets. He loved watching her work. She'd tie her hair back in a leather strap which was rarely up to the task, and her long red tresses would spill out bit by bit as she worked with the glittering metal.

Paul felt the addiction taking hold of him. He'd known her for just a few weeks, but she was constantly on his mind. He'd call her, ostensibly to read through their lines, but they wound up talking about other things, and he treasured every word he got from her, playing their conversations over and over again in his mind as he lay in bed.

Then the gifts began. On opening night, she surprised him with a gold bracelet she'd made for him. The following day, he found a basket of pine cones outside his door, and the day after that, she arrived in his room carrying a macramé belt.

"I stayed up all night making this for you," she said.

She pulled the belt he was wearing out of the loops of his jeans and began fitting the new belt through. It was slightly too wide, and the pressure of her fingers as she worked with the belt made him hard in an instant. He turned away from her, embarrassed.

She looked up at him from her seat on his bed.

"Paul," she said, her dark blue eyes big and sad. "I don't get it. Don't you want me?"

He looked down at her, startled. "I...*yes.* But I didn't think you..."

She groaned, curling her fingers into the pockets of his jeans. "God, Paul, I've been going crazy trying to figure out how to make you fall in love with me."

"I've been in love with you for weeks," he said. "Here. I can prove it." He pulled out the top drawer of his desk and handed her a poem, one of many he'd written about her in the past few weeks. It made her cry.

She stood up to kiss him, a far longer, far steamier kiss than the one they'd shared on stage. Then she walked over to his door and turned the lock. He felt his knees start to buckle and wondered how he would get through this. "I've never made love before," he admitted, leaning awkwardly against his desk. He'd had a number of girlfriends in high school, two in particular, who were drawn to his sensitivity and his poems, but he was still very much a virgin.

Annie, however, was not.

She smiled. "So *that's* it," she said, as though that explained everything. "Well, I've been doing it since I was fifteen, so you don't have a thing to worry about."

Her words shocked him at first. Disappointed him. But

then he felt relieved, because as she began kissing him, touching him, it was quickly obvious that she did indeed know what she was doing.

"You are to do absolutely nothing," she said. She undressed him to his boxer shorts and rolled him onto his stomach. Then she straddled him and began a long, deep massage, her hands soft and cool at first, heating up as she worked them over his skin. She rolled him onto his back and took off her T-shirt and bra. Paul reached up to touch the creamy white skin of her breasts, but she caught his hand and set it back down at his side.

"You may look but you may not touch," she said. "I told you, you have to just lie here. Tonight is entirely for you."

She made love to him the way she did everything in her life—generously, putting his pleasure ahead of her own.

In the weeks that followed, he realized that she could give endlessly, but she could not take. When he'd try to touch her during their lovemaking, she'd brush his hand away. "You don't need to do that," she'd say, and he soon realized that she meant it, that she'd be overcome with discomfort, thrown completely out of equilibrium, when he tried to turn the tables and give to her, in bed or out.

He bought her flowers once, for no particular reason, and her smile faded when he gave them to her. "These are way too pretty for me," she said, her cheeks crimson. Later that day, she gave the roses to another girl in the dorm who had admired them.

He bought her a scarf for her birthday, and the next day she took it back, slipping the twelve dollar refund into the pocket of his jeans. "Don't spend your money on me," she said, and she would not listen to his protests. Yet her gifts to him kept coming, and he grew increasingly uncomfortable accepting them.

One day he and Annie were eating lunch in the cafeteria when they were joined by a pretty brunette Annie had known in elementary school. "You were the nicest girl at Egan Day School," she said to Annie. Then she turned to Paul. "She was by far the most popular kid in the entire school. She was one of those girls you wanted to hate because she was so popular that she left no room at all for the competition, but she was so nice you just couldn't help but like her."

That night Annie lay next to him in his bed and told him how she had earned her popularity. "I have an enormous allowance," she said, her voice oddly subdued, almost flat. "I bought the other kids candy and toys. It worked."

He pulled her closer. "Didn't you think you were likable just as you were?"

"No. I thought I was an ugly little girl with terrible red hair. My mother fussed with my hair every morning, and she'd say how horrible it was, how bad I looked. I'd end up crying practically every day on my way to school."

"You're so beautiful. How could she do that to you?"

"Oh, well." Annie swept her arm through the air. "I don't think she meant to hurt me. She just...I guess she has her own problems. Anyhow, I really panicked when I got to high school and there were zillions of new kids to meet. I knew candy and toys weren't going to work anymore. I had to find some other way to get people to like me."

"Did you find a way?"

"Yes."

"Well?"

"I found a way to get the boys to like me, anyhow."

"Oh, Annie."

"Don't hate me."

He stroked her cheek. "I *love* you. You don't have to do that anymore. You've got me."

"I know." She snuggled close. "Hold me tighter, Paul."

He did, loving that she would confide in him, and he thought the time was right to ask her the question that had been on his mind since the first time they'd made love.

"Something bothers me, Annie," he said. "Do you ever come when we're making love?"

He felt her shrug. "No, but it doesn't matter. I'm content just to be close to you and see you enjoying yourself."

He was disappointed. Embarrassed. "I must be doing something wrong."

"It's not you, Paul. I never have."

He leaned away so that he could look at her. "You've made love since you were fifteen and you've never...?"

"I truly don't care. It's never been important to me. I'd see a guy and want to hold him, to feel good that way, warm and loved. If sex was what I had to do to get that, so be it."

He pulled her close again. "If you really want to make me happy, Annie, then let me make *you* feel good for a change."

"You do," she said. "You make me feel wonderful."

"You know what I mean."

She shrank away from him. "I figure it must not be possible for me," she said. "I think it would have happened by now."

He was unwilling to talk to his friends about something so personal, so he spent the next afternoon in the library hunting for a solution to Annie's dilemma. He found a book filled with advice and illustrations which he couldn't bring himself to check out from the wizened old gentleman behind the desk. So he sat in a secluded corner and read it, from cover to cover.

That night in her dorm room, he sat down on her bed and patted the space next to him. She joined him, wrapping her arms around him and planting a wet kiss on his neck.

"I read a sex manual today," he said.

"What?" She jerked away from him. *"Why?"*

"Because it's your turn tonight." He reached for the hem of her T-shirt, but she stopped him.

"No," she whined.

"Annie." He held her by the shoulders. "Do this for me if not for yourself, all right?"

"What if it doesn't work? You'll be disappointed in me... You'll..."

"I'm not going to be disappointed in you or stop loving you or anything else you're worried about. It'll be fine. But you have to relax."

She bit her lip. "Turn off the light," she said.

He did as he was told, and then returned to the bed where he undressed her, rather methodically, and sat behind her with his back against the wall.

"What are we *doing?* Aren't you going to take off your clothes, too?" she asked.

"Nope." He spread his legs wide and pulled her back against his chest. The illustration from the manual was burned into his brain. All day he'd thought of how it would feel to hold Annie this way, to touch her, to finally feel her respond. He wrapped his arms around her and kissed her shoulder. She was shivering.

"This is nice," she said. "You could just hold me like this. I'd rather do this than..."

"Shh. Rest your legs against mine. That's it."

"This is stupid. I feel ridiculous."

He stroked her arms, her shoulders. "You have to tell me

what feels good," he said, moving his hands to her breasts. "Let me know if anything hurts."

"That doesn't hurt." She giggled and seemed to relax in his arms, but she went rigid once he lowered his hands to her thighs.

"Come on, Annie, relax."

"I'm *trying*. I just don't like all the attention being on me. I don't see why... *Oh*."

His fingertips had found their mark. Annie drew in her breath and her legs suddenly opened wider, pressing hard against his own, her hands grasping the denim that covered his thighs. He slipped a finger of his left hand inside her and she shuddered.

"This feels good to me, too, Annie," he said, encouraging her, but it was unnecessary. She was letting herself go, letting herself *take*. When she came, he had one sudden pulse of terror that she might be faking, but then the waves of contractions circled his finger, and he felt her go limp.

That night was a turning point for them, not just that it made sex better—she continued to refer to sex as a "byproduct" of being close—but that it shifted their relationship to a different plane, one in which Annie allowed things to be done for her. The addiction, though still an addiction, was mutual now.

His family adored her. He and Annie visited Philadelphia twice that year, and Annie slipped right into that female dominated household as easily as if she'd been born into it.

"Your family's so warm, Paul," she told him. "You don't know how lucky you are."

She would not take him to meet her own parents, however, even though they lived no more than a half hour's drive from school. After much arm-twisting on his part, she finally agreed to take him home with her on her father's fiftieth birthday. "You talk about him all the time," he said. "I want to meet him."

She did talk about her father a great deal, her voice often swelling with her pride in his accomplishments as a physician. She worked for a month on his birthday gift—gold cufflinks she had designed herself—showing Paul the progress she was making on them each time he came over.

Paul held the small package containing the cufflinks on his lap as he and Annie turned onto the tree-lined street leading to her house. She had been quiet during the entire trip, tapping her fingers on the steering wheel of her red convertible.

"What time is it?" she asked, as they passed one enormous mansion after another.

Paul looked at his watch. "Ten past four."

"Oh, God. My mother will throw a fit."

"We're not *that* late."

"You don't understand. She has this thing about time. When I was little and she promised to take me someplace, she wouldn't do it if I was even a minute late getting ready."

Paul frowned at her. "You're kidding."

She shook her head. "Let's tell them your last name is Macy," she suggested.

"Why?"

"Just for fun."

He stared at her, confused. "It's not my name," he said.

She stopped at a stop sign and looked over at him. "I don't want to hurt your feelings, Paul, but my parents are very prejudiced." She lowered her hands to her lap and began kneading them together. "Do you understand? I mean, unless you're just like them, they... They'll like you better if they think you're..."

His cheeks burned. "Do you want me to lie about what my parents do for a living, too?"

She looked down at her hands. "This is why I didn't want you to meet them."

"I won't lie, Annie." Back then he never did. She said nothing, pressing her foot once more on the gas pedal.

"I thought you loved me," he said.

"I *do*. I just want them to love you too." She turned into a long driveway, and he caught a glimpse of a Tudor-style house far down the expanse of manicured lawn before it disappeared behind a row of pines. "They have my life planned out for me, Paul," she said. "I'm supposed to be majoring in something useful—we had a terrible fight when I told them I wanted to be an artist—and I'm supposed to marry one of the eligible sons of their elite little circle of friends. Do you understand now why I didn't want to bring you here?"

Yes, he understood, but she was a little late in telling him her reasons.

An elderly woman dressed in a dark uniform and white apron let them in. She kissed Annie's cheek and led them into the living room. "Your mum and dad will be down shortly, dear." The woman left the room, and Annie smiled at him nervously. He shivered. The living room was huge and cold, like a cavern.

"You get used to it," Annie said. She was perspiring despite the chill.

Her father walked into the room first. He was a thin, good-looking man, tan and fit and stern. His thick hair was mostly gray. He bussed his daughter's cheek.

"Daddy, this is Paul," Annie said, avoiding the surname issue altogether.

"Paul...?" Dr. Chase shook his hand.

"Macelli," Paul said, the name sounding suddenly dirty

to his ears. He shook the man's hand with a sense of defeat, imagining that he was already being ruled out as a serious candidate for the hand of his daughter.

Annie's mother made more of an attempt to feign warmth, but Paul felt the coldness in her hand when she touched her fingertips to his. She was a plain-looking woman, perhaps even homely, despite the heavy use of cosmetics. Her red hair was drawn back under serious control into a bun.

He could barely eat the slab of roast beef a second servant put on his plate after they'd sat down to dinner. He didn't balk at the probing questions about his family, however. Instead, he began to enjoy them, making it clear to Annie's parents that they had the son of blue-collar workers eating off their fine china, perhaps even sleeping with their daughter. He talked at length about the fireworks business and he told them about the time his mother cleaned the house of the mayor of Philadelphia.

During dessert—a birthday cake in the shape of a tennis racket—Annie presented her father with the set of gold cufflinks. "Why, thank you, princess." Dr. Chase leaned over to kiss Annie's cheek and then set the box next to his plate. Paul had the feeling the cufflinks would find themselves in the back of a drawer somewhere, if not in the trash.

"Annie's jewelry instructor says she's the best student he's ever had," Paul said.

"*Paul.*" Annie blushed.

Dr. Chase looked up from his cake. "Well, Annie's quite bright when she puts her mind to it," he said. "She could be anything she wants to be. She has the brains to do a lot more than twist little pieces of metal into jewelry."

Paul glanced at Annie. He saw the shine of tears in her eyes.

Dr. Chase set down his fork and looked at his watch. "I'm going to have to run, kids."

"But Daddy," Annie said, "it's your *birthday*." Her voice came very close to breaking. Paul heard the splintery little catch in the huskiness, but her parents didn't seem to notice.

Her father stood up and leaned over to kiss the top of her head. He nodded toward Paul. "Nice meeting you, Mr. Macelli. I'm sure we'll all think of you the next time we see a good show of fireworks."

Paul and Annie left shortly after dinner, and Annie was crying by the time they reached her car.

"Maybe I shouldn't have come," he said.

"It's not you," she said. "I always leave there in tears."

"I hate them. I'm sorry, Annie, but they're abominable."

"Don't say that, Paul, please. It doesn't make me feel any better. They're all I've got. You have your sisters and everyone, and I've got them. Period." She opened her car door and looked up at the house. "He never has time for me. He didn't when I was little and he doesn't now."

They spent the summer after their freshman year in New Hope, Pennsylvania, Paul living with a friend he'd known from high school, Annie with two girls from Boston College. Paul worked as a waiter during the day and in the summer stock production of *Carousel* at night, while Annie worked in a gallery, where she learned the basics of stained glass. It was a wonderful summer, both of them doing things they loved and spending their free time together. They were just nineteen, but Paul felt a maturity in their relationship. They talked about the future, about having children, little red-haired Italians they would name Guido and Rosa to torment her parents. *"Guido and Rozer,"* Annie would say, in her

Boston accent, which sounded strange to Paul's ears now that they were no longer in New England.

They took leisurely strolls around the little town of New Hope. Annie fell in love with a small blue cloisonné horse she found in one of the shops. Although she stopped by the shop to look at the horse every few days, Paul knew she would never buy it for herself. So when he had finally made enough money, he bought it for her as a surprise. It cost him nearly every spare cent he'd earned, and at first she wanted to take it back. He insisted she keep it, though, and she wrapped it in a soft cloth and carried it around in her pocketbook, taking it out to show anyone she met. She named it Baby Blue, after a Dylan song.

Her parents visited her in mid-July, and for three days he didn't see her. He finally went to the gallery where she worked, and he knew right away that she wasn't herself. She had circles under her eyes; her giggle was gone. He hated the way her parents poisoned her.

"They want me to change majors," she said.

"To what?"

"Something more useful than art." She straightened a picture on the wall. "If I don't change majors, they won't pay for me to stay in school. But I can't give up art. I'll have to lie to them." She looked at him. "I lied to them about you, too."

"What do you mean?"

"I told them I'm not seeing you anymore. I never did tell them you were here. They'd never let me stay here if they knew."

"But what about the future? What happens when we want to get married?"

Annie nervously wrapped a strand of her hair around her finger. "I don't know. I can't worry about that right now."

"Would they disinherit you if you married an Italian?"

"I wouldn't care if they did," she snapped. "It's not money I want from them, Paul. Don't you know that by now?"

It was true she didn't care about money for herself. She made her own clothes out of what looked like rags to him. She bought cheap shampoo that left her hair smelling like laundry detergent, and Paul could not go into the laundromat without thinking of her hair. Money was important to her only because it allowed her to help other people. She'd lay awake for hours at night, trying to determine who could use her money the most. At the end of the summer, she took the money she'd earned from her job at the gallery and threw a party for the kids at a nearby hospital.

Annie went off the pill just before they returned to school in the fall. She'd been taking it since she was fifteen. "It's bad to be on it for so long," she said. "I'm going to try this new sponge thing. It's more natural."

"I could use rubbers," Paul volunteered.

"No, you may *not*," she said. "You wouldn't enjoy it nearly as much." He knew better than to try to argue with her. Thus started Annie's long line of peculiar birth control methods, and there were times he secretly prayed they would fail. He loved the thought of having a child with her, of strengthening the bond that already existed between them.

When they returned to school, Paul moved into her dorm, one floor below hers. The placid tenor that had marked their relationship in New Hope followed them back to Boston and lasted nearly until the end of the year. That was when her parents received some forms from the school and discovered that Annie was still very much an art major. When they called her at the dorm to confront her with the lie, it was Paul who answered the phone in her room. He unwittingly identified himself, thinking it was one of Annie's professors calling. By the time Annie called her parents back that evening, they were in an advanced stage of fury. The phone battle went on for a good hour before Paul left the room, unable to tolerate Annie's meek apologies. A few hours after she'd gotten off the phone with them, her mother called back. Her father'd had a heart attack, she said. He'd collapsed shortly after talking with Annie and was now in the hospital. The doctors were not certain he would pull through.

She wouldn't let Paul go home with her, and she was gone a full week. She didn't return his calls, although he wasn't at all certain his messages were being delivered.

She was different when she came back to school. There was a distance between them which she wouldn't acknowledge, making it impossible for him to fight. "I don't know what you're talking about, Paul. I'm out with you, aren't I? I'm talking to you."

They went through the motions of their relationship—talking, going to the movies, eating together in the cafeteria, making love—but a part of Annie was missing.

Finally one night, very close to the end of the school year, Paul blocked her exit from his dorm room. "You can't leave until you tell me exactly what's going on in your head," he said. He sat her down on his bed, while he sat on his desk, far enough away from her that she would not be able to seduce him into touching her to avoid talking.

"My father almost died, Paul." She played with the silver bracelet on her wrist. "I caused it by making him angry at me, and I don't know how much longer I'll have him. He's so frail now. I can't bear seeing him like that. He said a lot of things to me in the hospital. He said he loves me... Well, not those words exactly. But he said I'm the most important thing in the world to him. He actually said that." Her eyes misted over. "He said he doesn't understand why I set my sights so low, that it disappoints him so much. 'Art's nice, honey,' he said, 'but you'll never be Picasso.' So I'm going to change my major. I've already filled out the forms."

"Change to what?"

"Biology."

"*Biology.* You have no interest whatsoever in biology."

She shrugged. "I think I could get into it. It would prepare me for nursing or maybe even medical school. Some career where I could help people. And my father would be so proud of me." She looked down at the bracelet again. "I'm going to give away all the jewelry I made."

"Annie..."

"My father said you're trying to pull yourself up in the world through me, but that you'll only succeed in dragging me down with you."

He wanted to throw something against the wall. "Do you believe that crap?"

"Of course not, but I feel like I'm killing him, Paul."

"He's trying to kill *you.* He's trying to make you a little clone of his goddamned fucked self."

She pressed her hands to her ears and he sat down next to her, pulling her close to him. "I'm sorry," he said. "Look, when you see your father, you get under his spell or something. It'll pass in a little while and you'll feel okay about yourself again. And about me. We'll be in New Hope again this summer and..."

She shook her head. "I'm not going to New Hope this summer."

He froze. "What do you mean?"

"I need to be by myself for a while. I need to think everything through."

"Will you stay with your parents?" He could not bear the

thought of her spending two months with them. She would be entirely brainwashed by the end of the summer.

"No," she said. "I thought I'd travel down the coast. From here to Florida."

"What do you mean, from here to Florida? Who would you go with?"

"Myself."

"You can't do that. What if your car breaks down?"

"I'm going to hitchhike."

Paul stood up. "You have this all planned out, don't you? You've been thinking about this for a long time and haven't said a word to me about it."

"I'm sorry."

"Annie, I can't be apart from you for the entire summer."

"Maybe it won't be that long. Maybe the first week it'll all come clear to me, and I'll write to you every single day."

He went to New Hope alone. He took a part in summer stock but was reviewed poorly, his first truly bad review ever. At first Annie sent him postcards daily from coastal towns in New York, New Jersey, Delaware, Maryland. She'd write volumes in the little space on the cards, her handwriting squeezed together almost unintelligibly, telling him about the beaches, the water, the arcades. She was meeting lots of interesting people, she wrote, which disturbed him. How many of those people were men? She'd sign the cards, *I love you,* though, and he tried to relax, to tell himself she would come back refreshed and free of her father's shadow. Little boxes wrapped in brown paper arrived for him several times a week and inside he'd find shells, a starfish, a seahorse. Annie and her gifts.

Suddenly, though, the gifts stopped, along with the postcards. He was sick with worry. After five days without a word from her, he called her parents.

"She decided to stay in North Carolina awhile," her mother told him.

"Well, I...I was hearing from her just about every day and then the cards stopped...and I just thought." He grimaced. He could imagine Annie's mother smiling with delight on the other end of the telephone. "Where in North Carolina is she?" he asked.

"The beach somewhere. I think they call it the Outer Banks down there."

Two more weeks followed without a word from Annie. He was in pain. His body literally ached when he got out of bed in the morning. He couldn't imagine she would leave him hanging this way, that she would cut herself off from him so completely. He read her last postcard over and over again, and the "I love you" at the end seemed just as sincere as it did in the first one. Maybe her mother was lying. Maybe Annie was in Boston. Maybe she wrote to him daily and her mother intercepted the letters.

Then the note came from Kitty Hawk.

Dear Paul,

I've written this letter in my mind a thousand times and it never comes out right, but I can't put it off any longer. I've met someone down here. His name is Alec and I've fallen in love with him. I didn't plan for this to happen, Paul, please believe me. I left B.C. with thoughts only of you, but also with the knowledge that things between us were not what they once were. I still love you—I think I always will. You're the one who taught me that receiving could be just as much an act of love as giving. Oh God, Paul, you're the last person in the world I would ever want to hurt. I doubt I'll return to B.C. in the fall. It's just as well we don't ever see each other again. Please, please forgive me.

Annie

He considered going to North Carolina to find her, claim her, but he didn't want her on those terms. He became obsessed with thoughts of harming himself. He could no longer drive at night without being tempted to slip his car across the white line into oncoming traffic, and he'd sometimes sit for hours in his kitchen, staring at the blade of a steak knife, imagining how it would feel to draw it through the vein in his arm.

He quit the play and moved home for the rest of the summer, where his sisters clucked over him and his parents tried to force him to eat. They treated him like the sick, withdrawing addict that he was. Still, he could not stand it when his sisters called Annie a two-faced bitch.

He returned to Boston College a walking dead man. He tried out for the junior play, but Harry Saunders said he was "lifeless," and cast someone else in the part Paul knew Harry had intended for him. He lost interest in acting altogether and switched his major to journalism. In November, one of Annie's friends told him that Annie had married Alec O'Neill in North Carolina. O'Neill. He supposed an Irishman was preferable to an Italian in her parents' eyes.

And in hers as well.

CHAPTER NINETEEN

Alec was calling Olivia in the evenings. The first time he had an excuse. He remembered her saying that she'd appeared on talk shows after the publication of *The Wreck of the Eastern Spirit*. He could picture her on TV, poised and attractive and persuasive. Only in his fantasy, it was the lighthouse she was talking about.

"Would you ever consider taking on one of the speaking engagements?" he asked her that first night he called. The kids were out and he was sitting alone in the living room, watching the sun melt into the sound. "We get a lot of requests, and after the brochure is put together we'll be inundated. There are too many for me to handle alone right now."

"But I don't know a thing about the lighthouse," she said.

"I'll tell you everything you need to know."

She hesitated, and he wondered if he was asking too much of her. "Why is the lighthouse so important to you, Alec?"

Alec looked across the room at the ten small, oval-shaped stained glass windows built into the side wall of the house. Their designs were barely visible in the dusky evening light.

"That's where I met Annie," he said. "I worked there the summer after I graduated from college. Annie was traveling down the coast and we just happened to be at the lighthouse at the same time one evening. It became sort of symbolic to me, I guess."

"Well, I'll do it, Alec. As long as the time doesn't conflict with my hours in the ER."

"That's great." He ran his hand over the arm of the chair. "By the way, I bumped into Paul in the grocery store yesterday."

"You *did?*" She sounded alarmed. "What did you tell him?"

"Oh, I just asked him a few questions about his fantasy life."

She was quiet for a moment. "I hope you're kidding."

"Of course I'm kidding." He frowned. "This really isn't a joking matter with you, is it?"

"No."

"Don't worry," he said. "We just talked about the lighthouse."

He didn't bother with an excuse when he called Olivia the following night. Or the night after that. On the fourth night, he got home late after driving Clay to Duke for a five-day orientation. It was ten-thirty, too late to call her, and he felt as though something was missing from his day when he got into bed. The emptiness of the bed overwhelmed him in a way it had not for several weeks, and he picked up the phone and dialed Olivia's number. He knew it by heart.

She sounded sleepy when she answered.

"I woke you," he said.

"No. Well, yes, but that's okay."

There was a silence, and an odd feeling passed through him that he was talking to her from his bed, and she from hers. He could picture her there. Silky-straight hair. Fair skin. Green eyes.

"I took Clay to Duke for an orientation today," he said. "It seems strange not having him around the house."

"Maybe this is a good time for you and Lacey to do something together."

"Ha. Fat chance." He felt a sense of dread about the next four days without Clay's presence to ease the tension between Lacey and himself.

It took Olivia three nights of phone calls to persuade him. He stopped by Lacey's room before breakfast that Wednesday morning. She was dressed for school in yellow shorts that were too short and a T-shirt from the sporting goods store where Clay worked. She was hunting on the floor of her closet for her other sandal.

He sat down on the corner of her bed. "Let's do something tonight, Lacey," he said. "Just you and me."

She looked up at him. "Why?"

"Like we used to. Remember? We used to spend a lot of time together."

"I'm going out with Jessica tonight."

"You see Jessica every night. Come on. Give your old Dad some of your time."

She leaned back against the wall next to her closet, the sandal in her hand. "What would we do?"

He shrugged. "Anything you want. You used to like to bowl."

She rolled her eyes.

"We could see a movie."

"I've seen every movie that's playing around here. They never change."

"Night fishing?" he offered. "You used to like that."

"Yeah. When I was about eight."

He sighed. "Help me out, Lacey. What can we do tonight?"

"I know." She suddenly looked excited, and he leaned forward. "I could, like, go out with Jessica and you could stay home with your lighthouse pictures."

He stared at her, hurt, and she sighed and set her sandal on the floor. "I'm sorry," she said, defeat in her voice. "We can do whatever you want."

He stood up. "Fishing then. I'll make the reservations."

She wore her radio headset in the car on the drive to the inlet. She slouched in the front seat of the Bronco, her feet against the dashboard tapping time to music he couldn't hear.

They arrived at the inlet and Lacey got out of the car, fastening the radio to the waistband of her shorts. She walked ahead of him, and his fantasy of spending a quiet evening in the company of his daughter fell apart.

"Lacey?"

She continued walking. Whether she was ignoring him or truly couldn't hear him with the headset on, he didn't know. It didn't matter. She was cutting him out one way or the other.

He caught up to her, stopping her with his hand on her arm. "Please don't take the radio on the boat," he said. "Leave it in the car, Lace. Please."

She muttered something under her breath, but returned to the car with him and left the radio on the front seat.

She was the only female on the boat. There were a dozen men from their early twenties on up, and they stared openly at Lacey when she boarded, forcing Alec to look at her with a more objective eye. Her clothes looked suddenly provocative. Her shorts were insanely short, her legs long and slender and remarkably tanned, given her delicate skin. She'd changed out of her T-shirt into some sort of tank top—a flimsy piece of white cloth with a scooped neck and a hacked-off length so that it didn't quite reach the waistband of her shorts. The nipples of her small breasts were visible beneath the thin white fabric. She was carrying a blue windbreaker that he wanted to wrap around her.

One of the younger men smacked his lips and grinned at her as she hopped from the pier to the boat.

"I'm her father," Alec said to the gawking young man. "Watch it."

"Dad," Lacey said. "See why I don't want to go out with you? You're so embarrassing."

He found a spot for them at the side of the boat, near the cabin and away from the other fishermen, who occasionally turned from their posts for a beer or fresh bait and stared in Lacey's direction. Was this what happened every time she went out on the street? If these guys were as blatant about it here, when she was with her father, what would they be like if he were not around?

Lacey baited her hook with a chunk of mackerel, effortlessly, as if she did it every day of her life.

"You were always better than Clay at this," Alec said. "He could never bring himself to touch the bait."

"Clay's a wimp sometimes." She sat down and leaned against the back of her chair.

Alec sat next to her and breathed in the scent of salt and seaweed as the coastline faded into the distance.

"Remember the one that got away, Lace?"

"Huh?"

"The blue you caught that jumped off the deck."

She nearly smiled, turning her face away from him so he wouldn't see. "A long time ago," she said.

"It was huge. I helped you reel it in and you were so excited, but once we got the damn thing off the hook, back it went."

"No one believed me," she said quietly, but with a certain indignation. "And you said you'd gotten a picture of it and..."

"And the film got wet and didn't turn out."

She laughed, but caught herself quickly. "Well, I don't think Mom ever believed it."

"Yes, she did. She just liked teasing you about it."

They were quiet for a few minutes. "I hate bluefish," she said. "As a matter of fact, I hate *fish*."

It grew dark quickly, and with the darkness came a sudden blustery wind. The sea began to kick up a little, the boat bouncing and rocking more than Alec would have liked. He and Lacey put on their windbreakers.

Lacey suddenly stood up. "I've got something, Dad." Her pole was bending, the reel clicking rapidly as the fish carried the bait out to sea.

"Just hold on, Lace. Let it run. That's it."

She hung on to the pole, the tip of her tongue caught between her lips in concentration. "It stopped!" she said.

"Okay, reel in the line. Get the slack out of it. Do you want some help?"

"Uh uh."

One of the young men came over and stood by her side. "Atta girl," he said as she cranked the reel. "It's probably gonna take off on you another time or two. Just..."

She yelped as the fish began stripping line from her reel once more, but it quickly tired of the battle this time, and she started reeling it in again, laughing.

Another of the men had come over to watch. "It's a blue," he said, as the fish thrashed wildly just below the surface of the water. "And a real beauty. Almost as pretty as the fisherman."

Lacey managed to grin at him as she struggled with her pole.

"Fisher*woman*," the first young man corrected him.

"Right," said his friend. "No doubt about *that*."

Lacey blushed. Alec thought she looked like a trembling mass of erogenous zones.

The first fisherman reached over the railing with the net as Lacey pulled the bluefish from the water. "Eight pounds, I'd say." He scooped the fish up easily and lifted it onto the deck.

"Don't let it jump back in!" Lacey screamed, and she lowered herself next to Alec, holding on to the fish with a rag while he extracted the hook from its mouth. One of the young men lifted the lid of the cooler, and Alec dropped the fish inside. Then, with one last look at Lacey, the fishermen returned to their own poles at the stern.

Alec and Lacey baited their hooks again and took their seats. Lacey was smiling.

"That was good work, Lacey," he said.

"We don't have to eat it, though, do we?" she asked.

"No. We can give it to Nola. She loves bluefish."

"No*ler*," she corrected him and he laughed. Annie, with her Boston accent, could never master those open "a"s. "I'd like you to meet my friend *Noler* and her daughter *Jessiker*," Lacey said, mimicking her mother's husky voice.

"She wasn't quite that bad," Alec said.

"I'm just glad she didn't name me Melissa or something."

He smiled at a memory. "She wanted to name you Emma, but I refused. I told her I'd only go along with it if she could say the name for a week straight without turning it into *Emmer*. But of course, she couldn't do it."

"*Emma.* God, Dad, thanks, you saved me."

The young man who'd called her a real beauty walked by, and Lacey turned to smile at him.

"I should tell them you're barely fourteen," Alec said.

Lacey shrugged. "Well, Mom was only fifteen the first time she...you know."

"How do you know that?"

"She told me."

"She did?" *Thanks, Annie.*

"I mean, she said it wasn't good to do it that young, but she turned out all right."

"She was lucky she didn't get pregnant. And there are diseases around now that she didn't have to worry about back then."

"I know all that, Dad."

He couldn't see Lacey's face, but he could practically *hear* her rolling her eyes, and he waited a moment or two before he spoke again. "So, does that mean you're planning to have sex next year when you're fifteen?"

"God, Dad, that really isn't any of your business."

He stopped himself from telling her it most certainly was his business. This was too good. She was actually talking to him. He probably should say something about birth control. If he brought it up, though, wasn't that tantamount to giving her the go-ahead?

"Jessica's done it," Lacey said suddenly, her eyes glued to the water.

"*What?*"

"God, I shouldn't have said that. You won't tell Nola, Dad, will you?" she pleaded. "Please don't. Jessica would kill me."

"No, I won't." Could he keep that promise? He would have to. He tried to picture sultry little Jessica Dillard in bed with someone and could not come up with a clear image. "Is she...being careful?"

"I guess." Lacey sounded irritated by the question and he decided not to push her further.

They caught a second and third bluefish before the rocking of the boat took the pleasure out of fishing. Alec was relieved when the captain turned the boat around and headed back to shore. Most of the other fishermen had reeled in their lines and were sitting down. A few of them moved inside the cabin as the wind whipped up.

"You're supposed to watch the horizon if you don't feel well, right?" Lacey asked.

"You're not feeling well, Lace?" He did not feel that well himself.

She drew her windbreaker tighter around her and shook her head. A rain was starting. He could see droplets of it fill her hair and sparkle in the light from the cabin.

Lacey suddenly moaned and stood up, grabbing for the railing. He stood next to her, lifting her thick hair away from her face as she got sick, and he remembered doing the same for Annie when she was carrying Lacey. A horrendous pregnancy, although she had always told Lacey it had been a delight-filled nine months, as though she was trying to change the memory of it in her own mind.

Alec took his handkerchief from his jeans pocket and wiped Lacey's eyes and mouth. "Let's move over here," he said. They sat down on the deck, leaning against the cabin to give them some protection from the wind and rain. Her teeth were chattering and he put his arm around her, pleased that she didn't protest.

One of the fishermen was getting sick somewhere on the other side of the cabin. Lacey whimpered at the sound of his retching, and leaned against Alec.

"Daddy," she said, "I feel so bad."

"I know, sweetheart." He looked out at the horizon. Through the haze he could make out the string of lights along the shore and, to the north, the pulsing beacon of the Kiss River Lighthouse. "Look, Lace," he said, "we're almost home."

She raised her head, but lowered it to his shoulder again, moaning, and he hugged her tighter. He was cold and wet and running the risk of Lacey getting sick down the front of his jacket, yet he had not felt this completely content in a very long time.

Lacey staggered to the car when they reached the inlet, while he carried the cooler of fish. He set it in the back of the Bronco and climbed into the driver's seat. He looked over at his daughter. "Still a little green around the gills," he said. "How are you feeling?"

"Mmm." She leaned her head against the window and closed her eyes.

She was quiet during the drive home. She did not even bother with the headset, and the radio rested silently in her lap.

Once in the house, Alec set the cooler on the kitchen table and took a good look at his daughter as she pulled off her soppy windbreaker. Her face was white, the skin around her eyes puffy. "I guess fishing wasn't the best idea," he said.

She set her crumpled jacket on one of the chairs and opened the top of the cooler. "Well," she said, lifting out the smallest bluefish, "Noler will be happy."

He smiled. "I'll take care of the fish, Annie. You go on up to..."

Lacey spun around to face him. "I am *not* Annie!" She threw the fish at him and it caught him on the cheek, cold and wet, before falling to the floor with a thud.

"I'm sorry, Lace," he said.

"You make me sick!" She turned on her heel and stalked out of the room, her red hair flashing in the kitchen light.

She was already gone by the time he got up in the morning, and the house felt empty. He carried the fish over to Nola's. She was out, but the house was unlocked and he put the fish in her refrigerator and left a note on the kitchen table. *Blues in the fridge,* he wrote, and imagined adding a second line—*By the way, your daughter is having sex.* How would he feel if Nola knew something like that about Lacey and didn't tell him?

He was putting together some information on the lighthouse for Olivia when Lacey came home that afternoon. He heard the back door slam shut and the thumping of her footsteps on the stairs as she ran up to her room. He'd been rehearsing what he would say to her all afternoon, what Olivia had coached him to say during their phone call the night before: He'd enjoyed her company last night, he would tell her. Please don't let his one mistake ruin it.

The door to Lacey's room was open, and at first he thought there was a stranger in the room—a young girl with jet black hair, sorting through the top drawer of Lacey's dresser.

"Lacey?"

She turned around to face him and he gasped. She had dyed her hair and cut it short, nearly to her scalp. In some places it looked practically shaved, the whiteness of her scalp clearly visible against the stark blackness of her hair.

"What did you to do yourself?" he asked.

She put her hands on her hips and narrowed her eyes at him. "I don't look a thing like her now, do I?"

CHAPTER TWENTY

"She cut off her hair and dyed it black," Alec said.

Olivia rolled onto her side, moving Sylvie out of her way. She knew when the phone rang at ten-thirty each night who it was, and she was sure to be in bed by then. He was the one who said it first—that he liked talking to her from his bed, that his bed was the loneliest place in his house since Annie died. Yes, she agreed, she knew exactly what he meant. She felt close to him, talking to him in the darkness. His lights were off as well; she had asked him that the first night. She'd stopped short of asking him what he slept in, not certain she wanted to know.

"She's tired of existing in Annie's shadow," Olivia said. She understood all too well how Lacey felt.

"It makes her look cheap," Alec said. "I keep thinking of those men on the boat. She was enjoying their attention a little too much. She told me her best friend is having sex. Maybe she's not as naive as I'd like to think. Annie was only fifteen her first time."

Olivia frowned. "Fifteen?"

"Yes, but there were extenuating circumstances."

"Like what?"

Alec sighed. "Well, she was raised with a lot of money but not much love," he said. "I guess she tried to find it the only way she knew how. She was pretty promiscuous as a teenager—she loathed that word, but I don't know what else you'd call it."

Olivia said nothing. She wondered if Annie had still been looking for love the night she slept with Paul.

"So how old were you?" Alec asked.

"I beg your pardon?"

He laughed. "I guess that was pretty blunt. You sounded so appalled when I said Annie was fifteen, it made me wonder about you. You don't have to answer."

Olivia wrapped the telephone cord around her fingers. "I was fourteen the first time," she said, "and twenty-seven the second."

It was a few seconds before Alec spoke again. "I've opened a can of worms."

"Well, I don't talk about this much."

"And you don't have to now if you don't want to."

She rolled onto her back again and closed her eyes. "I was raped when I was fourteen by an older boy in my neighborhood."

"God, Olivia, I'm sorry."

"It left scars. It made me...apprehensive about sex, and I didn't make love until I was twenty-seven. That's when I met Paul."

"There was no one in all those years you felt safe enough with?"

She laughed. "I didn't exactly have to fight men off with a stick. I was a very nerdy adolescent, and not much better as an adult. I avoided the whole issue of men and dating by focusing on my studies or my work."

"I can't picture you nerdy. You're so attractive and self-confident."

"In the ER, maybe, but it's not that easy for me to feel good about myself in the real world. Confidence is something I've always had to work at, and being dumped by my husband for a woman who is practically a figment of his imagination hasn't helped."

"I'm sorry I dredged up bad memories for you."

"You didn't. They're always there in one form or another."

"What did you parents do about the rape? Did you prosecute the guy?"

Olivia stared up at the dark ceiling. "My father was dead, and my mother was very sick—an alcoholic, actually—and she wasn't capable of much by then. I didn't tell anyone about it until I met Paul. You're only the second person I've told." She pulled Sylvie closer, until the cat's soft head was against her cheek. "Anyhow, I left home after it happened and moved in with one of my teachers."

"I had no idea you had such a difficult past."

"Well, I owe a lot to Paul." She had been able to tell Paul the entire story of her past, of the rape. She'd dated him for several months before she dared let him know the truth about her background, and during that time she'd seen him cry at sad movies and listened to him read poetry he'd written about her. She knew she could tell him anything.

He'd responded to her story with the compassion she'd expected. He was the gentlest of lovers, his patience infinite. He did as much as any man could to heal the scars of that day so long ago. In the process, he awakened something in her. *Your lascivious side,* he called it, and she knew he was right. She felt a wild need to make up for the time she'd lost, and Paul obliged her most willingly, nurturing that newly discovered part of herself.

But now he'd told her that he'd made love to Annie, a woman with twenty-five years' worth of lovemaking experience behind her. She was so *free-spirited,* he'd said. *So full of life.*

"Alec," Olivia said, "I need to get off."

"I've upset you."

"No, it just makes me remember what a caring husband I used to have."

"I don't understand his problem, Olivia. I feel like calling him up and telling him he has a beautiful wife who loves him and needs him and..."

She sat up. "Alec, you wouldn't."

"I think he's out of his mind. He doesn't know what he's got and how quickly he could lose it."

"Alec, listen to me. You only know my side of the story. You don't know what our marriage was like from Paul's perspective. It wasn't right for him or enough for him or—I'm not sure what. But, please, please, don't try to interfere."

"Relax. I'm not going to do anything." Alec was quiet for a moment before he spoke again. "When Paul finally gets his wits about him and comes back to you, do you think he'd mind if you talked to me from your bed every once in a while?"

Olivia lay back on her pillow again, smiling. "I hope I have that problem to worry about one of these days."

"I hope you do, too."

"I'd better get off."

"Olivia?"

"Yes?"

"Nothing. I just like saying your name."

CHAPTER TWENTY-ONE

He hung up the phone after talking with Olivia, knowing he would not be able to sleep. He got out of bed and pulled on the blue shorts he'd worn that day, zipping them up as he walked from the bedroom out to the second-story deck. He sat down on the glider, pumping gently with his bare feet, making the glider coast a little. The sound was dark. The water lapped gently against the beach in his back yard, and a damp breeze brushed over his chest and arms.

He needed to get Olivia and Paul back together again, quickly, before he told her anything more loaded than he liked the sound of her name. He couldn't shake the feeling that he was doing something wrong, something inappropriate, just by talking to her from his bed. But he knew the reason for his guilt.

The call had come on a Sunday morning, a couple of years ago. He'd been sitting out here on the glider, reading the paper and drinking coffee from a mug when he heard Annie answer the telephone in the bedroom. She spoke quietly into the phone, her voice unusually subdued, which made him turn his lead to listen, but he couldn't make out her words and he returned his concentration to the paper. After a few minutes she came out onto the deck and sat down next to him on the glider.

"That was the bone marrow registry," she said. "I'm a perfect match for a little girl in Chicago."

She had registered as a donor several years earlier and Alec had thought little of it at the time. Just another one of Annie's good deeds. He had never expected it to amount to anything. From what he'd heard, it was extremely rare to find a match for bone marrow outside of one's own family. Apparently, though, it was not impossible.

He set down the newspaper and took her hand, drawing it onto his thigh. "So what does that mean exactly?" he asked.

"I'll have to go to Chicago. The surgery's scheduled for Tuesday." She wrinkled her nose, and when she spoke again her voice was small, hesitant. "Do you think you could go with me?"

"Of course." He let go of her hand and smoothed her hair over her shoulder. "You're sure you want to do this?"

"You bet." She stood up and bent over to kiss him. "I'll start breakfast."

She was quiet for the rest of the day, and he didn't press her to talk. He sensed she was grappling with something that she needed to work out on her own. At dinner that night, she told the children as much as she knew about the little girl who would surely die without her help. Lacey and Clay were eleven and fifteen, and they listened carefully, with serious faces. They would stay at Nola's, Annie told them, and she and Alec would be home Wednesday night.

"How do they get the bone marrow out of you and into the girl?" Lacey asked.

"Well," said Annie, her face animated, "first they'll put us both to sleep so we don't feel any pain. Then they'll make a little incision in my back and take the marrow out with a needle and that's that. The doctor said I'll have a stiff back for a few days, but that will be the worst part. And I'll be saving the little girl's life."

That night she could not sleep. She tossed and turned, finally working her way into Alec's arms. "Please hold me," she said.

She trembled as he pulled her close to him, and when she rested her head on his bare shoulder, he could feel the warm dampness of her cheek and knew she'd been crying.

He held her tighter. "What's wrong?"

"I'm so scared," she whispered. "I'm so scared I'm going to die during the surgery."

He was alarmed. It was so unlike Annie to give a thought to herself. He leaned away from her, trying to see her eyes in the darkness. "Then don't do it," he said. "You don't have to do it."

"I *do*." She sat up, facing him, her hand on his chest. "It's a child's only chance."

"Maybe there were other matches."

"They said I was the only one."

"Christ. Nothing like a little guilt trip."

"The feeling is so strong." She shivered. "As though I'm definitely going to die. It would be punishment for all the bad things I've done."

He laughed and lifted her hand from his chest to his lips. "You've never done a bad thing in your life."

"I can't stand the thought of not getting to watch Lacey and Clay grow up." She began crying in earnest, and he knew her imagination was taking over as it so often did, tormenting her with the worst possible fantasy. "I'd never get to hold my grandchildren. I want to grow *old* with you, Alec."

She was pleading, as though there was something he could do to assure her of a perfect future.

"I want you to back out of this, Annie." He sat up too, holding her hands, squeezing them between his palms. "Blame it on me. Tell them..."

"I *can't*. The little girl needs..."

"I don't give a damn about the little girl."

She snapped her hands away from his. "Alec! How can you say that?"

"She's anonymous. I don't know her and I never will. You, on the other hand, I know very well, and you're too frightened. It's not good for you to go into surgery feeling this way."

"I have to do it. I'll be all right. I'm just..." She shook her head. "You know how nuts you can get in the middle of the night." She lay down again and snuggled next to him, and it was another minute before she spoke again.

"Let me just ask you something, though," she said. "Hypothetically."

"Mmm?"

"If I died, how long would you wait before you started going out with someone?"

"*Annie*. Cancel the damn surgery."

"No. I mean it, Alec. Tell me. How long?"

He was quiet for a moment, aware of how quickly he could lose her. She could, in a perfectly voluntary surgery, leave him forever. He pulled her closer. "I can't imagine ever wanting to be with anyone else," he said.

"You mean, sexually?"

"I mean period."

"Well, God, I wouldn't want you to be alone *forever*. But if I did die, would you wait a year please? I mean, that's not too long to grieve for someone you completely and thoroughly adore, is it? That's all I ask. Then you can do whatever you like, although it would be nice if you could think of me from time to time, and find your new woman lacking in almost every way."

"Why not in every way?" he asked, smiling. "Go for broke, Annie." He raised himself up on his elbow and kissed her. "Maybe we'd better make love one last time since you already seem to have a foot out the door." He slipped his hand to her breast, but she caught his fingers.

"You didn't promise yet, Alec," she said. "Just one year. Please?"

"I'll give you two," he said, certain then that it was a promise he would have no trouble at all keeping.

She felt better in the morning, a cheery optimism replacing her maudlin mood. Alec, however, felt worse, as though she had transferred her fear to him. By the time they boarded the plane for Chicago on Tuesday, he was sick with nervousness. He sat with his head flat against the seatback, trying to ignore the nausea pressing in on him, while Annie held his hand and rested her head on his shoulder. She read him the article she'd torn from the *Beach Gazette* that morning, the article describing her trip to Chicago, yet another one of Annie O'Neill's saintly deeds.

She had to stay in the hospital the night before the surgery and Alec took a room in the hotel across the street. He watched television the entire night. If he fell asleep he might miss the alarm, and Annie would be taken into the OR before he'd have a chance to see her.

He walked over to the hospital before dawn and went into her room as soon as they would let him. She looked beautiful, her hair falling around her shoulders, a smile of contentment on her face.

"Oh, Alec." She reached for his hand. "You didn't sleep."

"Yes, I did," he lied.

She shook her head. "You have circles under your eyes. You look awful."

He tried to smile. "Thanks."

The nurse came in, telling them it was time for Annie to be wheeled to the operating room. Alec leaned over to kiss her, leaving his lips on hers for a long time. When he pulled away she whispered, "Don't be scared." They wheeled her out of the room and he struggled to keep his tears and his terror in check as he watched her disappear down the hall.

The surgery went smoothly, and Annie was practically euphoric by the time he saw her back in her room.

"My first thought when I came out of the anesthetic was, *'I'm alive!'*" she told him with a tired smile. "I was sick as a dog. It was *wonderful*."

Sitting on the plane was not easy for her. She fidgeted, adjusting her seat belt in an effort to get comfortable, but she didn't utter a word of complaint.

"I've been thinking," she said, when they were somewhere over Virginia. "There are some changes I want to make about us."

"Like what?" he asked.

"We need more time together."

"Fine," he said.

"I propose that we meet for lunch one day a week."

"Okay."

"A two-hour lunch," she said. "In a motel."

He laughed. "I see."

"I really need this, Alec." She rested her head on his shoulder. "We never get time away together, without the kids around. It's so important. It's more important than you know, than I can possibly explain to you."

They met on Fridays, from twelve to two, in any motel

that would take them. In the winter it was easy to find a room, but during the summer, they paid an exorbitant price for the privilege of two hours in a prime-season motel. By that time, though, Alec knew those couple of hours were worth any amount of money. The intimacy they shared in the motel rooms spilled over to the other days of the week, and he saw a change in Annie. Her occasional moodiness, her periods of withdrawal, completely disappeared. Amazing that two hours a week could change so much.

"I've never been happier in my entire life than I've been this past year," she told him. They'd been meeting for well over a year by then, and her contentment was so complete that when the depression took hold of her late in the fall, it was impossible to miss. She grew nervous. Jumpy. She was tearful when they made love on those afternoons in the motel room, quiet as they ate the lunch she'd brought. She avoided his eyes when she spoke to him. Sometimes she'd cry for no reason at all. He'd find her weeping in the bathroom as she soaked in the tub, or he'd wake up in the middle of the night to hear her crying softly into her pillow. It seemed far worse than the other times, or maybe it was just that it had been so long since he'd seen that misery in her.

"Let me in, Annie," he'd say to her. *"Let me help."* But she seemed no more aware of the reason for her distress than he was, and so he settled for holding her close to him, for trying to still her trembling with his arms.

Then suddenly, she was gone. In the hospital that Christmas night, he'd remembered his promise to her and it had seemed ludicrous to him that she'd asked him to grieve for only one year. He couldn't imagine *ever* being interested in another woman. A year seemed no longer than one rotation of the lighthouse beacon.

Until he met Olivia, a woman as unlike Annie as a woman

could be. She's a friend, he told himself now as he coasted gently on the glider. She's married to another man and carrying that man's child.

Maybe he should call her earlier in the evening, before he got into bed, the bed that still seemed filled with Annie's presence. Maybe he shouldn't call her at all.

CHAPTER TWENTY-TWO

Tom Nestor helped Olivia load the bags of magazines and paperbacks into the trunk of her car after her lesson that Saturday. The Manteo Retirement Home wasn't far from the Battered Women's Shelter, and since she was volunteering there tonight, she thought it was about time she made good on her promise to get the magazines out of the studio.

"Thanks for doing this," Tom said.

"I meant to take them long before now," Olivia said as she got in behind the steering wheel.

"Hey, Olivia," he said, giving her shoulder a squeeze through the window. "The panel's a real peach."

She smiled at him and then glanced down at the panel she'd finally completed that morning, a geometric blend of colored and clear glass that was pretty enough to hang in one of her windows—one of the windows Paul would be unlikely to see if he stopped by the house.

She drove into Manteo and parked across the street from the retirement home, directly in front of a small antique shop. Her eyes were drawn to the sidewalk in front of the little shop, where three antique dolls dressed in satin and lace sat on three splintery old wicker chairs. This must be where Annie had bought her daughter's birthday gifts. She would have to tell Alec.

She got out of the car and shaded her eyes to look at the retirement home. It was a lovely old house, painted sky-blue with sparkling white trim. A broad porch ran its entire width. From the street, Olivia could see that several of the front windows were filled with stained glass panels, no doubt made and donated by Saint Anne.

She lugged the bags out of the trunk of the Volvo and walked across the street and up the sidewalk to the house. Although she'd been out of her air-conditioned car for only seconds, she was already perspiring. It was the hottest day of the summer so far and there was no breeze at all.

About a dozen sturdy-looking white rocking chairs lined the porch, but only a couple of them were occupied—one by a shriveled old woman who looked too frail to be sitting outside in the heat, the other by a white-haired woman wearing sneakers and holding a newspaper on her lap.

"Hello, there, young lady," the woman in sneakers said as Olivia started up the steps. "You're bringing us some magazines?"

Olivia set the bags down on the top step and shaded her eyes again. The woman sat clear-eyed and stick-straight in the rocker, but this close up, Olivia could see she was quite old, her face lined and leathery. Someone had carefully trimmed and shaped her short white hair.

"Yes," Olivia said. "Is there someone inside I should leave them with?"

"Sandy's in there."

"Eh?" The second woman leaned forward, and the woman in sneakers spoke loudly into her ear.

"She's brought us magazines, Jane, you know, like Annie used to do?"

Jane gave a slight nod before leaning back in her chair again and closing her eyes.

"You knew Annie?" Olivia stepped under the porch roof, out of the sun.

"Indeed I did." The woman held out one long-boned hand to Olivia. "I'm Mary Poor, keeper of the Kiss River Lighthouse."

Olivia smiled and shook her hand, struck by the strength in the woman's slender fingers. "I'm delighted to meet you, Mrs. Poor. My name's Olivia Simon."

"*Olivia*. Pretty name. Kind of old-fashioned."

"I think you know my husband, Paul Macelli," Olivia continued. "He interviewed you about the lighthouse."

Mary Poor narrowed her eyes at Olivia. "He's got you running around, doing Annie's old chores?"

Olivia was speechless for a moment, trying to figure out which of them was confused. "No," she said finally. "I'm taking stained glass lessons from the man Annie used to share her studio with and..."

"Tom, am I right? Tom what's-his-name. Wears his hair like a girl."

"Yes, that's right. Tom Nestor. Do you know him?"

"Oh." Mary smiled, displaying lovely straight teeth for a woman her age. "I met him once or twice," she said. "So it's Tom who's got you doing Annie's work."

Jane started to snore softly from the chair at Mary's side.

"Well, no," Olivia said. "I saw the pile of magazines, and Tom told me that Annie used to bring them over here, so since I'm volunteering at the women's shelter, I figured I could..."

"You're working at that hell hole?"

"It's not that bad."

"Oh, no, child, you shouldn't be there." Mary patted the arm of the empty rocker next to her. "Sit down," she said.

Olivia looked at her watch. She was running late, but she was curious about this old woman. She sat down in the rocker.

"You're a pretty girl," Mary said.

"Thank you."

"You remind me of my daughter, Elizabeth. She had your color hair—dark and silky—and eyes like yours, with a little sad look to them."

Olivia leaned away from her. She did not want sad-looking eyes.

"You don't look a thing like Annie, though."

"I know," Olivia said. "I've seen pictures of her."

"I bet you're not like her in any way at all."

Olivia felt insulted, and Mary did not miss her look of dismay. She hurried on.

"And that's just fine, child," she continued. "You be you, let Annie be Annie. Would you have done what she did? Jumped in front of a woman about to get her head shot off by her husband?"

Olivia had wondered about that herself. "Well, I like to think I..."

"The hell you would. Instinct takes over and you fight for yourself, for your own hide. And that's the way it *should* be." Mary licked her lips and looked out toward the street, toward the little shop where the dolls sat baking in the sun. "Annie was a really fine girl," she said, "but she could be a fool sometimes."

Olivia did not know what to say. She stared at the newspaper in Mary Poor's lap, folded to the crossword puzzle, which had nearly been completed.

"That husband of yours," Mary said.

"Paul?"

"Paul. He's a very high-strung sort, isn't he? You need to feed him kale with sea salt and lemon."

Olivia laughed.

"Kale with sea salt for those nerves of his. And you tell him it's about time he came back. I have plenty more I can tell him and Lord knows how much longer I can keep it straight in this old noggin." She touched her fingertips to her temple.

"You seem very lucid to me, Mrs. Poor." Olivia stood up. She bent down to pick up the bags, nearly straining her back with the weight of them.

"You make this the last time you bring magazines by here, all right?" Mary said.

Olivia frowned. "I don't understand," she said. "I thought..."

"You can come visiting anytime, child, but not doing Annie's chores for her."

Mary leaned back in the rocking chair after the girl had gone and closed her eyes. She had done enough of the crossword puzzle for now, and she knew that Jane would be asleep until suppertime. She should take a little rest herself, but her mind kept returning to the girl's face. Had she really looked like Elizabeth? Probably not. To be honest, she could barely remember Elizabeth's face at all. It was frozen in her memory at the ages she'd been in the few pictures she had of her. Three, eight, fifteen. That last picture had been taken the day before she ran away. She remembered well how she'd looked the very last time she'd seen her, though, two years ago, when she'd been lying in a casket. Mary never would have recognized her. Elizabeth had been fifty-eight years old, gray-haired and waxy-pale.

A friend of Elizabeth's in Ohio had sent Mary the letter, telling her that Elizabeth had collapsed at work and never regained consciousness. Mary wanted to go to the funeral, she told Annie. She needed to pay her last respects.

Annie drove her, and it took them a very long time to get there. Days, perhaps. Mary wasn't sure. She slept most of the way, while Annie sang along with the radio. Mary would catch bits and pieces of her songs, amused by the energy she put into them, as though she were on stage. It made Mary chuckle to herself. Then she'd feel a little guilty at the comfort she took in being with Annie, while her own daughter had died a stranger to her.

Annie took care of her on that trip, and for once Mary needed Annie's care more than Annie needed hers. Away from Kiss River for the first time in many years, Mary suddenly felt every bit her age—eighty-seven and one half years old. Almost as devastating as seeing the unfamiliar, lifeless body of her daughter was the sudden awareness of her frailty. She was confused, uncertain of the hour or the day. Sometimes uncertain of the year. In the restaurants, she stared at the silverware, trying to remember how to hold a fork, how to cut her meat. During the night in the hotel, she woke Annie half a dozen times to ask her why there were no bursts of light coming through the window.

The strangers she met at the funeral treated her like a very old woman, sometimes talking past her as if she were not there. Annie became her eyes and her ears and her memory. Mary would catch her dear young friend looking at her with a worry in her face she had never noticed before. Annie wept at Elizabeth's funeral, and Mary knew it was not Elizabeth she cried for, but her. She wanted to assure Annie that she was all right, that Annie did not have to fret about her. But the truth was, away from Kiss River she was a very old woman.

She was relieved to be back at Kiss River after that long and taxing journey. She stepped stiffly out of Annie's car and felt immediately rejuvenated by the cool, salt-filled air. She wanted to climb to the top of the lighthouse, but Annie dissuaded her. Annie made dinner for her before going home to her own family, fussing over her as if she were a helpless child.

Mary had only been back at Kiss River a day and a half when she fell. Looking back later, she wished she could say there'd been an obstacle in her path that night, but the truth was she was simply walking across the kitchen floor when she lost her balance and went down. Pain shot through her hip and arm, and her cheek smacked hard against the tile. She couldn't move. She couldn't lift herself a fraction of an inch from the floor.

For two days and two nights she did without food or drink. She messed herself. The floor grew as cold as the ground outside, while the fire in the living room turned to ashes and a cold front swept across Kiss River. Mary slipped in and out of consciousness, struggling to keep her mind working by remembering the names of the dozens of men who had worked at the lifesaving station over the years.

On the third night, Annie arrived. Mary heard her key in the front door. She heard her step into the living room, and she tried to call out to her, but her throat was too dry. Annie called her name as she moved from room to room, and Mary heard her gasp when she finally entered the kitchen.

"Oh, my God," Annie said, dropping next to her, the soft fabric of her skirt brushing over Mary's face. Did she have someone with her that night? Yes, of course. Mary remembered Annie speaking to the stranger who hung back in the shadows of the cold living room, telling him to call an ambulance. Then she lifted Mary's head into her lap and rocked her, as she must have rocked her children when they were younger.

"Oh, Mary," she whispered, her hair like a red veil in front of Mary's eyes. "You've gone and done it this time, precious. They'll move you out now for sure."

Mary hoped she would die right then. She squeezed her eyes closed and tried to force her soul from her body, but her effort only resulted in a deep and painless sleep. And when she woke up to the smell of antiseptic and sterile air, she knew she had left Kiss River forever.

CHAPTER TWENTY-THREE

Paul knew he should have backed out of tonight's meeting. He'd been sitting in his car on the tree-lined street in front of Alec's house for several minutes now, his windows rolled up and the air conditioner blowing in his face as he summoned up the courage to go inside. The first few meetings at the Sea Tern had been uncomfortable enough. He didn't know why Alec had suddenly suggested the committee meet here.

On the outside, the house was utterly Annie—yellow, with white trim, and surrounded by trees hung heavy with Spanish moss. It was a decade old—he knew that she and Alec had it built when Alec's practice was finally solvent. A couple of brightly colored sailboards were propped against the side wall, and he could see a fish-shaped windsock flying from the pier around back. The house was on the sound, on a little cul-de-sac of water, just as Annie had described it to him. *The sunsets, Paul. The colors. They would make you want to write. They'd make you want to cry.*

Paul started at a sudden rapping on his car window, and he turned to see Nola Dillard standing inches away from his face. He rolled the window down.

"Coming in, hon?" she asked. She was on foot. She must live close by.

He opened his door and joined her in the street, where her perfume masked the scent of the sound, and the setting sun played on the false gold of her hair. "I wasn't sure I had the right house," he lied.

"This is it, all right. You can tell by the sailboards if nothing else."

They were greeted at the door by a German shepherd on three legs.

"This is Tripod," Nola said.

Paul patted the dog's head. A dog and two cats, Annie had told him. Not much for a vet.

The personality the house exuded on the outside spilled over into the living room. Annie's touch was everywhere. The furniture was not the usual sturdy beach variety of the Outer Banks, but rather an overstuffed and eclectic collection of chairs and sofas upholstered in bold floral prints. The floor was nearly covered by patterned rugs, haphazardly layered on top of one another to form a comforting patchwork. Paul felt as if he'd walked into Annie's arms.

"Don't they have a wonderful view?" Nola was still at his elbow, pointing toward the huge window that looked out over the sound. The sunset was beginning to paint the sky, but Paul's attention was drawn to the adjacent wall where ten small, oval windows were scattered from floor to ceiling, each filled with an intricately detailed scene of a woman in a flowing dress. One held a parasol, another walked a greyhound, a third held a bloodred rose to her nose.

"Oh, my God," he said. He had not known, she had never told him, that these windows existed. "These are extraordinary."

"Mmm," Nola agreed. "She was a very talented lady."

He could have spent the rest of the evening in front of those ovals of glass, but Nola took his arm and steered him toward the kitchen.

"Let's say hello to Alec," she said.

The kitchen was again pure Annie. The floor and cabinets and countertops were white, but the walls were nearly entirely made up of windows, and the windows were filled with stained glass, so that even in the muted evening light, the room was awash in soft pastels.

Alec leaned against the counter by the sink, uncorking a bottle of wine. He smiled when he saw them. "Hi, Nola, Paul." He rested his hand briefly on Paul's shoulder.

"The bluefish was divine," Nola said. She kissed Alec on the cheek, touching his chest lightly with her hand in a way that gave Paul gooseflesh. Was there something between them? How could Alec have lost Annie such a short time ago and even let another woman near him? Nola, though, was looking at Alec with clear adoration that Alec seemed not to notice. Paul supposed he was the type of man some women would find attractive, with his piercing blue eyes and dark hair, and the smile that came as a surprise just when you thought he was incapable of any levity whatsoever.

He's so sexy, Annie had said during the first interview. Paul had taken her words as a warning, an indication that he didn't stand a chance with her this time around. He wondered later if she had only been trying to warn herself.

Alec arranged some wineglasses on a tray and handed the bottle to Paul. "Want to pour for me?"

"Sure." Paul tried to get the same level of energy into his voice that Alec had in his, but failed. He took the bottle from Alec's hand and began to pour, but his eyes were drawn to the decorative white shelves between the countertop and the cabinets. There, directly in front of him, was the small blue cloisonné horse he had bought Annie in New Hope. He spilled some of the wine on the tray and set the bottle down until he could pour it without his hand shaking.

Baby Blue. She had kept it all these years.

"Can you bring the tray out?" Alec asked, as he and Nola carried corn chips and salsa into the living room.

"Sure," Paul said again. He separated the glasses on the tray so they wouldn't rattle against each other when he lifted them.

He took a seat facing the wall of oval windows, but the light outside was quickly fading and from this distance he could not make out the scenes. Besides, he had to pay attention to what the others were saying. He had suddenly become the topic of their conversation.

Alec took a swallow of wine and lifted the file of material Paul had put together on the history of the lighthouse.

"Great work, Paul," he said. "You've more than earned your keep on this committee."

The others agreed, Brian Cass adding that they just needed a bit more information on Mary Poor to make it complete.

"I have a few things I need to get done for the *Gazette,*" Paul said. "But I'm hoping to get over to Manteo one day in the next week or so."

"No rush," Alec said. He took a deep breath and set down his glass. "Well, maybe I'd better wait till you've all had a bit more to drink before I move on to the next topic." He picked up another file. "I'm afraid this is it, folks. The Park Service has made their final decision."

"Oh, God," said Sondra. "They're going to move it."

Alec nodded, and Walter Liscott groaned and buried his head in his hands.

"Read it, Alec," Nola said.

Alec opened the file. A track would be built, he read, the

work to begin in late August and completed next spring. The lighthouse would be lifted up and onto the track and moved a quarter mile inland. Paul could not picture it. He could not imagine the spit of land at Kiss River in unrelenting darkness.

Walter stood up. "It's insanity!" he said. "It's a godawful jackass scheme!"

"It does sound impossible," Sondra said.

Brian Cass shook his head. "As far as I'm concerned, the historical significance of the lighthouse is down the tubes if they move it."

"What about the sea wall?" Walter gestured wildly. "Why the hell..."

"Walter." Alec's voice was calm, reasonable. "That argument's moot. This is what we have to live with."

Walter stared at Alec for a moment. "I'm sorry, Alec. I'm going to have to take myself off this committee. I can't be a party to that lunatic idea."

He started toward the door, but Nola stood up and grabbed his arm. "The engineers have been working on this for years, now, Walter. You know that. You know they wouldn't recommend moving it if they had the slightest doubt it would..."

"A bunch of little boys with a great big erector set," Walter said. "They're just playing. They're experimenting with something they have no right to tamper with." He turned to leave.

"Walter," Alec said. "We don't want to lose you. If you have a change of heart, please don't let pride get in the way of coming back."

Walter muttered something to himself and walked out the door.

The room was suddenly very still. An outboard motor

started up somewhere on the sound, and the three-legged shepherd yawned and rolled over at Alec's feet.

"Well," Alec said finally. "Anybody else want to leave?"

Sondra Carter folded her arms across her chest. "I want to, but I won't."

Alec continued the meeting, talking about a few speaking engagements he had lined up. Then the committee went over a couple of fund-raising ideas, but energy lagged as the reality of the Park Service report settled over them like a lead blanket.

The meeting ended abruptly at nine, and Paul found himself reluctant to leave. He hung back from the rest of the group, cleaning up a salsa spill from the coffee table, carrying the wineglasses into the kitchen. He set them carefully in the sink, his eyes fastened on the blue horse, as he listened to Alec bidding good-night to his other guests. Paul walked back into the living room, getting as close as he could to the oval windows, but it was too dark outside. It was nearly impossible to make out the designs.

"Annie finished them even before the house was built."

Paul turned to see Alec in the doorway. "It must have taken her forever," he said.

"Not really. Once she got a design down, she was pretty fast. Come outside. You can see them much better from there this time of night."

Paul followed Alec out the front door and around to the side of the house. They stood next to each other in the sand, Paul shaking his head in spellbound wonder. The windows were breathtaking.

"The thing that strikes me about her work is the realism," he said. "You'd swear these women were real, that their dresses would feel soft and silky if you touched them."

"That was her specialty," Alec said. "I don't think that

even Tom, the guy she worked with, ever mastered the technique she used."

Paul looked over at Alec, whose cheeks were splashed violet and gold from the window closest to his face. "Does it bother you to talk about her?" he asked.

"Not at all. She's one of my favorite topics."

Paul ran his fingertips over one of the windows, watching the color bleed onto his skin. "The night Olivia came home and told me Annie O'Neill was dead...I just couldn't believe it. She was so alive. She was wonderful to interview." He thought of the tapes he could not bring himself to listen to.

"It was unbelievable all right," Alec said.

"I guess you know Olivia and I are separated."

"Yes, she told me." He glanced at Paul. "Do you know that's not what she wants?"

"I know." Paul stared at the image of a white-gowned, raven-haired woman about to take a bite from an apple. "It was completely my fault, what went wrong. Completely my doing. I felt certain when I left that it was the right thing to do, but now...I miss her sometimes, although I still have my doubts we could ever make it work again."

"At least you have the choice. I envy you for that." Alec gazed down at the sand for a few seconds. Then he chuckled and looked up at Paul. "I have this almost uncontrollable urge to lecture you," he said. "You have a wife who's pretty and smart and alive and I get the feeling you don't realize how lucky you are and how quickly you could lose her...and I'm sorry. I don't have any right to tell you your business."

"Its okay," Paul said. "I guess I'd feel the same way in your shoes."

Alec slapped at a mosquito on his arm. "Let's go in," he said.

"Well, I should really get going." Paul's tone was

unconvincing. As much as he hadn't wanted to walk into Alec's house earlier that evening, now he didn't want to leave.

"Come on in for a while," Alec said. "It's not that late and my kids are out. I can use the company."

"I saw pictures of your kids at Annie's studio," Paul said, as they walked into the house. "Your daughter looks practically identical to her."

Alec laughed. "Not anymore. She cut off her hair and dyed it black." He stepped into a room off the living room. "Come in here," he said.

Paul walked into a small den. A computer rested on the desk facing the front window, and a broad work table like the one at Annie's studio took up half the opposite wall. The walls were covered with photographs, most of them family shots, taken on the pier, on the deck of the house, on the beach. Annie looked happy in every one of them without exception, the core of her family, and Paul felt a sudden self-loathing for trying to hurt that, for playing to her weakness.

He stared at a picture of Annie's children. Lacey and Clay. "She cut off that beautiful hair?" he asked, shaking his head.

" 'Fraid so."

Paul moved to another picture and this one gave him a start. A tanned white-haired man in tennis clothes standing next to a homely red-headed woman. "And who are these people?" he asked, although he already knew the answer.

The phone on the desk rang. "Annie's parents," Alec answered, as he picked up the receiver. He said a few words into the phone and Paul began to feel intrusive. He waved to Alec and mouthed the word *thanks* as he headed toward the door of the den, but Alec held up a hand to stop him.

"Wait a sec," he said, and then into the phone, "I'm leaving now." He hung up the phone and looked at Paul. "Are you squeamish?"

"Uh...no. I don't think so."

"Come with me, then." Alec picked up a set of keys from the top of his desk and started toward the door. "One of the wild horses was hit by a car near Kiss River. We might be able to use your help."

Paul followed him outside. They stopped in the garage, where Alec unlocked a cabinet and removed what looked like a tool chest and what was most definitely a shotgun.

Paul stared at the gun. "Are you going to... Do you think you'll have to shoot it?"

Alec looked at him, puzzled, before breaking into a smile. "With a tranquilizer dart," he said. "I'd use an injection if the horse needs to be put down, and that will most likely be the case, if it's not dead already by the time we get there. I haven't seen one of them survive a run-in with a car yet."

Paul got into the Bronco, next to Alec and the gun. "Annie told me the horses stay close to the road now that it's more developed around Kiss River," he said.

Alec backed the Bronco out into the street. "They think the grass has been planted just for them." He shook his head. "There are only ten horses left. Maybe nine, after tonight. We've plastered the road with warning signs, but some people still get behind the wheel with their brains in neutral."

They were quiet as they drove out of Southern Shores. What would Annie think if she could see this scene, Paul wondered, he and Alec cruising up to Kiss River like old buddies, a shotgun resting on the seat between them?

"You were starting to tell me about Annie's parents," Paul said.

"Oh, right." Alec turned on the air conditioner. Nightfall had done nothing to ease the heat of the day. "Her dad's dead now, but her mother still lives in Boston, where Annie grew up. I don't know why I have that picture of them hanging in the den. Annie insisted we put it up, but as far as I'm concerned we could have dropped it in the sound."

Even in the darkness, Paul could see the tension in Alec's jaw. "She mentioned that she came from a very wealthy family," he prompted.

Alec glanced over at him. "She said that?" He shook his head. "They had money, all right, but Annie never saw a dime of it once we were married. They cut her off."

Paul was beginning to perspire. He turned one of the air conditioning vents toward his face. "Why would they do that?" he asked.

"My parents owned a little Irish pub in Arlington—not much of a moneymaking enterprise—and I guess the son of a bartender wasn't good enough for their blue-blooded daughter." Alec's tone was quiet, confidential, and Paul could feel his hurt. "They said I was white trash."

Paul turned his head to the window. Annie had not married Alec to please her parents. She had left Paul for a man who was no more to their liking than he had been.

"There's the Kiss River Light," Alec said.

Paul looked ahead of them into the black night, and in a few seconds he saw it, too. *One, one-hundred...* So familiar. So constant. So... "Oh my God," he said.

"What?"

"What will happen to the light while they're in the process of moving it?"

Alec smiled. "I've thought of that myself. Doesn't feel too good, does it?" He turned the Bronco onto the narrow road leading out to Kiss River, and leaned forward, peering into the darkness. "There they are," he said.

Paul spotted two women on the side of the road, waving

them over with their flashlights. Alec pulled the Bronco onto the sandy shoulder. He handed the shotgun to Paul, and they got out of the car, Alec carrying the tool chest and flashlight.

The women walked over to them.

"It's one of the colts, Alec," the taller woman said. "He was on the ground when we called you. He's up now, but he's limping badly." She pointed into the wooded area at the side of the road and Paul could make out the dark silhouette of a young horse.

Alec set the tool chest down and put his hands on his hips, assessing the situation. "Where's the herd?" he asked.

"Across the street." The taller woman looked at Paul. "I'm Julie," she said.

"Paul Macelli," Paul said.

Alec touched the second woman on the shoulder. "And this is Karen."

"He was broadsided," Karen said. "The guy who hit him—with a Mercedes, no less—said the colt flipped up on the hood of the car and broke the windshield. He's got a right good gash on his left hindquarter."

Alec looked toward the horse. "Okay, fella," he said quietly, "let's see you walk."

The four of them stood waiting for some movement from the colt, but he seemed frozen in one spot. He lifted his head to look across the road, where a group of horses milled skittishly in the darkness, the light from the beacon brushing over them every few seconds. They were huge, Paul thought with a shudder. Menacing. He remembered Annie warning him to steer clear of them. *"They're wild,"* she'd said. *"They can be nasty."*

Finally, the colt took a few tentative steps, obviously favoring his left front leg. Then he stood still, alone in the woods, neighing—*crying,* really—a sound that hurt to listen to.

Alec took the shotgun from Paul's hand and gave him the flashlight. "Could you hold the light down here, Paul?" he asked as he knelt down to load the gun with something he took from the chest. Then he stood up. "Hold the light on him," he said, and Paul and the women trained the beams of their flashlights on the animal's bloody hindquarters as Alec moved quietly toward him.

Paul glanced over his shoulder at the enormous horses just across the road from where they stood. He felt somehow more exposed without Alec next to him.

Alec lifted the shotgun slowly to his shoulder and fired. The colt bucked and let out a cry. There was an answering whinny from the other side of the road, and Julie and Karen looked over at the herd.

"I'd better keep an eye on them," Karen said, walking back toward the road. "You two can help Alec."

There was not much to do as they waited for the tranquilizer to take effect. The three of them stood abreast, watching the frightened little colt stare back at them.

"How are you, Alec?" Julie broke the silence after a minute or two. Her question sounded loaded, one of those simple questions that took on greater meaning between old friends.

"I'm all right," Alec said. "Hanging in there."

After another few minutes of silence, the colt dropped abruptly to his knees, then rolled over on his side.

Alec lifted the tool chest. "Let's see what we've got," he said, as they started walking toward him.

Julie sat on the ground and pulled the colt's head into her lap, while Paul stood above them, holding the flashlight so that Alec could see what he was doing. He glanced nervously toward the road. How was Karen going to hold those horses back if they decided to protect one of their own?

Alec ran his hands carefully over the colt's legs, spending a long time on the leg the colt had favored. "Amazing," he said. "Nothing's broken. He's going to be sore for a while, though." He moved his hands slowly over the trunk of the horse. "No broken ribs. Hopefully no internal injuries, either. Looks like this is the worst problem." He turned his attention to the gash. "Come a little closer with the light, Paul."

Paul glanced across the road and reluctantly dropped to his knees. He was defenseless now. If the horses decided to stampede, the three of them were doomed.

He trained the light on the ugly wound. It was deep, and easily eight inches long. Alec washed it with a solution he took from his tool box.

"Do you have to stitch it?" Paul asked.

Alec nodded. "If it were winter, I'd let it go, but with this heat the flies are sure to get to it if I don't."

Paul wasn't certain he could watch this. He hadn't known what he was agreeing to when he'd told Alec he wasn't squeamish.

Alec rooted around in the tool chest for another minute. Then he took the flashlight from Paul and handed it to Julie. "You'll need to hold the edges of the wound together for me, Paul, okay?"

"Uh. You'll have to show me how."

Alec demonstrated, and Paul followed his example, wincing as Alec began to stitch.

"How's your baby doing, Jule?" Alec asked, keeping his eyes on his work.

"She's not a baby anymore," Julie said, "which goes to show how long you've been out of circulation. She's a hellion. Into everything."

Julie talked about the little restaurant she managed, and Alec talked about Clay going off to college in another month. Paul listened to their easy conversation, their comfort with one another. Alec's voice was so calm, so assured, despite the work he was doing on the colt, that Paul nearly forgot about the horses across the road.

"I wasn't sure I should call you," Julie said, after a brief silence. "I know you haven't been working lately."

"I'm glad you did," Alec said.

"Well, I thought twice about it, I can tell you that. But there just isn't anyone else I'd trust with one of these guys."

Alec glanced up at her with a smile. "This one's going to make it, Jule."

There was a silence as Alec continued his stitching. Paul moved his fingers along the edges of the wound to keep pace with him. The tension had left his body. The horses across the road seemed harmless as long as Alec was close by. For the first time he thought he understood. There was nothing mysterious about Annie leaving him for Alec. There had been no ulterior motive on her part, no hidden agenda, no succumbing to the demands of her parents. He could imagine her with Alec—Annie with her need to feel loved and cherished, safe and secure. Alec would have met those needs without even trying.

The pulsing light of the beacon seemed to slow, lingering on Alec's hand for several seconds before melting back into the darkness. Then his hands stilled, suddenly, the needle poised above the wound, and Paul looked up to find Alec staring at him.

"Are you all right?" Alec asked, as the soft white light swept over them again.

"Yes," Paul said, lowering his eyes to the horse. He wondered what Alec had seen in his face.

Okay, he thought, *you won. She was yours, not mine. She loved you, not me. You won, Alec. Fair and square.*

Chapter Twenty-Four

It was nearly eleven by the time Alec said good-night to Paul and walked alone into his house. Lacey and Clay were still out, and the emptiness was oppressive. Even Tripod did not bother to come downstairs to greet him.

He poured iced tea into one of the green, hand-blown tumblers Julie had given Annie for her birthday a few years earlier, and carried it into the living room, where he sat down on the couch and stared at the phone. It was after eleven. Too late to call Olivia, and that was just as well. He'd become a little too dependent on those phone calls. He'd see her in the morning, anyway. She had agreed to go windsurfing with him at Rio Beach.

He lay down, stretching out along the length of the sofa, a throw pillow beneath his head. It had been a long, long time since he'd worked on an animal. It had felt good—*powerful*—to be able to make a difference, to set something *right* for a change. He had expected to find a dead horse up there. Or worse, a dying horse. He supposed that's why he'd asked Paul to come along—to keep his mind off his jangling nerves.

Paul had to be the softest man he'd ever met. He'd gotten

misty-eyed over the colt. Alec could imagine him with Olivia. An image—thoroughly prurient—slipped into his mind of Olivia and Paul together, and he rested his arm over his eyes to try to block it out. The first erotic thought he'd had in months and he wasn't even a part of it.

God, he missed Annie. Sleeping with her, waking up with her. He missed those clandestine Friday "lunches" in motel rooms. She had been a different woman during those two hours each week. She'd never been a reluctant lover, but he knew it was usually the closeness she was after. The holding. The loving words. He'd learned long ago that he had a need for sex itself—for the purely physical pleasure it offered—that she didn't share. He'd adjusted. They had acknowledged their differences and worked it out. But during those weekly rendezvous, Annie had been impassioned, eager. Her body had given off steam when he touched her.

Alec finished the iced tea, wishing he'd poured himself something stronger, something numbing. He closed his eyes and breathed deeply, letting the hum of the air conditioner lull him to sleep.

When he woke up, he could not at first get his bearings. The dim light from the kitchen washed over the wall in front of him and he saw the ten oval windows. He was lying on the living room sofa. He had a throbbing erection, and its inspiration—Annie—no longer existed. *God damn it.*

He got off the couch in a rage, hurling the throw pillow to the floor. *Fuck* the Battered Women's Shelter. *Fuck* Zachary Pointer. He lifted the tumbler from the coffee table and heaved it toward the wall. Fuck *you*, Annie.

The tumbler sailed across the room, and he caught his breath as it connected with one of the ten small oval windows, splintering the detailed stained glass image of a dark-haired woman carrying a parasol.

Alec stared at the empty, oval-shaped hole in the wall. He closed his eyes and groaned, raking his hands through his hair.

The side yard was illuminated by lights under the eaves, and Alec could see some of the small, painstakingly cut pieces of glass as he walked barefoot through the sand. He sat on the ground beneath the windows and began picking up the pieces, collecting them in his palm.

A car stopped on the street in front of the house and he heard laughter, followed by the slamming of a door. In a moment Clay was walking toward him.

"Dad? What are you doing out here?" Clay looked down at the colored glass in his father's hand. "Who broke the window?"

"It was an accident." Alec followed Clay's eyes to where the green tumbler rested in the sand, and for a moment neither of them spoke.

"Did Lacey...?"

"No. It wasn't Lacey."

Clay stuffed his hands in the pockets of his shorts. "Well, look, Dad," he said. "It's late. You can worry about the window tomorrow."

"I don't want to leave the glass out here." Alec ran his fingers through the sand and found a small white triangle of the parasol.

"It'll be all right." Clay glanced around him as if he were worried someone in the neighborhood might be watching this scene. "Come on, Dad. You're freaking me out. I'll help you find the pieces in the morning."

Alec looked up at his son. A handsome young man. Black hair. Dark skin. Seventeen years old. In all likelihood he had made love to Terri Hazleton tonight. In another month, he'd leave home for good. He'd start his new life. His *own* life.

Alec stared into his pale blue eyes. "I miss your mother," he said.

Clay lowered himself to the sand, and leaned back against the house. "I know, Dad," he said quietly. "I do, too." He sifted his fingers through the sand and found a small red piece of glass, which he handed to Alec.

Alec closed his fingers around the fragments of glass in his palm. He rested his arms on his knees and looked out at the black water of the sound. "They're going to move the lighthouse, Clay," he said. "They're going to pull the damn thing out of the ground, and Kiss River will never be the same again."

CHAPTER TWENTY-FIVE

Alec could have asked Olivia to come to his house. He had the sailboards there; they could have set out right from the little cove that formed his back yard. As he drove toward Rio Beach, though, he realized that he hadn't wanted Olivia at his house in case Clay or Lacey were there. So what did that mean? Nola was over all the time, and he never gave it a second thought. But if they found Olivia there, he would have to offer an explanation for her presence. They might remember her from that night in the ER, or they might not. That wasn't it. He just didn't want them to see him with a woman other than their mother, no matter how platonic the relationship might be.

Olivia was leaning against her car in the little parking area adjacent to Rio Beach. She wore a white cover-up over her bathing suit and her legs were nearly the color of the jacket. This was a woman who worked entirely too much.

He parked next to her, and she shaded her eyes as he got out of the Bronco and began unstrapping the sailboard from the roof.

"I'm warning you, Alec," she said. "I can't swim a stroke."

He threw her a life vest from the back seat of the Bronco. "You don't need to know how to swim," he said. "You do need some sunscreen, though."

"I put some thirty on. This is the first time I've been out in the sun this summer."

"It looks like the first time in your life."

She made a face at him and took the end of the board to help him carry it through the tangled weeds leading out to the sound.

"How come there's just one board?"

"Because the wind is perfect for you today, but a little nonexistent for my taste. It's pretty shallow here. I can stay next to you and tell you what to do."

Rio Beach was nothing more than a scrap of sand at the water's edge, barely wide enough for the blanket Alec spread across it. He stood with his hands on his hips, looking out at the sound. The sun shimmered on the water, and he could see other windsurfers in the distance, but he knew none of them had put in here. Rio Beach was his little secret.

"Great day for this," he said, turning to Olivia. She was gnawing on her lower lip. "Are you ready?"

"As I'll ever be." She took off her jacket and laid it on the blanket. Her bathing suit was black and violet, conservatively cut at the thigh, but dipping gently over her breasts, and he remembered his erotic fantasy of her and Paul from the night before.

"What are you smiling about?" she asked.

He laughed as he took off his T-shirt. "Just glad to be out here," he said. "It's been a while."

She wore a long gold chain that fell softly between her breasts. The bone-whiteness of her skin made her look terribly fragile, but he would never have guessed she was pregnant. The slight rise of her belly would not give her away.

"So, did you call your doctor about windsurfing?" he asked. She had told him she was concerned about the advisability of windsurfing when pregnant.

She wrinkled her nose. "Yes. Turns out she's a windsurfer herself. She said the only risk she could see was that I might actually have fun for once and not know how to cope with the experience."

Alec laughed. "Your doctor's got you pegged."

He gave her a little demonstration, showing off a bit with a beach start, a couple of duck-jibes, before settling down to the tamer moves she would need to learn. The twelve-foot board felt sluggish, cumbersome beneath his feet. He was used to the small board he liked to take out in the ocean.

She shivered when she stepped into the water. Alec held the sailboard steady for her, and she climbed onto it, her face the picture of concentration. "Put your feet on either side of the mast," he said.

"Is this the mast?"

"Right." He held her hand to steady her as she rose to her feet. "Now hold on to the rope. You're going to uphaul to get the sail out of the water. Bend your legs. That's it. Keep your back straight and use your legs to pull the sail up."

She pulled in the rope, hand over hand, and the sail began to rise out of the water, taking wind, causing the board to turn suddenly beneath her feet. She screamed, falling backward into the water with a splash. He walked around the board to help her, but she surfaced laughing.

"I should have warned you about that," he said. "When the clew comes out of the..."

"What's the clew?" she asked, tossing the water out of her hair.

"This part of the sail right here," he said, and he got onto the board once more to show her how it was done.

She spent more of her time in the water than on the board, but she was nothing if not a good sport. She laughed a couple of times to the point of tears. It was a side to her he had not seen, a side he imagined she rarely saw herself.

She was climbing gamely onto the board for what seemed like the hundredth time, when her bathing suit slipped from her shoulder and he saw the sharp white line it left on her skin.

"You're burning," he said. "We'd better get you out of here."

Olivia sat down on the blanket, her teeth chattering. Alec wrapped her towel around her, rubbing her arms through it, briefly, letting go as he realized the intimacy of the touch. The gold chain clung softly to the pink swell of her breasts, and he looked away.

He got the green and white striped umbrella from the back of the Bronco and set it up over Olivia's half of the blanket. Then he lay down next to her, relishing the warmth of the sun on his skin. "So, how come you never learned to swim?" he asked. He had spent most of his childhood canoeing and water skiing on the Potomac.

"I never lived near any water." The umbrella caught her words and floated them down to him.

"Where did you grow up?"

"In the central part of New Jersey. Have you heard of the Pine Barrens?"

"Isn't that where everyone intermarries and produces, uh—" he was not sure how to word it "—less than brilliant offspring?"

She made a sound of mock disgust. "Well, you're think-ing of the right place, but your view of it is a little colored by its press. Intermarriage is far more the exception than the rule."

"That's where you grew up?"

"Yes, and I know what you're thinking. Just because I can't master windsurfing does not make me less than brilliant."

He smiled to himself, staring up at the clear sky, a dazzling blue he had seen nowhere outside the Outer Banks. "Paul was at the lighthouse meeting at my house last night," he said.

She sat up, abruptly. The gold chain swung free for a moment and then clung once more to the slope of her breast. "You didn't say anything, did you?"

"No." He looked up at her worried face. "I told you I wouldn't. *He* said something you might find interesting, though."

"What? Tell me *everything* he said. Every word, okay?"

Alec smiled. "He's a nice guy, Olivia, but he's not *God*. I'm sorry, but I neglected to take notes. I didn't realize I'd be tested on the material."

She was quiet for a moment. "Are you angry with me?"

"No." He shaded his eyes to see her more clearly. The bridge of her nose was burned. "Do I sound mad?" Did he? Was he? "He said that whatever was wrong between the two of you was his fault, and that he thought he might have made a mistake when he left you."

Olivia pressed her fist to her mouth. "He said *that?*"

"Yes. He seems depressed to me. There's a...*heaviness* about him."

She looked out at the sound. "I can't believe he said he might have made a mistake. Was that his exact word?"

Alec sighed. "I think so. I'll tape him next time, Olivia, I promise."

She lay down again. "It's just that I was about to give up."

He told her about the horse. "He got sort of choked up while he was helping me."

"It sounds as if you spent half the night with him. I'm very jealous." She suddenly gasped. "Don't ever tell Paul I'm taking stained glass lessons, Alec. You haven't mentioned it to him, have you?"

He frowned at her. "What are you so afraid of?"

"It's too hard to explain," she said, looking away from him. "Just please don't tell him."

They were both quiet for a few minutes, and when she spoke again her voice was subdued. "I'm having an amnio-centesis done Thursday," she said.

He looked over at her. "Are you nervous about it?"

"No. Well." She shrugged. "I guess you always have to face the possibility that something could be wrong. I just hate having to go through it—not the procedure so much as the waiting for results—without Paul."

"You know, Olivia, I think one of us *should* tell him we're friends. It might open his eyes a little to the fact that you're not going to just sit around waiting for him forever."

"Except that I would. Wait around forever, I mean." She let out a weary-sounding sigh. "What about you, Alec?" she asked. "Do you go out at all?"

"No." He shut his eyes against the brilliant yellow sunlight. "It's not time yet, and there really isn't anyone. There's one woman who has designs on me, but I'm not interested."

"Who is she?"

"A neighbor. Nola." He ran a hand through his hair. It was almost dry. "She's been a family friend for many years. Annie always said she had her eye on me, which I didn't believe at the time. I do now, though. She brings us food. She calls to check up on me."

"And you're not interested?"

"Not in the least." He stretched, ready for a change of subject. "Well, listen. I've been asked to speak on both a radio show and at a meeting of lighthouse enthusiasts in Norfolk this coming Saturday and I'd love to talk you into taking on one of those jobs. Any chance of that?" He looked over at her. "Do you have Saturday off?"

"I do have it off," Olivia said, "but now that you've told me Paul's having second thoughts, I think I'd like to try to spend the time with him."

"Oh, right," Alec said, disappointed. "You should." He leaned up on his elbow to face her. "Tell him about this." He touched her still visible hip bone lightly with his fingertips, wondering if he was out of line. "Tell him about the baby."

"No." She sat up, smoothing her hair away from her face with her hands. "It's got to be me he's coming back for."

"Well." Alec sat up too and reached for his T-shirt. "I think it's about time you got to see a little more of the Outer Banks. We'll see how much fun you can tolerate."

He took her to Jockey's Ridge. She had seen the enormous sand dunes from the road many times, she said, but it had never occurred to her to actually *walk* on them. She'd put a pair of shorts on over her bathing suit and Alec lent her a T-shirt. He dug around in the glove compartment of the Bronco until he found a tube of zinc oxide—in neon green—and painted it on her nose. The wind was up and the dunes were practically shifting in front of their eyes as they climbed. They reached the highest peak, out of breath, and sat on the ridge to watch a group of helmeted people learning to hang glide.

Then he took her to the Bodie Lighthouse. They walked around the site, looking up at the black and white horizontally striped tower, while he told her the history of this particular light. He felt some guilt over not taking her to the Kiss River Lighthouse, especially since he was asking her to speak about it. It was too far from where they were, he told himself, although his real reason was clear to him—the Kiss River Lighthouse belonged to him and Annie. He was not at all ready to share it with someone else.

They had an early dinner, then started the drive back to her car at Rio Beach. They were quiet. Content, he thought. A little tired.

"When are you going back to work, Alec?" Olivia asked when they were a block from the beach.

"Not you, too," he said.

"Well, it doesn't seem healthy to take so much time off."

"That's because you're a workaholic."

"And I need the income."

He pulled into the little parking lot and turned off the ignition. "Annie had a life insurance policy." He looked over at her. "It was ridiculous. Three hundred thousand dollars on a woman who earned about fifteen thousand a year and gave most of it away. Or," he laughed, "spent most of it on insurance premiums, I guess. It was a shock to me. Tom found it when he was cleaning up her stuff at the studio."

"Why did she do it?"

Alec watched the windsurfers on the sound. "I have two theories," he said. "Either she knew I'd be so devastated if she died that I wouldn't be able to work for a long time. Or else, some insurance salesman got to her and she just wanted to make his day. She needed people to like her." He shook his head. "I think that was why she gave so much of her work away. She never lost that insecurity. She never thought people would care about her just for herself."

"Well, money's not the only reason for working," Olivia said. "You loved treating that horse last night, Alec. You lit up when you were talking about it. Why don't you go back a day or two a week?"

He hesitated. "It scares me. I'm not in such great shape, though I'm a lot better than I was before you told me about that night in the ER." He looked at her. Her cheeks were red. The zinc oxide had faded from her nose. She would be hurting tonight. "But it gets stressful at the animal hospital, especially in the summer," he continued. "Lots of emergencies— Well, look who I'm talking to about emergencies, and I'm just talking about dogs and cats."

"Yes, but they still suffer. And so do the owners."

"Right. It never used to bother me, but since Annie..."

"It's like getting back on a horse, though," Olivia interrupted him. "You've got to do it, and the longer you wait the harder it becomes. After something terrible happens, I sometimes force myself to go into work the next day even if I'm not scheduled. I went in the day after Annie died, even though I didn't have to."

He stared at her. "You push yourself too hard, Olivia."

"Don't change the subject," she said. "Just one day a week, okay?"

He smiled. "If you'll call Paul and try to see him this weekend."

Paul thought he'd made a mistake in leaving her.
Olivia drove from Rio Beach to the little shop across the parking lot from Annie's studio, where she bought the Jenny Lind crib she'd had her eye on for weeks. The sales clerk helped her load the box into the trunk of the Volvo, and she

drove home with a long-forgotten sense of hope and well-being—and the beginning sting of a fierce sunburn.

She lugged the box into the house and rolled it on its sides through the hall until she reached the little room she would make into a nursery. There, she rested it against the wall, stopping short of taking it apart and setting up the crib. She wouldn't tempt fate by being overly optimistic.

She would call Paul tonight, ask to see him, talk to him. She was rehearsing the conversation in her mind as she walked out to the mailbox to pick up her mail, and it was there she found the note, scribbled on the back of a used envelope.

"Stopped by on my way to Washington," Paul had written. *"I'll be up there for a week or so working on a story about oil drilling off the Outer Banks. Call you when I get back."*

She stared at the envelope, at the familiar handwriting. She turned it over, peered inside. Then she balled it up in her fist, crushed it between her palms. She wanted to track him down, call him at his hotel, scream at him. *"Didn't you just tell Alec O'Neill you'd made a mistake?"*

But she knew she would do no such thing. Instead, she walked back into the house, where she soaked a few teabags to nurse her burn. Then she called Alec to tell him she'd be happy to accompany him to Norfolk on Saturday.

Chapter Twenty-Six

Wednesday was Jonathan Cramer's birthday, and Olivia agreed to take his night shift, hoping it would keep her mind off the amniocentesis scheduled for the following morning. Around six, Alec dropped off a blue folder filled with lighthouse information she would need to know for the radio interview on Saturday. The waiting room had been full then, and there was little time to talk as he handed her the folder across the reception desk.

"What time are you done here?" he asked.

"Midnight." She returned his look of disappointment. They would not be able to talk on the phone tonight.

It was close to eleven when a teenage boy was brought in by his friends. Olivia heard him before she saw him.

"I'm gonna have a fucking *heart* attack," he screamed, as Kathy and Lynn wheeled him into one of the treatment rooms. Olivia joined them and began questioning the boy—a good-looking kid with sun-streaked blond hair. He was seventeen, he said, and he had been at a party, drinking a little, when his heart started racing, beating so loudly he couldn't hear anything else. He reeked of alcohol. His blue eyes were glassy, frightened.

"Start a monitor," she said to Kathy. Then to the boy, "What did you have besides alcohol?"

"*Nothing.* Just a couple of beers."

He was lying. He was too agitated, too wired, his palpitations too wild. "I know you had something else. I need to know what it was to be able to treat you properly."

"My heart's gonna fucking *burst.*"

She glanced at Kathy. "He has friends here?"

Kathy nodded. "In the waiting room," she said. "I asked them what he took, but they claim he was just drinking and then started complaining of a rapid heartbeat."

Olivia left the boy under Kathy's care and walked into the waiting room. There were three of them, two girls and a boy, and they sat close together on the blue vinyl couch, sharing a stony, defensive demeanor. They had probably talked on the way over here, agreeing with one another about how they would answer any questions asked of them. Olivia felt their fear, though, as she neared them. Behind their hardened features, their faces were ashy pale.

"I'm Dr. Simon." She pulled up a chair, glad the waiting room was empty now, save for these three. "And I need to get some information from you about your friend in there."

They stared at her. The boy looked about eighteen. He was barefoot and blond, his hair brushing his shoulders. The blond girl wore skin-tight jeans and a white T-shirt, the sleeves and midriff cut into fringes, while the other girl had on a scoop-neck jersey and a light blue miniskirt. Olivia was so astonished at being able to clearly see the girl's floral underpants that it was a moment before she noticed her hair. It was very dark, and looked as if it had been cut by a butcher. Olivia knew without a doubt who was sitting in front of her.

The girl may have tried to rid herself of her mother's red hair, but there was little she could do to mask those freckles and dimples and dark blue eyes.

"Lacey?" Olivia asked.

The blond girl drew in her breath. "How does she know your name?"

Lacey struggled to avoid Olivia's eyes.

"I need to know what your friend in there took," Olivia said.

"Just beer," said the boy, his voice deep, challenging.

"No," Olivia said. "He did not have just beer. This is serious. Your friend could die. I need to know what I'm dealing with."

"Crack," said Lacey, and the boy threw his hands in the air and stood up. He swung around to glare at Lacey.

Olivia leaned over to squeeze Lacey's hand. "Thank you," she said. "I'll let you know how he's doing. In the meantime, please give the receptionist his phone number and the name of his parents."

Olivia returned to the treatment room. The boy was hooked up to the monitor. He had settled down, his eyes closed. His heartbeat was rapid, but rhythmic, and there was little they could do except observe him for now. Within a half hour, Olivia felt certain he was out of danger and she returned to the waiting room to tell his friends.

The two girls were still close together on the sofa, while the boy leaned against the wall, smoking a cigarette.

"He's going to be all right," Olivia said. The three of them looked at her stonily, no emotion showing in their faces. "Lacey, I'd like to see you for a moment in my office."

Lacey looked at the boy before she got to her feet and followed Olivia through the waiting room door. She said nothing as they walked down the hall and into Olivia's office.

"Have a seat," Olivia gestured to a chair in front of her desk. She sat down herself, a little overwhelmed by the odor of alcohol and tobacco that had accompanied Lacey into the room.

Lacey gave Olivia a narrow-eyed glare across the desk. The loss of the long red curls had transformed her into a tougher, more arrogant-looking young girl. "How did you remember me?" she asked.

"I remember you very well," Olivia said. "It was a terrible night, and it really stayed in my mind." What she knew now that she had not known then was that Lacey had been with her mother when she was shot. "It must be very difficult for you to be here in the ER, Lacey. It must bring back some terrible memories for you."

Lacey shrugged. "It's no big deal."

"Your friend could have really gotten himself into trouble," Olivia said. "Not just with his health, but with the police as well. Maybe you're getting in with the wrong crowd of people. It could have been you in there."

"The hell it could. I wouldn't touch that stuff. None of us would. And I've never even met him before. He's a friend of Bobby's from Richmond. He brought the crack down with him, but he's the only one who used it."

"I'm glad to hear that," Olivia said. The blue folder Alec had brought her was in front of her on the desk, and she touched it lightly with her fingertips before she spoke again. "How did you get to the ER?"

"Bobby."

"Well, I think Bobby's had a bit too much to drink to drive you home. Why don't I call your father to come get you?"

"No." Lacey suddenly lost her tough-kid facade. Her eyes filled. "Please don't."

Olivia looked down at the folder. The idea of calling Alec was appealing, but he would not be pleased to find Lacey in this situation, and Lacey was clearly terrified of having him know what had occurred here tonight.

"How about your brother?" Olivia asked.

Lacey shook her head, dropping her eyes to her lap.

"Well, let's go talk to your friends and see if we can come up with a way to get you home safely."

Olivia stood up, and Lacey took off out the office door, obviously relieved to be dismissed. Olivia stared after her for a moment before she followed, wondering if there was anything in the world quite as fragile as a fourteen-year-old girl.

CHAPTER TWENTY-SEVEN

Paul had forgotten the feel of a Washington summer. It was only seven o'clock in the morning, and already his T-shirt stuck in wet patches to his back and chest as he walked through Rock Creek Park. He had walked this same route with Olivia several times a week, and he could still feel her presence on the path. There was the expansive, thick-trunked oak tree she had claimed as her own, never failing to admire it no matter how many times she passed beneath its branches. There was the spot where she'd found a perfect robin's egg nestled in the grass at the side of the path. She'd picked it up in a tissue and made Paul climb the tree to put it back in the nest. It was not possible to walk along this path without thinking of Olivia.

The branches of the trees hung low to the ground from the weight of their leaves, and everything around him, as far as he could see, was green. The color soothed him, despite the heat. This is what he missed in the Outer Banks. Greenness. Lushness. Sand and water and blue sky were not enough.

The work he had to do up here this week was unbearably boring, not his type of material at all. He had already made up his mind to refuse the next assignment like it, although he didn't have much choice on a little paper like the *Gazette*. He missed the *Post*. He missed just about everything he didn't have right now.

He reached the end of the path and crossed the street to the deli he and Olivia had frequented. He stepped inside, breathing in the scent of onions and garlic and cinnamon. So strong, so utterly comforting.

It was early, and only two other customers were in the deli, sitting at a small table near the back of the store.

"Mr. Simon!"

Paul smiled as he recognized Joe, the round-faced, balding owner of the deli who was working alone behind the counter. Joe had learned Olivia's name many years earlier and assumed that since Paul was her husband, his name was the same. He and Olivia had never bothered to correct him.

"Haven't seen you in months!" Joe grinned.

"How've you been, Joe?" Paul asked, approaching the counter. "Olivia and I moved to North Carolina. The Outer Banks."

"Ah," Joe said. "It's beautiful down there. You really get the weather, though, don't you?"

"A bit."

"Have a seat." Joe gestured to the tables. "You want the onion bagel with salmon cream cheese?"

"You've got quite a memory."

"Some people stick in your mind, you know what I mean?" He set a cup of coffee on the top of the deli case and Paul carried it to the nearest table.

"So how is Dr. Simon doing?" Joe asked as he worked on Paul's bagel. "She's still doctoring, I hope."

"Uh huh. She's working in an emergency room down there. I'm up here by myself on business." At some point he was going to have to come up with a way of saying they were separated. He could imagine Joe's reaction. He could almost picture the pain and disappointment in his eyes.

"She liked cinnamon and raisin, right?"

"Right."

Joe shook his head as he carried the plate to Paul's table. "You give her my best," he said, setting the bagel next to Paul's coffee. He wiped his hands on his apron, then reached into his back pocket and pulled out his wallet. He glanced toward the door before sitting down across the table from Paul. "Let me show you something," he said. He took a picture from the wallet and set it on the table in front of Paul. A small, dark-haired girl, about five years old, grinned up at him. "Know who that is?"

"One of your grandkids?"

"That's right. Lindsay. The one who wouldn't be here if it wasn't for that wife of yours."

"Oh." Paul lifted the picture to get a better look at the child. "I'd forgotten."

"A crazy coincidence, wasn't it? You and Dr. Simon were sitting right here when that beeper of hers went off, like it did more times than not, right? And she zipped off like she always did, no matter if she'd gotten her bagel yet, and you and I were saying what a shame it was she always had to take off like that. Remember?"

Paul nodded.

"And it turns out it was little Lindsay in the emergency room they were calling her for."

Paul did remember that morning, as well as the morning after when all of Joe's family came into the deli to meet Olivia and the bagels were on the house. Paul had been proud to be her husband.

"Drowned in the bathtub," Joe said. His eyes had filled.

"The gal in the ambulance said she was as good as dead till your wife got to her." Joe tapped the picture. "You take this to her—to Dr. Simon. Show her what good work she did that morning."

Paul swallowed. "All right," he said. He pulled out his own wallet and slipped the picture inside. "Thanks, Joe. She'll be happy to see it."

There was a sudden rush of customers, and Joe returned to his place behind the counter. Paul wrapped the bagel in his napkin. His throat had constricted. He couldn't eat. He waved good-bye to Joe and went outside, the air hitting him in the face like a hot, wet rag as he walked quickly across the street and back into Rock Creek Park. He knew exactly where he would sit to finish his breakfast—on the lush green grass beneath Olivia's favorite old oak.

CHAPTER TWENTY-EIGHT

"How did it go today?" Alec asked. "The amnio?"

Olivia held the phone against her ear as she rolled onto her side. She'd hiked her nightgown up to her hips, and her hand rested on the bandaid below her navel.

"It was all right." She was relieved to hear Alec's voice, relieved to talk to someone who knew about the baby. She had felt more alone today than at any time since Paul left her. She'd wept on the far-too-long drive to Chesapeake, as well as on the way back, and she'd gone to bed early tonight—nine-thirty—as though she could hasten Alec's call just by being there. "Today was the easy part," she said. "Now comes the waiting."

"I thought of you driving up there alone. I should have offered to go with you. Didn't think of it till too late."

Olivia smiled. He was so sweet. Thoughtful. And his voice was sleepy. Warm. Like the triangle of moonlight that crept across her bed, and her legs, and her hand where it rested on her belly. More than likely his room was drenched in moonlight too. It was in his eyes, perhaps. On his chest. She could see the wedge of white light playing with the softly curled hair of his chest. She had not stared at his body the other day at Rio Beach. She had barely noticed it, but right now she found she could remember it in detail.

"Olivia?"

"Yes?"

"You're very quiet. Are you sure you're all right?"

She lifted her hand from her stomach and watched the diamonds in her ring soak up the moonlight. "My bed just feels particularly empty tonight."

"Oh," he said. "Do you know how to reach Paul? Maybe you should call him."

"Actually, you're a lot easier to talk to than Paul these days."

"Yeah, but I can't do much about filling your bed."

She cringed, and rolled onto her back again. "Where is this conversation going?" she asked.

"Shall we change the subject?"

"Actually, this subject has been on my mind a lot lately. I think it began when you told me about Paul saying he might have made a mistake. I started thinking about him— you know, about *being* with him—and then he takes off for D.C."

"Maybe when he gets back."

"Maybe. Alec? How do you..." She struggled for the right words. "How are you coping with celibacy?"

He laughed. "That's pretty damn personal, Dr. Simon."

"Sorry."

Alec sighed. "Mother Nature has a way of taking care of things," he said. "Having your spouse die seems to obliterate any libidinous urges, temporarily at any rate. At least I'm assuming it's temporary." He chuckled. "Actually, I'm *sure* it is. I guess it doesn't work that way when you're only separated, huh?"

"No," she said.

"Are you still getting massages?"

"It's not the same thing," she said grumpily.

Alec was quiet for a moment. "What would happen if you showed up in Paul's hotel room?"

"I don't want to be humiliated."

"I'm certain he still cares about you."

Almost unknowingly, she had moved her hand to the warm delta of her pubic hair. She parted her legs a little. She could do this. She could listen to Alec's voice and...

"Oh, *God.*" She sat up abruptly, tugging her nightgown to her knees.

"What's the matter?"

"Talking about this is definitely *not* helping, Alec." She propped her pillow up against the headboard and sat back, lifting the blue file folder from her night table to her lap. "Why don't you just quiz me on the lighthouse?"

Mike Shelley walked into her office late the following afternoon.

"Do you have a minute?"

She closed the patient chart she'd been working on as he sat down on the other side of her desk. He looked a little tired, but he was smiling. He leaned back in the chair.

"I wanted to let you know I'll be leaving the ER in September."

"No." She was genuinely distressed. She depended on the calm efficiency Mike brought to his job as director of the emergency room.

"I'm afraid so. My parents are in Florida, and they haven't been well this past year. I'd like to be closer to them and I've been offered a job down there." He paused. "So, obviously, that leaves my position here open. I wanted to tell you that

you're in the running, along with Jonathan and two candi-
dates from outside."

The ambition Olivia had tried to temper when she started
working in this small, sedate ER suddenly reared its head.
She smiled. "I'm honored to be considered."

"Between you and me, Olivia, you're my first choice. Jonathan's clinically good, but your past experience is far more
varied and you handle everything that comes through the
door with a cool head. That's critical in this job. I don't want
you to get your hopes up, though. You still have the least
seniority of anyone on the staff." He stood up and sighed.
"Jonathan wants this badly," he said, and she thought she
detected a warning in his voice. "He may be a bear to work
with until this is over."

Olivia smiled. "What else is new?"

She reached for the phone the instant Mike left her office
and dialed Paul's number, but she succeeded only in reaching
his answering machine. She'd forgotten he was in Washington. She listened to his voice on the tape, imagining it filling
his little cottage, resonating off the colored images in Annie's
stained glass.

She didn't bother to leave a message. Instead she called
Alec and was pleased when he suggested they go out to
dinner to celebrate.

"Except," she said, "there's really nothing to celebrate yet."
Mike had warned her not to get her hopes up, and already
she was picturing taking his place.

"Sure there is." Alec sounded unusually cheerful. "More
than you know."

"What do you mean?"

"I'll tell you when I see you."

He picked her up at the emergency room after her shift
and drove her to a small restaurant she'd never even noticed

before. It was tucked between a few acres of amusement park rides on one side and a trailer park on the other, but inside it was cozy and dark. The candlelit tables were draped in mauve tablecloths, and the waiter laid her napkin across her lap as she sat down. The setting was undeniably romantic.

They ordered their meals, Alec turning down wine out of obvious deference to her condition. Olivia looked at him across the table as the waiter walked away. "So," she said, "what did you mean there's more to celebrate than I know about?"

He lowered his own napkin to his lap. "I went in to work today," he said, grinning.

"Oh, Alec, really? How was it?"

"It was great till the animals started showing up."

She gave him a sympathetic smile before she realized he was joking.

"It was actually painless," he said. "Thanks for persuading me. I'm going to work three days a week for now."

"You look as though it agrees with you," she said. He had not stopped smiling since they sat down, and she could barely remember the haggard look he'd worn that first day she'd met him in the studio.

They filled their plates at the salad bar. "You must have had a sonogram with the amnio yesterday, huh?" Alec asked as they walked back to their table.

"Right."

"No twins?"

She took her seat again. "Just one unbelievably tiny fetus," she said. "Sex indeterminate."

"What was it like being a twin?" Alec cut a cherry tomato neatly in half. "You must have been very close to your brother."

"When we were kids, yes, we were close, but probably

not the way you would imagine." She sipped her water, set the glass down again. "I was born first, but my mother'd had no prenatal care and the midwife wasn't prepared for twins. The cord was wrapped around Clint's neck for quite a while before she even realized he was there. He suffered some brain damage."

"Oh, no."

"It wasn't severe. He was mildly retarded, but he also had a wealth of physical problems." She pictured her brother as a child, his skin so white, so translucent that the veins were clearly visible at his temples. "He was always small for his age and he was asthmatic. Quite frail. So I didn't have the usual twin experience. I had to look out for him."

She had sat up with Clint during his middle-of-the-night asthma attacks. She'd beaten up kids who made fun of him. She'd even done his homework for him, until one of her teachers told her she couldn't protect Clint from everything. *You have to look out for yourself, Livvie,* she'd said, and Olivia had finally done exactly that. Once she left home, she neatly, permanently cut Clint out of her life. In the early years of her marriage, Paul had encouraged her to get in touch with Clint, but even with Paul's support she had not been able to make the phone call or write the letter that would have brought her brother back into her world.

"How did he die?" Alec asked.

"Respiratory problems and something with his liver. My mother died a few years after I moved out, and Clint and my older brother, Avery, stayed on in the house in the Pine Barrens." Clint had idolized Avery, but Avery had been a dangerous boy to look up to.

The waiter set their meals in front of them, and Olivia took a bite of tender, perfectly cooked salmon.

"Was it growing up with Clint that made you want to be a doctor?" Alec asked.

Olivia shook her head. "I wasn't even a pre-med major when I started college. I was going to Penn State, and I was living with a woman who was a doctor. She was the sister of..." How much should she say? "This is confusing. She was the sister of a teacher I had in high school, the teacher I moved in with after I left home." She took another bite of her salmon, chewing slowly, before she continued. "I've always had a tendency to be very influenced by the women around me. My mother wasn't much of a role model, so I grew up a little unsure of myself as a female. My brothers were my strongest influence when I was young. I could beat up nearly anyone on the playground by the time I was twelve." She smiled. "But when I became a teenager I realized that wasn't appropriate behavior for a girl, so I started looking to my teacher for clues to how a woman should act. I started to... *emulate* her, and it became a pattern. When I lived with her sister while I was at college, I began modeling myself after *her*. That's why medicine started to look so appealing."

"Good thing she wasn't a trash collector."

Olivia laughed.

They ate in a comfortable silence for a few minutes before Alec began talking about Lacey and Clay. Olivia thought of Lacey's tough-looking appearance in the emergency room a few nights earlier. Alec had his hands full with her.

"Do they have grandparents?" she asked suddenly, wondering if he was getting any help from the rest of his family. "Are your parents still alive?"

"No. They died a long time ago, before the kids were born."

"How about on Annie's side?"

Alec made a sound of disgust. "They never even met them," he said bitterly.

"Bad topic," Olivia said.

Alec set down his fork. "Annie's parents had her life planned out for her. She had to do the whole routine—private schools, the debutante ball. They'd picked out the guy they wanted her to marry and no one else would do. They completely cut her off when she married me, not just financially, but emotionally as well." Alec picked up his fork again, holding it above his plate. "I tried to contact them. I called them several times, but they wouldn't even come to the phone. I wrote them letters using the animal hospital as a return address so Annie wouldn't know, but I never heard a word from them. Finally," Alec smiled at whatever he was remembering, "I came up with what I thought was a foolproof plan."

"What was that?"

He leaned toward her across the table. "This was about five years ago, during one of Annie's bouts of withdrawal. I always figured those moods of hers were connected with her thoughts about her family. So I went to Boston, armed with pictures of Annie and the kids, and I made an appointment to see Annie's father, who was a cardiologist."

"You mean, a medical appointment?"

Alec laughed. "Pretty damn clever, huh? You should have seen his office. Incredibly posh. A lot of gaudy antique reproductions. It was nauseating. So his nurse took me into one of the examination rooms and asked my why I was there. I told her I'd been having chest pains, and she made me take off my shirt to do an EKG, which had not been in my plans. I had not planned on having to meet my father-in-law for the first time half naked."

Olivia smiled, remembering exactly how he looked shirtless.

"So, of course I had this perfectly normal EKG. The nurse left and then Dr. Chase himself came in. He asked me what my problem was, and I said, 'I'm not sick. I'm your son-in-law.'"

"What did he say?"

"He turned purple, and he told me in no uncertain terms to get the hell out of his office. He left and slammed the door in my face. I left too, but before I did, I gave the nurse the envelope with the pictures in it and asked her to give it to him."

"Did he get them? Did you ever hear anything from him?"

Alec ran his fork through the crabmeat on his plate. "The next thing we heard, he had died of a heart attack. An old friend of Annie's wrote to tell her about a month after it happened, and when I figured out the date he died I realized it was the day after I'd gone to see him."

Olivia shifted back in her chair. "Oh," she said.

"So, of course, I never told Annie what I'd done. She was so upset she hadn't known in time to go to his funeral. Jesus." Alec shook his head. "Her mother had the audacity to show up at *Annie's* funeral, though. I wouldn't even talk to her, although there were certainly plenty of things I wanted to say. Fucking bitch." He looked up at Olivia. "Pardon me."

She laughed, and Alec smiled. "How did I get on the subject of Annie again? Back to Olivia. Are you all set for your debut as a connoisseur of the Kiss River Lighthouse tomorrow?"

"I think so."

"I'll pick you up around ten."

The waiter cleared their plates away and they ordered

coffee. Olivia watched Alec drop two lumps of sugar in his cup. He was smiling to himself.

"Alec?" she said.

"Hmmm?"

"You're different tonight."

"Am I? Is that good or bad?"

"It's wonderful," she said. "You seem happy. Even when you're talking about painful things, like Annie's parents, you seem removed from the sadness somehow."

He nodded. "I feel better. Every day's a little improvement from the day before." The candlelight flickered in his pale eyes. "I owe a lot of how I feel to you. You've let me talk, let me cry on your shoulder, or at least in your kitchen. Going in to work today topped it off. Thank you."

She felt his knees touch hers beneath the table, and this time she didn't bother to move away.

Outside, the air was filled with screams and music from the amusement park next door. The sky above the rides was lit up from the colored lights. Alec rested his hand lightly on Olivia's back as they crossed the parking lot to the Bronco, and she was exquisitely aware of every fingerpoint of pressure.

Three teenagers walked toward them, probably cutting across the parking lot to get to the amusement park, and they were very close before Olivia recognized them as Lacey and her two friends from the emergency room.

"Dad?" Lacey stopped, frozen, a few yards in front of them.

Alec stiffened at Olivia's side, dropping his hand quickly from her back. "Hi, Lace," he said. "Jessica." Alec stared at the boy walking between his daughter and her friend, while Lacey stared at Olivia, nothing short of stark terror in her face.

Olivia broke the silence. "I like your haircut, Lacey," she said. "It really looks different than it did back in December." She looked hard into the girl's eyes, letting her know she had said nothing to Alec about Lacey's visit to the emergency room.

"This is Olivia Simon, Lacey," Alec said taking a step away from Olivia. "Do you remember her?"

Lacey gave a quick nod, but Alec didn't seem to notice. He thrust his hand toward the boy. "I'm Lacey's father," he said.

"Bobby," the boy said, solemnly shaking Alec's hand.

"Where are you kids off to?" Alec asked.

"The rides, Dad." Lacey walked past her father, and Jessica and Bobby quickly followed.

"Well, have fun," Alec called after them. He glanced at Olivia, and they started walking toward the Bronco again, this time a few feet apart. It felt like miles.

Alec was quiet as they got into the car. He turned to look behind him as he backed out of the lot into the street, and in the garish, blinking lights from the amusement park, his knuckles glowed white on the steering wheel. He turned toward Kill Devil Hills. He wished he were rid of her now, she thought. He wished he did not have to drive her back to the ER before heading home.

They had driven four blocks in silence when she finally spoke. "Is it any woman you don't want Lacey to see you with, or just the one who couldn't save her mother's life?"

Alec looked at her sharply, then back to the road. He sighed. "Sorry. My kids have never seen me with a woman other than Annie and that just felt weird. I don't want her to read anything into seeing me with you. I think she'd feel like I'm betraying Annie."

"We're friends, Alec. Aren't you allowed to have friends?"

He didn't seem to hear her. "That boy she was with looks far too old for her."

Olivia twisted her wedding ring around on her finger. "Maybe she needs to be restricted a little more than she is."

He shook his head. "No way. Annie would never have tied her down."

She weighed her words carefully before she spoke. "Annie's not here," she said quietly. "The situation's different from any the two of you had to handle when she was alive. You don't really know what she would have done."

Alec pulled the Bronco into the emergency room parking lot. "Well, soon enough you'll have your own kid and then you can raise him or her any way your heart desires, but Lacey's done just fine all these years and I'm not going to change things now." He turned off the ignition and got out of the car, walking around it to open her door for her. By the time she had stepped out, her eyes had filled. She looked up at him.

"I understand that you're embarrassed Lacey saw us together," she said, "but please don't take it out on me."

He looked crestfallen. "I'm sorry," he said, nearly whispering, and she was glad they were under the bright lights of the parking lot, glad they couldn't touch. She got into her own car and pulled out of the lot, glancing back to see him standing in the pool of white light, watching her drive away.

There were four messages on her answering machine when she arrived home, all left by the same reporter—an eager-sounding young woman—from the *Gazette*. Each message was more urgent than the one preceding it, and the last was marked by an almost threatening quality, as the reporter finally stated the nature of her call: "It's *critical* that I speak with you *tonight,* Dr. Simon," the woman said. "It's regarding Annie O'Neill."

Olivia bristled. She pressed the erase button. What could possibly be so urgent about a woman who was already dead, a woman Olivia had no interest whatsoever in discussing tonight? She knew reporters, though. This young woman would not give up until she had Olivia on the line.

She followed the phone cord to the wall and unplugged it. In the kitchen, she lifted the phone from the wall and set it on the counter. She pulled the cord from the jack in her bedroom as well, knowing as she did so that she was cutting herself off from the possibility of hearing anything more from Alec that night. That was just as well. If he didn't try to call her tonight, she didn't want to know.

CHAPTER TWENTY-NINE

"She's the doctor who killed Mom," Lacey said as she poured milk on her puffed rice.

Alec frowned at his daughter across the table. "No," he said carefully. "She's the doctor who tried to save your mother's life."

Lacey looked up at him. "Mom had this one tiny little speck of blood on her shirt. That was it, but by the time that doctor got through with her, she'd bled to death." Lacey's lower lip trembled, and he watched her fighting to still it. She looked down at her bowl, bobbing the puffed rice in the milk with her spoon. A tiny stripe of red was growing in the part of her black hair.

"Lace," he said. "Look at me."

She tried. She lifted her eyes to his for the briefest of moments, then turned her head toward the window.

"Sweetheart." He rested his hand on her wrist. "We've never really talked about this. About what actually happened that night."

Lacey pulled her hand away from him. "She's dead," she said. "It doesn't matter."

"Well, I think maybe it does. I had a lot of questions, Lacey, and I bet you do, too. That's how I know Dr. Simon. I bumped into her a few weeks ago at the studio. She's taking stained glass lessons from Tom, and I had a long talk with her about what happened to Mom."

Lacey looked at him, her nose red. "Are you, like, *dating* her?"

"No."

"Then why were you with her last night?"

"She's become a friend."

"You had your *arm* around her."

He did not know what to say. He couldn't even explain last night to himself. "She's married, Lace," he said. "She and her husband are separated right now, but they're probably going to get back together. Her husband is the guy who wrote that article about Mom in *Seascape Magazine,* remember?"

She wrinkled her nose. "He got my age wrong."

"Did he?"

"Don't you remember? He said I was twelve. *Twelve.*" Her eyes grew huge. "I was thirteen and a half."

Alec smiled at her indignation. "Well, I guess that sort of mistake happens all the time."

Lacey began dipping her spoon in and out of the cereal again. So far none of the puffed rice had made it to her mouth. "So," she said, "what did you and that doctor talk about last night?"

"The lighthouse." Alec leaned back in his chair. "She's going to help out with the speaking engagements. She has a lot of experience doing that sort of thing. As a matter of fact, she's driving up to Norfolk with me this morning."

Lacey rolled her eyes and stood up to carry her bowl to the sink.

"Aren't you going to eat that?" Alec asked.

"I've lost my appetite." She began running water into the bowl.

"Who's Bobby?" Alec asked.

"A friend." She kept her back to him as she put the bowl in the dishwasher.

"Well, why don't you ask him over sometime so I could get to know him?"

Lacey turned around to frown at him. "Get a *life,* Dad." She dried her hands on a paper towel and left the room.

Alec smiled as he pulled into Olivia's driveway. She was sitting on her front deck in a pale, apricot-colored suit that looked out of place on the rustic wooden deck, but would be perfect for her interview in Norfolk. He was wearing a suit himself.

He got out of the Bronco and walked around to open the door for her, and he was relieved to see her ready smile after their tense words of the night before.

"You look beautiful," he said as he took his seat behind the wheel once again. "Sophisticated."

"You too," she said. "First tie I've seen you in. Looks nice."

Alec quizzed her about the lighthouse as they drove over the long bridge to the mainland, and they had crossed the state line into Virginia before either of them mentioned the night before.

"I'm sorry about the way I acted when we bumped into Lacey," he said. "Are you still angry with me?"

"No. I know it was awkward for you."

"I tried to call you to apologize, but you didn't answer." He had dialed her number several times, finally giving up at eleven o'clock.

"I'd unplugged my phone."

Alec frowned at her. "So I couldn't get through?"

"No, Alec." She smiled. The peeling bridge of her nose made her look very young. "A reporter from the *Gazette* was trying to reach me and I just didn't feel like talking to her."

"What did she want to talk to you about?"

Olivia shrugged and looked out the window where a delapidated barn sat in the middle of a wide, jade-green field. "I have no idea," she said.

They reached Norfolk a few minutes after noon, and they ate lunch at a restaurant near the radio station where Olivia would be interviewed. Olivia ate her own tuna salad sandwich as well as a couple of bites of his.

He grinned at her. "Are you one of those people who eats a lot when they're nervous?"

"I'm eating for two, remember?" she said, then added a bit defensively, "And I'm not in the least nervous."

He walked her to the door of the radio station, feeling guilty about leaving her to wait out the forty-five minutes before her interview alone. Then he drove to the public library, where the Mid-Atlantic Lighthouse Friends were meeting.

He had taken the easier assignment, he thought as he spoke to the appreciative audience of thirty or so fellow lighthouse fanatics. They could not have been more receptive, and by the time he had finished, several of the men and a couple of the women had written hefty checks for the lighthouse fund. He left after a short period of questions and answers, and once back in the Bronco, turned on the radio to catch the last ten minutes of Olivia's interview. Olivia and her interviewer, Rob McCain, were laughing, and he knew it was going well.

"Obviously," Olivia said, "the vagaries of nature are only a small part of what we're dealing with. Any decisions made with regard to the lighthouse have political and technological and economic implications as well."

Alec stopped for a red light, smiling, impressed.

"But the sea wall concept seemed to have so much support behind it," Rob McCain said. "Was that support politically motivated?"

"No more than for any other solution," Olivia said. "The *interest* in saving the Kiss River Lighthouse cuts across political boundaries, and so the need for funding is completely nonpartisan. We've received donations from schoolchildren and grandmothers and executives and politicians. Anyone who cares about saving a piece of our history."

He liked that she was using the word *we* to describe the committee, despite the fact that he usually felt possessive about the little band of lighthouse zealots he'd put together. After today, Olivia most definitely belonged.

She stood on the sidewalk in front of the radio station, watching for the Bronco. The interview had gone exceedingly well. She'd done a little extra reading on her own beyond the information Alec had given her, and it had increased her comfort, her confidence.

The Bronco turned the corner and came to a stop in front of the radio station. Olivia climbed into the passenger seat to find Alec grinning at her.

"I caught the tail end of it," he said as he pulled out into traffic. "You were great."

"Thanks," she said. "I enjoyed it."

It was hot in the car. She wished she could take off her suit jacket, but she'd had to pin the waistband of her skirt closed this morning. She'd been stunned that the safety pin barely managed to span the gap between the hook and the eye. Her jacket would have to stay on no matter how warm it got.

"Air conditioner's starting to act up, I'm afraid," Alec said.

She opened her window a crack and turned to look at him. "How did yours go?" she asked.

"Fine. They were very enthusiastic, but I think you should take all the speaking engagements from now on." He glanced over at her. "You *floored* me, Olivia. I don't think I believe that stuff about you not feeling confident outside the ER. I think you were *born* confident."

She smiled. "The teacher I moved in with after I ran away from home was in charge of the debate team at my high school."

Alec was quiet for a moment. "You ran away?" he asked finally. "You'd told me that you *left* home, not that you..." He looked over at her. "Why, Olivia? Why would you do something like that?" His tone was very soft. Curious, not accusatory.

Olivia gnawed on her lower lip, wondering how to answer him. Alec looked at her again, his eyebrows raised.

"I'm debating whether to tell you the abridged or un-abridged version," she said.

"I'd like the unabridged. We still have a long drive ahead of us."

She drew in a breath, resting her head against the back of the seat. "Well," she said, "I left home—ran away from home—the day I was raped and I was afraid to go back, so I never did."

"But why would you leave your family at a time like that?" Alec's eyes were on the road, but he was frowning.

She was quiet for a long moment, trying to find the words.

"Do you want to tell me?" He glanced at her.

"Yes."

"Try, then."

"It's too hot," she said, and even she could hear the child-like tone of her voice.

Alec turned the failing air conditioner up another notch, and it gave out a promising stream of cool, light air. They were driving through Chesapeake, past the fast food restaurants, the hospital. It was one of the hospitals she had looked into when she decided to leave Washington General, but the offer in the Outer Banks had come first.

"The house I grew up in was a real rat's nest," she began slowly. "It was very tiny. Just one bedroom, which I shared with my two brothers. My mother slept on the couch in the living room—or rather, that was where she passed out. She never remarried after my father died. She was...heavyset, and she used to say the only man who would fit on the couch with her was Jack Daniel's." Olivia felt her lips curve into a smile. She glanced at Alec, whose somber expression didn't change as he stared at the cars ahead of him.

"I came home late from school one day. It was winter, and I remember it was already dark out. The boy who lived next door to us—Nathaniel—was in my room with my brothers. I was uncomfortable around him to begin with, because he was enormous. He was seventeen and probably six and a half feet tall and two hundred and fifty pounds, and his idea of fun was to shoot dogs and cats with a pellet gun. Anyhow, when I walked into the room, the three of them suddenly stopped talking and I knew they were up to something. I tried to leave, but Avery blocked the door and Nathaniel started circling around me, saying I looked good, I was really...filling out, was what he said. He started touching me as he walked around me. Just little touches—" she touched her fingertips to Alec's shoulder, just for a second "—like that. But all over. Surprising me. I didn't know where the next touch would get me. He was really frightening me. I started beating on Avery to try to get the door open. At one time I could actually beat Avery up, but he'd gotten too strong for me—he was almost seventeen then—and he just laughed. Someone said something—I don't remember what—but I realized then that I was part of a deal. Nathaniel had done something for them or given them something and I was payment."

"Jesus," Alec said.

The air conditioner had grown sluggish again. She could barely breathe. She opened the window a few more inches, but the hot, noisy air was intolerable and she rolled it up again. "All of a sudden, Avery grabbed me and held me back against him by my arms and Nathaniel tore my blouse open." The buttons of her blouse had landed on the wooden bedroom floor with little clicking sounds, rolling beneath the beds and the dresser. "I was fighting like crazy, kicking at him, but he didn't even seem to feel it. He pushed my bra up." She turned her head to look out the window again, remembering the sharp pain of her embarrassment. She had only recently taken to dressing in the closet, away from her brothers' eyes.

"Olivia." Alec shook his head as he turned the Bronco onto the jughandle by the tall, sky-blue water tower. "You don't have to tell me any more. I shouldn't have asked."

"I *wanted* you to ask," she said. She wanted to tell him all of it, to get it all out. "I want you to understand."

He nodded. "All right."

"Nathaniel started touching my breasts. He was really rough and I screamed for my mother, but I knew that was useless, and I screamed for Clint to help me, but he was just sitting on the bed, staring at the floor. The next thing I knew, *I* was on the floor and Avery somehow pulled my blouse back in a way that trapped my arms so I couldn't move." She shuddered. "That was the worst part, not being able to use my arms or my hands. I still...I can't stand to feel trapped. Paul once held my arms down when we were making love—not to scare me, he didn't mean it to frighten me, but I started screaming." Paul had cried when he realized how he'd fed into her terror. "Poor Paul," she said. "He didn't have the vaguest notion what he'd done."

She rested her temple against the warm glass of the car window and shifted uncomfortably in her seat. She would need a rest room soon. Her bladder seemed perpetually full these days.

"So," she continued, "Nathaniel pushed my skirt up and took off my underpants and Avery crammed them in my mouth so I couldn't scream. I felt like I was choking and it was so...humiliating. I was kicking at Nathaniel with all my strength and finally Avery told Clint to help hold me down." She looked at her hands where they rested in her lap, and an old ache started deep in her chest. "I feel sorry for Clint when I remember this," she said. She could still see the confusion in her twin's face as he struggled to figure out to which of his siblings he owed his allegiance. A year earlier, it would have been Olivia for sure, but now, at fourteen, his older brother's approval meant everything to him. "He was crying himself, but he got down on the floor and held one of my legs while Avery held the other."

Nathaniel had loomed above her like a giant and she remembered the scene as if it had happened in slow motion, his meaty hand pulling down the zipper of his pants, reaching inside to draw out his huge, dagger-straight penis. She had screamed then, the sound muffled by the cloth in her mouth. "The next thing I knew, all two hundred and fifty pounds of him were on top of me, but he couldn't get inside." His body had hammered against her unyielding flesh, his face growing red with frustration. "He said it was like trying to...fuck a brick wall, and I kept praying he'd give up, but he didn't. I was crying and gagging and I couldn't use my *hands*." She lifted her hand to her throat. "He was so heavy. He was crushing me. I remember Clint saying, 'Maybe you should stop, Nat,' but I don't think Nathaniel even heard him. Finally," she shrugged, "I felt as though I...split open. The pain was so bad and it took him forever. I passed out, I guess, because when I woke up I was alone in the room. There was blood on my skirt and my legs. There was blood on the doorknob."

Alec took his right hand from the steering wheel, reaching toward her to slip his fingers into the cup of her palm. His thumb traced the bones in the back of her hand, and she closed her own fingers gratefully over his.

"I ran to Ellen Davison's house. She was my science teacher. I didn't tell her what happened. I *never* did, but she must have known somehow. She acted as though she'd been waiting for me to show up. She had a spare room, the bed made up and everything. I just moved in, and she switched me to a school outside my neighborhood. I never saw anyone in my family again."

"Good lord, Olivia."

"I worried about Clint," she said, "but I only thought of myself after I left home. I learned about my mother's death during my first year of college, and I knew I should go back to make sure Clint was all right, but I just couldn't. I was so terrified of Avery, and..." She wrinkled her nose. "I felt as though if I went back after all my hard work to get *away* from there, I would somehow be stuck there again. That I would become the old, scared Olivia. I know it doesn't make sense, but..."

"How could you still care about Clint after what he did?" Alec interrupted her.

"He really wasn't part of it."

Alec glanced at her sharply. "What do you mean, he wasn't part of it? He held you down while another man raped you."

"But he..."

"You said he was only mildly retarded. Didn't he know the difference between right and wrong?"

"Yes, but... Paul used to say I should give him a chance to redeem himself, that he was just a kid then, and..."

"*No.*" Alec squeezed her hand hard. "What happened was too big, too much to forgive, *ever.*"

Olivia bit her lip. "Annie would never have turned her back on her brother," she said, "no matter what had happened in the past."

"Annie did many asinine things in the name of charity."

"Clint *needed* me, though. Once I was on my feet, once I was established as a physician, I really should have tried to see him. Avery certainly didn't know how to take care of him. My own *mother* didn't know how. We lived in a *sewer*, Alec. You'd be sick if you could see where I lived, and I just left him there to rot." She pulled her hand out of Alec's and brushed her bangs off her forehead. "A couple of years ago, Ellen wrote to tell me she'd heard he had died. Most likely he was an alcoholic, like my mother. No one ever told him it could kill him. If I'd helped him, he'd probably still be alive." She looked at Alec. "I deserted him."

"To *survive.* You had no damn choice."

She closed her eyes, trying to take in his words, to believe them. Then she sighed. "I could really use a rest room," she said. She pulled down the visor to look in the mirror, groaning when she saw her face. Her nose was red; her mascara had run onto her cheeks in elongated gray triangles.

"We'll stop at the next gas station," Alec said.

He waited for her in the parking lot of the small gas station. He cleaned the windshield of the Bronco and took off his jacket and tie before getting behind the wheel again. There really was something radically wrong with his air conditioner.

He could not scrape the image from his mind of Olivia's brothers holding her down while the leviathan seventeen-year-old raped her. Only in his mind, it was his daughter he saw on that floor. Maybe Olivia had been right the night before when she'd said that Lacey should be reined in a little more. He had no idea where she was at night, who she was with. He was not being much more help to her than Olivia's mother had been passed out on the couch.

Olivia got back in the car, her face scrubbed clean of makeup. Her recent sunburn had all but disappeared, and she was once again anemically pale, her green eyes and dark lashes a dramatic contrast to the whiteness of her skin. She was still pretty, though. Perhaps even more so.

"You okay?" he asked, as she buckled her seatbelt.

She nodded. She was perspiring, her bangs damp across her forehead.

"Why don't you take off your jacket?"

"I can't. My skirt is pinned together."

He laughed, and it felt wickedly good—a sudden, welcome release—but Olivia didn't smile. "Do you think I care?" he asked. "Take it off. It's too damn hot in here."

He held the jacket while she leaned forward to slip her arms out of the sleeves. He folded it and set it on the back seat.

"Better?" he asked, and she nodded. They were both quiet

as he began driving again, and it was a few minutes before he realized she was crying, her face turned to the window, her sniffing practically silent. He pulled the car onto the shoulder of the road and turned off the ignition.

"Olivia." He undid her seatbelt as well as his own and pulled her into his arms. For a moment, she clung to him and he felt the dampness of her skin beneath her thin white blouse.

"I'm sorry," she said, when she could finally get the words out. She had pulled away from him slightly, her face lowered, the top of her head brushing his lips. He shut his eyes and rested his lips there, in the warm silk of her hair.

"I haven't talked about it for so long," she said. "I haven't even thought about it." She looked up at him, tears glistening on her dark lower lashes. "Thank you for saying there was nothing I could have done about Clint. I've always thought I should have been able to rise above what happened to me somehow. Put the past aside and help him, but..."

"But you knew you couldn't do that and take care of yourself at the same time."

She nodded. "God, I was *lucky* I was raped. It got me out of there."

"No," he said. "You were *not* lucky. You would have found some other way out."

"I don't know." She let go of him, sitting back in her seat, her eyes closed. "It got me out of there, but it took such a toll." She opened her eyes, and there was a faraway look in them as she stared out the window of the car. "It left me afraid of men and terrified of sex and feeling more worthless than I already felt."

Alec studied the steely edges of her profile. "You've overcome all that, though, haven't you?"

She nodded. "Paul changed it for me. He was so incredibly patient."

Yes. He imagined Paul would be that way.

Olivia smiled, that dreamlike look still in her eyes. "I was so *nervous,*" she said. "I'd gotten it in my mind that I didn't heal properly after the rape, that I couldn't let anyone casually touch me, or try to make love to me, because I didn't know how I would react, physically or emotionally. Paul was the first person I met who I knew I could trust, who would bear with me. I wanted to make love so badly, but it still took about four or five nights for us to...complete the act. He'd get in a little further each time before I'd freeze up." She blushed, red blotches forming quickly on her white cheeks, and looked over at him. "Am I embarrassing you, talking this way?"

"No." His voice was more of a whisper than he'd intended. "I like listening to you, and I need you to remind me about Paul, because sometimes when I'm with you I forget about him."

She held his eyes for a moment before continuing. "He'd write poetry," she said. "Every day he'd show up with a new poem, chronicling our progress. Sometimes they'd be sweet and touching, others were metaphorical—a hunter with his spear closing in on his prey." She laughed. "Finally we did it. I was twenty-seven years old and it was my first orgasm ever, and I'd had no idea it could be so...*powerful.*"

"You came the first time you made love?" He knew the question was tactless the moment he'd blurted it out, but Olivia seemed unperturbed.

"Yes," she said. "That's pretty easy for me. I can't *not* come."

"You're lucky. Annie..." Alec hesitated, discovering he could not talk about this quite as openly as Olivia. "It was always hard for Annie," he said, "though I figured out after a while that she just didn't care. Sex didn't mean much to her. She only wanted to feel close, to feel cared about. She said being close was the medicine she needed to feel good, and sex was just a side effect."

Olivia frowned. "All those years you were married to her, you had to put your sexual feelings on hold?"

"No. You forget I was married to the world's most generous woman. I never went without." He had a sudden stab of guilt for talking about Annie so candidly. "Whew," he smiled weakly. "I can't believe we're having this conversation."

Olivia returned his smile. She stretched her arms out in front of her and sighed. "How about dinner?" she asked. "I'm starving, and I could use the air conditioning."

They stopped for dinner, switching to the safe topic of the lighthouse and their respective speaking engagements. Back in the Bronco, Olivia fell asleep, her head cradled between the seat back and the window. He woke her as they crossed over the bridge into Kitty Hawk. The sunset was too beautiful to miss, the sky surrounding them with purple and gold. They rolled down their windows to let the Bronco fill with the damp evening air and the scent of the sound. Olivia undid her seatbelt and turned around, getting to her knees to look out the rear window. There was a skewer-thin run in her stocking where it covered her calf, and her blouse puckered above the safety-pinned waistband of her skirt in a way that touched him, that made him reach over to lightly run the back of his fingers over her hair.

She sat down again as they drove into Kitty Hawk, and Alec turned onto Croatan Highway in the direction of her house.

"Will you be all right alone tonight?" he asked.

"Yes." She reached into her purse for her keys. "As soon as

you woke me up and I got a whiff of Outer Banks air, I felt better." She leaned her head back against the seat and looked over at him. "Even though I only have one friend here— namely, you—it feels like home."

Alec smiled at her. Then, on an impulse, he made a U-turn at the next intersection.

"What are you doing?" Olivia asked.

"I'm taking you someplace. You've earned the right to see it."

"The lighthouse!" she said as he took the right turn off the highway toward Kiss River.

The road leading out to the lighthouse was dark, the trees forming a green-gray tunnel for the Bronco. Alec pulled into the small parking lot, surrounded on all sides by shadowy bayberry bushes. Night had fallen quickly over Kiss River, and the beacon was already on. It flashed as they got out of the Bronco, illuminating Olivia's white, awestruck face.

"It's spooky out here," she said. The keeper's house was dark, and no one was in sight as they walked across the field of sea oats, Olivia craning her neck to look up at the light. "Two hundred and ten feet is taller than I'd imagined."

Alec held up one of the keys on his key ring. "I'm not supposed to have this," he said. "Mary Poor gave it to Annie years ago." He opened the door and stepped into the dark hallway, feeling on the wall for the light switch.

"Oh, my God," Olivia said as light filled the hall and il- luminated the circular staircase. She walked forward and looked up. "Two hundred and seventy steps."

"They'll probably be better to manage with your heels off." He waited for her to slip off her shoes before he started up the stairs. "You don't have a problem with vertigo, do you?" His voice echoed off the sloping, white brick walls.

Olivia looked straight up at the eerily lit circles of stairs above her. "I guess I'll find out," she said.

They stopped at the third landing for Olivia to catch her breath. From the narrow window they could just make out the outline of the keeper's house, asleep in the darkness.

The circle of stairs grew tighter and he could hear Olivia's breathing as well as his own. "We're almost there," he said.

They had reached the narrow landing, and he unlocked the door to the gallery, stepping back to let Olivia out first.

"It's *extraordinary,*" she said as a warm wind swept across their faces. She looked up. "Look how close we are to the stars. *Oh.*" She started as the lens directly above them flashed its light over their heads, and Alec laughed.

He leaned his elbows on the railing and looked out at the ocean. The moon lit up the water, and the waves looked like glittering strips of silver rushing toward the shore.

"Once I locked Annie and myself up here for the night," Alec said. "I dropped the key to this door over the railing."

"Intentionally?"

"Yes." It seemed unbelievable that he'd once had such a spontaneous idea of fun. "We couldn't get down until morning, when Mary Poor let us out." He smiled at the memory and felt suddenly close to Annie. If Olivia were not here, he would talk to her.

Olivia leaned on the railing next to him. "Thanks for this," she said. "For letting me come up here. I know you think of the lighthouse as yours and Annie's."

He nodded, acknowledging the truth in her statement. "You're welcome."

They watched the lights of the boats slip across the horizon for a while longer. Then Alec filled his lungs one last time with salt air. "You ready to go down?" he asked.

Olivia nodded and stepped back through the door to the

landing, but something on the ground caught Alec's eyes. "Just a sec," he said. He walked around to the sound side of the gallery and gripped the cool iron railing in his hands as he stared into the darkness between the keeper's house and the woods. The flash of light cut a path between him and the ground, and in that clear white light he saw a bulldozer standing next to two fresh, deep scars in the earth.

He walked Olivia to her front door. He held one arm out to her, and she stepped into his hug. He softly kissed her temple.

"Thanks for your help today," he said.

She took a step away from him and smiled. "Thank you for *yours*. It was a little more than you bargained for." She unlocked her door, then turned to face him again. "You don't have to call me tonight, Alec."

"Are you saying you've had enough of me for one day?"

"No." She hesitated for a moment. "It's just that I feel very close to you today, and I'm not so sure that's good."

His heart did a little flip before he thought of Annie. *Will you wait a year?*

He nodded. "I'll talk to you tomorrow, then."

His house was empty when he got home. He heated a slice of frozen pizza in the microwave and sat down at the kitchen table to eat it, that morning's *Beach Gazette* spread out in front of him. There, in the upper right-hand corner of the front page, was a picture of Annie. Alec set the pizza down and lifted the paper. The headline was bold, the letters enormous: K.D.H. EMERGENCY ROOM ACCUSED OF COVER-UP IN O'NEILL DEATH. He read through the article twice, the muscles in his hands contracting into fists. Then he picked up his car keys and stormed out of the house.

Chapter Thirty

Olivia was relieved to get out of her suit and stockings and into the shower, where she scrubbed away the more painful remnants of the day. Then she put on her robe, poured herself a cup of tea, and sat down at the kitchen table with the pieces of stained glass she had cut at the studio the week before. She was wrapping the smoothed edges of the glass with copper foil when there was a knock at her front door. She looked up, startled by the anger in the sound.

She set down the piece of glass she'd been working on and walked into the living room. The room was dark, just a dim pool of light spilling across the carpet from the kitchen. She walked quietly to the window nearest the door, where she peered out to see Alec standing in the porch light. He was dressed in white shorts and a navy blue T-shirt, and he was raising his fist to knock again.

She tightened the sash of her robe and opened the door. "Alec?"

He walked into the living room and thrust a copy of the *Gazette* in front of her.

"Have you seen this?" he asked. He was angry, and she

stepped away from him, away from the unfamiliar flame in
his eyes.

She took the paper, raising it into the stream of light from
the kitchen, and read the headline: K.D.H. EMERGENCY
ROOM ACCUSED OF COVER-UP IN O'NEILL
DEATH.

She frowned at him. "A cover-up?" she said. "I don't have
any idea what they're talking about, Alec."

He pulled the paper from her hands. "It seems as though
you left out a few details when you told me what happened
the night Annie was brought to the ER." He spoke with a
controlled sort of calm, yet she could hear anger behind the
words.

She pulled her robe more snugly around her, remembering the messages from the reporter on her answering machine the night before. She was afraid she *did* know what lay
below that headline. There certainly had been no "cover-up"
of Annie's treatment in the ER, but everyone involved had
known better than to discuss the case publicly. There were
people—including some of the ER staff—who thought her
attempt to save Annie had been preposterous. Reckless. Alec
knew enough about medicine that, with the facts presented
to him by someone other than herself, he might draw a simi-
lar conclusion.

Right now, he had the same accusatory look in his eyes
that he wore in that photograph in Annie's studio, and she
wished there was a way to change that, to bring back his
smile. She was about to lose something that had become precious to her. Alec's friendship. His trust.

"Shall I read it to you?" he asked, and he began reading without waiting for her reply. "Olivia Simon, one of the
Kill Devil Hills Emergency Room physicians vying for the
position of medical director, was involved in a cover-up in

the death of one of the Outer Banks' most beloved citizens, Annie Chase O'Neill. So states Dr. Jonathan Cramer, another emergency room physician who is also in the running for the director's position. 'Dr. Simon has made serious mistakes in judgment,' Cramer said yesterday. 'She often acts as though she owns the emergency room.' He cited in particular the O'Neill case. Ms. O'Neill was shot last Christmas while working as a volunteer at the Manteo Battered Women's Shelter. Cramer stated that, 'in that type of case, usual procedure is to stabilize the patient and send them by helicopter up to Emerson Memorial, where they have the facilities to deal with severe trauma. We can't handle that sort of thing here. I argued that we should prepare the patient for transport, but Dr. Simon insisted we treat her in the ER. Annie O'Neill didn't stand a chance.'"

"Oh, Alec, that's *crazy*," Olivia said, but Alec continued reading, and Olivia knew this one article was enough to kill any chance she'd had at the directorship position.

"Dr. Simon worked in the emergency room of Washington General in the District of Columbia for ten years prior to coming here. 'She's used to the heavy stuff in D.C.,' Cramer said. 'She doesn't understand the limitations of a small facility like this.'

"Michael Shelley, current director of the free-standing emergency room, denied any cover-up and said the entire case was being blown out of proportion. Dr. Simon could not be reached for comment.

"Because," Alec said with a biting touch of sarcasm, "as we all know, Dr. Simon had unplugged her phone." He dropped the paper on the coffee table and stared at her. "Why didn't you tell me there was some question about how to treat her?" he asked. "Why did you hide the facts from me?"

Olivia sank wearily into the nearest chair and looked up

at him. He stood in the center of the room, directly in the light spilling from the kitchen, like an actor caught in the spotlight.

"Alec," she shook her head. "There was no cover-up. I didn't tell you there was a question about treating her because in *my* mind there *was* no question. Jonathan Cramer dislikes me and he's afraid I might be selected over him for the director spot. He's looking for a way to hurt me."

"Right this minute I don't give a damn what he's doing to *you*," he said. "I want to know what happened to my *wife*."

"I've explained everything that hap..."

"You made it sound like you only had one option."

"I felt like I did."

He paced, out of the spotlight, into it again. "It's always struck me as *insane*—the idea of one lone physician performing open heart surgery, whether you had the necessary instruments or not. I tried to put that thought out of my mind, but this article just..." He shook his head and turned to look at her again. "Why didn't you send her up to Emerson?"

This way her blood's on your hands.

"I didn't think she could possibly make it, and..."

Alec gestured toward the newspaper on the coffee table. "*This* guy obviously thought her chances were better if she went up, and he'd been working there longer than you. Didn't you stop to consider that he might have known what he was talking about?"

"I really thought that surgery..."

"You don't *do* that kind of surgery in that kind of setting, Olivia. You don't have to be a Rhodes Scholar to figure that out. You'd intubate her, put a couple of IV lines in her, and get her out of there as fast as you could." He stood directly above her now, and his voice had risen, hurting her ears.

"If you'd sent her to Emerson, maybe she would have had a chance. Maybe she'd still be alive."

Tears spilled over Olivia's cheeks. She looked up at Alec. "Jonathan was scared," she said. "He'd never seen that kind of wound before, and he had no idea what to do with it. Think about it, Alec. *Please.* She had two *holes* in her heart. Jonathan neglected to mention that to the press. How do you stabilize a person with two holes in her heart? I had no choice but to operate. She would have died in that helicopter. I have absolutely no doubt about it. She was losing blood so quickly."

Olivia paused. Above her, Alec was breathing hard, his eyes still narrowed, angry, but he was listening to her, hearing her out.

"Jonathan walked out on me when I said we should operate. He left me alone to take care of her. I realized that I was taking a risk when I elected to do surgery, especially by myself. Maybe it *was* crazy of me to try. I knew I was walking a fine line, legally and medically. But *not* ethically." She brushed the back of her hand across her wet cheek. "Sending her up, making her someone else's responsibility, would have been the easy way out, but she would have died. I did what I thought was right, and if we could have somehow closed that hole in the back of her heart she might very well have made it." Her hand started to throb, her fingers grew hot with the memory. She looked up at Alec again. "It was the hardest thing I've ever done."

His chest rose and fell rapidly with his breathing, but his eyes had softened while she spoke. He reached down to touch her shoulders, pulling her up to him, pulling her silently into his spotlight, into his arms.

"You don't know how hard it was, Alec," she whispered against his shoulder. "You can't know."

"I'm sorry." He kissed the top of her head. "I'm really sorry, Olivia. I read that article and just...lost it. I thought you'd lied to me. Kept things from me." He sighed. "I guess I still need someone to blame."

She pulled her head away to look at him. "Please, Alec, talk to Mike Shelley. Talk to the nurses who were on duty that night. I need you to believe me."

"I do," he said. "I believe you." He pulled her head to his shoulder again and held her that way for a minute, maybe longer. She closed her eyes, gradually becoming aware of the depth and pace of his breathing. He drew away from her slightly, tipping her head back with his fingers to kiss her temple, her eyes, her wet cheeks, and she turned her head to catch his next kiss on her lips.

His anger was gone, and in its place was a heat. He slipped his hands between them and untied the sash to her robe, letting it fall open a few inches. Then he stepped back and stroked the back of his fingers between her breasts.

"This is nice," he said, tracing the line of her gold chain with his fingertip. He pulled off his T-shirt and opened her robe further, until the satin had slipped over her breasts and she was bathed in the white light coming from the kitchen. Her body was so hungry for this. Alec raised his hands to her breasts, and she arched forward to meet the lightness of his touch.

He lifted the robe from her shoulders and let it drop to the floor in a soft pile around her feet. She was melting, liquid. She drew her hand to the front of his shorts, tentatively resting the back of her fingers against the unmistakable firmness of his erection beneath the cloth.

"Yes," he said, his breath warm against her ear. "Please."

She turned her hand and felt a tremor run through his body as he pressed hard against her palm. He lowered his hands from her breasts, and she parted her legs slightly, waiting for his touch, aching for it, but his fingers froze on the swollen rise of her belly, and everything in him seemed to cool at that moment. She tightened her hand on him, but he was already drawing away from her, and he slipped his fingers into hers and lifted them up, holding them just below his chin. The light from the kitchen glimmered on his braided gold wedding band. He looked at her squarely.

"What are we doing, Olivia?" He shook his head. "I mean, you're a married woman. I *feel* like I'm still married. Your husband's a friend of mine. You're going to have his baby."

His hair brushed her thigh as he bent down to pick up her robe. He slipped it onto her arms and up over her shoulders, closing it across her breasts, tying the sash. Her cheeks flushed with embarrassment that he, not she, had been the one to stop. She had been so eager, so willing.

She hugged her arms across her chest as he looked into her eyes, his face once again as serious, as unsmiling as when she first met him.

"Maybe we'd better not see each other for a while," he said. "Today was a little too intense, all the way around. It was one thing when I felt as though we were just friends, but friends don't do what we just did and it's... You're vulnerable, I'm vulnerable. I'm working with your husband..." He stared at her in exasperation. "Olivia, *say* something."

She looked down at the floor, still hugging her arms. *My husband made love to your wife.* The words were so close; she could barely hold them in. She wanted him to understand why that night in the ER had been so hard. She wanted him to share the pain with her.

"All right," she said, raising her head, but she found she

could not look at him, and she bent down instead to pick up his T-shirt.

He pulled the shirt over his head. "I'd better go," he said. She followed him to the door, her legs shaking, and a great, vast hollowness in her chest. Her head was light. She wondered if she was about to be sick.

Alec opened the door and turned to look at her, the porch light catching the pale blue of his eyes. "Maybe you should come to the lighthouse meetings," he said. He reached forward to lightly touch her arm. "It would help me to see you and Paul together, and it would probably be good for the two of you. You know, a shared interest."

"No," she said, recoiling from the image of the three of them together. "I couldn't." She glanced behind her at the coffee table. "Do you want your paper?"

He looked past her, back into the shadows of her living room, and shook his head. "Throw it away," he said, and then with the barest hint of a smile, "Why don't you use it to line Sylvie's litter box?"

He wished she had tried to resist him, but that was hardly a fair expectation. If he hadn't felt the small, firm sphere of her belly, that reminder of her husband beneath his palm, he would have taken it all the way. Then at the next lighthouse meeting he would not have been able to look Paul in the eye.

He punched the buttons on the car radio, trying to find a song he could sing along with to clear his head, but the airwaves were filled with classical music and advertisements and songs he didn't know. He took a shower when he got home, the water just cool enough to chill him, but by the time he had dried himself off, all he could remember was the sensation of Olivia's hand on him, squeezing him, stroking him through his shorts. He wanted to obliterate the feelings in his body, the thoughts in his head. He hunted through the pantry until he found what he needed—a bottle of tequila, left over from one of his and Annie's parties last summer when they'd served margaritas. He uncapped the bottle and took a swallow. *Shit.* The stuff was poison. He forced down another mouthful and went into his bedroom, where he undressed and got into bed, still clutching the neck of the bottle in his fist.

He remembered that party. Annie had grilled chicken for fajitas, while he made the margaritas. Tom Nestor had gotten ferociously drunk, and Annie had watched him carefully, finally telling Alec to water down his drinks. Tom was one of those people who underwent a complete change of personality after one drink too many. He'd grow weepy, pouring out his personal problems to anyone who would listen, and on that night he was bemoaning a fight with a woman he was seeing, clearly sapping the life out of the party. Annie had tried to shut him up. "You say too much when you're drunk, Tom. You say things that will get you into trouble once you're sober." Tom, however, could not seem to help himself, and he continued his lamentations until the early hours of the morning. Annie wouldn't let him drive home. She made up the guest room for him, but in the morning they found him curled up on the floor of the living room, beneath the oval stained glass windows.

Alec lay perfectly still, letting the memories come and go, but the alcohol was having no effect whatsoever on his erection. Instead, it was garbling his thoughts, taking away his control over the images that came into his head: Olivia's breasts, white and smooth in the light pouring from the other room; the thin line of liquid gold as it dipped between them; the firm nuggets of her nipples beneath his fingertips. He swallowed another mouthful of tequila, struggling to conjure up Annie's face, Annie's presence, but without success. He slipped his hand beneath the sheet with a sense of resignation, knowing that it would not be his hand he sank into, but the imagined warmth and comfort of Olivia's body.

He came, explosively, angrily, a warm stream of tears slipping into his hair. "Annie," he whispered. "I don't want to be alone anymore."

He fell into a deep, restless sleep. He dreamt they were lifting the lighthouse from the ground, twenty men or more, lifting it to their shoulders, then setting it, wobbling and creaking, onto the track. People cheered, while Alec's heart pounded in his ears. The men attached a system of ropes and pulleys to the lighthouse, and the noble, tall white tower began its slow journey inland along the track. Alec was first to hear the cracking, first to see the mortar between the bricks turn to powder. He waved his arms at the men, screaming for them to stop, but they couldn't hear him over the cheers of the crowd. Huge chunks of the lighthouse broke off, crashing to the sand in slow motion. Alec started to run toward it, but Annie was there. She caught his arm, and he saw her mouthing the words, although he couldn't hear them above the crashing sound of the lighthouse: *"...we should just let it go."*

"No!" Alec sat up in the bed. He was sweating. Breathing hard.

"Dad?" Lacey was calling to him from outside his bedroom door. It must have been her voice that woke him up.

He ran his hands over his face, trying to rub away the dream. "Yes?" he answered, his voice so soft and tight that he wondered if it would carry through the door.

"Can I come in, please?" She sounded like a child. If he

opened the door she would be standing there with her curly red hair, six or seven years old.

Alec's head throbbed. The room was black except for the light from the digital clock. 2:07. There was a cold circle of wetness next to him on the mattress, and for a moment he thought he'd gotten so drunk that he'd wet the bed, until he remembered. The room smelled of tequila and sweat and semen. He could not let Lacey in here.

"Daddy? I need to talk to you, Daddy, *please*."

"Give me a minute, Lace, and I'll come out." He got out of bed and hunted in the darkness for his shorts. He pulled them on as the room spun around his head. He was going to be sick. He made it to the bathroom in time and vomited twice before lowering himself to the floor and leaning back against the welcome coolness of the tile wall. He would sit for just a few minutes until the room stopped spinning.

He stood up after a while, testing his legs, testing his equilibrium. He was okay. He brushed his teeth, then found his T-shirt. The clock on the night table read 3:15. *3:15?* He must have passed out. He opened his bedroom door, but the hallway was dark. One of the cats whisked by his legs, startling him, as he made his way down the hall to Lacey's room. He knocked on her door, opening it when there was no answer. Her overhead light was on, but she lay fully dressed and asleep on top of her bedspread, one of her china-faced dolls clutched tightly in her arms. The smell of beer emanated from her, as if she'd bathed in it.

Alec got a blanket from her closet and laid it over her, tucking it around her shoulders. Then he sat on the edge of her bed and gently shook her arm.

"Lacey?"

Her eyes remained shut, her breathing deep and regular. He'd really blown it. She'd wanted to talk to him tonight.

She'd *needed* to, isn't that what she said? She'd even called him Daddy, but he had not been there for her.

She'd been drinking. It was undeniable now. He would have to talk to her, somehow preventing the discussion from turning into one more fight. It was good she was asleep. It would give him time to think through how to handle this. He wouldn't come down hard on her tomorrow. He wouldn't come from a place of anger. He would try to handle it the way Annie would have, and he'd tell her he loved her before he said anything else.

He leaned forward to brush the dark hair off Lacey's forehead and saw the clean, straight line of red roots at her scalp. He stood up with a sigh and turned out the light, leaving his daughter alone, with her chin pressed against the cold china cheek of her doll.

CHAPTER THIRTY-ONE

The call from Nola woke him the next morning. "Did you get a chance to see yesterday's *Gazette,* hon?" she asked.

Alec rolled over to look at the clock, wincing as the bottle of tequila connected with his ribcage. It was nine-thirty, and there was a jackhammer in his head.

"Yeah, I did," he said.

"I got so furious when I read it. I can just imagine how terrible you must feel, Alec. Do you think you should sue?"

He looked up at the ceiling. "I've spoken to Olivia Simon," he said. "It was a judgment call, and she did what she thought was best. I'm convinced she was right. By the way, do you know who she is?"

"Olivia Simon?"

"Yes. She's Paul Macelli's wife."

"You're kidding. I didn't know he was married."

He thought he detected some disappointment in Nola's voice. Perhaps she'd been interested in Paul herself. "They're separated, but I think it's temporary." He drew in a breath, bracing himself for her reaction to what he was about to say. "She went up to Norfolk with me yesterday."

Nola was quiet for so long that he wondered if she was still on the line. "She did?" she asked finally.

"Mmm. She's had public speaking experience, so I had her take the radio interview."

Nola hesitated again. "I could have done that, Alec."

He had not even considered asking Nola. He could not imagine spending that much time alone with her. "Well, Saturday's your big day at work."

"True, but what does Olivia Simon know or care about the lighthouse? And with this brouhaha about her mishandling of Annie's treatment—it's a little like sleeping with the enemy, don't you think?"

He laughed. "No, Nola, your metaphor's a bit off base."

"Well, hon, I think there are going to be some repercussions from this. I got a lot of phone calls yesterday from people who are upset over it and want to do something about it."

Alec sighed. "Try to diffuse it, okay, Nola? Annie's gone. Nothing's going to bring her back."

Clay was alone at the kitchen table when Alec came downstairs. He was eating half a cantaloupe filled with cottage cheese, and Alec's stomach turned at the sight. He put a couple of pieces of bread in the toaster and poured himself a cup of black coffee before taking a seat across from his son.

"Is Lacey up yet?"

"Uh-uh." Clay looked up at him. "You look like you crawled out of a toxic waste dump."

"Thanks." Alec rubbed a hand over his chin. He hadn't bothered to shave this morning. Hadn't even showered yet. He didn't want to miss seeing Lacey.

Clay stuck his spoon upright in the cantaloupe. "I've made a decision, Dad," he said. "I'm not going to college this year."

Keeper of the Light

"What?" The toast popped up in the toaster, but Alec didn't bother to take it out.

"I'm going to stay home a year. Lots of kids do that."

"You have a straight-A grade point average and a scholarship to Duke and you're going to stay home and sell surfboards?"

Clay looked down at his cantaloupe. "I think you need me here," he said. "I think Lacey needs me."

Alec laughed. "You and Lacey get along like oil and water."

"That doesn't mean I don't care what happens to her. I'm afraid if I go away I'll come back and she'll be pregnant and using coke or something."

Alec reached across the table to lay his hand lightly on his son's arm. "Clay, what is it? Are you afraid to leave home?"

Clay drew his arm away. "Yeah, I'm afraid, but not for myself."

"You're going to college. I can certainly take care of a fourteen-year-old girl."

Clay looked up at him, and Alec was surprised at the tears in his eyes. He had seen Clay cry only once since he was small, and that was the night Annie died. "You used to be the greatest father in the world," he said, "but now I'm not so sure you *can* take care of a fourteen-year-old girl. I'm not so sure you can even take care of *yourself.*" He leaned forward, his elbows on the table. "Dad, listen to me, all right?" he said. "I was at a party last night and some guys I know came in and told me they'd just come from a party where they saw Lacey. She was ripped, Dad. Wasted. They said she went into one of the bedrooms with some guy and then later with another. And that's just while they were there."

The coffee started to burn a hole in Alec's stomach. He stared wordlessly at his son.

"They didn't know who the guys were or I would have found them and beat the shit out of them."

"Okay," Alec said. "Thank you for telling me. Let this be my problem, though, all right? I'll handle it. I'm her father, not you." He reached for the toast, thinking of Annie. She would never have forced Clay to go to school if he didn't want to. "The choice is yours about college, Clay, but don't stay here because of Lacey."

He turned on his answering machine to take the calls from friends and acquaintances incensed over the way Olivia had managed Annie's case in the ER, angered by something they knew nothing about. Then he showered and shaved in an attempt to pull himself together, struggling unsuccessfully to keep his mind off the image of Lacey in a strange bedroom, being pawed at. Used.

He woke her at noon. Her face was puffy and pale, and she groaned when she opened her eyes. He'd left the overhead light off and the shades pulled, but still the faint light made her wince. She sat up slowly, leaning against the headboard, the china doll lying face down at her side.

"You wanted to talk to me last night," he said. He would be careful not to call her Annie.

"I don't remember," she said in the sullen voice he had come to equate with her lately. There was a string of hickeys, red and round, on her neck, disappearing under the neckline of her T-shirt.

"I think we do need to talk."

"Not now. I don't feel well."

"You're hungover, and that's one of the things we need to talk about. You're way too young to be drinking." He cursed himself as she frowned. Wasn't he going to start this conversation by telling her he loved her?

"I only had one beer," she said, and tempted though he was to accuse her of lying, he bit his tongue.

He picked up the doll and rested it on his lap. Its brown eyes were painted on; they stared blankly at the ceiling. Alec looked back at his daughter. "I was thinking last night that it's been a while since I told you I loved you," he said.

She dropped her eyes to the blanket covering her knees and picked at a thread coming loose from the binding. She'd made a tactical error in cutting her hair—it was no longer long enough to cover her eyes.

"I do, Lace. Very much. And I'm worried about you. Clay told me that some of his friends saw you...go into a bedroom with a couple of different guys last night."

Her face shot up. There was alarm in her eyes, but she attempted a laugh. "They must have me mixed up with someone else."

"You're a smart kid, Lace, but I think drinking throws your judgment off and you end up doing things you wouldn't ordinarily do. Guys will take advantage of you. You're too young to..."

"I'm not *doing* anything, and even if I was, so what? Mom turned out okay."

"She did start young, that's true, but it was because she was searching for love. You know what her parents were like— she never felt loved by them. You know *you're* loved, don't you Lace? You don't have to have sex to get guys to like you."

"I'm *not*."

Alec's eyes were drawn to the wall above Lacey's head where a long-haired musician, his leather pants stitched into a genital-hugging cup at the crotch, smirked at him. He looked back at his daughter. "I guess we should talk about birth control," he said.

Lacey flushed, her cheeks the color of the welts on her neck. "Please shut up."

"If you need birth control, you can get it. Do you want me to make a doctor's appointment for you?"

"*No.*"

He looked down at the doll, touching the delicate little white teeth with the tip of his finger. "Well, maybe it's not negotiable. If you're getting involved with...boys, you probably should see a doctor whether you want birth control or not."

She stared at him incredulously. "*Mom* would never have made me go."

He felt his patience slipping. "Look, Lacey, if you want to act like an adult, then you're going to have to face the responsibilities that come along..."

"Mom would never have gotten on my case like this, either," she interrupted him. "She would have believed anything I said. She would have trusted me."

He threw the doll down hard on the bed and stood up. "Well, I'm not Mom," he said, unable to keep the anger out of his voice. "And she's not here. You're stuck with me because she thought a bunch of goddamned battered women needed her more than we did."

Lacey flung her blanket aside and jumped to the floor, turning to glare at him across the bed. "Sometimes I think you wish Zachary Pointer had killed me instead of her," she said. "I bet you lie awake at night and think, why couldn't it have been Lacey? Why did it have to be Annie?"

He was too astonished to speak. He stared after her as she ran out of the room, her footsteps quick and sharp in the hallway, and the bathroom door slammed shut so loudly he winced.

He stood there for a few minutes more before beginning

to make her bed. He folded the edge of the sheet neatly over the blanket, tucked the spread under her pillow, and sat the doll up against the headboard. Then he walked downstairs to the den, where he could spend the rest of the day lost in his work on the lighthouse.

CHAPTER THIRTY-TWO

They gave her the tourists in the emergency room over the next couple of days, because the locals—at least those coherent enough to be choosy—refused to see the doctor who had taken Annie O'Neill from them.

On the Tuesday after Jonathan's vitriolic story appeared in the *Gazette,* Mike Shelley asked to see her. He was on the phone when she walked into his office, and he gestured for her to sit down. She watched the lines deepen in his forehead as he listened to his caller. Whatever he had to say to her wasn't going to be good.

She had felt very much alone these past couple of days, despite a reserved sympathy from most of the ER staff. "We're behind you," Kathy Brash said to her. "We know what you went through that night," Lynn Wilkes added, but their voices were whispers, as though they were afraid of being too public with their support. Jonathan had his allies as well—people who watched her every move, who waited for her to make another error in judgment.

She had heard nothing from Paul since he'd left for Washington, and nothing from Alec since the night she'd stood naked and willing in his arms. She cringed to remember that night. He'd been serious when he said they should avoid each other. For the past couple of nights she lay in bed, waiting for ten-thirty to come, hoping that the phone would ring. She'd finally drop off to sleep, waking up in the morning to the realization that he hadn't called. Perhaps by now he blamed her too.

Mike hung up the phone and gave her a tired smile. "I need to show you something I received this morning," he said. He pulled a sheaf of paper from a large envelope and pushed it across the desk to her. "A petition. Three hundred names, all asking for your resignation. Or, I guess, asking me to force you to resign."

She looked down at the yellow lined paper. Across the top of the first sheet someone had typed: *In light of her inadequate handling of the medical emergency which resulted in the death of valued community member Annie Chase O'Neill, the following people call for the immediate resignation of Olivia Simon, M.D."*

She let her eyes brush over the names, lifting the second sheet, the third, trying to determine if Alec's signature was among the many, but she could not read that quickly, and the names began to blur in front of her. She looked up at Mike.

"I have no intention of asking you to leave, Olivia, but I thought you should know what we're up against. I'm sorry this has gotten so out of hand."

Mike had made his own statements to the press, and although he vehemently denied any cover-up, he was reserved and cautious in the words he used. Olivia understood. His position was political as well as medical, and he couldn't afford to alienate the community. It didn't matter what he said, anyway. People were hearing only what they wanted to hear. Even after all these months, they wanted a scapegoat, someone to blame for the loss of their beloved Saint Anne.

"Have you heard anything from her husband?" she asked. "Do you know where he stands?"

"Well, I don't thinks he's behind this petition. I just hope he's not talking to a lawyer."

"Mike, I'm sorry."

"Don't be. What you did may have been unwise from the standpoint of liability, but it took courage. I'm not at all certain I would have had the guts to do something for her here."

She stood up, and he followed her to the door.

"Keep your chin up," he said. He gestured toward the petition on his desk. "I'll figure out what to do about this. You just concentrate on your work."

She stopped by the studio that evening to show Tom her design for a new stained glass panel—multicolored hot-air balloons above a green meadow. A little more of a challenge. She could already picture it in the window of the nursery.

Tom looked up from the work table when she walked into the studio.

"Hi." She pulled the roll of graph paper from her tote bag and set the bag itself on the empty chair by the table. "How are you doing?"

"I'm not sure." Tom's voice sounded tight, and when she looked down at him, he crossed his arms across his chest.

"What's wrong?"

"I've been giving it a lot of thought, Olivia," he said, "and I'm just not sure I can teach you any longer."

She stared at him, wondering if his signature was on the petition. "Because of the things Jonathan Cramer's been saying about me?"

"Because I don't know what to believe. Because I think you took a risk with the life of a very good friend of mine.

A very precious friend." There were actual tears in his eyes, ready to spill onto his pale eyelashes.

Olivia put her hands on her hips. "I did everything I could for her, Tom. I didn't kill her. I feel like people are blaming me because Zachary Pointer's too far away and too invisible—blaming him doesn't give them much satisfaction. So I've become the scapegoat, but I swear to you, Tom, I did the best I could."

"Maybe you did, Olivia. I can't judge. All I know is, I can't sit here with you week after week, letting you use Annie's glass and Annie's tools and Annie's..."

"All right." She reached for her tote bag. "You've made your point."

"I could give you the names of a few other people who could teach you, but I have to warn you that the art community here's pretty tight, and I really doubt any of them would be willing to take you on right now."

She slipped the graph paper back into her bag, and without another word, left the studio. She let the door slam behind her, and a few people in the parking lot turned to stare at her. Did they know who she was? Did everybody know? She got into her car, and just in case someone was watching, waited until she was out in the street before she let herself cry.

Her shift in the emergency room was nearly over the following night when they got a call about a head-on collision out on the main road. One driver had walked away with scratches, but the driver of the other car, a woman in her early twenties, was seriously injured and was being brought in by ambulance.

"We'll need a second physician," Olivia said to Kathy as she readied the treatment room.

"I know," Kathy said, her voice hesitant, "but it's Jonathan who's on call."

Olivia was at the scrub sink. "Well," she said, "you'd better get him over here."

The injured driver and Jonathan arrived at the same time. Jonathan plowed into the treatment room, barking orders, looking as though he were already director of the ER. The patient—a twenty-one-year-old woman—was brought in taped to a backboard and wearing a cervical collar. There was a dark bruise already spreading across her abdomen. She was conscious, though not too coherent, and she moaned with pain.

"Wasn't wearing a seatbelt," said the paramedic. "She was lucky she got caught on the steering wheel or she would have gone through the window."

"Get a C-spine," Olivia said to Kathy, "and a CBC and type and cross. And do a blood alcohol level, while you're at it." She thought she smelled alcohol on the young woman's breath.

Jonathan started an IV in the woman's arm. "Is the helicopter on its way?" he asked Lynn Wilkes, who nodded. "We'll stabilize her and send her up," he said. Then he looked across the patient at Olivia, his voice heavy with sarcasm. "Or do you want to play doctor on her?"

Olivia did not respond. She felt uncertain of their next move with this patient. Her blood pressure was ninety-five over sixty. She was a slender woman who appeared to be in good physical condition. Was that pressure normal for her or an indication of something more ominous? "Pulse is one-ten," Kathy said, glancing at Olivia.

Olivia carefully palpated the woman's abdomen. "Abdomen's firm," she said, moving her fingers to the woman's left side. Suddenly the woman groaned, trying to roll away from

Olivia's touch. Was she simply recoiling from pressure on the bruise, or could her spleen be ruptured?

"Let's tap her abdomen," Olivia said.

Jonathan scowled at her. "We don't have time. You want another dead lady on your hands?"

Olivia said nothing more. She followed Jonathan's lead, helping him prepare the woman for transport, and she felt dizzy as she watched the emergency technicians transfer her to the waiting helicopter. By the time she returned to her office, her legs were weak and rubbery. She sat down at her desk, leaning back in the chair and closing her eyes. She'd been a coward. Why was she letting Jonathan intimidate her?

She should have fought him, but she was terrified now— not of Jonathan, not of losing her job—but of her own judgment. If anyone were to ask her just at that moment, as she sat nauseated and trembling at her desk, if she was certain she'd made the right decision in Annie's case, she could not have said.

She called Emerson Memorial that night and learned that the woman had indeed suffered a ruptured spleen. Jonathan had been right—the extra minutes it would have taken to tap her abdomen could have cost the young woman her life. Olivia wept, partly from relief that the patient was all right, and partly from the realization that she'd been wrong, that right now she could not trust her own ability to make sound decisions in the ER.

She went to bed, overwhelmed by her solitude. At twelve-thirty, she lifted her phone from the night table to her bed and dialed Alec's number. His voice was thick with sleep when he answered, and she hung up without saying a word.

Chapter Thirty-Three

August 1991

Paul walked across Connecticut Avenue, struggling to pull the District of Columbia's thick, sodden night air into his lungs. You needed gills for this sort of weather. The pink neon sign for Donovan's Books sprouted from the side of a building half a block in front of him, and he quickened his pace.

Once inside the store he stood by the door for a moment, mopping his forehead with his handkerchief and drinking in the unmitigated splendor of his favorite bookstore in all the world. Olivia's favorite as well. He missed living here, and he was beginning to miss Olivia.

Nine-thirty at night and the store was packed. *Joy.* What was open in the Outer Banks at nine-thirty except, perhaps, the bait shops?

He walked slowly through the store, touching books with his fingertips. He'd had poetry readings here on a fairly regular basis. Sunday afternoons, Tuesday evenings. The crowd was always eclectic, always appreciative. Always on his side.

He reached for the stairs in the rear of the store and climbed up to the loft, where he ordered mineral water and a slice of cheesecake from the man at the service counter. Then, carrying his tray, he searched among the small, crowded tables for an empty seat. Two men were just vacating a table near the railing. They offered it to Paul, and he sat down, realizing as he surveyed the store below him that this was the table where he and Olivia had always tried to sit. For the first two years of their marriage, they had lived in an apartment directly across the street. Even after they'd bought the house in Kensington, they'd meet a few times a week at this table, spending hours over mineral water and avocado sandwiches as they worked together on *The Wreck of the Eastern Spirit*. God, how he had loved writing that book with her.

He'd been at Washington General to cover the illness of a senator when he got word of the train plunging into the Potomac. He was the first reporter to reach the emergency room, and in the chaos of that moment, and during the hours that followed, no one seemed to notice him or monitor his actions.

He saw Olivia for the first time when she was meeting a stretcher-borne victim of the train wreck at the automatic doors to the ER. She was grabbing her long brown hair up into a sloppy, off-center ponytail, slipping a rubber band from her wrist to her hair to hold it in place. Then she and the paramedics whisked the elderly woman past Paul on their way to the trauma room, Olivia pressing a piece of bloody gauze to the wound in the woman's side, talking calmly to her all the while. Dozens of doctors and nurses worked hard in that ER over the next few days, but Paul could not shift his focus from Olivia. He watched her tell families that their loved ones would either live or die. He watched her softly touch their arms, or hold them when they needed to be held. By the end of those few frightening days, her hair hung limply down her back and her bangs were swept by sweat and grime off her forehead. Her green scrubs were streaked with blood, and dark circles ringed the delicate alabaster skin around her eyes. He thought she was entirely beautiful.

He wished he'd been drawn to Olivia because he was finally ready for someone new, but he knew it was her utterly selfless compassion in the ER that had seduced him, because it reminded him of Annie. The comparison was ridiculous. Annie, with her disregard for time and her totally chaotic approach to life, would have created havoc in an emergency room. It was Olivia's cool, clinical efficiency that made her so good. It took him a while to realize she was not at all like Annie, but by then he had genuinely fallen in love with her.

Some evenings he and Olivia would sit at this table and page through books she'd plucked from the shelves on her way through the store. She usually selected books on nature, or medicine. Early in their relationship, she went through a phase of reading every book she could find on sex. Having denied any sexual thoughts or feelings for much of her life, she was unstoppable once she'd been set free. Sex with Olivia had been like teaching a child a new game—at first she'd been uncertain of her ability, but once the rules were mastered, she wanted to play it continually. And she'd played it very well indeed.

During the last few years of their marriage, though, the books she'd bring to the table were filled with the sobering, sometimes hopeful, sometimes disheartening information on infertility.

Paul ate the last bite of his cheesecake, letting it melt in his mouth as he studied the gold band on his finger. He had put it on just that morning, and although he had not worn it in many months, it comforted him to see it on his hand. He and Olivia would not have drifted away from each other if they'd been able to have a family. He'd felt cheated when he learned she was incapable of conceiving. He struggled not to let his feelings show. It was not in any way her fault, and her own disappointment was keen. He was nearing the point of pulling himself together from that blow when she announced she had received the job offer in the Outer Banks.

He was incredulous. He knew Annie lived in the Outer Banks with her husband and two children, and he was filled with an odd mixture of excitement and terror. He tried to talk Olivia out of taking the offer, but she returned from her interview raving about the uniqueness of the area and the quiet challenge of the position being offered to her. It's too isolated, he said. Too far from his family and their friends. He knew in retrospect his argument had been weakly offered, that in truth, he was electrified by the idea of being close to Annie. As his fantasies grew of what it would be like, how he might see her, might just bump into her at the grocery store or on the beach, he withdrew further and further from Olivia. When he spoke to her at all it was with a sharp edge to his voice. He was angry with her for putting him in this situation.

Once the move was complete, he managed to wait all of a week before looking up O'Neill in the phone book. She was listed both at her home address and at her studio. He waited another day before driving past the studio, and one more before going in.

She'd been alone, adjusting a photograph on the far wall, and the look on her face when she turned to see him could not have been more horror-filled if he had walked in sporting two heads.

"Don't panic," he said quickly, holding up a hand to ward

off anything she might say. "I'm not here to cause you any trouble. I'm married too. Happily. My wife is a physician at the emergency room in Kill Devil Hills." He rambled on about Olivia, partly to fill the silence, partly to convince her he had no intention of being a threat to her or her marriage.

She flattened herself against the wall of photographs as she listened to him, her arms folded protectively across her chest. Her hands hugged her elbows so tightly that he could see the whiteness of her knuckles from where he stood on the other side of the room.

She looked extraordinary. A little heavier than the last time he'd seen her. Not overweight, but she had a woman's body now. Still the same hair, though not quite so wild, and the red was softened by those occasional strands of silver. Her skin was as dewy and fair as it had been when he first met her.

When he finally paused for breath, she spoke. "You'll have to tell her you can't stay here," she said. "It won't work, Paul. Please. It would be impossible for you to live here without us constantly bumping into each other."

Her words only served to encourage his fantasy. Why would she care where he lived if she didn't fear being tempted by him?

"I didn't want to move here, believe me," he said. "I tried to talk Olivia out of taking the job, but she was sold on it."

"Does she know about me?"

He shook his head. "She doesn't even know about the summer I lived here. I started to tell her about you once, long ago, but Olivia's one of those people who wants to leave the past in the past." Olivia's own past had been so weighty, so painful, that it had absorbed nearly all their energy in the early days of their relationship. He'd had to undo all that had been done to her, and after that she wanted to put the past behind her. She knew only that he'd had a very serious relationship long before he met her. She wanted to know no more than that.

He walked to the back wall of the studio to study the breathtaking stained glass. "Your work is beautiful, Annie. You've come a long way."

"I've changed, Paul," she said. "I'm not the woman you used to know. Please don't have any illusions that you and I can have a relationship again."

"Just friendship."

"No. It's impossible." She lowered her voice, and he knew someone else must be in the studio. "There was too much between us for us to simply be friends."

He was close enough to her now to see fine lines at the corners of her eyes and mouth. He wanted to see her laugh, to hear her ringing giggle bounce off the glass.

"I'm working for the *Gazette,*" he said, "and freelancing. I'd like to do an article on you for *Seascape Magazine.*"

"No."

"I've already spoken to the editor about it. Please, Annie. It would help me get my name known here."

He started as a door creaked open behind him, and he turned to see a large, ponytailed man walk into the room from what must have been a darkroom. Annie stepped toward him. "Tom," she said. "This is Paul Macelli. He's a journalist who wants to do a story on me in *Seascape.*"

"Hello," Paul said as he shook Tom's hand. He would play her game. He would act as though they were strangers to one another if that was what she wanted.

"Well, you couldn't pick a better person to write about," Tom said. "She's a real Jill-of-all-trades. Anything going on in the community, she's a part of it, and you can see for yourself what a talented artist she is." He talked on, telling him little details about her work that Paul began jotting down in a notebook, while Annie lowered herself behind the work table, looking up at both of them, her eyes resigned and unsmiling.

The interviews began. He let her talk about her son and daughter, about Alec. Those meetings fed the roots of his obsession. He sent the *Seascape* photographer to her studio and demanded he take dozens of pictures, far more than Paul would ever need for the article, so that he could keep them for himself. He could pretend the smile she showed the camera was meant for him, because he was seeing so little of it in real life. She wanted him again; he was certain of it. There was no other reason why she should be afraid of his being nearby. She had to want him.

He had no friends. A growing number of acquaintances, but no one to confide in, and he was bursting to talk. And there was Olivia, ready to listen.

Olivia. How had she tolerated him all those weeks, those months, when he was wrapped up in Annie, when he spoke of nothing else?

It had been a terrible sickness in him. From this distance he could see it for what it was: a pathetic obsession that was costing him his sleep, his self-respect, his marriage. A few days earlier, Gabe had called him at the hotel to tell him about the *Gazette* article in which Jonathan Cramer accused Olivia of mishandling Annie's case. He'd thought about it all night and he knew Cramer was wrong. He only had to think back to the wreck of the Eastern Spirit to know how wrong he was. He would trust Olivia with his own life, with the lives of anyone he loved. Annie had stood a better chance of survival under Olivia's care than she would have with any other physician in the state. He could see that now, from this distance, as surely as he could feel Olivia's presence in this bookstore. He had been satisfied during those years he and Olivia lived up here. With Olivia, he had finally been a man in control of himself and his demons, and he'd been grateful to her for freeing him from his obsession.

For her trouble he'd repaid her with pain, with coldness, with cruelty. Now she was handling harassment by the paper he worked for, as though he was still hurting her even when he was not physically there.

He looked at his watch. She would still be up by the time he got back to the hotel if he left right now. He paid the bill and hurried out into the hot night air.

CHAPTER THIRTY-FOUR

The phone rang at ten-thirty-five. Olivia was lathering her hair in the shower, and she stepped out quickly, drawing a towel around her as she raced into the bedroom to answer it before the machine picked it up.

It was Paul's voice, not Alec's, that greeted her, and for a split second, she was disappointed.

"Are you back?" she asked.

"No. I'm in a hotel in D.C. I'll get back tomorrow." He sounded tired. A little tense.

"How are you?" she asked.

He was quiet for a moment. Then she heard a slight laugh, or maybe a cough. "Physically, I'm fine. Emotionally, I'm coming to grips with the fact that I've been out of my mind."

The shampoo was beginning to drizzle down Olivia's back. "What are you talking about?" She stretched the phone cord down the hall to the linen closet, where she pulled out a towel and draped it around her neck.

"I talked to Gabe at the *Gazette* and he told me about the flak on Annie's case. I'm sorry, Olivia. I didn't think the

Gazette was capable of yellow journalism. Maybe if I'd been there I could have prevented it somehow."

She walked back into the bedroom and sat down on the bed. "You thought I was to blame too," she said.

"For Annie dying? No, Liv, I know you too well to have seriously thought that. I did wonder how you could have done it, though. How you could work on her when I'd been so obnoxious about the way I felt about her, but I know you did your best. I'm sorry I ever accused you of anything less."

She cradled the receiver between her palms. "It means a lot to me to hear you say that."

He was quiet for a moment. "I've been doing some thinking up here," he said. "D.C.'s loaded with memories of you—of us together. I stopped in Donovan's Books tonight."

"*Oh.*" The sights and sounds and warm-coffee smell of Donovan's filled her head.

"I wish we'd never left here. Things were good for us here."

"But we agreed we didn't want to raise a family there, whether we had our own children or adopted or..."

"I know, I know." He paused. She heard him let out his breath. "Can I see you when I get back?"

"Of course."

"I mean, a date? We'll go out someplace, get to know each other again."

"I'd like that." She matched the tenderness in his voice with her own.

"I should be there around five."

"I work until seven." She cringed, waiting for him to chastise her for allowing her work to interfere with her marriage again.

"Seven is fine," he said, then he hesitated for a moment.

"Liv? Why aren't you fighting this thing with Cramer? It's so unlike you to just sit back and take it."

She ran her hand over her bedspread. He was right. She usually took her adversaries head-on, battling them just as she had battled every other obstacle in her life.

"My only recourse would be to ask for a medical review panel," she said, "but I'm not sure I have the strength right now to go through that process."

"*Do* it, Liv. I'll be behind you all the way. I promise."

She thanked him, surprised and somewhat guarded, unable to completely trust his words, his warmth. Yet by the time she'd hung up the phone, she'd made a decision, and despite the hour, she called Mike Shelley.

Mike listened quietly as she told him her plan. She could guess what he was thinking. A review panel would not only put her on the line, but the emergency room itself.

"Please hold off a day or two on taking any action, Olivia," Mike said finally. "Let me think about it a bit."

She got off the phone, feeling better, feeling less helpless than she had a half hour earlier. She stood in front of the full-length mirror on her closet door. Her hair was white with lather. She let the towel drop to the carpet and turned to look at her profile. There was no denying the slight protrusion of her belly. If Paul touched her, he would know. It had been enough to make Alec pull away from her.

Instead of putting on her nightgown, she dressed in a T-shirt and the only pair of jeans she could still zip closed. Then she walked outside to the storage closet and took a couple of screwdrivers and a wrench from the small hardware kit Paul had left her when he moved out. She carried them into the nursery, along with the radio and a glass of ginger ale, and settled in for a long and satisfying night of crib construction.

★ ★ ★

At the change of shift the following evening, Mike called Olivia and Jonathan into his office. Jonathan sat near the window, wearing the sour smirk that was a permanent part of his demeanor these days, while Olivia took the chair closest to the door.

Mike leaned forward, his forearms on his desk. "Jonathan," he began, "I want you to retract your 'cover-up' statement to the press."

"I'm not going to retract something I think is the truth."

Mike shook his head. "Olivia is planning to request a medical review panel, and if that occurs, I will be telling that panel the truth as *I* see it, which is that *both* of you were right in the O'Neill case." Mike spoke slowly, as if he expected Jonathan would have difficulty following him. "Olivia was right to take the action she did because she has the skill and the experience to perform that type of surgery. A case could be made for malpractice if she had *not* attempted to save Ms. O'Neill's life in that way. But *you*, Jonathan, were also right. Do you know why?" He didn't wait for Jonathan to respond. "You were right because you do *not* have the skill or experience to perform that procedure. It would have been malpractice if you *had* attempted it. So." Mike sat back again, his eyes on Jonathan. "Is that what you'd like this community to hear?"

Jonathan's eyes had narrowed. There was a thin bead of sweat above his upper lip. "You're twisting the..."

"I'm twisting *nothing*," Mike growled, leaning forward again, and Olivia was as surprised as Jonathan by the force of his reaction. "You make that retraction or Olivia is calling for a review panel to clear her name. And clear it she will, which isn't going to make you look too good, is it?"

She felt Jonathan's eyes on her, felt his burning, penetrating glare. "Don't bother," he said to her, standing up. "I'm re-signing, effective immediately. Then you can tap abdomens till your heart's content, for all I care." He took off his stetho-scope, and in a exaggerated gesture, slapped it down on the desk before storming out of the office.

Mike looked at the stethoscope, and Olivia thought he was trying not to smile. He raised his eyes to hers. "I apologize for not doing that sooner, Olivia. Please wait on the review panel until we see what the outcome of this is." He nodded toward his phone. "Shall I call the *Gazette* and tell them the news?"

She changed her clothes in the lounge for her date with Paul, ignoring the rumors that were already crackling through the ER about what had taken place in Mike's office. She dressed in a blue skirt that masked her expanding middle, and a white, short-sleeved sweater. When she stepped out of the lounge, she spotted Paul in the waiting room and felt a nearly forgotten flutter of longing for him.

He'd brought her a delicate blue tea rose in a silver bud vase, and she recognized it as the rare variety she had grown in the yard of their old house in Kensington. Her throat ached to see it, the remnant of a happier time.

"I cut it this morning," he said as they walked out to his car. "Snuck into the yard before the sun was up."

His out-of-character wickedness made her smile.

He started the car and pulled out of the parking lot, glanc-ing over at her once they were on the road. "You look good," he said.

"Thanks." She noticed he was wearing his wedding ring again. He was serious about this, about missing her, about getting back together. She studied his profile. He had a lovely chin with the suggestion of a cleft, and a fine, straight nose, but he really did not look well. He had lost a good deal of weight these last few months. His skin was sallow, his cheeks drawn, and she felt a little sorry for him.

She told him about her meeting with Jonathan and Mike, thanking him for his encouragement. "I'd gotten sort of paralyzed, I guess," she said.

"What's it been like for you since the story came out in the *Gazette?*"

She described the bilious letters to the editor that had appeared in the last two issues of the *Gazette*. Their irate tone and the mushrooming of negative sentiment toward her were humiliating. She told him about her stiffness at work and her sudden lack of faith in her own judgment, surprising herself with her willingness to talk to him so openly. Then she told him about the petition. "I expected to see your name at the top," she said. "I figured the only reason you weren't on it was because you were out of town."

He reached over to squeeze her shoulder. "Forgive me for ever thinking you wouldn't do your best with her. It hurts me to see your name dragged through the mud this way, Liv. Really, it does."

At the next stoplight, he pulled out his wallet and handed her a picture of Joe Gallo's granddaughter. He told her about his conversation with Joe and how proud he had felt to be her husband, but she only half listened.

She would have to tell him she'd gone to Norfolk with Alec, that she'd done that talk show. He was sure to hear about it at the next lighthouse meeting, and it would be better if he heard it from her. Not now, though. She didn't want to damage the closeness she felt to him here in his car.

When they pulled into the restaurant parking lot, she turned to lay her sweater on the back seat of the car and saw the small oval of stained glass attached to the window. It was too dark to see the design, but she had no doubt it was one of

Annie's, and the hope she'd felt these last twenty-four hours was abruptly tempered by reality.

She carried the rose into the restaurant, exchanging it for the carnation on their table. After their drinks had been served, she folded her hands on the edge of the table and drew in a breath.

"I was on a radio talk show in Norfolk last Saturday," she said. "About the lighthouse."

"What?" His eyes widened behind his glasses. "What do you mean?"

"Alec O'Neill called me. He was supposed to make two appearances up there on the same day, so he asked me if I'd be willing to handle one of them since I had experience doing that sort of thing."

"That's ridiculous. You don't know a thing about the lighthouse."

"I do now."

Paul pumped the stirrer up and down in his drink. "Did you and Alec drive up together?"

"Yes." He let out his breath, ran a hand over his chin. "What have you told him, Olivia? I mean, does he have any idea why we're separated?"

"He doesn't know anything about you and Annie."

"Well, what did you talk about for...what is it, two hours each way?"

She thought back to all she had told Alec, to how thoroughly she had let him into her personal life. "We worked on our presentations going up and talked about how they went coming back. That's all."

Paul sat back in his chair and shook his head. "I don't get this at all. Why you? Why do you care about the lighthouse enough to speak about it?"

"Why do *you* care so much?"

He colored quickly. "I've always had a fascination with lighthouses," he said. "You just didn't know about it because we lived in the District, where lighthouses are few and far between." He bent his stirrer between his fingers until it snapped. "It just makes me uncomfortable to know you're talking to O'Neill. Do you have any more of these speaking engagements lined up?"

"No."

"Don't take any more, all right?"

She folded her arms across her chest. "If I have the time and interest, I'm going to do it, Paul. You really have no right to tell me not to."

The woman at the next table glanced over at them, and Paul lowered his voice. "Let's not talk about this now, okay?" he said. "I wanted tonight to be good. Let's talk about Washington."

"All right." She leaned away from the table as the waitress set her salad in front of her.

"I felt good there, Olivia. I haven't felt that way in so long. I've been back just a few hours and I'm already tensing up. It's this place." He shuddered. "The Outer Banks. It reminds me too much of Annie here. It's too small. Everywhere I go there are reminders of her. The way the air smells makes me think of her."

"I love the way it smells," she said, alarmed with herself for baiting him. The way the air smelled made her think of Alec and the evening they stood on the balcony of the Kiss River Lighthouse, the beacon pulsing above them. Every time she stepped outside now, she breathed in the air in huge, cleansing gulps.

Paul looked down at his salad. "If you and I get back together, we'll have to leave here."

She felt stricken. "I love it here, Paul, in spite of the fact that half the populace would like to see me lynched. I'm hoping that will blow over. I think this would be the perfect place to raise a family."

"*What* family?" he asked, and the woman at the next table could not resist glancing at them again. "You're thirty-seven years old and the surgery only gave you a twenty percent chance of conceiving. Not very good odds."

Olivia leaned closer to him to avoid being overheard. "I'm more convinced than you are that I could conceive. If I don't, we could adopt. We've talked this out before. It's nothing new."

"Things have changed since the last time we talked about a family."

The waitress delivered their entrees, and Olivia watched the muscles in the side of Paul's jaw contract as he waited out the intrusion.

"You don't understand," he said, once the waitress had left. "I have to get out of here, Olivia, that's all there is to it. Whether it's with you or without you, I have to leave. I drove down here today feeling good and optimistic about us and looking forward to seeing you, but as soon as I crossed the bridge into Kitty Hawk, this black cloud dropped over my head. My mood got worse and worse as I drove down the island, and by the time I got to my house and out of the car..." He shook his head. "It's like she's still here, more powerful than she ever was when she was alive."

Olivia felt her patience slipping. "What do you expect? Your house is full of reminders of her. Maybe if you got rid of...all the *icons,* all the tangible evidence that you ever knew her, you'd start to forget about her."

He looked, briefly, angry, and she suddenly realized she could not just forgive him and go on. She was filled with her own anger.

"There's nothing I want more than for us to get back together," she said, "but I refuse to live in Annie's shadow again."

"Then we have to leave here."

"I'm not going to leave a place I've come to love until I see real evidence that you're over her. Throw out the stained glass. Break it into pieces."

He started visibly.

"Oh, Paul." She crumpled her napkin and set it next to her plate. "You're not ready, are you?"

"Not to destroy the stained glass, no." He looked exhausted, his eyes red and half-closed behind his glasses. She thought of Annie as a succubus, coming in the night to drain the life out of him. Perhaps Annie was more Paul's nemesis than she was hers.

He drove her back to her car in the emergency room parking lot after dinner. She was glad he was not driving her home, where she would have felt the need to invite him in, where the night before she had worked on the crib until she was giddy. He walked her to her car, holding her hand. He kissed her lightly on the lips, and she turned abruptly to unlock the door of the Volvo. She would give him no chance to touch her, no chance to discover her secret.

She arrived home to find a message on her answering machine from Clark Chapman, the medical director of Emerson Memorial. She frowned as she listened to his deep, resonant voice.

"Please give me a call when you get in tonight," he said. He left a number and told her he would be up until eleven. It was not quite ten now.

She dialed his number, curious.

"Dr. Simon!" He sounded delighted to hear from her, as if they were old friends. "How *are* you?"

She hesitated, wondering if perhaps she *had* met him somewhere and had forgotten. "I'm fine, thank you," she said.

"You're wondering why I'm calling, right?"

"Well, yes."

"I'd rather have this conversation in person, of course, but I didn't want to put it off that long. I've been following your story, Dr. Simon. It was more than idle curiosity on my part, of course, since your patient—Mrs. O'Neill—would have ended up in our trauma center had you opted to transport her."

"Yes."

"And you and I both know she would have come to us DOA."

Gratitude and relief rushed through her, and her eyes threatened to fill. She cried too easily these days. "You and I seem to be the only people who are certain of that," she said.

"I've spoken to some colleagues of mine at Washington General," Clark Chapman continued. "People who can attest to your clinical skill and sound judgment. You made the far more difficult choice with Mrs. O'Neill, didn't you? You demonstrated initiative and courage, at considerable personal risk." There was a smile in his voice. "Are you wondering what I'm leading up to?"

"Yes."

"I'm offering you a job. You'd be co-director of our trauma team. It's a great group of people. They already think you're a bit of a hero."

It was perfect. One of those weird serendipitous occurrences that suddenly made everything fall into place. She and Paul could be together in a new location, without the rush of Washington, yet without reminders of Annie for either of them. Still, aside from feeling vindicated by Clark Chapman's words, she felt no enthusiasm.

"I'm very flattered," she said, "but I'm not sure I'm ready to leave the Outer Banks. I don't want to simply run away from my problems here." It was not exactly the truth, but Clark Chapman seemed to accept it.

"It's an open invitation," he said. "Come visit us." He gave her his work number, and she jotted it down in her appointment book. "The position would be created for you," he added. "It doesn't exist right now, but we've got a few extra bucks for that department, so it's yours whenever you say the word."

She hung up the phone, feeling strangely flat. Wary. She couldn't allow herself to hope, couldn't give herself over to a new dream of the future when she didn't yet trust her husband to be a committed, contented part of it. But Paul was back, she told herself. Paul had missed her. Surely they would be able to work things out.

Once in bed, though, once she had closed her eyes, all she could see was that telltale oval of glass on the window of his car.

Chapter Thirty-Five

Paul Macelli was back, more nervous than the first time, if that was possible. Mary had been waiting weeks for him and was beginning to think he wouldn't come again, that he'd lost his courage after his first visit. She hated waiting. She was ninety years old. It seemed like all she did these days was wait.

Paul adjusted his glasses and took the tape recorder from his briefcase, setting it once again on the broad arm of Mary's rocking chair. He pressed the button to begin recording.

"I'd like to hear about *you* today," he said. "They used to call you the Angel of the Light, didn't they?"

"So they did," she said, a little surprised, but pleased all the same. "What do you want to know?"

"You said you met your husband in Deweytown. Is that where you grew up?"

"Oh, yes. Deweytown was just about cosmopolitan compared to Kiss River, I can tell you that. My father owned a little grocery store over there. Caleb was worried I wouldn't want to leave Deweytown, but I had plenty of spunk in those days. I thought it would be an adventure living in Kiss River."

"And was it?"

Mary smiled. "At times, yes. At other times—well, it didn't matter. I was always one for having a good imagination. I knew how to keep myself occupied when there was nothing more exciting going on than watching the beacon go round." Mary clamped her lips shut. She'd better watch how much she said. She looked over at him as he adjusted his glasses again. He was jiggling one leg up and down, sending an irritating vibration into the floor of the porch.

"So," he said. "Tell me how you came to be known as the Angel of the Light."

"Well." Mary looked out at the street. "I guess you could say I had a way with people, and living out at Kiss River, you got real hungry for company. So any time I'd hear someone in the village was sick, I'd take them food and make sure they had whatever it was they needed. Sometimes I'd carry them across the sound to the doctor in Deweytown in our little boat. I guess I just got a reputation for helping people out."

Mary shifted in the rocker. It had bothered her that people thought she was so good. They hadn't known her, really.

"Caleb and I made a good team," she continued, looking once again at Paul. "We were both hard workers, and we both loved the lighthouse. Anytime I'd see a ship, I'd go out on the gallery and wave. So I guess I got myself a reputation that way, too. Sailors would ask each other who that lady on the lighthouse was, and they'd say, why, that's Mary Poor, who's always friendly, always doing a good turn for someone. Sailors watched for me then, hoping I'd be out waving when they went by."

She looked toward the harbor and closed her eyes to block

out the view of the boats, imagining in their place the towering white spire of the lighthouse.

"I could cook, too." She opened her eyes again and smiled. "I was a bit famous for my persimmon cakes and puddings. I believe you've had a taste of one of my persimmon cakes, haven't you?"

"Uh." Paul dropped his pen, bent over to pick it up. "I don't recall," he said, straightening up again.

"Too bad I couldn't make one right now," Mary said, "but they don't allow us to cook. Or drink. Or smoke. You have a cigarette with you today?"

"Sorry, no. I don't smoke." He shifted in the rocker and pushed the recorder a little closer to Mary. "Tell me about the work you did with the Life Saving Service."

Mary felt herself color and hoped that Paul Macelli did not notice. "Well, I guess that's another reason they got to calling me the Angel. A more important reason, really." She sat up taller in the chair, straightening her spine. "I was very strong, you see. I could swim better than most men. I'd be out in the ocean nearly every day, swimming back and forth, back and forth. My arms were solid as brick, and my legs too, from climbing up to the top of the tower." Mary smiled to herself. "I had a dream of working with the Life Saving Service, you see. We knew a lot of the men who worked over at the station and I'd ask to go out with them when they were rescuing someone. Of course they just laughed at me. But in 1927, I finally got my chance. Caleb and I were down a mile or so on the beach because we heard there was a boat stranded on the bar. When we got there, the boys from the Life Saving Station had just sent out their power boat to try to save the crew. It was real squally that day, and the power boat got hit straight on by a big breaker and started going to pieces. There were just a few of the men left on the beach with their old surfboat. They quick got in and headed out to sea, and I saw my chance." Mary smiled to herself. "I just jumped in with them, in my skirt and all. They were too shorthanded and too shocked to stop and tell me to get out. I'll tell you, those oars felt right natural to me, and we managed to load the fellas from the power boat into the surfboat without a hitch. I was stiff in the shoulders for a few days, but I didn't care. After that, the Life Saving crew sometimes called on me—unofficially, of course—when they needed an extra pair of hands."

Mary rested her head against the back of the rocker. All this talking was wearing on her.

"Would you like to stop for today?" Paul asked.

Mary shook her head. "I'm not finished just yet," she said. There was one last story she needed to tell—and a story it was, more fiction than fact. She'd told it this way for so long now, she could hardly remember the truth anymore. "You see, in the end it was my courage—or maybe my foolhardiness—that cost me my husband. In July of 1964, I was up in the tower when I spotted a man swimming off Kiss River and it looked like he was in trouble. I ran down to the beach and went in after him. He was unconscious when I got to him and he was just too heavy for me and I started getting crampy and going under. Caleb somehow caught sight of us and he came out to the beach and jumped in after the both of us. He managed to get us out, too, but it was all too much for him. He was sixty-four years old. His heart stopped right there and he fell out on the sand."

"I'm sorry," Paul said. "That's a tragic way to lose someone."

Mary stared into space for a moment. "Yes, it was," she said finally. She raised her hands and dropped them on her thighs. "Well, that's all for today, I think."

"Of course." Paul turned off his recorder and stood up. "Thanks again for your help," he said.

Mary watched him walk down the sidewalk to his car. The stories had tired her, made her remember things about herself she did not like to remember. And they made her remember a night long ago when she'd told those same stories to Annie.

She'd known Annie for only a few months then, but already she'd felt a comfort with her young friend she'd never known with another soul, woman or man. She had never had the luxury of a close woman friend, and despite the difference in their ages, she knew she could confide in Annie. She could tell Annie the truth.

It was on a cold evening in January, one of many evenings Annie had spent with her back then. Alec was struggling to make a go of a veterinary practice, but the Outer Banks were so sparsely populated that he spent most of his time treating farm animals on the mainland. He was gone often in the evenings, pulling calves, or tending to colicky horses, leaving Annie with entirely too much time on her hands.

She had Clay with her, as she often did, on that night in January. Clay would totter around the keeper's house, talking gibberish and getting into things. Finally, Annie would lay him down in the small upstairs bedroom, setting pillows at the edge of the bed so he couldn't roll out. She'd sing to him in that soft, dusky voice that made Mary's heart ache as she listened to her from the chair by the fire. She could picture the room—the room that had been Caleb's as a child—filling with light every few seconds. Annie might pull the shades and draw the curtains, but the light would still find cracks to pass through, and Clay would slip under its hypnotic spell. He would be asleep quickly, more quickly than he ever fell asleep at home.

After a bit, Annie would come downstairs, where Mary had the fire raging and the brandy poured. For the first time in a decade, she had a bond with another human being.

Most nights were filled with Annie's chatter, and Mary loved listening to her, to the way she mangled words with her accent. She spoke about Alec, whom she adored, or about Clay, or the stained glass. Sometimes she spoke of her parents, whom she had not seen since meeting her husband. Her phone calls to them were not returned, she said; the letters she wrote them were sent back unopened. Once, she and the baby flew to Boston, thinking her parents surely wouldn't pass up an opportunity to see their only grandchild. But she was turned away at their front door by a maid who told her she was no longer welcome in her parents' home.

She worried about Alec, driving so much in foul weather, working outdoors with huge animals. His hands were chapped and raw most of the time, she said, and once his arm had been broken by the ferocious contractions of a cow in labor. She'd gone with him a few times, but he'd said it was no place for her—and certainly no place for Clay—out in the middle of nowhere with the wind tearing at their clothes and stinging their eyes. So she ended up with Mary at the keeper's house more often than not.

As Mary felt the brandy warm her on this particular night in January, it was her voice, not Annie's, that echoed softly in the living room of the house. The fire crackled and spit, and the ocean roared not far from where they sat, but Mary's voice was calm and steady. She could not have said why she poured it all out to Annie that night, that secret side of herself she had never bared to a soul, except that with Annie's silence, her loving gaze, she spurred her on.

Mary told her the same tales she'd told Paul Macelli—how

she had come to be known as the Angel of the Light through her acts of kindness and caring.

"You remind me of myself in that way, Annie," she said. "You have such a good heart. You go out of your way for folks, with never a thought for yourself." She sipped her brandy, feeding herself courage. "But that's where the comparison ends. You're really a far better person than I ever was. A far better woman."

Annie looked over at Mary, her cheeks flushed from the heat of the fire. "Why do you say that?"

Mary shrugged as though what she had to say next was easy for her. Insignificant. "I had another side of me," she said, "a side I never let anyone see." She looked hard into Annie's eyes. "You see, my husband was the best husband a woman could ask for. Patient and kind and strong. But it never felt like enough for me. Maybe it was the isolation. I don't know. But I wanted to..." She pursed her lips, staring into the orange flames in the fireplace. "I wanted to have other men," she finished.

"Oh," said Annie. "And so...did you?"

"Only in my imagination." Mary shut her eyes. "It was the strongest feeling. The strongest yearning. I'm ashamed to talk about it."

"You don't need to be ashamed. Lots of women think about..."

Mary brushed away whatever Annie was about to say with a wave of her hand. "Not the way I did. I'd lie awake at night, imagining being with other men I knew. I'd be with Caleb...*lying* with Caleb...and I'd imagine he was someone else. Sometimes I couldn't do my work. I'd go up in the tower to polish the lens, and instead I'd sit on the gallery and daydream. I'd wave to the sailors and imagine them returning at night, coming up on the beach to look for me. I used to think about hanging a red cloth from the gallery to let them know when Caleb was gone, when I would be...available. Once I went so far as to buy the cloth."

Mary felt the color in her cheeks. How foolish she must seem, a seventy-three-year-old woman talking this way.

"But you never hung the cloth?" Annie prodded.

"No."

"It must have hurt," Annie said, "wanting to do something so badly, but thinking that you couldn't."

Mary smiled. Annie *did* understand. "That was the *real* reason I wanted to work with the Life Saving crew," she said, "so I could be around the men, so I could feel the excitement of what might happen. But I'd come to my senses every time I came close to going through with it. What right did I have to be so dissatisfied, I'd ask myself? To want more than I had?"

Mary tapped her fingertips against the glass. She would have liked a cigarette, but she knew it distressed Annie when she smoked.

"Sometimes I'd force myself to stop thinking about other men, but it felt like I was cutting off a leg or an arm, it was so much a part of me. We'd go to church and even *there* I couldn't stop myself from imagining. People would say that Caleb wasn't good enough for me. Some of them would ask me what I saw in him, me being such a fine woman—so they thought—and Caleb just a plain man, solid and steady." She shook her head. "He was a thousand times better than I was."

Annie leaned forward in her chair, the fire throwing gold light into her long red hair. "You are far too hard on yourself, Mary."

Mary took a full swallow of the brandy, thick as honey as

it warmed her throat. She looked up at Annie. "It was my nonsense that killed Caleb," she said.

"What do you mean?"

Mary shook her head. "Even at sixty-three, my head was still full of that schoolgirl silliness. No one knows this—the truth of how Caleb died, I mean. Can you keep it here in this room?"

Annie nodded.

"Well, there was a fisherman who'd taken a shine to me when I was in my thirties, and we talked off and on over the years, teasing each other about how one day we'd do more than just talk. Finally he persuaded me. He told me I wasn't getting any younger, and I thought to myself, He's right. It's got to be now or never. We planned to meet one evening when Caleb was away for the night. Only Caleb didn't go. So when I went out to the beach, it was to tell Chester it was off for that night. He didn't believe me, I guess. Thought I was weaseling out of it. So he started kissing me right there on the beach, and I was fighting him, afraid Caleb might be up in the tower. And that's just where he was. He saw it all and thought Chester was attacking me. He flew down those stairs and out to the beach and started sparring with Chester. Two gray-haired old men." She shook her head. "They ran into the water, pounding each other in the waves. Caleb was just too old for that. They *both* were really, two old coots going at it like a couple of wild Indians. By the time Caleb drug himself out of the water, he couldn't get his breath and he just fell dead at my feet." Mary winced, recalling her initial disbelief that Caleb was dead, and, later, her self-loathing.

"A few weeks after Caleb was buried, Chester had the nerve to ask me to marry him. Needless to say, I turned him down. I'd finally found the cure for my wicked imagination, but it came with a big price tag."

Mary talked a while longer and felt a change in Annie, a silent drawing in. Annie had wrapped a shawl around her shoulders and now she pulled it tighter, staring at the flames as Mary spoke. After a while, they heard a faint cry from upstairs.

"He's awake," Annie said softly.

Mary nodded. "You'd better get home."

Annie rose, letting the shawl drop from her shoulders to the chair. Her footsteps were heavy and slow on the stairs. Mary listened to her reassuring Clay with her cooing and clucking.

When Annie returned downstairs, she handed the baby to Mary, resting him on the older woman's lap. "Let me stoke the fire for you before I go," she said, as she always did. She stirred the wood for many minutes, and Mary watched the flames leaping around her head. When Annie finally stood up and lifted Clay into her arms, her face was flushed, and heat poured from her hands and her clothes. She didn't meet Mary's eyes, and for a moment Mary wished she had not spoken so freely. She had risked too much in telling her. She had risked this special friendship.

Mary stood up and walked Annie out onto the porch. Annie turned to face her, hugging her baby close to her against the wind.

"Mary," she said. "Your longings...your fantasies...they didn't make you a bad person."

Mary breathed in a quick, silent sigh of relief. "No," she said.

She watched as Annie walked through the darkness toward her car. Halfway there, she turned back to Mary, and in a voice so soft she could barely be heard over the sound of the sea, said, "Mary. We are more alike than you know."

For just a moment she was illuminated by the beacon of

the lighthouse and Mary saw the shine of her cheeks, the stubby hand of her child coming up to touch her chin, and then the world was dark again.

CHAPTER THIRTY-SIX

Paul's car was in her driveway when she got home from the emergency room that Thursday evening. Olivia felt a disconcerting mix of joy and anger. Should he be allowed to come and go as he pleased? What if he'd walked into the room that was to become the nursery and discovered the crib?

Inside, the house smelled of garlic and olive oil and wine, familiar smells of Paul's cooking. She walked into the kitchen, and he smiled at her from the stove where he stood over the skillet, a fork in his hand like a conductor's baton and his old red smock apron tied around his waist.

"Hi," he said. "I thought I'd surprise you. Scampi." She had told him once, long ago, that his scampi was an aphrodisiac.

She set her purse on the table. "Could you let me know before you come over in the future?" she asked. "I don't think it's fair for you to...just walk into this house."

He looked surprised that her first words were critical, that she did not appear overjoyed to see him. "I'm still paying my share of the mortgage," he said.

"It isn't a matter of money," Olivia said. "You left me. I'm entitled to at least some privacy." She wanted to look down at her stomach to see if there was any telltale bulge.

He rested the fork on the counter and turned to face her. "You're right. I didn't think. I just wanted to surprise you. I wanted to do something nice for you, Liv. Do you want me to leave?"

She shook her head. "No." There was a surly edge to her voice that surprised her as much as it did him. "I want you here," she said, gently now. "Let me change my clothes."

Once in her bedroom, she put on the one pair of jeans she could still fit into and a long, baggy T-shirt. Soon, she was going to have to give in and buy maternity clothes. People would know then. *Paul* would know.

She returned to the kitchen. "Can I help?" she asked.

"It's ready," he said. "Just sit down." He gestured toward the kitchen table. She still had not replaced the table in the dining room.

She sat down, and Paul set a plate covered with fat garlicky shrimp and wild rice in front of her. He was a natural cook, one of those people who could turn out stunning meals without ever consulting a cookbook. He had always been far more domestically inclined than she. Their plan had been for him to stay home with their children while she went off to work.

He tilted the bottle of wine above her glass but she held her hand over the rim. "No thanks," she said, and he looked down at her in surprise. "I've stopped for a while."

"Why?"

It would have been easier just to let him pour the wine. She didn't have to drink it.

"Cleaning up my act a little," she said.

He sat down. "I was hoping to get you drunk tonight so I could seduce you."

She felt her cheeks redden and looked down at her plate.

Paul leaned across the table to rest his hand on her arm. "You're really furious with me," he said.

"You've done some things that are hard for me to simply overlook."

He nodded and leaned back again, pouring wine into his own glass. "I guess I can't blame you," he said, "but I did something today you'll approve of."

"What's that?"

"I donated two of Annie's stained glass panels to the library."

She was truly surprised. "You did?"

He sipped his wine. "I can't just quit cold turkey, Liv, but I'm working on it. The two underwater scenes in my living room. Plus the little oval in my car. The librarian was thrilled. Those panels are probably worth a lot more now that she's...been gone awhile." He pursed his lips for a second, as though acknowledging that Annie was dead still hurt him. "I'll get rid of the rest of them in a week or two, as soon as I find the right place to donate them."

"That's good, Paul." She tried to smile at him. "Whether we get back together or not, you really need to put her behind you."

He flushed. "What's your game, Olivia? Are you playing hard to get or what?"

"I'm not playing any game at all." She looked at him, at the warm hazel eyes behind his glasses. "This is hard for me, trying to figure out how to behave with you. I'm terrified of trusting you, of letting my guard down around you. I'm afraid to commit myself to you when I'm not certain you can make a commitment yourself."

"It worked before," he said. "We just need to get away from here."

She ate in silence for a moment before looking up at him again. "I've received a job offer," she said. "At Emerson Memorial." She described the call from Clark Chapman, as a smile spread across Paul's face.

He set down his fork and leaned across the table again, reaching for her hand this time. "It's a sign, don't you think? A good omen. We move to Norfolk and start over. Start fresh. Tell him yes, Liv. Call him tonight and tell him."

She shook her head, but left her hand in his. "I need to think about it," she said. "I can't jump into it that quickly."

After dinner, he served her strawberry mousse in the living room, she on one end of the sofa, he on the other. She wondered how she could get him out of the house before he tried to touch her. He seemed to have no intention of leaving. He took off his shoes and raised his legs to the couch.

"I reread *The Wreck of the Eastern Spirit* last night," he said.

"Why?"

"I wanted to feel good. To feel close to you. It made me remember how I felt during those days when I was watching you in the ER and falling in love with you. Remember how wonderful it was?"

She laughed, bitterly. "It was wonderful all right. Forty-two people died. It was fantastic." She regretted her nastiness as soon as she spoke. Paul stood up, a hurt expression on his face.

"You've changed," he said. "You've become...callous."

"I'm just afraid to feel close to you."

"What do I have to do, Liv?"

"To start with, you could get rid of the rest of the stained glass."

He nodded. "All right. Tomorrow."

An arrow of fear passed through her, as she realized that

even if he got rid of every tangible trace of Annie O'Neill, she still might not want the man who was left. "You made love to her," she said softly. "That's what hurts most. You can't throw that away, and I'm always going to feel like that memory is still with you. If we ever make love again, I'll think you're comparing me to her. Or imagining I'm her."

He looked stricken. "Oh, no." He sat down, pulling her into a hug. "I love you, Liv," he said. "I just lost my mind for a while, that's all." He tipped her head back to kiss her and she allowed the kiss, hoping she would feel something tender for him, but she wanted to bite his lips, to draw blood. She pulled her head away, awkwardly crossing her arms low on her stomach to keep him from touching her.

He leaned away from her. "I guess you don't want me to stay over tonight."

She shook her head.

"I miss you."

She looked up at him. "I miss you too, Paul," she said. "I've missed you very, very much, but I need to be sure of you. Call me again when you're over Annie, when you're one hundred percent finished with her."

She stayed seated on the sofa while he put on his shoes. Then he leaned over to squeeze her knee, not speaking to her, not looking at her, and she knew he was close to crying, that once outside, he would probably let the tears come.

She unzipped her jeans when he left, sighing with relief as she drew in a long, deep breath. She rested her hand on her gently rounded stomach and her eyes went to the phone. It was ten-thirty-five and it hadn't rung.

Alec.

She had to admit the truth to herself: She was four months pregnant by a man she was no longer certain she loved, and she loved a man still in love with his dead wife.

Chapter Thirty-Seven

The baby moved.

Olivia lay very still. Outside her bedroom window, the first pink light of dawn tinged the sky above the sound.

Again. The flutter of bird wings.

It stopped. She closed her eyes, resting her hands flat on her stomach. Had she dreamt it? No. Too real. Paul's child.

When she opened her eyes again, the sun was full in the sky, and her room glowed with a clear yellow light. She lay still for a moment, struggling to feel...*something*. Maybe it *had* been a dream. Maybe her imagination.

She had the day off, and so she was still in her robe a half hour later when she picked up the *Beach Gazette* from her front deck and carried it into the kitchen. She'd been tense reading the paper lately, but this morning there should be some mention about Jonathan leaving the ER.

Indeed, there was an article on the front page. Jonathan Cramer had resigned suddenly, the article stated, offering little else except a recap of the mud-slinging situation, leaving readers to draw their own conclusions about his sudden retreat. This would not be enough, she thought, disappointed.

She was halfway through her blueberry muffin when she came to the letters to the editor. She would skip over them today. There were usually half a dozen furiously assailing her for her handling of Annie's case. She was about to turn the page when she noticed the name at the bottom of the last letter. Alec O'Neill. She flattened the page out again and began to read.

I'm writing to express my dismay over the negative press and outpouring of hostility toward the Kill Devil Hills Emergency Room physician who tried to save the life of my wife, Annie Chase O'Neill. As a veterinarian, I'm well aware of human fallibility in making medical decisions, particularly under the stressful conditions a trauma case presents. Even so, I feel assured that the best possible decisions were made in Dr. Simon's attempt to save Annie's life. I understand the anger and readiness to find a scapegoat in the community because I've experienced those feelings myself in the last seven months, but those of you familiar with Annie's generous spirit know that she never would have maligned another person or harmed his or her career. If you trace Annie's activism in the Outer Banks, from her advocacy for the Kiss River Lighthouse keeper, Mary Poor, to last year's fight to keep a child with AIDS in school, you will see that she focused her energy only on helping others. Attacking the very person who risked her own well-being to try to help her is not a way to honor Annie's memory.

It's ludicrous to think that a woman with two holes in her heart could possibly have survived the forty-five-minute flight to the nearest trauma center. Dr. Simon went beyond the call of duty to treat Annie in our local emergency room rather than wash her hands of the case by transporting her to Emerson and certain death on the way. She deserves our support, not our criticism.

Olivia read the letter through twice, her muffin forgotten. She called Alec's house, but hung up when the message on his machine clicked onto the line. She called the animal hospital, panicking when the receptionist answered the phone. She couldn't interrupt him. Surely he was busy.

"I'm concerned about my cat," she said, realizing as she spoke that she had learned this idiotic ruse from Alec himself when he'd told her he'd made an appointment to see his father-in-law. "I was wondering if I could get in to see Dr. O'Neill today?"

"What's the problem?"

"Some skin thing." Olivia glanced into the living room where Sylvie was curled in a contented ball on the rattan chair. "She's been scratching madly for a few days now."

"We could squeeze you in around four-thirty this afternoon. Can you make it?"

"Yes."

"And your name?"

"Mrs. Macelli." She was afraid the name Olivia Simon would be too familiar to this young woman.

There were three dogs in the waiting room at the animal hospital, and Olivia wondered if she was being fair to Sylvie to use her this way. The cat trembled in her arms, but she settled down once they had been moved into the small examining room to wait for Alec. This was a mistake, Olivia thought. She would not appreciate anyone intruding on her work time with personal business. She had her hand on the doorknob when Alec walked in from the opposite side of the room.

"Olivia?" He looked puzzled. He also looked extremely well. It had been nearly a week and a half since she'd seen him, and his tan was deep in contrast to his white coat. "What's wrong with Sylvie?"

"Absolutely nothing." Olivia smiled foolishly. "I'm sorry, Alec. I just wanted to thank you for writing that letter to the *Gazette,* and there was no answer at your house, and I felt like I couldn't wait."

Alec smiled. He reached out to take Sylvie from her arms and the little cat curled up against his chest while he stroked her ears. "You didn't need to make up an excuse to see me," he said.

She felt the color rise in her cheeks. This was so adolescent. "Your letter was such a relief to me," she said.

"You haven't deserved the public flagellation."

"Well, whether your letter changes that or not, I just wanted you to know how grateful I am that you wrote it. That you feel that way. I wasn't sure."

Alec looked down at Sylvie. She had started to purr, kneading her paws against the chest pocket of his white coat. "I'm sorry I haven't called you," he said, raising his eyes to Olivia again. "I'm sure you could have used some support the past week or so, but..."

"Don't apologize. I didn't come here to get an apology out of you."

"We were just getting a little too close for comfort," he said.

"You must think I'm horrible for letting it go as far as I did."

"Of course I don't think you're horrible. You haven't had

much of a husband lately, and I haven't had anything in the way of a wife, and... Are you upset about it?"

"Embarrassed."

"Please don't be."

"Well, let me get out of here so you can see your real patients." She reached for Sylvie, but he turned to keep the cat in his own arms.

"Not so fast," he said. "Tell me how you've been."

The crush of news from the past week raced through her mind. Paul was back; Paul was remorseful. But she didn't want to talk about Paul.

"I was about to start on a new stained glass project," she said, "but Tom's decided he can't teach me any longer."

"How come?" Alec's eyes suddenly widened. "Not because of the situation with Annie, I hope."

She nodded.

Alec scowled. "That's ridiculous. I'll talk to him."

"No, please don't. It might just make things worse."

"What will you do about the stained glass then? Are you going to quit?"

"I'll find a way."

"I've got a bunch of Annie's old tools just sitting at the house. Why don't you stop by and see if there's anything you need."

The relief she felt was completely out of proportion to his offer. "Did she have a grinder at home?"

Alec nodded. "Come over tonight." He handed Sylvie back to her, and his fingers lightly brushed the top of her breast through her blouse. "My kids will probably be there. They can chaperone us. Keep us out of trouble."

She set her hand on the doorknob, but made no move to leave. She looked up at him. "I felt the baby move early this morning."

He narrowed his eyes at her, and she couldn't read his expression. She shrugged, embarrassed. "I just wanted to tell someone," she said as she opened the door.

"Olivia," he said, and she turned to look back at him. "It's Paul you should be telling."

CHAPTER THIRTY-EIGHT

He took Annie's tool case and grinder down from the hall closet for the first time in seven months and carried them into the den. The case was made of soft brown leather, dusty now, and the sight of it was enough to start an aching deep in his chest. He dusted it off with a tissue before opening it, spreading it flat on Annie's old work table, steeling himself against the odor, an old, familiar smell, at once metallic and soapy, a mixture of Annie and her tools.

The tools were not in their little pockets but strewn haphazardly as she had left them. Pliers, glass cutters, rolls of solder and copper foil, three-bladed scissors. He was a little embarrassed to have Olivia see this, to see exactly what Annie had been like in all her disorganized glory. He could picture her sitting here in the den, continually fighting with her hair as it slipped into the path of her work. She'd grab the bulk of it in her hands, give it a twist, and toss it over her shoulder, an unconscious gesture he had seen in her since the first night they'd met. It would be good to have Olivia take some of these tools. Put them to good use. Give them a second life.

"Why do you have Mom's tools out?"

He turned to see Lacey standing in the doorway. Her hair was growing out into an almost comical pattern of red and black.

"Olivia Simon's going to borrow some of them."

"Why can't she use Tom's?"

"Tom's not teaching her right now, and she's to the point where she needs some tools of her own, so I suggested she come over to take a look at Mom's."

"She's coming *here?*" Lacey's eyes widened. "I thought you weren't going out with her anymore."

"I was never actually going out with her, Lace. She's a friend. I explained that to you." He wondered if asking Olivia over here tonight had been a mistake. He could have dropped the tools by her house. The memory of the last time he was in her living room slipped through his mind, and he shook his head. Well, he could have dropped them by her office.

The doorbell rang, and he heard Clay sprint down the stairs to answer it. He'd spoken to Clay earlier, letting him know Olivia was coming over and why, and Clay had responded with an uncharacteristic, positively lecherous grin. Now Alec heard Olivia's voice in the living room, and Clay's laughter in reply.

"I have to study," Lacey said, taking the door that led to the kitchen rather than the living room so she would not have to pass Olivia on her way upstairs.

Olivia and Clay walked into the den.

"I'm on my way out, Dad," Clay said.

Alec looked up from the tools. "Okay. Have fun."

Olivia smiled as she watched Clay leave the room. She had on a pink and white striped jersey dress with a dropped waist.

It was perfect for her, he thought, the perfect camouflage. No one would know if she were pregnant or not.

"Your son looks so much like you it's uncanny," she said, setting her tote bag on the chair by the work table. She dropped her eyes to the tool case. "Wow."

"These are kind of a mess," he said. "Annie would have been able to pick out what you need without any problem, but I can't begin to tell you."

"I think I can figure it out." She glanced up at him and caught sight of the oval windows through the door of the den. "Oh, Alec." She walked into the living room and over to the windows. It was still light enough outside so that the designs and their colors were vivid. "They're beautiful."

He stood next to her. "Your husband was fascinated by them, too."

"Was he?" She pointed to the one in the center. "Why did she make this one clear?"

"She didn't. I broke it a couple of weeks ago. I threw a glass at it."

She looked at him. "I didn't think you were the violent type."

"I'm not, ordinarily."

"Were you aiming at someone?"

"At God, I think." He laughed, and she touched his arm.

"Tom's trying to put it back together for me." He started toward the kitchen and she followed him. "Want some iced tea?"

"Please."

He took the pitcher of iced tea out of the refrigerator and got two of the green tumblers from the cabinet over the sink. "So, how's Olivia doing?" he asked as he poured. "I really haven't spoken to you since the day we went to Norfolk."

She took the tumbler of iced tea from his hand and leaned

back against the counter. "Olivia's a little mixed up." She looked down at her glass, and her eyelashes lay dark and thick against her cheeks. "A lot's happened since the last time we spoke, besides the fact that I've become the least popular physician in the entire Outer Banks."

He shook his head. "I'm sorry."

"But the other day I got a job offer. The medical director of Emerson Memorial called to offer me a position in their trauma unit up there."

"Really?" Alec set his tea on the counter, a little disconcerted. "Will you take it?"

"I don't know. I like it here, and I'll like it even better if I begin to feel trusted as a physician again. But there's more." She sipped her tea, looking at Alec over the rim of her glass. Her eyes were the same green as the tumbler. "Paul returned from his trip a changed man," she said. "He's being very attentive."

Alec's smile froze into place. "That's great, Olivia. Is he over...old what's-her-name?"

"I don't think he's completely through with her, but he's really trying. The thing is, he says the Outer Banks make him think of her, so he wants us to leave here."

"Ah. So the job in Norfolk would be ideal." He picked up his tea and started walking toward the den. "I thought it was just a matter of time," he said. He wanted to know more. He wanted to know if they'd made love. "Have you told him about the baby?"

"Not yet."

They were back in the den, back above Annie's old tools, and the scent of them was almost too much for him. "That would do it, Olivia," he said. "Paul's such a romantic. If you told him..."

"I can't yet."

364   DIANE CHAMBERLAIN

"He's going to figure it out soon enough, don't you think?"

She glanced down at the pink and white stripes of her dress where they hung loosely across her stomach. "Is it that obvious?"

"Not at all to look at you. But...I'm assuming...he's your husband..." He felt himself flush, and Olivia smiled.

"I'm not letting him get that close to me yet."

"Ah, I see." He moved her totebag from the chair to the table. "Well, have a seat."

The phone rang just as she sat down, and Alec picked it up on the desk. There was an emergency at the animal hospital, the operator told him. A dog with a burr in its eye.

He hung up and explained the situation to Olivia, smiling. "You're the one who talked me into going back to work," he said. "Take your time with this." He gestured toward the tools. "I don't know how long I'll be, so don't feel as though you have to wait. Lacey's here if you need anything."

He went upstairs to tell Lacey he was going. She was sitting on her bed, books and papers spread out in front of her and nerve-jangling music blaring from her radio. "I have an emergency at the hospital," he said. "Olivia's still here looking through Mom's stained glass stuff. I'm not sure when I'll be back."

"Dad," she whined. "Make her *go* if you're not going to be here."

"She just got here, Lace. I'll call if I'm going to be really late."

He left her room before she could offer anymore objections and walked down the stairs. He stopped in the doorway of the den, but Olivia was deep in concentration. A sheet of graph paper lay on her lap, and she bent over it, her lower lip caught pensively between her teeth and a pair of Annie's scissors in her hand. He left without disturbing her.

Outside, the damp, salty air enveloped him. It covered Olivia's Volvo with a faint mist, glistening in the pink light of the sunset, and he ran one hand down the warm, slick side of the car as he walked out to the street and his Bronco.

Lacey appeared in the doorway of the den. Olivia looked up from the tool case and was struck by how much older she looked than fourteen. "Hi, Lacey," she said. "How are you?"

"Okay." Lacey slipped into the den and pulled her father's chair from his desk to the work table. She sat down, hugging her knees, her bare feet up on the chair. It was difficult to look at her hair and keep a straight face. "What are you working on?" she asked.

Olivia thought for a minute. She couldn't tell her she was making a panel for a nursery—she could hardly let Lacey know she was pregnant when her own husband had no idea. "I'm making a panel for one of the bedrooms in my house," she said.

"Do you have a design? Mom always worked with a design."

"Yes." Olivia lifted the graph paper from her lap to the table. The hot-air balloons probably looked simplistic to Lacey after the kinds of things her mother had done. But Lacey smiled.

"That's nice," she said, and she sounded sincere. She watched as Olivia pulled a roll of copper foil from the case. "You never told my father you saw me in the emergency room," she said.

"No."

"Why not?"

"Because what happens in the ER is confidential." She looked up at Lacey. "How's your friend doing? The boy who used crack?"

Lacey wrinkled her nose. "He wasn't my friend. He's gone back to Richmond. He was an asshole, anyway."

Olivia nodded. "He took a major risk with his life."

"He didn't care. Some people's lives are so screwed up they don't care." Lacey picked up one of the spools of solder and began playing with it. Her fingernails were chewed short; a couple of her fingertips looked red and sore. There was a scared little girl behind that tough facade.

"Your father told me you have a collection of antique dolls," Olivia said.

"Yeah." Lacey didn't look up from the solder. "My mother used to give them to me for my birthday."

"Could I see them?"

Lacey shrugged and stood up, and Olivia followed her up the stairs. They passed what had to be the master bedroom, the bed a beautiful four poster covered by a quilt. Lacey opened her bedroom door and Olivia could not prevent a laugh. "Oh, Lacey, this is great," she said. There was a shelf going three fourths of the way around the room on which delicate, ruffle-dressed dolls sat, wide-eyed and prim. Above and below the dolls were posters of rock groups—young men in leather pants and vests, bare-chested, long-haired, earringed and insolent-looking.

Lacey smiled at her reaction.

"Is this room a good description of you?" Olivia asked.

"What do you mean?"

"I mean half angel, half devil."

"Three quarters devil, I guess."

Olivia saw the textbooks on her bed. "What are you studying?"

Lacey groaned. "Biology and Algebra."

Olivia picked up the biology text and skimmed through the pages, remembering how enthralled she'd been by her own biology book in high school, how she had read the entire book by the end of the first week of school. "What are you up to?"

"Genetic stuff." Lacey picked up a worksheet from her bed. "This is my homework. I *hate* this stuff. I'm supposed to make this pedigree study into some kind of chart or something. It doesn't make any sense to me."

Olivia looked at the sheet, then at Lacey. "Let me help you with it."

The girl colored. "You don't have to."

"I'd like to." She kicked off her shoes and sat down on Lacey's unmade bed. "Come on," she said, patting the space next to her.

Lacey joined her on the bed, and Olivia talked about Punnett squares and dominant and recessive genes until Lacey had a grasp of the concepts herself. They were comparing earlobes and trying to roll their tongues—which she could do, but Lacey could not—when they heard Tripod barking downstairs.

"Anybody home?" A female voice called out from the kitchen.

"It's Nola," Lacey said. She raised her voice. "We're up here, Nola."

They heard footsteps on the stairs and then an attractive blond woman dressed in a dark blue suit appeared at Lacey's door, holding a pie in her hands. This was the woman who had "designs" on Alec, Olivia remembered.

"Oh, excuse me, Lacey," Nola said. "I didn't know you had company."

Olivia leaned forward on the bed and lifted her hand to shake Nola's. "I'm Olivia Simon," she said.

"She's a friend of Dad's," said Lacey.

"I'm just helping Lacey with her biology." Olivia felt as though she owed Nola some sort of explanation. "Alec had an emergency at the animal hospital."

"Oh." Nola looked a little lost. She patted a strand of her pale hair back into place above her ear. "Well, I brought this pie over for him. You'll let him know, Lacey?"

"Sure."

"I'll leave it on the kitchen counter. It's his favorite, strawberry rhubarb."

Nola left the room, and neither of them spoke again until they heard the back door open and close downstairs. "She's my best friend's mother," Lacey said. "I think she wants to be *my* mother, too."

"You mean...marry your father?"

"Exactly."

"Would you like that?"

"Yeah, about as much as I'd like to die in a stampede of elephants."

Olivia laughed.

Lacey drew little circles in one corner of her homework paper. "I don't think my father will ever get married again."

"No?"

Lacey shook her head. "He loved my mom too much."

Olivia looked up at the row of dolls. They were a little spooky-looking, with their huge, watchful eyes. "It's nice you have all these dolls to help you remember her," she said. "Do you have a favorite?"

Lacey stood up and walked over to the other side of the room to take one of the dolls—a beautiful black-haired toddler—down from the shelf. She plopped back on the bed and set the doll in Olivia's lap just as they heard a car pull into the driveway.

"Dad's home," Lacey said, but she didn't move from Olivia's side.

"Olivia?" Alec called from the den.

"We're up here," she and Lacey chorused, and Lacey giggled.

They heard him climb the stairs and then he appeared in the doorway, unable to mask his surprise at finding the two of them looking like lifelong buddies, Lacey clutching her biology book, Olivia with the raven-haired doll in her lap.

"Well... Hello." He smiled.

"How's the dog?" Olivia stood up.

"She'll survive."

"Olivia helped me with my homework."

"And Nola stopped by with a pie for you," Olivia said. She had a pleasant sense of belonging in this house, standing there in bare feet, a welcome guest in the bedroom of Alec's daughter. "It's your favorite," she said. "Strawberry rhubarb."

"She worked her fingers down to bloody stumps hulling those strawberries just for *you,* Dad."

"Don't be catty, Lacey," Alec said, but there was laughter behind his smile. He looked at Olivia. "Want some pie?"

"Yes." Lacey jumped up from her bed. "I'll go cut it."

Alec looked after Lacey as she raced out of the room and down the stairs. He turned to Olivia. "She's acting like a human being," he said. He ran his fingers down her arm and squeezed her hand before letting go. "What did you do?"

Olivia's mood was light on the way home. She was humming when she pulled into her driveway, smiling as she walked up the front steps. But she nearly stumbled over an enormous floral arrangement sitting on the deck. The fragrance of the flowers filled her head as she knelt down to read the card propped up against the vase.

Wish you were here so I could give these to you in person. I love you, Liv,

Paul

CHAPTER THIRTY-NINE

The committee meeting was again at Alec's. Paul would have preferred to meet almost anywhere else, but he supposed this was some sort of test to see if he could be in Annie's home without succumbing to his memories again. He had given away two more of the panels that morning, leaving him with just the large one in his bedroom and a few smaller panels scattered throughout his house. This was probably the most difficult thing he would ever have to do in his life, but it was absolutely necessary. He couldn't go on the way he'd been.

He'd watched Olivia on the news the night before. A reporter was interviewing her in front of the emergency room, discussing the shift in public opinion since Jonathan Cramer's resignation and the publication of Alec's letter in the *Gazette.*

"What we should learn from Ms. O'Neill's case is how critical the need is for better emergency services in the Outer Banks," Olivia said. "Whoever becomes director of the Kill Devil Hills Emergency Room should work toward that end."

She looked very pretty, very sexy in her scrubs, and she

sounded bright and in perfect command of the interview. Seeing her in that forum inspired him to write a poem about her—how long since he'd done that?—which he left in an envelope in her mailbox on his way to the meeting.

Now in Alec's kitchen, he had a sense of déjà vu. Alec was filling baskets with pretzels and popcorn, while Paul poured wine into glasses on a tray. Only this time, he intentionally avoided looking at the blue cloisonné horse on the shelf in front of him.

He glanced over at Alec. "Olivia mentioned that you and she had speaking engagements in Norfolk a few weeks ago."

"Yes," Alec said. He was taking napkins out of the cupboard above the sink. "She did a great job."

"Thanks for writing that letter to the *Gazette*," Paul said. "It's really made a difference for her."

"It was the least I could do."

Paul tipped the bottle over another glass. "I know these last few months have been hell for Olivia," he said. "I haven't been much help to her. I have a lot of making up to do."

Alec had started toward the living room with the baskets and napkins, but now he stopped and looked at Paul, a smile coming slowly to his lips. "Take good care of her, okay?" Then he looked past Paul's head, and Paul turned to see a girl in the doorway between the kitchen and den. "This is my daughter, Lacey," Alec said. "Lacey, this is Paul Macelli. Dr. Simon's husband."

Alec left the kitchen then, and Paul smiled at the girl. She was tall and fair-skinned, with Annie's blue eyes, but her hair was half black and half red. She eyed him as she took a handful of pretzels from the bag on the counter.

"You're the one who got my age wrong." She leaned back against the cabinets.

"What do you mean?" he asked, setting the bottle down. Her hair was absolutely ridiculous.

"In that article about my mother in *Seascape*. You said I was twelve, but I was actually thirteen. I'm fourteen now."

Paul frowned. "I could swear your mother said you were twelve."

She popped a few pretzel sticks in her mouth. "Everybody got on my case about it," she said, chewing. "I mean, *twelve,* God." She gave him a narrow-eyed look of disapproval as she swept past him. "I'm going out, Dad," she called into the living room, and then she disappeared through the back door.

Paul stared after her. He would swear on a stack of Annie's stained glass panels that she'd said her daughter was twelve.

He was anxious during the meeting. Alec talked about the progress being made on moving the lighthouse. The track was already under construction, he said, and the site was swarming with engineers and surveyors.

Paul barely listened. Mothers didn't get confused about the ages of their children. His mother could rattle off all six of their ages at any point in time. There was only one reason he could think of for Annie to have lied about Lacey's age.

The moment the meeting was adjourned, he thanked Alec and nearly ran out to his car. He drove home in a trance, and once inside his little cottage, began digging through the box of tapes he kept in the spare room. He found the three tapes he'd made of his interviews with Annie and carried them, along with his tape recorder, into his bedroom. He sat down on the bed and skimmed through the tapes with the fast for-ward button until he found the one he was after. Drawing in a long breath, he leaned back against the wall and pushed the play button.

He could hear the clinking of silverware from another

table in the Sea Tern. Then his question. "Tell me about your kids."

"Well..." Annie's voice cut through him. It had been so long since he'd heard it. A little husky, and here, a little halting. He thought now that he understood the reason for the slow, careful manner of her speech. "What would you like to know about them?"

"Everything," he said. "I assumed you didn't name them Rosa and Guido."

Paul winced now as he heard himself ask that question, as he remembered the angry look she'd shot him.

"You promised not to..." Annie said, and he interrupted her quickly.

"I'm sorry. Okay. Clay and...?"

"Lacey."

"Lacey. How old are they?"

"Clay is seventeen, and Lacey is twelve going on twenty."

Paul pressed the rewind button. "...twelve going on twenty," Annie repeated.

Paul turned the machine off and closed his eyes. There was only one reason she'd lie. He thought of the girl in Alec's kitchen, the girl with Annie's eyes, Annie's red hair pushing out the black, and once he started thinking, he couldn't stop.

He'd received his master's degree in communications when he was twenty-four years old. He suddenly saw his future mapped out in front of him, and there was a gap in it only one person could fill. He hadn't seen Annie in over four years, not since she'd left him at Boston College to set out on her own. He could not look for a job, he couldn't commit himself to his own future until he'd made one last attempt to include her in it.

He moved to Nag's Head in late spring, renting an efficiency apartment two blocks from the water. He auditioned
for a role in *The Lost Colony,* a play on the history of the
Outer Banks that ran each summer in Manteo, and easily
won a part. He found Annie and Alec's number in the phone
book, but didn't call. Instead, he drove to the address listed in
the directory—a little soundside cottage in Kitty Hawk. He
arrived very early in the morning and parked a block away,
sipping coffee, his eyes on the house. Around seven, he saw
a tall dark-haired man leave the cottage and get into a beat-
up truck standing in the driveway. That had to be Alec. Paul
felt a mixture of hatred and envy as he watched him drive
away. He waited another fifteen minutes to be sure that Alec
hadn't forgotten anything he would need to return for. Then
he started his car and drove the block to the cottage, studying himself in the rearview mirror. He hadn't changed much
in the past four years. He still wore the same wire-rimmed
glasses. His hair was a little shorter, but that was about it.

He got out of the car and walked quickly to the front
door, knocking before he had a chance to change his mind.

Annie opened the door. For a moment, she didn't seem to
recognize him. Then she let out a squeal of delight. "Paul!"
She threw her arms around him and he hugged her, laughing
with relief. Behind her, a toddler sat quietly watching them
from a playpen. Even from this distance, Paul could see the
pale blue eyes that he imagined belonged to his father.

He hugged her a fraction of a second too long, and she
pried herself free, her face flushed. "Oh, Paul," she said,
holding one of his hands in both of hers. "I'm so sorry for the
way I handled things when we split up. Really, it's *haunted*
me. I'm so glad I've got this chance to tell you." She pulled
him into the room. "Come in, come in." She stood away

from him, her hands on her hips, her eyes appraising. "You look *good,* Paul," she said.

"So do you." She looked incredible.

"This is Clay." She reached into the playpen and pulled the little boy up into her arms.

Paul touched the boy's hand. "Guido," he said softly. Annie looked confused, and then she laughed.

"I'd forgotten about that. And Rosa, right?"

"Yeah," he said, feeling terribly sad. "Rozer."

Annie looked at her son. "Can't you say hi, precious?"

The little boy buried his head in the tempting hollow of her throat.

"He's sleepy," she said to Paul. She laid Clay back in the playpen and covered him with a light blanket.

"What are you doing here?" she asked. "Are you on vacation? Who are you with?" She didn't wait for any of his answers. "I'd like you to meet Alec—unless that would be difficult for you." She plunked down on the sofa. "Oh Paul, how did you ever forgive me? It was terrible, the way I did it, but I was so mixed up with my father being sick and all."

"I know." He sat down next to her on the sofa and took her hand. "I'm here at least for the summer," he said, and there was a discernible crack in her smile that he tried to ignore.

"The whole summer?" she asked.

"Yes. I've got a role in the *Lost Colony* play."

"That's wonderful," she said, but her voice was uncertain.

"And I'm staying in a little apartment in Nag's Head."

"Are you alone?"

"Yes."

And then she seemed to catch on. "Why here? Why the Outer Banks?"

"Why do you think?"

She shook her head and pulled her hand away. "I'm *married*, Paul."

"Happily?"

"Very. I've changed a lot. I'm not so...*wild* anymore. I'm a wife and a mother. I have responsibilities."

"Well, could I see you sometime? Just two old friends meeting for lunch?"

"Not if you want something more from me." She had folded her arms across her chest and shifted away from him on the sofa.

"I'll take whatever you're willing to give me, Annie. If that means one lunch during the entire summer, then that's what I'll settle for."

He wrote his number on a notepad on the coffee table, hugged her once more and left, determined to wait at least a week before he tried to see her again.

The play was his salvation. His role was demanding, and the camaraderie of the cast absorbed his time during the day when they were rehearsing. At night, though, he couldn't stop himself from imagining Annie in her little cottage, contentedly bedding down with her tall, pale-eyed husband.

The Lost Colony opened on a steamy night that made the heavy costumes intolerable, but the crowd of tourists was enthusiastic. Paul felt good when he stepped backstage for intermission. He had just taken a bottle of Coke from one of the backstage hands when he spotted Annie by the dressing rooms, her eyes fixed on him. One of the male cast walked past her, reaching out to touch her hair. She smiled at the stranger, absolving him, as though she understood he had been powerless to keep his hands to himself.

Paul walked over to her. "I'm glad to see you," he said.

"You were *spectacular*, Paul," she said. "These tights really do something for you." She touched his hip, and a jolt of electricity shot through him. He looked into her eyes and saw that she knew exactly what she was doing.

"Annie..."

"Shhh." She touched her fingertips to his lips. "After the show," she said, smiling. "There's a place we can go. A friend of mine's. You can follow me. I have a red VW convertible. You'll see me."

He did see her, sitting cross-legged on the hood of the VW under a light in the parking lot. He declined the invitation to go out with the rest of the cast to celebrate. Instead, he followed Annie closely in his own car, hypnotized by the way the air lifted her red hair in the darkness. They drove over the bridge into south Nag's Head and turned onto Croatan Highway, and he hugged the rear of her car for the next fifteen miles. Where the hell was she taking him? She finally pulled into a sidestreet, where she stopped her car and turned around to call to him.

"Park here and get in my bug," she said.

He obeyed her and had barely shut the VW's door before she made a U-turn and was out on the road again.

"Where does your friend live?" he asked as they passed through Southern Shores.

"You'll see."

They drove another few miles between dark, shadowy dunes. Paul hunted for a light on the horizon, but aside from the swath of light cut by Annie's headlights, they were in total darkness.

"Where's Alec tonight?" he shouted against the wind.

"Working on the mainland. He does a lot of work with farm animals these days."

"Where's your little boy?"

"Neighbor." The car bounced in a rut and he held on to the armrest.

"Where the hell are we going, Annie?"

She pointed into the darkness ahead of them and in a moment he saw a flash of light.

"A lighthouse?"

"The Kiss River Light. We're going to visit the keeper."

He fell silent, surrendering. He would let her be his guide.

She turned onto a dirt road and they bounced through the darkness for a few minutes before coming to a clearing. Annie pulled into a small area of packed sand close to the light and closer still to a large white house. Paul got out of the car and looked up at the dizzying tower above them just as the beam of light brushed over his eyes.

"It's phenomenal," he said.

"I know. Come on." She took his hand and they walked up the brick path to the house. Lights were on in a few of the downstairs windows, but he couldn't get a good look inside.

Annie knocked briskly on the door and after a moment it was opened by a tall, elderly woman dressed in a long dark skirt and white blouse.

"Come in, Annie," she said, stepping aside.

"This is Paul Macelli, Mary. Paul, this is Mary Poor, the keeper of the incredible Kiss River Lighthouse."

Paul nodded solemnly at Mary. What the hell was going on? Were they going to spend the evening talking with an old woman?

Annie kissed Mary's cheek. "Do you need anything, sweetie?"

"No, no." Mary waved her hand. "You go on up."

Annie grabbed Paul's hand and led him up the stairs to a small bedroom with a quilt-covered double bed. She closed the door and swung around to kiss him. "Oh, God, Paul you were so beautiful on that stage. I'd forgotten." She started unbuttoning his shirt, but he caught her hands.

"Annie, I don't understand..."

"Shh." She pulled her own blouse, still buttoned, over her head and took off her bra. "Hold me," she demanded, and he held her, the sun-filled scent of her hair achingly familiar, and the bare skin of her back warm against his hands. Every few seconds the white light of the beacon flooded the room, catching the red of her hair, the creamy whiteness of her skin, but otherwise it was too dark to see.

"Touch me," she whispered. *"Everywhere."*

He stripped off his own clothes and laid her down on the bed to carry out her order. Her body was more alive than he'd ever known it, and he did not like to think that he owed her new fervor to her husband. She wrapped her legs around him. "I need you close to me, Paul," she said. "As close as you can get."

He slipped inside her, briefly aware of the bed creaking, of the old woman downstairs, but surely Mary Poor knew what was going on up here. He put the sounds out of his mind and focused on Annie. He was with her, inside her, after all this time. She rocked with him, but when he slipped his hand between their bodies to touch her, she shook her head.

"Doesn't matter," she said.

He was insistent. Persistent. And finally she came, the spasms of her body propelling him over the edge.

He started to roll off her after a few minutes, but she held him fast. "No," she said. "Stay close."

"I love you, Annie."

"Hold me."

"I am. I'm right here." He concentrated on holding her tightly enough to still the trembling in her body. Then he did roll off her, halfway, so that when the light filled the room he could see her face. "I don't understand this arrangement, Annie," he said. "The old woman..."

"Mary. She knows I need to see you. I visit her a lot when Alec works. I've told her all about you."

"Can we meet again?"

"We *have* to. Afternoons might be better. Can you make it in the afternoon?"

"Of course. But let's meet at my apartment."

"No," she said. "It has to be here. People might see me with you. A lot of people know me, Paul. I'm too familiar a face. Way out here, we're safe."

And so it continued. It was Paul's most blissful summer, with the possible exception of the summer he had spent with her in New Hope. She would let him know in the mornings, by hanging a red scarf from the corner of the little front deck of her studio, whether she could meet him that day. She asked him never to come into the studio—she didn't want to have to explain his presence to Tom Nestor.

A few times during the summer, he would see her from a distance with Alec. He spotted them together in the grocery store, and once throwing a frisbee on the beach. She laughed a lot with Alec, the dimples deep in her cheeks, and Paul would not be able to get the image out of his mind until he was with her again.

The scarf hung from the deck more often than not. Annie and Paul met at Mary's house and spent the afternoons in the upstairs bedroom. They spoke often of the past, but never of the future. He was careful of his demands on her, but by the middle of the summer he could no longer tolerate the clandestine nature of their relationship. He wanted more.

"I think it's time you left Alec," he said one afternoon, after they had made love.

Annie's head shot up from his shoulder. She looked stunned by his request. "I'll never leave him, Paul. *Never.*"

"Why not? I could support you better. And Clay. I'd adopt Clay. I could..."

"Don't talk that way!" She sat up. "You said you'd take whatever I was willing to give. This is it."

"But I love you."

"And I love Alec."

For the first time, he was furious with her. He pushed her aside and got out of the bed, but she quickly grabbed his arm. "I'm sorry, I'm sorry, I'm sorry. I didn't mean that to sound the way it did."

"You hardly ever see him. He's gone all the time, leaving you with a baby and..."

"Because he worries about money. It's the only kind of work he can get right now. If we wanted to live in a city, he wouldn't have to work so hard, but we want to live here. So that's the price we have to pay."

He looked down at her. "You're *using* me."

"*No.*"

"You are. I'm just filling a need when Alec's not around, right? Good old Paul."

"Don't say that." She began to cry, reaching for him, wrapping her arms around his waist, and he put the argument aside.

She held his hand when she walked him out to his car that night. "I'll never leave Alec, Paul. If you want me on those terms, you can have me. Otherwise, don't come here again."

Of course he continued to come, enduring the knowing nod from Mary Poor, the telltale creaking of the bed. He never lost the hope that Annie would reconsider. *The Lost Colony* play closed on Labor Day and he got a job as a waiter in Manteo. It was hardly what he'd been trained to do, but he could not leave. Then things suddenly, abruptly changed.

For several days in a row, the red scarf did not appear. He worried she was ill, or angry with him, and he had made up his mind to call her when he spotted the scarf hanging once again from the corner of the deck. He drove to Kiss River that afternoon, greatly relieved.

"She's upstairs," Mary Poor said when she met Paul at the door. Paul could never look this woman squarely in the eye. He felt disliked by her, his presence merely tolerated. "She's not feeling well."

Annie looked terrible. Her hair was tied back and the skin around her eyes was puffy. There were lines in her face he had never noticed before, at the corners of her mouth and across her forehead.

"What's wrong?" He touched her forehead for fever, but it was cool. "Poor Annie. You look awful." He tried to draw her into his arms, but she pulled back.

"We can't make love," she said, sitting down on the bed.

"Of course not. Not with you feeling so bad."

"No, that's not it." She was agitated. Hot-wired. "We need to talk."

Alec must have found out. This would be it, then. Things were finally coming to a head and in the next few minutes, Paul would learn either that he had won or lost.

Annie kneaded her hands together in her lap. "I can't do this anymore," she said.

"What's happened? Does Alec know?"

"No. I'm just...disgusted with myself." With that she jumped up from the bed and ran down the hall to the tiny upstairs bathroom. He heard her getting sick. He thought then of how she wouldn't let him use rubbers because they could interfere with his pleasure. She'd assured him, though, that he didn't need to worry, that she had replaced the strange bevy of birth control devices she'd used in college with a diaphragm. Exactly how foolproof was a diaphragm?

Her skin was damp and gray when she returned to the room. He forced her into his arms, and she clung to him, weeping.

"You're pregnant." He spoke quietly into her hair.

"No!" She pulled away, wild-eyed. "Please Paul, just leave the Outer Banks and don't come back."

"I won't go. Not until you tell me what's wrong."

"Please." She started sobbing, far too loudly. She pleaded with him to leave, all the while clutching his arm. He heard Mary Poor's slow footsteps on the stairs, and he grabbed Annie's hands to try to calm her as the door swung open.

Mary walked into the room, and suddenly she did not seem the old woman Paul had thought her to be. She stood very tall, a light burning in her blue eyes. "Get out now and stop upsetting her," she said. She sat down on the bed and pulled Annie's head against her shoulder, and Annie clung to her. "Hush, Annie. You'll make yourself sick again." Mary looked up at Paul. "Get out," she said, her voice soft now, not unkind, and Paul felt his own tears starting.

"Don't I have a right to know why?"

"Leave now," Mary said.

Annie clung more tightly to Mary, drawing her knees up, trying to fit all of herself into the protection of the old woman's arms, and Paul had no choice but to leave. He returned to his apartment, where he packed up his belongings. He left the Outer Banks that same night, after taping his family's address and phone number in Philadelphia to the door of Annie's studio.

Twelve going on twenty. Of course she'd been pregnant. What other reason could there have been for her secretive behavior and his sudden dismissal? If she had told him during the interviews that Lacey was thirteen, he would have done the math. He would have figured it out.

Oh, Jesus. He opened the drawer of his night table and pulled out the stack of photographs the *Gazette* photographer had taken of Annie at her home. There was one of Lacey and Clay that had not been used in the article, and Paul stared hard at the young girl. She looked like Annie. He needed to see her again. He needed to search her face for traces of himself and his sisters. He needed to know for certain, and there was only one person alive who could tell him.

He inserted another tape into the recorder and pressed the play button, leaning back against his headboard, eyes closed, to lose himself in Annie's voice.

CHAPTER FORTY

Olivia was moved by the poem. It reminded her of the poems he'd written about her in *Sweet Arrival*. She could imagine Paul reading it to her in the voice he saved for his poetry, the voice that could still other voices in a crowded room and draw all eyes to him. She remembered the pride she'd felt listening to him at readings, and the wrenching sort of love his carefully crafted verses elicited in her. No wonder he missed Washington. There were many people there who appreciated his gift.

The doctor's office had called her earlier that afternoon to tell her that the results of the amniocentesis were completely normal—and that she was carrying a boy. Only when she felt the wild surge of relief wash over her did she realize how frightened she'd been that something might be wrong. Now she could think of little except the baby.

She read the poem over several times, even though the first reading had convinced her that the old Paul, the Paul she had married, had returned. It was time to tell him about the baby. Time to accept him back, to do her best to forgive him and begin moving toward the future again.

She dialed his number, but reached only his answering machine. Alec had mentioned a lighthouse meeting tonight. Most likely he was there.

"I love you, too, Paul," she said, after she heard the tone on his machine. She rested her hand on her stomach. "Please call me when you get in. I have something important to tell you."

She worked on the stained glass panel at the kitchen table, waiting for the call, which never came. The phone didn't ring at all until after she had gone to bed, and she knew before she picked it up that it would be Alec, not Paul, on the line.

"Was Paul at the meeting tonight?" she asked him, after a few minutes of small talk.

"Yes. He was first to leave, though. Seemed like he was in a hurry."

"He wrote a poem about me and left it in my mailbox. I think he might truly be ready to come home and start over."

There was a short silence on Alec's end. "I think you're right. He said something about needing to make up to you for the hell he's put you through."

"He said that?"

"Something like it."

She smiled. "I've decided to tell him about the baby."

"It's about time."

"It's a boy, Alec. I got the amnio results and everything's fine."

"That's wonderful." He sounded a little flat.

"Paul's always talked about having a son. He grew up surrounded by females." She sighed. "I'm nervous about telling him, though. Once I do, there's no turning back. I left a message on his machine to call me."

"Oh," Alec said. "Then I'd better let you go."

"No. Please don't get off." She bit her lip as another few seconds of silence filled the line.

"I spoke to Tom," Alec said finally. "He said to tell you he's sorry for his behavior, and he'd like to teach you again."

"Really? That's great. Thank you."

"Do you have all the tools you need now?"

"I could use a soldering iron. Did Annie have one?"

"A couple of them."

She closed her eyes. "Oh, God. Paul will have a fit when he finds out I'm doing stained glass."

"Why?"

She clutched the phone. She had slipped, forgetting that Alec did not know the whole story. "I'm not a very artistic person. He'll think I'm wasting my time."

"It's not a waste of time if it's something you enjoy."

There was one more brief, loaded silence before Alec spoke again. "If you don't see Paul tomorrow night, you're welcome to come over here and use the soldering iron or whatever."

"All right," she said, but she knew she would see Paul. She *had* to. Suddenly she wished she could split herself in two. "Oh, Alec," she said, "you've been the very best of friends."

"You sound as though we'll never see each other again."

"No, I don't want that to happen." She knew it would have to be that way, though, that she would have to cut herself off from Alec. It was too dangerous. She might confide in him when she should be confiding in Paul. She might compare Paul to him, and there was enormous risk in doing that, in the possibility she would find Paul lacking. At some point she would have to break away from Alec completely. But not right now. Not yet.

"Alec?" she asked. "Are you in bed?"

"Yes."

"What are you wearing?"

He laughed. "I'd better get off the phone and let your husband take care of you."

With that he was gone. Olivia lay awake a while longer, waiting for the phone to ring a second time, but it never did.

Paul didn't call the following day either. She wondered if he might have lost her number at the ER, but even if he had, it wouldn't be that difficult to track her down. By late afternoon she was certain his machine had somehow eaten her message and she left another. Then she tried his office.

"He's not in today," the receptionist said. "He took it as a personal day."

When seven o'clock came with still no word from Paul, she drove over to Alec's.

"Maybe he had to go out of town?" Alec suggested. He was sitting at his desk, sorting slides of the lighthouse for a presentation he needed to make the following week, while Olivia studied the directions for the soldering iron resting on the work table.

"That must be it," she said.

"Hi, Olivia."

Olivia turned to see Lacey in the doorway. She wore short denim shorts and a tank top that hugged her small breasts and exposed her midriff.

"Hi, Lacey. How did you do on your biology homework?"

"I got an A. Or I guess *you* got an A."

"Not true," Olivia said. "You did the work yourself. I just got you pointed in the right direction."

"I'm going out." Lacey looked at her father.

Alec glanced up from his slides. "Have fun," he said.

Lacey turned to leave the room, the denim snug across her small, rounded bottom.

"What time does she need to be in?" Olivia asked, when she heard Lacey close the front door behind her.

Alec shrugged. "When she stops having fun."

Olivia stared at him. "What if that's five in the morning?"

Alec turned around at the challenge in her tone. "It won't be. She rarely pushes her limits."

"But how do you know she's okay? I mean, how do you know when to start worrying?"

"Haven't we had this discussion before?" he asked. "Lacey's learning to make her own choices and take responsibility for her own actions."

"Is that Alec talking or Annie?" Olivia knew by his stunned expression that she'd taken the debate one step too far. She sighed. "I'm sorry, Alec. It's really none of my business."

He stood up and pulled a book from the shelf by the window, and he touched Olivia's shoulder lightly before sitting down again. "It's all right," he said. "You don't understand. I think it's impossible for anyone who didn't know Annie to understand."

It was slow in the ER the next day and Olivia spent much of the morning obsessively checking her answering machine at home, but there were no calls from Paul. She tried his work number again, and this time the receptionist told her he'd called in sick. She called his home, beginning to worry. There was no answer, but there was little she could do about it until she got out of work.

She had just finished stitching the eyebrow of a hang gliding novice when Kathy told her there was a girl in the waiting room who was asking to see her. Olivia walked into the reception area to see Lacey leaning against the waiting room wall, thumbing through a magazine.

"Lacey?"

Lacey looked up at her and stood at attention, her arms stretched out to the sides. "See?" She grinned. "I'm alive and well. Dad said you were worried about me going out last night, so I thought I'd stop by and show you I'm still in one piece."

Olivia smiled. "How did you get here?"

"Bicycle."

"Where's your helmet?"

Lacey rolled her eyes. "God. You're, like, obsessed with this safety stuff. Chill out."

Olivia opened the door between the waiting room and the reception area. "Come in," she said. "Would you like some coffee?"

"Coffee?" Lacey followed her into the hall. "I'm fourteen, Olivia. Aren't you afraid it'll, like, stunt my growth or something?"

Olivia led Lacey into her office, where she poured them each a cup of coffee and closed the door.

"So," she asked as she watched Lacey empty three packets of sugar into her cup, "did you have fun last night?"

Lacey shrugged and took a sip of her coffee. "I guess."

"What time did you get in?"

"I don't know." She held up her left arm. "I don't own a watch. My mother didn't believe in them."

"How can someone not believe in watches?"

"You didn't know my mother."

"How do you ever get up for school on time?"

"I just do. My mother said you develop an internal clock, and it's true. Every once in a while I'd be late, but none of my teachers ever cared. They knew my mother." She dumped another packet of sugar into her coffee, then returned her eyes to Olivia. "My father has to take Clay to Duke on Friday. He has to stay overnight, so he wants me to stay at Nola's, but I was wondering if..." She wrinkled her nose. "This is, like, *forward* of me, but could I stay with you while he's gone?"

Olivia was taken completely off guard. "You hardly know me, Lacey."

The girl blushed. "Well, but, I mean, you're nice and I don't think my father would mind since obviously you're not going to let me run the streets until morning, right?" She grinned again and Olivia could not help but smile back. It would interfere with any time she might have to spend with Paul, but she could not possibly turn down a fourteen-year-old girl who needed something from her.

"I'd be delighted to have your company," she said. "But we need to clear this with your father first."

"I'll tell him."

"You'll *ask* him."

Lacey giggled.

"Let him know it's fine with me, Lacey."

She drove to Paul's cottage as soon as she got out of work. His car was in the driveway, but there was no answer when she knocked on the door. That worried her. She tried the knob, and the door opened easily. She stepped into the living room, pulling the door closed behind her. The house was quiet.

"Paul?"

There was no response. The room looked bigger without the stained glass in the windows. It relieved her to see the clear windows, the deep evening blue of the ocean in the distance.

She walked into the kitchen, calling his name, her apprehension mounting. Where was he? She headed toward the bedrooms in the back, not certain which was his and a little afraid of what she might find.

The door to the first bedroom was open, and when she stepped inside she was immediately surrounded by color. One of the windows was still hung with a stained glass panel of two vivid tropical fish. The double bed was half made, the spread and sheets twisted into a knot. Two pillows were propped up against the headboard. The room smelled of food, an odd mixture of scents. A half-full carton of Chinese food sat on the night table, next to a wine glass tipped on its side and an empty bottle of chardonnay. A dirty plate and crusty fork rested on the top of a pizza box in the middle of the floor.

Olivia's pulse began to race. Something was certainly wrong. Paul was fastidious. Except for the stained glass, she would never have guessed this was his room. Could he have rented it out to someone else?

Then she saw the pictures strewn across the bed. Annie, all of them. Olivia picked one up and scowled. She was sick of that face, the red hair, the pert nose, the pale freckled skin. A tape player rested in the midst of the photographs. There was one tape inside it and two stacked next to it. She picked one of them up and read the label. *Interview with ACO, #1.* She shook her head. Three tapes and dozens of pictures for a simple magazine article. She hit the play button on the machine. There was laughter, then a few seconds of silence before Paul asked:

"Do you ever use the lighthouse in your work?"

"Kiss River?" Annie asked, her voice surprising Olivia with its depth, its huskiness. "I have, yes. It's a very special place to me. It's where I first met Alec."

Olivia heard Paul sharply suck in his breath. "I didn't know that," he said.

"Yep. I sure did."

There were another few seconds of silence.

"Jesus, Annie, how could you—"

"Shut *up*, Paul."

Olivia turned at the sound of the front door opening. She quickly stopped the machine and stood waiting by the bed. She heard him walk through the house. He must have seen her car; she would not be a complete surprise to him. In a moment he stood in the doorway of the bedroom. He did not look well. His green T-shirt was wrinkled and stained; his hair hung limply over his forehead. The sunlight filtering through the stained glass turned his face a sickly yellow, and she wondered how she must look, bathed in the colors of this room. He stared at her for a long moment, then looked down at his bed.

"Your car was here, but there was no answer when I knocked," she said. "The receptionist at the *Gazette* told me you were sick, so I was worried when you didn't come to the door."

He cleared his throat. "I was walking on the beach," he said.

She gestured toward the bed. "I see you've been having a little...Annie fest."

His lips started to move, but he didn't answer.

"You're not through with her." Her voice was soft, and she heard the weariness in it. "You're never going to be through with her."

"I just need a little more time," he said.

Olivia stalked past him, walking briskly through the hall and the living room, not stopping until she reached her car. She rammed the keys into the ignition, and her tires squealed as she pulled out onto the road. Once on the highway, though, she slowed down, focusing on the heavy summer traffic, reminding herself that inside her slept her normal, healthy son.

CHAPTER FORTY-ONE

Lacey was talkative as she helped Olivia make up the bed in the guest room. A little nervous, Olivia supposed. A little high-strung, which for some reason reminded her of the old lighthouse keeper's advice to feed Paul kale and sea salt.

Alec had called her the other night to apologize for Lacey's forwardness. "I'm sure you'd rather spend the time with Paul," he'd said, and Olivia, who had just returned from Paul's cottage, fought tears as she described what she had found there.

"He's *wallowing* in the memories of her, Alec," she said. "He's surrounded himself with take-out food so he doesn't have to budge from his room and he can stare at her pictures for hours on..."

"Olivia?" Alec had interrupted her.

"What?"

"Please give me your permission to talk with him."

"*No.*"

"He sounds like he needs help."

"I know, but he won't take it."

"What if I just stopped by his house on the pretense of talking about the lighthouse?"

"Please don't, Alec."

Alec had finally given in, but not before he told her that he wished things were settled between her and Paul. "For my sake," he'd said, his voice quiet, solemn, "if not for yours."

Lacey tucked the blanket into the foot of the bed. "I'm thinking of getting my nose pierced," she said, looking over at Olivia, waiting for a reaction. Her red and black hair was beginning to remind Olivia of a checkerboard. "What do you think?"

"I think it sounds revolting." Olivia lifted the spread from the armchair to the bed. "Would your father let you?"

"My father will let me do anything I want, haven't you figured that out yet?"

The bed was finished and Olivia looked across it at her house guest. "Let's go get some dinner," she said. "You can choose the restaurant."

Lacey selected the Italian Palace, a family-style restaurant with pasta dishes that, to Olivia's surprise, were better than passable. "This is my favorite restaurant," Lacey said, her eyes half closed in a mock swoon over the taste of her lasagna. Then she suddenly sat up at attention. "My father gave me the money to pay for this," she said.

"Well, that was nice of him, but hardly necessary."

"He said I'm not supposed to take no for an answer."

"Okay." Olivia smiled and lifted her water in a toast. "Here's to your father."

Lacey grinned as she tapped her water glass against Olivia's.

"I have a stained glass lesson with Tom tomorrow morning," Olivia said. "Would you like to go with me?"

"Sure," Lacey said. "I haven't seen Tom since I cut my hair. He's gonna freak."

"Tom doesn't have much room to criticize someone else's hair, does he?" Olivia asked.

Lacey laughed. "I guess not." She took a swallow of her Coke. "What's your sign?" she asked.

"My sign?" Olivia frowned, confused for a moment. "*Oh*. Aquarius."

"Oh, that's *excellent!*"

"Is it?"

"Yes. I'm a Cancer. You know, the sign of the crab. A *water* sign, just like yours. You fit in really well with my family. My mother thought water signs were best. My father's a Pisces—"

Like Paul, Olivia thought.

"—and my mother was an Aquarius, just like you, only she was a *weird* Aquarius and you're—well, it's hard to believe you're the same sign. Clay, unfortunately, is a Scorpio. I don't know *how* that happened. But anyhow, when my mother discovered she was pregnant with me and realized I'd be a water sign, she celebrated by taking a long swim in the ocean, even though it was, like, almost winter and the water was really cold."

Olivia smiled as Lacey paused to take another bite of her dinner. This kid was wound up.

"My mother wanted more children than just us two," she continued, "but she said it wasn't fair to the environment. She believed that two people should only replace themselves, or we'd all run out of food and water. She and Dad talked about adopting some handicapped kids, but they never did. I'm sooo glad." Lacey rolled her eyes again. "I'm very different from my mother. I'm really selfish. I didn't want to have

Keeper of the Light 399

to share my parents with another kid. Sharing them with Clay was bad enough."

"Do you and Clay get along?"

"I mostly ignore him. He's been a complete prick this summer because now I, like, go to some of the same parties as him and he hates having his little sister around."

Olivia frowned at her. "You *are* a little young to be hanging around with graduating seniors."

Lacey smirked at her. "Graduating seniors," she said, mimicking Olivia's voice. "God, Olivia, sometimes you sound like an old lady."

"Well, that's what Clay is, right? A graduating senior? When do those parties get over?"

"What do you mean?"

"I mean...I understand you don't have a curfew. So what time do you usually get home?"

"One or two."

"*Lacey.* That's outrageous. You're fourteen years old."

Lacey gave her an almost patronizing smile. "It's *summer,* Olivia, and summer school's over. It's not like I have to get up early in the morning or something."

"Did you stay out that late when your mother was alive?"

Lacey poked her fork in the lasagna. "I...no," she said, pursing her lips. "I didn't need to, but she wouldn't have gotten on my case if I did."

"What do you mean, you didn't need to?"

Lacey looked up at her. "I *liked* being home then. My parents were *fun.* My friends practically lived at my house, they liked being around my parents so much." She tightened her lips again. "You should have known my father then. He was really funny, and he always had ideas for what we should do. Once he got us all up in the middle of the night and drove us to Jockey's Ridge and we climbed out on the dunes in the *dark* and then laid down in the sand to watch the stars. He was always doing things like that. He used to take me and my friends up to Norfolk for concerts. Nobody else's father would ever do that. He was so cool." She looked out the window at the darkening parking lot. "He's changed so much. That's part of why I stay out late. I don't like being around him, 'cause he reminds me of how fucked up everything is." She looked over at Olivia. "Excuse me for saying that. Fucked up, I mean."

Olivia sat back from the table. "I want to buy you something," she said.

"What?"

"A watch."

"You're *kidding*." Lacey smiled uncertainly. "Why?"

"Someone your age should have one."

"My mother..." Lacey stopped herself. "Could I pick it out?"

"Yes, but it comes with a contingency."

"What's a contingency?"

"Something you'll have to do in order to get the watch."

Lacey looked intrigued. "What?"

"You'll have to call me every night at midnight, no matter where you are, to let me know you're okay."

"What?" Lacey laughed.

"That's the contingency." She knew she was undermining Alec, but perhaps Alec needed to be undermined.

"I'll wake you up," Lacey said.

"Yes, you probably will, but I'll fall back to sleep knowing you're safe."

Lacey stared at her solemnly. "Why do you care whether I'm safe or not?"

Olivia studied her own plate for a moment. Her manicotti had hardly been touched. She looked up at Lacey again. "Maybe you remind me a little of myself at your age," she said.

"Well," Lacey set down her fork and looked coyly at Olivia. "There's a contingency about me calling you."

Olivia smiled. "What's that?"

"I'll call you if you'll stop working at the Battered Women's Shelter."

Olivia was touched by the unmistakable concern behind Lacey's request. She shook her head. "I like working there, Lacey. You don't need to worry about me. I'm not very much like your mother. I don't think I would ever have the courage to risk my own life to save someone else's."

They stopped in the drug store on the way back to Olivia's to look for a watch. Lacey tried on six or seven, carefully avoiding those in the higher price range, before finally selecting one with a glittery silver face and a black band adorned with silver stars.

They picked up a carton of ice cream and, once back at Olivia's, built themselves huge banana splits. They carried the sundaes into the living room, where they sat cross-legged on the floor to eat them. Sylvie curled up, purring, in Lacey's lap as they dug into the ice cream. Every minute or so, Lacey raised her left hand to study her watch.

"I can't believe that you're fourteen years old and that's the first watch you've ever owned," Olivia said.

"If my mother was buried, she'd be rolling over in her grave right now."

Olivia cut off a chunk of banana with her spoon. "Was she cremated?" she asked.

"Yes. Well, of course, first every little speck of her that could be used by someone else got donated. Then what was left was, you know..." Lacey waved her hand through the air.

"Clay and my father threw her ashes into the ocean at Kiss River."

Olivia shuddered, the imagery almost too much to bear.

"I didn't go to the funeral," Lacey said.

"How come, Lacey?"

"I wanted to remember her like she was alive." Lacey's face suddenly darkened. She looked down at Sylvie. "I don't get why some bad people can live to be a hundred years old and someone as good as my mother dies so young. She hated— what do you call it when you go to the electric chair?"

"Capital punishment?"

"Yeah. She hated that, but if I could see the man who killed her and I had a knife, I'd slice him up." Her hands were balled into fists as she spoke, and Sylvie opened one eye to observe the unprotected bowl of ice cream on the floor in front of her. "I could do it," Lacey said. "I could kill him and I wouldn't ever feel bad about it."

Olivia nodded, certain Lacey meant what she said.

"I keep imagining what it must have felt like to have that bullet shoot into her chest."

"Your father told me you were with her when it happened. That must have been terrible for you."

Lacey poked at her ice cream. "I was standing right next to her," she said. "I was in charge of the green beans, and she was in charge of the salad. This man rushed in and started yelling at this lady in the food line. Mom could never stay out of *anything.* She stepped right in front of the lady and said, 'Please put the gun away, sir. It's Christmas.' And he shot her. *Bam.*" Lacey winced, and a visible shiver ran through her arms. "I keep seeing her face. Sometimes when I'm in bed at night, that's all I can see. Her eyes got real wide, and she made a little noise like she was surprised, and where the bullet went through her shirt, there was a little speck of blood." She looked up at Olivia. "I blamed you for a long time, because I was so sure she'd be all right. I couldn't imagine her dying. Then it seemed like once you got to her you made things worse. My father says you didn't, though. He said you tried really hard to save her."

"He's right, Lacey. I did."

Lacey ate a few more mouthfuls of her sundae before looking at Olivia from under a shock of two-toned hair. "Do you like my father?" she asked.

"Very much."

Lacey lowered her eyes again. "He's been a little better since he started...being friends with you," she said. "He used to walk around like he was sleepwalking or something. He hardly ate anything and he didn't care what he wore and all his clothes got too big for him. He looked like a scarecrow, and all he'd do was carry around his stupid old pictures of the lighthouse and stare at them every chance he got. He used to sleep with my mother's old *sweatshirt*."

Olivia ached for Alec. She was embarrassed by this glimpse into his dark and private world.

Lacey took the last bite of her banana, now swimming in a chocolate soup. She swirled her spoon around in the bowl with her stubby fingers and their chewed-off nails. "I met your husband at the lighthouse meeting the other night," she said, glancing up at Olivia. "I thought he looked kind of nerdy. No offense."

Nerdy? Olivia supposed that a forty-year-old man with wire-rimmed glasses and cerebral good looks would probably strike a fourteen-year-old as nerdy. "No offense taken," she said.

"Do you think my father's handsome?"

Olivia shrugged noncommittally, aware she was treading on dangerous ground. "I suppose so."

"My mother used to say he was *hot*. They were, like, completely and totally in love." Lacey moved her wrist back and forth, her watch sparkling in the light from the table lamp. "Nola would love to get into my father's pants," she said, her eyes glued to the watch.

"That's sort of a crude way to say she's interested, don't you think?"

Lacey grinned at her. "I think you're kind of *prissy*. I mean, if you think my father's handsome, don't you sometimes wonder what it would be like to go to bed with him?"

Olivia struggled to keep the shock from her face. She leaned forward and spoke slowly. "What I think, or what your father thinks, or what Nola thinks about that sort of thing is very personal, Lacey. It's not your place to speculate about it."

Lacey's eyes filled in a half-second's time. "I'm sorry," she whispered, crimson patches forming on her throat and cheeks. Her lower lip trembled in a way Olivia could not bear to watch. She set her own bowl of melting ice cream on the floor and moved forward to take Lacey in her arms. Lacey held her tightly, her delicate shoulders shaking with her sobs.

"It's okay." Olivia kissed the top of her head. She remembered being held this way a lifetime ago by Ellen Davison, who never pressed her to tell her why her body ached and bled, who never once suggested she go home again. She remembered the surprising strength in Ellen's slender arms, strength that let her know she could finally turn her burden over to a grown-up who would keep her safe.

"My father hates me," Lacey wept.

"Oh, no, honey. He loves you very much."

"There was just that drop of blood on her shirt, so I told him she'd be all right. He was so scared. I wasn't used to

that—I'd never seen him look scared of anything before—
and I kept telling him not to worry. He *believed* me that she'd
be okay. He blames me for getting his hopes up."

Olivia felt Lacey's fingers on her back, clutching her
blouse.

"It could have been me," Lacey said. "I was thinking the
same thing my mother was, that I should just jump in front
of that lady. Maybe he wouldn't have shot a kid, and then
nobody would've gotten hurt. I think my father wishes I'd
been the one to get shot. For the longest time after she died,
he wouldn't talk to me. He wouldn't even *look* at me and
he kept calling me Annie." Lacey stiffened beneath Olivia's
arms. "I *hate* him. He forgot my birthday. He thinks Clay's so
wonderful because he's smart and got a scholarship to Duke
and everything and I ended up having to go to summer
school. He just wishes I'd go away. He wouldn't care if I
stayed out all night long. He wouldn't care if I never came
home."

Olivia's own tears fell onto Lacey's hair. It was *Alec* Lacey
should be talking to, Alec who needed to listen to his daughter's fears. It was Alec who needed to tell her he would do
everything in his power to make her world right again.

But Alec wasn't here, and perhaps he wasn't capable of
listening to Lacey yet, or of coping with fears that were so
much like his own, and so Olivia pulled Lacey more tightly
into her arms. She would hold her for as long as it took to
make her feel safe.

CHAPTER FORTY-TWO

Every time Alec glanced in the rearview mirror, he saw the lines across his forehead and the deepening crow's feet at the corners of his eyes. Maybe he'd spent too much time in the sun over the last few years. Or maybe he was just getting old.

He'd left Clay at Duke a few hours earlier and he had not expected the crush of emotion that came over him as he said good-bye to his son. There had been other students in the lounge of Clay's dorm, and so he'd hugged him loosely when what he really wanted to do was hold him close. It had been a one-sided hug, anyway. He could see the light in Clay's eyes, the excitement he felt at this new chapter in his life about to begin. Only one of them was truly going to miss the other.

He turned off the highway into Manteo as a light rain started. He drove past the Manteo Retirement Home in its blue splendor, thinking that he should call Mary Poor soon to arrange the tour of the keeper's house. On a whim, he turned the car around and stopped in front of the Home. Might as well do it now.

As he got out of the car, he noticed the small antique shop across the street, where a few antique dolls sat in front of the window on ancient-looking chairs. A gray-haired woman was moving some of the dolls inside, out of the rain. Olivia was right. This must be the store where Annie had found Lacey's dolls.

There was no one sitting on the broad front porch of the Retirement Home. He rang the bell and a young, blond-haired woman answered.

"I'm looking for Mary Poor," he said.

"Come in." The woman stood back to let him pass. "She's in the living room working on a crossword puzzle, as usual."

She led him into a room where several elderly women were watching television. Mary Poor sat apart from them in a wing chair in the corner, holding a folded newspaper under the beam of light from a floor lamp. "Mary?" the blond woman said. "There's a gentleman here to see you."

The old woman rested the paper in the lap of her blue skirt as she looked up into Alec's face, a surprising sharpness in her blue eyes. She was wearing tennis shoes.

"Mrs. Poor?" Alec held out his hand. "I don't know if you remember me. I'm Alec O'Neill. Annie's husband."

The woman squinted up at him for a moment before shaking his hand. "So you are," she said. "So you are."

Alec sat down in a second wing chair, noticing with some admiration that Mary was working the puzzle in pen.

"I stopped by to ask if you'd be able to give some of us on the lighthouse committee a little tour of the keeper's house. I guess you know we're putting together a booklet on the lighthouse. Paul Macelli's been talking to you, and it's really coming together, but I think he should get a firsthand look at the house so he can describe the rooms, and I'll take some pictures." He looked at the thin skin covering Mary's blue-veined, fine-boned hands. "Would it be possible? I mean, are you able to get around?"

"Well enough, well enough," Mary said. "When would this be?"

"Sometime in the next few weeks. That will give Paul time to write it up and me time to develop the pictures before we have to get all the material to the printer."

"You just call when you want me, and I'll get one of the girls to drive me over."

"That'll be great. Thanks." He glanced over at the television, then back at Mary's face. "How are you? Is there anything you need? I know Annie used to bring you things."

The old woman smiled. Her teeth were beautiful, and Alec wondered if they were her own. "She was one for giving things, all right," Mary said. "I miss that little girl." She pointed to the window behind Alec's head, and Alec turned to see a stained glass panel of the Kiss River Lighthouse, its beam of light cutting through the dark blue ribbons of a night sky. It was stunning in its simplicity, and for a moment he was speechless.

"I've never seen that one before," he said finally. "It's beautiful."

"She gave it to me years ago and I brought it along when they moved me here."

He stood up for a closer look, hypnotized by the dazzling white of the glass lighthouse. He thought he had seen all of Annie's work and he felt as if he'd just discovered another dimension of the woman he thought he'd known so well.

Mary followed his gaze to the window. "You'll call me, then?" she asked.

He forced his eyes back to hers once more. "Yes," he said, reluctantly turning to leave. "I'll be in touch."

He stopped by Olivia's to pick up Lacey. He watched them hug on the front deck, a prolonged hug that made him feel oddly excluded.

"Thanks, Olivia." Lacey picked up her duffel bag and headed toward the Bronco.

Alec smiled up at Olivia. "Thanks from me, too," he said. "Any word from Paul?"

She shook her head. "I was very glad for Lacey's company."

He got into the Bronco and pulled out onto the road, while Lacey pushed the buttons on the radio, finally settling on a mind-numbing cacophony.

"Did you have a good time?" he asked.

"Uh-huh." She tapped her palms on her thighs in time with the music, and he noticed the watch.

He touched her wrist. "What's this?" he asked.

She lifted her arm to look at the glittery face of the watch. "Olivia bought it for me," she said. "I'm supposed to call her at midnight on the nights I go out."

He frowned. "What for?"

"Just to let her know I'm okay."

"That's crazy. You'll wake her up."

"It was a *contingency*." Lacey's voice started to rise. "She would only buy me the watch if I agreed to call her."

"Why do you want a watch all of a sudden? You've never wanted one before."

"*You* wear one. What's the big deal?"

He didn't want to fight with her. In a few minutes they would walk into the house and feel Clay's absence. They only had each other now.

He pulled into their driveway and turned off the ignition. He lifted her wrist so he could study the watch. "It suits you," he said.

She pulled her hand away and made a face at him. "What is *that* supposed to mean?" She reached into the back seat for her duffel bag and got out of the Bronco, walking ahead of him toward the front steps.

"Lace."

She swung around to glare at him.

"I like the watch on you. That's all I meant." He looked at her across the hood of the Bronco. "It's just you and me, now, Lacey," he said. "Let's not start out on a sour note."

"*You* started it. I was perfectly happy just listening to the radio. *You're* the one who wanted to talk." She stalked up the steps and into the house.

He called Olivia at nine, from the den, too annoyed with her to wait until ten-thirty. He didn't want to feel all that close to her tonight.

"I'm upset about the watch," he said.

"It wasn't expensive."

"It's not the money." He raked his fingers through his hair. "It's not even the watch, actually. It's this bit about her calling you at midnight. I'm capable of taking care of her, Olivia."

Olivia didn't answer right away. "She needs some...*guidelines,* Alec," she said finally. "She needs to know you care enough about her to want to know what she's doing."

He shook his head. "I know the way this house has always been run strikes you as weird, but I'm not about to change it. If I started changing the rules on her now, she'd take off. She needs the familiar—the same structure she had when Annie was alive."

"*What* structure? The two of you allowed her to do anything she wanted. She's a *child,* Alec. She needs a *parent.*"

"So you're taking it on yourself to be one for her, is that it? You spent one night with her, Olivia. That doesn't make you her mother."

Olivia was quiet and Alec closed his eyes, regretting his words. He was, he knew, a little jealous of her sudden, easy relationship with his daughter.

"I'm getting off," Olivia said.

"Olivia, I..."

"Let's just drop it, all right? Good-bye."

CHAPTER FORTY-THREE

Lacey called her at midnight, four nights in a row, twice from home, twice from someplace else. Olivia woke up when the phone rang, groggy and a little nauseated, but she wasn't about to tell Lacey not to call.

"My father says I don't have to call you," Lacey said on the first night. She was at a friend's house, and Olivia could hear laughter and loud music in the background.

"Well, he's right," Olivia said. "You don't have to, but I'd like it if you did so I don't worry about you."

"Okay," Lacey said, easily. "I will."

Alec had called her a couple of times since the night they'd argued about the watch. He'd apologized for blowing up, and she'd allowed the subject to die. Still, it had soured the air between them, just a little, just enough to keep her from feeling too close to him again. And that, she thought, was fine.

On the fifth night after Lacey started calling her, Olivia woke up automatically at midnight, reaching for the phone before she realized it hadn't rung. Maybe Lacey had stayed home. Probably she had fallen asleep, safe and sound in her own bed. Olivia watched the neon-green numbers change on her night table clock. Finally, at twelve-thirty, the phone rang. She picked it up to hear Lacey sobbing on the other end, speaking unintelligibly. Olivia sat up in bed to give the girl her full attention.

"I think you've had too much to drink, Lacey."

Lacey cried for a moment into the phone. There was a ripple of laughter in the background. "I'm scared," she said finally.

"Of what?"

There was another pause while Lacey struggled for control. "I haven't gotten my period."

"Oh. How late are you?"

"I'm not sure. I lost track."

"Where are you, Lacey? I'm coming to pick you up."

Lacey didn't resist. She gave Olivia a muddled set of directions to a house near Kiss River and said she would wait for her out front.

The road was nearly deserted, and Olivia was relieved when she finally spotted the beacon ahead of her in the darkness. She drove on slowly, knowing the horses were out here somewhere. She found the intersection Lacey had told her about and turned onto a road of packed sand, praying her car would not get stuck. She could just imagine being stranded out here in the middle of the night.

Lacey's directions had been poor, but after a few hundred yards on the sand road, Olivia heard music. She followed the sound to a small white house, where Lacey sat alone on the concrete front stoop. She looked up as Olivia pulled into the grassy driveway, then started walking toward the car.

Olivia opened the door for her. She was clearly drunk, and her clothes smelled of beer and tobacco. It took her three attempts to get into the car, where she closed her eyes and rested her head back against the seat.

Olivia leaned over to snap Lacey's seat belt in place. "Have you had anything besides beer?" she asked.

"Uh uh."

"Have you gotten sick?"

Lacey nodded, her eyes opening to half mast. "Three times," she whispered.

"Let me know if you're going to get sick again so I can pull over."

"Mmm." Lacey closed her eyes again. She slept for most of the drive to Olivia's house. Olivia set her up in the guest room, deciding there would be time in the morning to pursue Lacey's concern about her late period. She went back to her own bedroom and called Alec.

"It's Olivia, Alec. I'm sorry to wake you."

"No problem," he said, his voice thick with sleep. "What's up?"

"I have Lacey here with me."

"Why?"

"She was at a party and had too much to drink and she called me, very upset. So I picked her up and brought her here."

She heard the heaviness of his breathing. She pictured him sitting bare-chested on the edge of his bed, rubbing his face, trying to wake himself up.

"I'll come get her," he said.

"No, don't. She's asleep. I'll bring her home in the morning."

"I don't want you to have to go to all that trouble."

"It's all right. I'm off tomorrow. Go back to sleep, Alec. We'll talk more about this in the morning."

Lacey was pale and red-eyed the next morning. She sat at the table in her foul-smelling jeans and T-shirt, dumping spoonfuls of sugar into her coffee. She was sober and very quiet. Olivia put a plate of toast in front of her and sat down on the other side of the table.

"When you called last night, you said you were concerned that your period was late."

Lacey looked up, startled. "I said *that?*"

Olivia nodded.

Lacey groaned and leaned back in the chair. "I can't believe I told you that."

"Do you know when you were due?"

Lacey shook her head back and forth against the chair, her eyes closed.

"Have you had sex since your last period?"

Lacey made a face, her cheeks reddening. "I can't talk to you about *that,*" she said.

"Well, just tell me if there's a possibility you could be pregnant."

She nodded.

"We'll go into the ER this morning and get a test done."

Lacey opened her eyes and looked directly at Olivia. "Oh, God, Olivia, what if I am? I'd have to have it. I don't think I could ever have an abortion. My mother would have killed me. She *hated* abortions. She said they were murder."

"But you and your mother are different people."

Lacey looked surprised by that thought. "Still," she said, shaking her head, "I don't think I could do it."

"Let's wait and see what we're dealing with, Lacey. We don't need to borrow trouble."

They waited in Olivia's office while Kathy Brash ran the test. Lacey did not want to talk. She sat in the chair by the window, playing with the cord from the blinds, and she jumped when the phone rang.

Olivia picked up the receiver.

"Negative," said Kathy.

Olivia thanked her and got off the phone. She looked across her desk at Lacey.

"You're not pregnant."

Lacey covered her face with her hands and started to cry. "I was so scared," she said. "It was just about all I could think of. I almost told you when I stayed over that night. I wanted to, but I thought you'd think I was a slut or something."

Olivia shook her head. "I don't think any less of you, Lacey." She leaned forward on her desk. "Look at me," she said.

Lacey lowered her hands to her lap and looked at Olivia.

"You have to tell your father."

Lacey's red eyes opened wide. "Tell him *what?*"

"That you thought you might be pregnant."

"But I'm *not*. Why should I get him all upset? There's absolutely no reason for me to tell him."

"There's a very good reason. He's your father. He needs to know how serious things are with you."

"What if I don't tell him?"

"Then I will."

Lacey jumped from the chair. "I thought I could *trust* you."

"You can trust me to do whatever I feel is best for you."

"Oh, God, you're a *bitch*." Lacey dropped to the chair again. "He'll kill me, Olivia. He'll..." She shook her head, fat tears rolling down her cheeks.

Olivia stood up. "He needs to know, Lacey." She took her car keys from her purse. "Let's go."

Lacey followed her with a heavy air of resignation. She stared out the window of Olivia's car on the drive to Southern Shores, shooting occasional, evil-eyed looks in Olivia's direction. "But I'm not even pregnant," she'd growl. "I thought I could trust you."

Lacey let herself into the house ahead of Olivia and brushed past her father on the way upstairs to her room. Alec looked expectantly at Olivia.

"Could we go in the den?" she asked.

He nodded, leading her into the den and taking his usual seat at the desk. She sat down at the work table.

"She was afraid she was pregnant," Olivia said.

Alec looked surprised for an instant, then shook his head. "Oh, no," he said.

"She's not. I had her tested this morning at the ER. She knows I'm telling you this and she's not happy about it, but I thought you needed to know."

He nodded. "Christ." He looked up at the ceiling, and when he spoke there was anger in his voice. "Okay, Annie," he said, "so what would you do now?"

Olivia stood up. "*Forget* what Annie would do or what Annie would think or what Annie would feel. Has it ever occurred to you that maybe Annie was *wrong?*" Olivia grabbed her purse from the work table and stalked to the door of the den, where she turned back to look at him. "Your barely fourteen-year-old daughter who's been raising herself all these years thought she was *pregnant.* Forget about Annie. Lacey needs *you* right now. She needs *Alec.*"

She let herself out the front door, nearly knocking Tripod over in her rush to leave. From her car, she looked up at the window she knew was Lacey's, wondering if in the last hour she had lost both Alec *and* his daughter.

Alec sat alone in the den for a long time, aware of the stillness in the house. *She's afraid of what it will be like when it's just the two of you.* Wasn't that what her school counselor had told him? He rose to his feet and started up the stairs.

He knocked on the door and pushed it open. Lacey sat cross-legged on her bed, clutching a dark-haired china doll to her chest. She looked horrid, her two-toned hair uncombed, her cheeks tear-streaked. She smelled like stale beer.

"I'm sorry, Daddy," she said.

He sat down on the bed and pulled her into his arms, and for the first time in far too long she didn't struggle to get away from him. She wept against his shoulder, her back shivering beneath his hands. He stroked her hair, afraid to speak, afraid his voice would give out.

Finally he drew away from her. He pulled a tissue from the box on her night table and held it to her nose.

"Blow," he said, and she did. Then she looked up at him, with Annie's blue eyes, waiting for him to speak.

"You must have been terrified to think you were pregnant," he said.

She nodded, lowering her eyes quickly, and her tears flicked from her long lashes onto the back of his hand.

"Would it have been that boy's? Bobby's?"

She didn't lift her head. "I don't know whose it would have been."

Something rolled over in his gut, and he struggled to keep his voice soft. "Oh, Lace," he said, pulling her close again. He waited for her tears to stop before he finished his thought. "There are some changes we're going to have to make," he said.

"What do you mean?"

"I want you in at twelve on Friday and Saturday nights and ten on weekdays."

She pulled away from him, staring at him in bruised disbelief. "*Dad.* It's *summer.*"

"There's still no reason for you to be out later than that. And I want to know where you're going to be. I want phone numbers, and I want to meet the kids you're going out with, too."

"I *knew* you'd do this. You're going to make me into a prisoner. You can't keep me from having sex."

"I know that," he said quietly. "I wish you wouldn't, though. You just don't know—you can't possibly understand what you're doing. It should be *special*, Lacey. What's it going to mean to you when you find someone you really love?"

"It meant something to Mom even though she did it when she was really young. She told me that with you she finally felt complete."

Alec sighed. It seemed to him that Annie and her openness had a way of sabotaging every move he made with Lacey.

"Well, if you're going to do it, you need to do it responsibly." He stood up, frustrated. "But it's really not a good idea to start on the pill so young. And you shouldn't smoke if you take it...and, damn it, Lacey, *why?* You're only fourteen. Is it because Jessica does it?"

"No."

"Are you afraid the boys won't like you if you say no?"

She looked down at her doll. "I don't have any idea in the world why I do it."

Her tone made him feel enormously sad. He took a step toward her bed and leaned down to kiss the top of her head. "Maybe you need to think about it a little, Lace, instead of just doing it." He walked to the door and turned to face her again. "You can have anything you need in the way of birth control," he said, "but please do me a favor and give it some thought. You're too valuable to just give yourself away."

Chapter Forty-Four

There was no way out of it—Paul would have to speak to Mary Poor. His work was beginning to suffer. Sal Bennett, the editor of the *Gazette,* chastised him for being late with one article, inaccurate on another.

"Are you having some personal problems?" Sal asked, and Paul knew the obsession must show in his face. His thoughts were full of Annie, and of the girl he was coming to think of as his daughter.

He'd tried twice to get a look at her. He'd lurked in her neighborhood like a mad rapist, following her once to the beach, another time to the movies, where she'd sat with a boy who managed to slip his hand under her shirt sometime during the first hour, eliciting in Paul an unfamiliar paternal fury.

He'd held off on going to see Mary, hoping that by some sign from Lacey, some distinctive mannerism or familiar inflection in her voice, he would know the truth. Asking Mary required courage he did not have, but now that his job was being threatened as well as his sanity, he knew he could no longer put it off.

He found Mary at the retirement home, sitting as usual in one of the rocking chairs on the porch, the folded newspaper on the arm of the chair. She looked up as Paul sat down next to her.

"Where's your recording machine?" the old woman asked.

"I don't have it with me today," Paul said, tapping his fingers on the arm of the rocker. "This isn't an interview. I just have a few things I need to get straight with you."

Mary rested the paper on her knees. "Such as?"

"Such as, exactly how well do you remember me?" He lowered his voice. "I mean, I guess you remember that I was Annie's...friend, long ago."

Mary nodded. "I can't remember yesterday, sometimes, but I remember fifteen years ago well enough."

"Then...do you remember the last time I was with Annie at your house at Kiss River? The day you kicked me out?"

"Yes."

Paul sat on the edge of the chair, turning to face her. "I need to know...was she pregnant then? Is that why she wanted me to leave? She has a daughter who's fourteen years old. Lacey. Is she my child?"

"What difference does that make? Annie's husband is Lacey's father now."

"It makes an enormous difference. She may be the only child I'll ever have, and she should know who her real father is." He looked into the old woman's clear blue eyes. "She's mine, isn't she?"

Mary lifted the paper to the arm of her chair again. "Think what you want," she said, turning her attention back to the crossword puzzle.

Paul watched her for a moment before getting to his feet.

He didn't leave the porch, though, and after a while Mary looked up at him again.

"I can't get free of her," he said quietly. "Annie's ruining my life."

CHAPTER FORTY-FIVE

Mary watched Paul Macelli drive away, knowing this was not the last time she would see him. He would not be able to rest until he knew the truth, and maybe one day she would have to tell him.

She could understand someone's need to do all they could for a daughter. She had felt that way about Annie, and it had led her to aid and abet her in a way she had come to regret. *You're my savior, Mary,* Annie had said to her more than once, but the truth was, she'd done Annie far more harm than good.

She remembered well the day she banished Paul from Kiss River, and she remembered even more clearly the events that occurred a few days after his leaving.

There'd been talk of a storm back then—a brutal one—and some of the residents of the Outer Banks had already packed up their most treasured possessions and moved inland. Mary listened to the radio off and on during the day, and by late morning they had withdrawn the warning. "Looks like it's going to miss us completely," said the meteorologist, a mixture of relief and disappointment in his voice.

Mary stared disgustedly at the radio as she put the kettle on to boil. Why did she even bother to listen? She opened the back door and stepped outside. The sky above the dunes was white, with no sign of the usual gulls or pelicans or geese, and the sea oats stood arrow-straight in the still, heavy air. The ocean had that ominous swollen look, the nearly black water billowing into waves that broke high up on the beach. Mary sniffed the air and shook her head once more. They were fools, she thought, all of them. Tomorrow they would defend themselves, talking about how unpredictable storms could be, how there was simply no way they could have known.

Inside once more, Mary brewed herself a pot of tea and set about preparing for what she knew was coming. Caleb had taught her what to do, just as he'd taught her how to read the wind and the water. Mary filled the lanterns with kerosene and set them on the kitchen table. She took three jugs from the cupboard and carried them upstairs, where she filled them with water and left them on the dresser in her bedroom. Then she placed the old rubber stopper in the drain of the clawfoot bathtub and turned on the faucet, all the while thinking of Annie. When she woke up this morning and opened her bedroom window, she knew the storm was well on its way, and she'd called to warn her.

"Don't go today, Annie," she'd said. "The storm will hit while you're driving back."

"They're saying it'll miss us." Annie's voice was soft, a little frightened, although Mary knew it wasn't the storm she feared. "I have to go while I've got my courage up," she said.

Mary offered to go with her, but Annie laughed at the suggestion. "Don't be ridiculous," she said. "I'll be fine." Mary could just imagine the burden a seventy-seven-year-old woman would have been on her today, but every time she thought of Annie trying to drive home in the state she'd be in, she wished anew that she'd refused to take no for an answer.

The rain started around four that afternoon, while Mary was struggling to board up windows. She had done it by herself all the years since Caleb's death, but she was not as strong as she used to be, and she had only enough plywood for those downstairs windows that faced the ocean. That would have to do, she thought, exhausted from the work. She brought the hanging plants in from the porch and carried her old photograph albums up to the second floor. She checked all the windows, cracking a few, remembering Caleb's voice as she did so: "Houses can explode during a hurricane," he had said to her that first year they were married, and he'd gone on to tell her stories of houses that had done exactly that.

Mary made one last tour of the yard for anything she might have neglected to batten down before returning to the house, securing the front door behind her. Then she sat down in the rocking chair in front of the fireplace to wait.

She turned the radio on after a while, smiling ruefully as the meteorologist admitted his error and once again advised his listeners to evacuate, but her smile faded as she thought of Annie. Where was she now? Perhaps she'd heard the new warnings and would find someplace on the mainland to spend the night. Mary hoped so. She had suggested Annie take a room so she wouldn't have to drive home, but Annie'd refused to even consider the idea. "I'll be too anxious to get home to Alec and Clay," she'd said. Mary didn't see how she would be able to face her husband and child tonight. "I can do it," Annie reassured her. "I'll just say I have a bellyache and take to my bed for a day or two. Women do this all the time."

She knew Annie, though. She knew it was not the physical pain that would crush her spirit.

The wind picked up suddenly. It whistled through the upstairs, and rain began to spike against the plywood on her windows. The lights inside the house flickered but stayed on. Mary stood in front of the window next to the fireplace and watched the world darken in a few seconds' time, dark enough to trick the lighthouse into thinking it was dusk, and the beacon suddenly flashed to life. She could make out the frothy whitecaps of the ocean, swelling ever nearer to the lighthouse, licking hungrily at the dunes.

Then she saw the headlights of a car bouncing through the rain and darkness toward the house. The car pulled up within a few feet of the front porch, and only then could she make out that it was Annie's. She grabbed her slicker from the coat rack and struggled to push open the front door. The wind ripped it from her hands and flung it against the house with a *bang,* and she had to grab hold of the railing to keep from being blown off the porch herself.

Annie was crying as Mary pulled the car door open. She managed to wrap the slicker around the younger woman's shoulders and pull the hood up over her head as they ran from the car to the house. Mary tugged the front door shut, breathless from the effort. When she turned around, Annie was already sitting on the couch, hunched over, clutching the wet slicker around her. She was sobbing, her face buried in her hands. Mary left her alone as she went into the kitchen to put the kettle on once more. She took two cups out of the cupboard just as the lights went out, leaving the house as dark as the world outside.

"Mary?" Annie called from the living room. She sounded like a child.

"I'm lighting the lanterns," Mary called back, fumbling

on the kitchen table for the matches. "I'll be there in a minute."

She left one lantern glowing in the kitchen and carried the other into the living room. She looked out the window, but all she could see was blackness. Even the beacon could not tell her how close the water was, how soon they should move upstairs.

"I couldn't go home," Annie said. Her face was gray in the lantern light and her teeth chattered as Mary helped her take off the slicker. "I just couldn't face Alec."

"I should call him to let him know you're all right," Mary said.

Annie looked at the phone on the desk in the corner. "Maybe I'd better," she said. "He'd think it's weird if I don't talk to him."

Mary moved the phone to the sofa so Annie didn't have to get up. She had to dial the number for her, Annie's hands were trembling so fiercely.

"Alec?" Annie said. "I stopped by to make sure Mary was all right, but it's gotten so nasty that I think I'd better just stay put."

Mary watched Annie's face. Her voice would not give her away, but if Alec could take one look at the pain in her eyes, he would know instantly what she had done. It was good she had not gone home.

"Can I speak to Clay?" Annie asked. "Oh. Well, that's good. Maybe he'll sleep through the whole thing... Yeah, we're fine, just sitting here, drinking tea." She laughed, but tears were streaming down her cheeks and she wiped at them ineffectually with the back of her hand. Mary felt the threat of her own tears, and she breathed deeply to hold them back. "Alec?" Annie said, twisting the phone cord around her fingers. "I love you so much."

Annie hung up the phone and curled herself into a ball in one corner of the couch. She was shivering convulsively. Mary found a wool blanket in the chest in the downstairs bedroom and wrapped it around her. She brought Annie the tea, holding the cup while she sipped. Then Annie looked up at her.

"Oh, God, Mary," she said. "What have I done?"

Mary sat down next to her. "Maybe there's a lesson in this," she said. "For you and me both. I've made it too easy for you. I've let you live out my own dreams, which were never meant to see the light of day. I'm just as guilty as you are."

"Shh, Mary. Don't talk about guilt." Annie shook her head, kneading her hands together in her lap. There was no color at all in her face. "It hurt so much," she said. "They said it wouldn't be bad, but it was *horrendous,* and I deserved every single solitary ounce of the pain."

"No, you didn't," Mary said. "You..."

Something crashed against the outside wall of the house and Annie jumped. "I don't *like* this," she said. She drew the blanket tighter around her shoulders as the wind whistled eerily through the room.

"We should go upstairs," Mary said.

Annie was slow on the stairs, in more pain than seemed normal for such a thing. Mary settled her into the small bedroom she had come to think of as Annie's. She watched as her young friend climbed into the bed, fully clothed and still shaking, covering her ears against the sound of the wind as it screamed through the upstairs rooms. She was beginning to babble, not making much sense at all, and her skin felt hot to the touch. Mary soaked a washcloth in cool water and bathed Annie's face and hands. She would lace her next cup of tea with Southern Comfort.

"It's stopped," Annie said suddenly, sitting up in the bed to listen. Indeed, the rain *had* stopped. The wind was still, and when Mary looked out the window, she could see stars.

"Yes," Mary said, shivering herself. She would let Annie believe what she wanted, although she knew it was only the eye of the storm passing over them. Soon it would all begin again.

By that time, though, Annie was asleep. Mary kept watch by her bed, sitting up the entire night, listening to the house strain at its roots.

Annie's color was better in the morning, and the fever had broken. Mary left her sleeping while she surveyed the damage. Rain had swept under the doors and through the cracked windows, but otherwise everything inside was in one piece. The electricity was still out, and her phone had died sometime during the night. Outside, she found the crushed metal lid to a garbage can resting against her front porch. The shape of the beach had changed overnight, the sea oats closer to the water, the pitch of the sand steeper. The lighthouse looked unscathed, although she would have to check the lantern room later.

When she returned to the kitchen, she found Annie mopping the rainwater from the floor.

"Here," Mary said, taking the mop from Annie's hand. "You shouldn't be doing that."

Annie sat down weakly at the kitchen table, folding her white hands in her lap. "I dreamt last night it was Alec's," she said quietly.

Mary stopped mopping to look down at her. "Annie, you felt very certain it was Paul's."

Annie closed her eyes, nodded.

"Now, I admit I don't know much about this topic," Mary said, leaning on the mop, "but that diaphragm you're using

to keep from having babies just isn't fail-proof enough for—"
she hesitated, hunting for the words "—for someone like
you."

Annie ignored her. "I'm going to get pregnant again as
soon as I can."

Mary looked at her squarely. "You can't bring that baby
back."

"I know," Annie said in a small voice. "But I'm going
to try. And this one will be Alec's for sure." She must have
seen the doubt in Mary's eyes, because she added, "I *swear* it,
Mary. This one will be his."

The crossword puzzle had fallen from Mary's knees to
the porch, and she did not bother to pick it up. She thought
about Paul Macelli, still burdened by things that had happened so long ago. She thought of Annie, and of herself, and
she knew that whatever lesson the three of them had learned
back then had been all too quickly forgotten.

CHAPTER FORTY-SIX

There were a dozen yellow roses waiting for Olivia in the emergency room when she arrived for work Friday morning.

"Are they from Paul?" Kathy asked her, as Olivia opened the card.

You were right, and I was wrong—Alec.

Olivia smiled. "No," she said, slipping the card into the pocket of her white coat. "They're not."

It had been just twenty-four hours since she'd left Alec and Lacey alone to hash out their differences without her. And without Annie. When Alec didn't call her last night, she figured that either things had not gone well or he was angry with her for her tirade. It relieved her to see that neither was the case.

Mike Shelley called her later that afternoon. He wanted to take her out to dinner after her shift, he said. "Not a date," he added, laughing. "My wife's standing right here, ready to intervene. I just have something I want to talk with you about. Is seven okay?"

"Fine," she said, wondering exactly what she was agreeing to.

He took her to a small seafood restaurant in Kitty Hawk and waited until their entrees were served before satisfying her curiosity.

"The personnel committee's made its decision," he said.

"Oh?" She could not tell from the tone of his voice whether she should smile or frown.

"It was hairy there for a while, but I think deep down each of us knew who we wanted. We held off making a decision until the whole Annie O'Neill fiasco had died down. We were all impressed with the way you handled that situation, Olivia. As Pat Robbins on the committee said, Olivia Simon knows how to keep her wits about her in *and* out of the ER."

She smiled at him. "You're saying I've got it if I want it?"

"Yes," Mike said. He looked at her quizzically. "Do you have some doubts about taking it?"

Olivia looked down at her plate. "I've appreciated how you've stuck by me through everything, Mike. I want to be thrilled. I *am* thrilled, but at the same time..."

"What?"

"It's my husband. He doesn't want to stay here."

"I thought...you're separated, aren't you?"

"Yes, but I keep hoping..." She shrugged. "Well, I guess this will be the big test. I'll tell him I've got the offer and see what happens. Maybe he and I need a crisis—we just plod along, not together, but not totally apart either. I suppose this will move us in one direction or another. May I have a few days to decide?"

"Absolutely." He leaned back in his chair. "I'm not one of those people who thinks you should put career over family,

Olivia, regardless of what sex you are. So whatever you decide, I'll understand."

"Thanks."

"At the same time, though, you're the one the ER needs. It's going to expand—it's *got* to—and we need someone there who can handle the changes."

She felt a hunger in her that had been missing for a long time. There was a challenge in front of her, tempting her, waiting for her to grab it. She wished she could say yes and be done with it.

"Mike, there's one more thing you should know."

"What's that?"

"I'm pregnant. The baby's due in January."

Mike's eyes widened. "Wow."

"I don't intend to take much time off, if everything goes well. Maybe I should have told you before, but I..."

He shook his head. "It doesn't change anything with regard to the offer."

She smiled, relieved. "Good."

"Well." He leaned back in his chair. "I'm supposed to bring you home with me for some dessert when we're through with dinner, on order of the director of my household. Okay with you?"

"I'd love it," she said.

For the first time, Paul was looking forward to the meeting at Alec's. It might give him a chance to really get a look at Lacey, and sure enough, she was standing in the kitchen with her father and Nola when he arrived. She was drinking a Coke from the can, and she looked at him with more than a passing interest when he walked into the room. Could she possibly know? Was there a chance Annie had told her something?

He said hello to the three of them, unable to take his eyes from Lacey's face. He tried to imagine her without the Halloween hair. She was Annie, through and through. He could see no one else in her features; certainly there was no trace at all of Alec.

"Wine's already in the living room, Paul," Alec said as he walked past him, with Nola close on his heels.

"I'll be there in a second," Paul said. "I just want to get a glass of water." He reached toward the cabinet over the sink and looked at Lacey, who had boosted herself onto the countertop. She was wearing a short, hot-pink T-shirt and white shorts. Her feet were bare. "Glasses in here?" he asked.

"Next one," she said. "To your right."

He filled the glass with water and took a long drink. Then he leaned back against the counter to study her. "I checked the notes I made when I interviewed your mother, Lacey, and for some reason she did say you were twelve."

Lacey wrinkled her nose. "That is totally weird," she said.

"Maybe she was a little nervous about being interviewed."

The girl shook her head. "She never got nervous over anything." She swung her bare legs out in front of her and studied her pink toenails. "Your wife is really nice," she said.

He frowned at her. "How do you know... Oh. You met her at the hospital the night your mother died."

"Yeah, but that's not really how I know her." Lacey took an annoyingly long drink from her can of soda, and when she finally set the can on the counter, there was a coyness in her smile. "Actually," she said, "I talk to her every night."

"To my wife? To *Olivia?*"

"Yeah. She insisted. See, what happened was, one night I slept over her house and..."

"You stayed at her house?"

"Uh-huh, and then she said I had to call her at midnight every night, and she somehow talked my father into making all these rules for me." Lacey grinned, rather happily. "She's positively wrecked my life, but she's kind of hard to stay mad at." She held up her hand to show him a black and silver watch. "She bought this for me."

"Paul?" Alec called from the living room. "We're about to get started."

"I'll be right there," he called back, but he didn't make a move toward the door. "Why did you sleep over her house?" he asked.

"Because my father had to take my brother to college and was going to be gone all night. So Olivia is, like, really close friends with my father and she said I could stay there."

Paul stared at the cloisonné horse on the other side of the room. "I didn't realize she was friends with your... I guess she's helped him with the talks he gives on the lighthouse, right?"

"Well, they only did that once." Lacey held the can to her lips again, leaning back to swallow the last of the soda. "They go out sometimes," she continued. "You know, to dinner or whatever, and sometimes she comes over here at night to use my mother's stained glass stuff."

"Your mother's...?"

Lacey let out an exasperated sigh. He must be sounding as dense as he felt. "Her stained *glass* stuff," she said. "You know, her *tools* and things."

There was laughter from the living room. Paul set the empty water glass in the sink, his hand shaking badly. He struggled to make his face unreadable as he turned back to Lacey.

"But Olivia doesn't work with stained glass," he said.

"God, you must not have seen her in a while. She takes lessons at my mother's studio every Saturday morning from Tom Nestor. He's the guy who..."

"I know who he is." Paul tried to picture Olivia at Annie's work table in the studio. He tried to imagine her out to dinner with Alec, laughing with him, telling him...what? She'd been here at Alec's house. *Annie's* house. Playing mother to Annie's daughter.

"Paul?" It was Nola this time, an irked quality to her voice.

"I'd better go," he said.

"Yeah," Lacey grinned. "You don't cross Nola Dillard and live to talk about it."

He knew the moment he sat down on the sofa that he could not stay. His confusion was turning to anger. What the hell did Olivia think she was doing?

Alec was talking about the upcoming tour of the keeper's house, now scheduled for the following Tuesday.

"Alec?" Paul interrupted him, standing up, and everyone raised their eyes to him.

"I'm sorry," Paul said, "but I'm going to have to leave. I'm not feeling well. I thought I could make it through the meeting, but..." He shrugged his shoulders.

"Do you want to lie down for a while?" Alec asked.

"I have some aspirin," Sondra Carter offered.

"Is it something you ate?" Nola asked.

"No." He began backing away from them, the color rising in his face. "I'm sure I'll be all right once I'm out in the fresh air."

They were quiet as he walked the few steps to the front door and let himself out. Once outside, he wondered what they were saying about him. Probably not much. They would probably just get on with the meeting, and later Alec would call him to make certain he was all right. That would be exactly like Alec. He wondered what kind of sympathy and understanding he'd been giving Olivia these past couple of months.

He drove south toward Kitty Hawk, fifteen miles over the speed limit, trying to think of what he would say to her when he finally saw her face-to-face. Anything he said was sure to come out as a growl. There was no way he could do this calmly.

The house was dark when he arrived, her car gone. *Damn.* He was ready. He was bursting to have this out with her.

He sat down on the front deck. Where was she? Who was she off with tonight? Maybe she was at the Battered Women's Shelter. He could go over there. He closed his eyes, smiling ruefully at the image of yet another irate husband creating a stir at the shelter.

He sat on the deck for nearly an hour before he gave up and drove home to his little cottage in South Nags Head. He would find her in the morning. Saturday morning. Lacey had told him where she would be.

Olivia arrived home around ten. She thought of calling Paul to tell him about Mike's offer, but she needed time to think it through herself. Besides, she did not look forward to talking to Paul these days.

She had just gotten into bed when Alec called.

"The roses are beautiful, Alec," she said. "Thank you."

"I really owe you for your help with Lacey," he said. "It changed things overnight. She's talking to me, and I suddenly feel as though I have some control in my house."

"She's basically a good kid."

"I know that." He sighed. "This morning she told me she doesn't want to do anything about birth control, that she doesn't want to have sex again for a while. I don't know if that's realistic, though. Once a kid starts, how does she stop?"

"If she's getting more from you, maybe she won't need so much attention from guys at parties."

"I hope you're right." He was quiet for a moment. She thought she could hear him stretching, turning, and she knew he was in bed. "Well," he said, "how are you doing?"

"I was offered the director position tonight."

"You're kidding! Why didn't you call me the second you heard? That's fantastic, Olivia."

She could see the moon from her bed. It was nearly full and surrounded by stars. "I'm afraid to tell Paul. It's going to bring things to a head."

"He didn't stay for the meeting tonight."

"What do you mean?"

"He just came for a few minutes and then left. He said he wasn't feeling well."

"Did he say what was wrong?"

"He didn't offer any details. When are you going to tell him about the job?"

"Sometime tomorrow. I need to think about what I really want before I talk to him."

Alec was quiet for a moment. "I wish you'd take it," he said. She heard him draw in a long breath and let it out again. "Olivia," he said, "are you in bed?"

"Yes."

"You know...sometimes I want to say things to you that I'm not sure I should say."

"Like what?"

"Well, that I appreciate you and admire you. That I miss you when I haven't seen you for..."

Her beeper went off, and he stopped talking.

"I heard that," he said. "I'd better let you go."

Olivia closed her eyes. "I'm sorry."

"I have to go to the studio tomorrow to pick up the oval window and make an enlargement of a print. Could you have lunch after your lesson?"

"Yes," she said. "I'll see you then."

She hung up the phone and called the ER. There'd been a fire in one of the soundside cottages in Kitty Hawk. Three burn victims were coming in. Expected time of arrival: ten minutes.

She quickly got out of bed and pulled on her pink and white striped jersey dress. She brushed her teeth, ran a comb through her hair. It wasn't until she was in her car on the way to the ER that she allowed herself to think about Alec.

She wished he'd gotten to finish what he'd started to tell her.

Tomorrow, she thought. *Tomorrow at lunch.*

CHAPTER FORTY-SEVEN

Through the studio door, Olivia saw Alec and Tom standing by the work table. Tom was taping the small oval window between two pieces of cardboard, and Alec was laughing. They looked up when she opened the door.

"Morning, Olivia," Tom said, as he set the packaged window down on the table. "I have to give Alec a hand in the darkroom, so go ahead and get set up here and I'll be back in a minute."

Alec didn't say a word to her, but he didn't need to. The warmth in his smile said enough.

Olivia sat down at the table and pulled the piece of glass she'd been working on from her tote bag. She would need Tom's help on this. She'd already destroyed two pieces of glass trying to make this particular shape.

She cut out the pattern piece with her three-bladed scissors and had just glued it to the glass when Tom came out of the darkroom. He sat down next to her, and laughed when she told him the problem she was having with the cut.

"Well, you're trying to do something impossible here," he said, pulling a piece of scrap glass from the pile on his desk.

He showed her a different way to score the glass, and she was attempting to follow his instruction when the studio door suddenly burst open. Olivia looked up to see Paul charging toward her, his face red, his eyes angry, and she dropped her hands from the glass to her lap.

"I don't *believe* this," Paul said, his voice far too loud. "I heard you were doing this, but I thought it couldn't possibly be true."

She glanced toward the darkroom. Alec must have heard Paul's voice, because he opened the door a few inches. Olivia could just make out the frown on his face.

"Stained glass, Olivia?" Paul had his hands on the work table, and he leaned toward her, his face inches from hers. "The Battered Women's Shelter? Taking care of Annie's daughter? What are you trying to do, turn yourself into her?"

"Paul..." Olivia stood up, trying to think of the words that would put an end to his outburst, that would erase what he had already said, but her voice wouldn't work. Everything in the room seemed frozen. Next to her, Tom had stopped breathing, and Alec stood fast in the doorway of the darkroom, his hand locked on the knob. Only Paul moved, his arms thrashing in the air, his face tinted blue one minute, yellow the next.

"I hear you're great friends with her husband," he said. "Are you sleeping with him too, Olivia? Are you doing it in Annie's bed?"

"Stop it, Paul." Olivia's voice was a whisper compared to his. "You have no right to..."

Paul stalked toward the door, but whipped around once more to face her. "You think *I'm* nuts," he said. "What you're doing is *sick,* Olivia. Really crazy." He turned on his heel and stamped out of the studio, slamming the door behind him.

The stained glass panel hanging from the door swung loose for a moment, and Olivia cringed as it crashed against the door knob, splintering several of the small pieces of glass..

She sat down again as a stillness filled the studio, a silence so complete that when she began turning her ring on her finger, she could hear the faint chafing sound it made against her skin.

Alec pushed the darkroom door open and stepped into the room. "It was *Annie*," he said. "The other woman, right? Paul's obsession?"

She looked up at him. His smile was gone. There was an iciness in the faded blue of his eyes. "Yes," she said.

"You told me you were trying to be more like her, like the other woman. You *used* me, Olivia."

She shook her head.

"Paul used me too, didn't he? He got to see Annie's house and...the oval windows, and the pictures in the den. *Jesus.*" Alec pounded his fist on the work table. "He picked my brain about her. You did too." He raised his voice an octave to imitate her. " 'What was she *really* like, Alec?' You had me spilling my *guts* to you."

"Alec, I know it must look that way, but..."

"Well, I'll tell you something, Olivia." He was standing right in front of the table, and she forced herself to look up into his eyes. "If you were trying to be like Annie, you've failed miserably. You'll never be anything like her, and I'm not just talking about your lack of artistic talent." He lifted the graph paper on which she had carefully drawn the design of hot-air balloons and crumpled it between his fists before throwing it to the floor. "I'm talking about the way you lie and deceive and manipulate. Annie was always open, always honest. She couldn't have lied if her life depended on it."

She could see nothing except the anger in Alec's eyes. The rest of the room had blurred, darkened.

Alec picked up the wrapped oval window from the work table and looked down at Tom. "I'll come back for the enlargement tomorrow," he said. "Right now I need to get out of here."

Olivia watched him leave, and then she was alone with Tom, uncertain how to break the silence.

"You know," he said, his voice very soft after Alec's rage, "I knew Paul had more than a casual interest in Annie. I'd be in here sometimes when he'd come in to talk to her, and it would be obvious. Annie thought it was my imagination, but I, uh..." He ran his big hand over his face, as though he suddenly felt very weary. "Well, let's just say I understood how Paul felt."

He pulled a cigarette from the pack in his shirt pocket and lit it before he continued. "After she died, he couldn't stop buying her work. He spent a small fortune. I'd try to slow him down, but he had one thing on his mind, and that was Annie. I didn't think you knew, though, so I kept my mouth shut about it."

He took a drag on the cigarette and looked toward the front door. "In all the years I've known Alec, I've never seen him that angry. I should remind him that he's the one who asked you to go to lunch with him. I was a witness, remember? It wasn't like you went after him."

Tom's voice was soothing, the odor of tobacco in his hair and on his clothes, suddenly comforting. She wanted to rest her head on his shoulder, close her eyes.

He stood up to retrieve the crumpled graph paper Alec had thrown on the floor. "So," he said, as he sat down again, spreading the paper flat on the table. "Are you still interested in stained glass or was that just an attempt to be more like Annie?"

Olivia turned her eyes away from the simplistic design. It suddenly looked like a drawing in a coloring book. She stood up and began packing her belongings into the tote bag. "I *was* interested," she said, "but I guess I'm not very good at it."

"He's just angry, Olivia." Tom stood up, too. He lifted the tote bag to her shoulder, squeezed her hand. "Even Annie had to start somewhere."

She drove directly to Alec's house, and she could not have said if she was relieved or chagrined to see the Bronco in the driveway.

Lacey answered the door. "Olivia!" She grinned.

"Hi, Lacey. I need to see your father."

"I don't know if that's such a good idea," Lacey said. "He came home a while ago with a real attitude."

"I know, but I need to talk to him."

"He's around the side," Lacey pointed out the door. "He's putting in the little window."

She thanked Lacey and walked around to the side of the house. Alec was working on the window, at about the height of his chest. He glanced toward her as she approached, but that was all it was—a glance—and he said nothing to make the next few minutes easier on her. Last night he had told her he missed her, he admired her, and he had been about to tell her more. He had to feel like a fool.

She stood next to him in the sand. "Please let me talk to you," she said.

He didn't answer. He was caulking around the small, delicate window, and he didn't bother to take his eyes from his task.

"Oh, Alec, *please* don't be angry with me."

He looked at her. "Can you possibly blame me?"

She shook her head. "I want to explain, but it's...so complicated."

"Don't worry about it. I'm not going to believe a word you say, anyway." He ran his finger over the caulk.

"I couldn't tell you," she said. "In the beginning, there didn't seem much point to it and I thought it would only... disturb you. Then you started working with Paul. How could I possibly tell you then?"

He didn't answer, and she continued. "*Yes,* I wanted to understand Annie better. Paul idolized her, you loved her, Tom Nestor thought the sun rose and set on her, the people at the shelter—*everyone*—adored her. I wanted to understand what she had that I didn't. I wanted to know what made her so special in Paul's eyes that he would...that after nearly ten years of a good marriage he could suddenly forget I existed."

Alec looked out at the sound, where a speedboat was pulling a water skier smoothly across the water, close to the pier. Then he took a rag from his jeans pocket and focused on the window again, carefully wiping a smear of caulk from the yellow dress of the woman in the glass.

"Annie seemed like such a wonderful person," Olivia said, fighting for his attention. "I *did* want to be more like her. I wanted to be generous and talented. That's why I started working at the shelter, but now I truly enjoy it, Annie or no Annie. And that's why I started doing stained glass, but I enjoy that, too, even if I'm not turning out any masterpieces." She gestured toward the oval windows. "I've never had a...a *hobby* before. I've never take the time to..." She dropped her hand to her side, frustrated, as Alec crouched down in the sand to clean the nozzle of the caulk gun. Had he heard a word she'd said?

"I didn't ever use you, Alec. Not intentionally. You came

to me first, remember? And I know Paul wasn't using you, either. He's always been fascinated by the Kiss River Lighthouse. He had no idea you were involved on the committee, and he almost quit when he found out."

Alec suddenly stood up and looked her straight in the eye. "You told me bold-faced lies, Olivia," he said. "You said the woman Paul was interested in had moved to California."

"What could I say?"

"The truth, maybe, or was that out of the question?" He wiped his hands on the rag. "The night Annie was in the ER..." He closed his eyes, and deep lines appeared between his brows, as if he were in pain. She touched his shoulder, but he shook her hand away as he opened his eyes again. "You knew who she was that night, didn't you?" he asked. "You knew while you were working on her. You knew she was the reason Paul left you."

"Yes," she said, "I knew who she was, but Paul didn't leave me until that night. He went crazy when I came home and told him that she died."

"You can't tell me you didn't feel some joy right then? That she was dead?"

Olivia sucked in her breath, and the tears she'd been holding in for the last hour spilled onto her cheeks. "Is that the kind of person you think I am?" She turned to leave but he caught her arm, his fingers pressing hard against her wrist.

"I don't have any idea *what* kind of person you are," he said. "I don't *know* you."

"Yes, you do. You know things about me I've never been able to tell anyone except Paul. I've felt close to you. I've felt...*attracted* to you." She wiped her cheek with the back of her hand. "Paul once told me that his relationship with Annie was hopeless because she loved you too much," she said. "I'm not sure if I'm any closer to understanding why

Paul fell in love with Annie, but I understand why Annie would love *you*, Alec. I understand that completely."

She turned to leave, and this time he let her go.

She was in bed at ten, but she could not sleep. The baby was as restless as she was tonight. His featherlike flutters seemed frenzied, unending, and every time she changed position in the bed, he let her know of his displeasure.

She'd heard nothing from Paul, and she was not yet ready to initiate a conversation with him herself. But *Alec*. What more could she do—short of hurting him with the truth of Paul and Annie's brief liaison—to make him understand? Ten-thirty came and went, and she lifted the receiver of the phone to her ear to be certain it was working.

At quarter to eleven there was a knock on her front door. She slipped her robe over her cotton nightgown and walked downstairs to the dark, silent living room. She turned on the front light and peered out the window to see Alec standing on the deck, his hands in the pockets of his jeans.

She pulled open the door. His smile was uncertain. "I was going to call you," he said, "but thought I'd stop over instead."

She stepped back, and he walked past her into the living room. She closed the door and leaned back against it, tightening the sash of her robe.

"I was overwhelmed this morning, Olivia," he said. "I'm sorry."

It was so dark in the room she could only make out the whites of his eyes, the white stripes of his rugby shirt. She didn't want to turn on a light, though, didn't want him to be able to read her face all that easily tonight.

"I was wrong to keep things from you," she said. "I've been walking a fine line between you and Paul. I omitted a fact or two when I spoke to you, and then another fact or two when I spoke to him. Then, suddenly, it all snowballed on me. I am not deceptive, Alec. I'm not generally a liar."

He was quiet for a second or two. "No," he said. "I don't think you are."

Her eyes were adjusting to the darkness, and she saw the sadness in his smile.

"How did Paul know?" she asked. "How did he figure out what I was doing?"

"Lacey, I think. He was talking to her before the meeting last night. That's probably why he left right away." He ran a hand over his chin. "Poor Annie," he said. "She was so down for those few months before she died. Now I'm wondering if Paul was part of the reason—if he was hassling her in some way."

Olivia caught her lower lip between her teeth. "I think he may have been, Alec."

He frowned. "Do you think he was trying to get her to sleep with him?"

She shrugged, looking away from him, as though considering the possibility. "I guess only Paul could answer that question."

Alec walked to the front door and looked out toward the street. "Why didn't she tell me he was bothering her?" he asked, his voice rising. "I asked her over and over again what was wrong. I hated it when she'd get like that. It scared me, she seemed so...*lost* inside herself." Alec seemed lost himself. He was no longer in this room with her. "I asked her to let me help her, I *begged* her, but she..." He shook his head. "Oh, hell," he said tiredly. "What does it matter at this point?"

Olivia rested her hand on the back of the rattan chair. "Why don't you sit down?"

He shook his head. "I don't want to sit down." He took a

few steps toward her and wrapped his arms around her, pulling her head against his shoulder. He smelled of his familiar aftershave, and she closed her eyes. They stood that way for a long time. Minutes. She felt a little dizzy with her eyes closed, a little high, and she let the feeling build, let it consume her until she needed to hold on to him to keep herself upright.

After a while, Alec lowered his hands to her hips and pulled her gently against him, against his rock-hard erection. She thought of freeing it, taking it in her hands, her mouth. She locked her fingers behind his back to keep them from drifting down to his belt.

"What is it about this room?" Alec spoke softly in her ear. "It always seems to have this effect on me."

She untied her robe and opened it so there was one less piece of cloth between her body and his, and when she pressed against him once more, she could feel her own heartbeat pulsing low in her belly. Maybe she should say something. Maybe she should tell him she wanted this, she wanted *him*. No doubt Annie had been a verbal lover.

"Olivia," he said. "Where's your bedroom?"

She drew away from him and took his hand, leading him up the stairs, down the hallway, and by the time they'd reached the dark refuge of her room, she had lost control. She sat down on the edge of her bed and turned to unzip his jeans, drawing her hands inside and bringing his erect penis to her lips.

Alec caught his breath. "*Christ,* Olivia." His fingers combed through her hair, down the nape of her neck and up again, while she worked feverishly at his body. She barely heard him when he asked her to stop. The request was gentle, almost polite, and he repeated it as he pulled away from her.

She was shaking, uncertain if she had done something

wildly inappropriate in his eyes, or if he was about to leave her again. He would tell her they were both too vulnerable. Walk out her door. She looked up at him. "What's wrong?" she asked.

He sat down next to her on the bed, his arm around her shoulders. "Nothing's wrong," he said. "You just surprised me. I wasn't expecting...*that*, exactly, and it's been a very long time for me. If you were to keep on doing what you were doing, it would all be over in seconds, and I'm not that anxious to get this over with." He stroked his fingers over the skin beneath her eyes. "Why are you crying?"

She touched her fingertips to her eyes and felt the wetness. "I don't know," she whispered.

He leaned over to kiss her, softly—*too softly;* she could not tolerate moving this slowly—and she deepened the kiss with her tongue as she turned to straddle his thigh.

Alec ran his hands under her nightgown, up her thighs. He leaned back to look up at her. "Are you always like this?" he asked. "Or is it just that you've gone without for too long?"

"I'm *always* like this," she said, tugging his rugby shirt out of his jeans.

He laughed, shifting her off his thigh and back to the bed. He stood up, and she watched him as he undressed. Her curtains let in the pool of moonlight reflected off the sound, and she could see the distinct lines on his body, separating dark from light, the public Alec from the private. His stomach was tight and ridged with muscle, and she imagined his erect penis was still glistening from her attempt to please him.

She rose to her knees on the bed and took off her robe, but when she reached for the hem of her nightgown, he caught her hands.

"Leave it on," he said, closing his arms around her.

He didn't want to see her body. She imagined how her

rounded belly would look to him in the white light of the moon.

Alec bent down to take the hem of the nightgown in his own hands. He lifted it up, his palms running slowly over her thighs and hips. The cotton caught softly on her nipples as he raised the nightgown over her breasts, then over her head, until she stood as she had weeks earlier, naked and ready in his arms. He began kissing her again, and now there was a hunger, a heat in his mouth that she welcomed, that she shared. He stroked her body as they kissed, his hands skimming over her shoulders, her breasts, her hips. He slipped his hand between her legs, and despite the fact that he had seemed driven only seconds earlier, his fingers were tender as first they probed, then began stroking her, so softly that she groaned and pressed against his hand for more.

"Sit down," he said, and she lowered herself to the bed. He laid her back on the blanket and then knelt by the side of the bed, drawing her legs over his shoulders and letting his mouth finish the work of his hands. She understood immediately what he had meant about it being over too quickly. It had been so long since she'd been touched this way, this intimately. Her orgasm was sudden, and almost unbearably intense, bringing with it a fresh rash of tears she didn't understand.

He lifted her more fully onto the bed and was quickly inside her, pinning her beneath him in a way that gave her one brief, irrational moment of panic, that made her wonder if he was still angry. No. The thrusting of his body was careful and controlled, and it felt good. *Very* good. He moved in a way that was new to her, with a depth and pressure that took her straight back to a climax and renewed her weeping as she wrapped her legs around him to spur him on to his own release.

The stillness of the room was nearly overwhelming after the frenzied activity of the last few minutes. She tried to keep the sound of her tears out of her breathing. She did not want him to know. He had touched her everywhere. He had explored her body in intimate ways, yet he had carefully avoided her stomach, carefully avoided the evidence of her husband.

She turned her head to kiss his jaw. He was so still, so quiet.

He lifted himself from her before she was ready to lose him, briefly touching his lips to her forehead as he slipped out of her and rolled onto his back. His semen seeped from her body to the blanket, and the cool air of the house hit the dampness of her skin and made her shiver.

"Alec?" she said softly.

He found her hand in the darkness and held it on his stomach. "I didn't leave a note for Lacey," he said. "I should probably get going."

He sounded empty. She closed her eyes. "What was this all about?" she asked quietly, forcing the words past the tightness in her throat. "Why did you come here tonight? Was it vengeance? Were you using me because you thought I used you?"

He raised himself up on his elbow to look at her. The reflected moonlight filled his eyes, made them look like translucent glass, blue marbles. "Did you feel used?" he asked. "Is that how it felt to you?"

She shook her head. "But you seem very distant. You seem...let down, as though it was Annie you wanted and Olivia you got, and I just don't measure up in bed any more than I did in her studio."

"Olivia," he said, his voice a quiet reprimand. He smoothed her hair back from her face.

She drew the edge of the blanket over her breasts. "When Paul and I made love back in April, he told me he had to imagine I was Annie before he could...feel anything. I thought maybe that's what you were doing, and then..."

Alec interrupted her. "Oh, Olivia," he said, smiling. He shifted a little on the bed so there was more blanket for her, and he tucked it beneath her shoulders. "Do you ever have it wrong. Want to hear how wrong you have it?"

She nodded.

He lifted her hand to his lips, and the moonlight shimmered in the gold braid of his wedding ring. "For the past month or so, when I try to think about Annie, you always get in the way. I'd try to remember making love to her, and the only image I get in my mind is of that night in your living room."

"Then why are you suddenly so distant? Why do you want to leave?"

He didn't answer right away.

"Is it the baby?" she asked.

He nodded. "Partly, yes." He sighed and rolled onto his back again, looking up at the ceiling. "Everything's wrong about this, Olivia. *Everything.* Here we are, making love in your husband's bed. He could come over here any second. What would I do then? Hide in the closet? Climb out the window?"

"Paul and I are *separated,* Alec."

"It makes me feel...*sleazy.*"

Olivia winced. She did not feel sleazy. She felt no guilt at all.

"Paul still loves you. You can see that, can't you? If he didn't, he wouldn't have been so angry when he saw you in the studio," Alec said. "He wouldn't care that much. It's Paul who should be here in this bed with you, not me. This is just plain wrong." He let go of her hand. "But that's still not all of it."

He stood up and began to dress. Olivia pulled herself up to sit against the headboard of the bed. When he'd zipped his jeans he sat back on the bed and looked over at her. "Annie's been gone such a short time," he said. "Just eight months. After nearly twenty years, eight months is nothing. I'm still too much...Annie's husband, and I feel as though I'm betraying her somehow." He chuckled, but the clear blue of his eyes had clouded over. "This sounds a little...I don't know, melodramatic, I guess, but a few years ago Annie had to have surgery and she thought she might die. She asked me to promise that if she died, I wouldn't get involved with anyone for at least a year. She needed to know she was so well-loved that I couldn't even consider seeing someone else." He smiled at the memory. "Well, of course I never thought she'd die. Even if she did, I couldn't imagine being able to care enough about another woman to get involved again for a very long time. When I came over here tonight, I put memories of Annie out of my mind, but when we finished making love, it just hit me. *Wham.*" He looked out at the sound. "I can see her face. I can remember her asking me..." He shook his head quickly, then looked over at her. "See what I mean?" He smiled. "It's just too soon for me, Olivia." He stood up again, picking up his rugby shirt from her dresser, and Olivia wiped the tears from her face while his back was turned.

"I'm sorry," he said as he straightened the collar of his shirt. "I didn't mean to use you any more than you meant to use me." He sat on the edge of the bed again to put on his tennis shoes. "I'm going to call Paul tomorrow, just to clear the air. He and I are into this lighthouse thing too deeply for either of us to just walk away from it. And I want you to tell him about the baby. Please, Olivia. For my sake, all right?"

He finished tying his shoes and looked over at her. "Because once he knows, it will straighten him out. He'll want you back. We both know that, and once you're back with him, I'll be able to get on with my life without thinking about you every damn minute of the day. Will you tell him?"

Her voice was thick when she answered. "As soon as he's calmed down enough to hear it," she said, knowing she would not want to tell him even then, because Alec was right. Once Paul knew, he *would* want her back, but she was not at all certain that she wanted *him*.

"Make that very soon, okay?" Alec stood up and walked to the door, where he stopped and looked back at her. He had stepped out of the moonlight and he was no more than a shadow in the doorway.

"I've been thinking lately that maybe Annie was wrong about some things," he said softly. "She was such a powerful person—such a *charismatic* person—that I went along with her whether I agreed with her or not. It was just...easier. I always found her endearing—her wackiness, her disorganization, the way she could never get anywhere on time. You are entirely her opposite, Olivia. There's no way you could ever be like her, don't you see that? I've appreciated all those things in you that are unlike her. Sex with you was different. I knew it would be. You actually *like* it." She could not see him, but she heard the smile in his voice. "I feel *guilty* that I appreciate that in you, because then I have to admit that maybe things weren't as good with Annie as I tried to make myself believe they were." He paused. She heard the air conditioner come on, felt the cool shaft of air on her throat.

"I'm rambling," Alec said. "I guess what I'm trying to say is that I think I at least owe her the year I promised her. And you owe it to Paul to tell him he's going to be a father." He paused again, and she hugged her knees to her chest. "You're very quiet," he said.

"I love you, Alec."

She followed his dark shadow as he walked toward her, as he slipped back into the light, real again. He leaned down to kiss her, his lips light and warm against her own. Then he turned and left the room.

CHAPTER FORTY-EIGHT

Lacey was asleep when he got home. She had been sticking to her curfew. Friday night she didn't even go out. Olivia had been right. Although Lacey offered verbal protests, she seemed to welcome the restrictions on her freedom. He'd hear her on the phone, complaining to her friends. "My dad won't let me stay out that late," she'd tell them, a sort of perverse pride in her voice.

It was nearly one. Really too late to talk to Paul, but he would not be able to sleep until he did. He needed to have this discussion behind him. He went to the den for his address book and sat down at the desk to dial Paul's number.

"Hello?" Paul sounded wide awake. Alec heard music in the background. Something instrumental. Classical.

"It's Alec, Paul, and it's one o'clock in the morning, so let me start by apologizing if I woke you up."

"I'm awake," he said. "Is something wrong?"

Alec laughed. "That's an understatement." He flipped idly through the pages of his address book while he spoke. "Look," he said, "you need to know that I was at the studio when you came in this morning. I heard everything you said."

There was silence on Paul's end of the phone, and Alec continued.

"I wish you'd been honest with me," he said. "You had a thing for Annie. I would have understood. She was very easy to have a thing for."

"Did...had Olivia already told you that?"

"No. She'd told me you left her because you were in love with someone you couldn't have. She never told me who it was."

"Did she... What did she tell you? I mean, did she explain to you that it was just..."

"Relax." He felt sorry for Paul. "She told me it was platonic, if that's what you're worried about."

Paul was quiet for a minute. "You were lucky to be married to her," he said. "I'm jealous of you for that."

"You have nothing to be jealous about. Olivia's a wonderful person. She's pulled my family back together." He remembered Paul asking Olivia if she had slept with him. He hoped the question did not come up now.

"I don't understand what got into her, with the stained glass and all," Paul said. "That's so unlike her. She really went off the deep end."

"If you think she's behaved strangely, maybe you need to take a look at yourself. You left her because you had a crush on a dead woman, for Christ's sake." He looked at the picture of Annie on the wall above his desk. She was sitting on a split rail fence, winking at him, grinning. "Have a little compassion, okay?" he continued. "Olivia was so upset when you walked out that she would have tried anything to get you back."

Paul sighed. "I haven't been able to get Annie out of my mind."

"Annie's dead, Paul, and I'm the widower. You have a wife who's alive and beautiful and who still cares about you. You're throwing away something that's real for something that doesn't exist."

"I know that," he said quietly.

He'd come to the *S*'s in his address book, and he let his fingers pause there, on Olivia's name. "There's something Olivia needs to tell you," he said.

"What?"

"Just talk to her. Tomorrow." He yawned, suddenly tired. "And by the way, don't forget that Mary Poor's giving you and Nola and me a tour of the keeper's house Tuesday morning."

"You still want me on the committee?"

"Of course."

Paul hesitated. "Someone else could write up the part about the keeper's house."

"No one on the committee writes the way you do. I'll see you about nine then?"

"All right."

Alec was exhausted when he got off the phone. He fell into bed, but could not sleep. Olivia's scent was still on him, and for some reason every time he closed his eyes he saw her in the emergency room, telling the man with the lacerated arm that the ER was not a McDonald's. The memory made him laugh out loud.

He should never have gone to her house tonight. He knew what would happen—he'd *intended* it to happen. He hoped Olivia could have her soul-baring talk with Paul without throwing in that minor detail. It was one thing to covet a man's wife; it was quite another to sleep with her.

He woke up tired in the morning, his sleep interrupted by nightmares about the lighthouse and fantasies of Olivia. He got out of bed and frowned into the bathroom mirror. It had been a while since he'd seen those dark circles around his eyes. He looked like someone out of a horror movie, someone haunted.

Downstairs, he took Annie's tool case from the closet in the den and carried it into the kitchen, setting it by the back door. Then he poured himself a bowl of cereal and a cup of coffee.

He had to see the lighthouse today. He needed more pictures of it before they moved it, because once it was moved it wouldn't be the same. The view would be different. The air around the gallery wouldn't smell the same. It wouldn't *feel* the same.

He opened the drawer next to the refrigerator and took out the stack of lighthouse pictures. It had been many weeks since he'd looked through them. He propped them up against his juice glass and sat down to eat.

"Dad?"

He looked up to see Lacey in the doorway of the kitchen.

"Hi, Lace," he said.

"Are you okay?"

"Sure. Why?"

"You look...I don't know." She sat down at the table and hugged her arms across her chest. Her eyes fell to the photographs on the table. "Why do you have *them* out?"

"Oh, I don't know," he said, lifting the top picture, one he had taken from inside the lens itself. The landscape was upside down in the curved glass. "I was looking through them to see if I've missed anything. I want to make sure I've got every angle of it before they move it."

Lacey scrunched up her face. "You have every possible angle anybody could ever have, Dad."

Alec smiled. "Maybe."

Lacey took an orange from the fruit bowl in the middle of the table and began rolling it back and forth between her hands. "Do you want to do something today?" she asked.

He looked across the table at her, surprised. "What did you have in mind?"

"I don't know. Anything. You can choose."

"Do you want to go to the lighthouse with me?"

"Dad." She looked bruised, and he thought she was going to cry. "Please don't start going there all the time again. *Please.*"

"I haven't been in a long time, Lacey."

"I *know.* So why do you have to go today?" She did start crying now. She raised her feet to the chair and hugged her legs to her chest. The orange rolled off the table and she didn't seem to notice. "I don't get it," she said. "I get up this morning and all of a sudden everything's, like, gone back the way it was."

"What do you mean, back the way it was?"

Her eyes had found Annie's tool case by the door. "Why is that there?" she asked, pointing.

"I'm going to drop it by the emergency room for Olivia."

"She can come *here* to use it."

He shook his head. "She can't come over here anymore, Lace. She needs to spend her time with her own family, not with us."

"She doesn't *have* a family."

"She has Paul."

Lacey made a disdainful noise. "He's an asshole."

Alec shrugged. "Regardless of what you think of him, he's still her husband."

"I thought you liked her."

"I *do* like her, Lacey, but she's a married woman. Besides, Mom hasn't been gone all that long."

"Mom's *dead*." Lacey glared at him. "She's burned up into fifty million little ashes that the sharks probably ate for dinner the night after her funeral. She's nothing but *shark* shit, now, Dad."

If he'd been sitting closer to her, he would have slapped her. So it was just as well the table was between them. Her cheeks reddened quickly. She had frightened herself.

"I'm sorry." Her voice was small and she kept her eyes glued to the table. "I'm really sorry I said that, Daddy."

"She was a very special person, Lace," he said, gently. "She can't be replaced."

Lacey was quiet for a moment. She drew invisible lines on the table with her fingertips. "Can I still call Olivia?"

"Sweetheart." He set down the picture. "You have a reasonable curfew now, so I really don't see much point to you disturbing her every night, do you?"

"But...when would I get to talk to her?"

She looked waiflike, with her funny hair and red nose, and her big, sad blue eyes. "I'm sorry, Lace," he said. "I let things get out of hand and you got caught in the middle. Why don't you call her...not today, though, she has some things to work out today...but in a few days, and then you and she can arrange how and when you can talk. You're welcome to talk with her if she's willing, but I'm not going to be seeing her anymore."

Olivia was taking a quick lunch break in her office when Kathy brought in the tool case and set it on her desk.

"Alec O'Neill left this for you," she said.

Olivia nodded. "Thanks, Kathy."

"And there's a compound fracture on its way in."

"Okay. I'll be right there."

She set down her peach as Kathy left the room, and opened the case, spreading it flat. The tools were neatly arranged, as she had left them the last time she was at Alec's. Tucked into one of the pockets was a white envelope with her name on it, and inside she found a note in Alec's handwriting.

Tools are for you, for as long as you want them. Put them to good use. I spoke to Paul last night—he knows you need to talk to him. Lacey's upset to learn you aren't coming over anymore. I told her she could call you in a few days. Hope that's okay with you. I wish you the best, Olivia.

Love, Alec

She was not going to cry again. Absolutely not. Still, she needed a minute to herself. She hit the lock on her office door and turned to lean her back against it, eyes closed, arms folded across her chest, and she stood that way until the distant sound of the ambulance siren brought her back to life.

CHAPTER FORTY-NINE

A young girl was standing on the sidewalk in front of the retirement home. Mary had just finished the crossword puzzle when she looked up from the rocker to see the girl shading her eyes and looking, Mary thought, directly at her. The girl started up the walk, and Mary dropped the folded newspaper to the floor.

"Are you Mrs. Poor?" the girl asked when she reached the porch. She had very odd hair. Bizarre. Red on top and black at the ends. Mary knew who she was. She recognized the vibrant red the girl had tried to cover up. She knew that fair, freckled skin, and those wide blue eyes and deep dimples.

"Yes, young lady," she said. "What can I do for you?"

The girl pointed to the rocker next to Mary. "Is it okay if I sit here?"

"Well, now, I wish you would."

"My name is Lacey," she said, sitting down. "I'm Annie O'Neill's daughter... Do you remember her?"

Mary chuckled. "As well as I remember my name," she said. "You look like your mama, don't you?"

Lacey nodded, then touched her hair. "Except for this," she

said. She glanced out at the waterfront and then returned her eyes to Mary, leaning sideways in the chair. "This is going to sound pretty weird, I guess, but I know my mother used to talk to you when she had a problem, so I was wondering... Well, I just thought I could, like, try it, too."

"What kind of problem can a young girl like you have?"

"It's really complicated." Lacey looked at her uncertainly, thinking, no doubt, that Mary was older than she'd expected her to be, too old to help a young girl out of a predicament.

"You don't happen to have a cigarette, now, do you?" Mary asked.

"What?" Lacey looked stunned. Then she stood up and pulled a crushed pack of Marlboros from the pocket of her shorts. "I don't really think I should give you one," she said, holding the pack away from Mary. "Aren't you, like... I mean... Isn't it bad for your health?"

"No worse than for yours." Mary held out her hand, and Lacey rested the beautiful tube of tobacco on her fingers. Mary lifted the cigarette to her lips, inhaling deeply as Lacey lit it for her. She began to cough—*hack, actually*—until tears ran down her cheeks, and Lacey patted her worriedly on the back.

"I'm all right, child," Mary was finally able to say. "Oh, that's lovely, thanks." She gestured toward the rocker next to her. "Now sit down again and tell me your problem."

Lacey slipped the cigarettes back in her pocket and sat down. "Well." She looked at the arm of the chair, as though what she had to say was written there. "My father got really depressed after my mother died," she said. "He'd just sit around the house and stare at pictures of the Kiss River Lighthouse all day long, because they reminded him of Mom, and he didn't go to work and he looked awful."

Mary remembered the year following Caleb's death. Lacey could have been describing her back then.

"Then my Dad started being friends with a woman named Olivia, who was also the doctor who tried to save my mother's life in the emergency room the night she was shot..."

"She *was?*" Mary remembered the young woman who'd dropped magazines off at the home. She'd had no idea Olivia was a doctor, much less the doctor who'd tried to help Annie. And married to Paul Macelli, wasn't she? Good Lord, what a mess. She drew again on the cigarette, cautiously this time.

"Yes." Lacey had taken off her sandals and raised her feet to the seat of the chair, hugging her arms around her legs. It was a position Annie might have squirmed her way into. "Anyway," she continued, "she's married to Paul Macelli, the guy who's been talking to you about the lighthouse. But she's really in love with my father."

Mary narrowed her eyes. "Is she now?"

"Oh, definitely. I can tell by the way she talks about him and stuff. And the thing is, he really likes her too, but he says he won't see her anymore, partly because she's married, even though she's actually separated, but mostly because he thinks it's too soon since my mother died for him to feel that way." Lacey stopped to catch her breath. "She's not much like my mother," she said, "and that bothers him, I guess. I really loved my mother, but everybody talks about her like she was a *goddess* or something."

Lacey looked up as Trudy and Jane walked out onto the porch. Their eyes bugged out when they caught sight of Mary's cigarette. Mary nodded to them, and they seemed to understand she wanted time alone with her young visitor. They walked down to the end of the porch and sat in the rockers there.

"Well, anyway," Lacey said, "so now my Dad's gone back

into this little cocoon he was in before he got to be friends with Olivia. He looks bad, and he thinks about the lighthouse all the time, and I can't stand being around him. He gets so weird. And *Paul.* I don't understand why Olivia would like him more than my father. He's so dorky."

Mary smiled. She was not sure what *dorky* meant, but she was certain the girl's assessment was accurate.

"Excuse me for saying that. I guess he's, like, a friend of yours since you've been talking to him about the lighthouse and all."

"You can say whatever's on your mind, child."

Lacey lowered her feet to the porch and sat back in the chair, her head turned toward Mary. "Did I explain this well enough? Can you see what the problem is?"

Mary nodded slowly. "I can see the problem far better than you can," she said.

Lacey gave her a puzzled stare. "Well," she said, "my mother always said you were a very wise woman. So if she came to you with a problem like this, how would you help her?"

Mary took in a long breath of clean air and let it out in a sigh. "If I had truly been a wise woman, I would never have helped your mother at all," she said. But then she leaned over to take the girl's hand. "You go home, now, child, and don't worry yourself over this. It's a matter for grown-ups, and I promise you I'll attend to it."

CHAPTER FIFTY

Mary had a plan. Some might say it was cruel, but she could think of no other way to change the destructive legacy Annie had left behind her. Three people's lives were in turmoil. Four, actually, if she counted Annie's daughter. She would have to play the old, eccentric fool—a role she was not fond of, but which she knew how to employ when necessary. It would be necessary tomorrow, when she took the members of the committee on their tour of the keeper's house. And it would be necessary now, when she called Alec O'Neill to make her demand.

She steeled herself for the phone call, using the private phone in Jane's room so that no one would hear her and wonder what the hell was going on with old Mary. It rang three times before Alec answered it.

"Hello, Mary," he said. "We're all set for nine o'clock to-morrow. Is that still a good time for you?"

"Perfect," Mary said. "Perfect. Now who did you say is coming along?"

"Myself, and Paul Macelli, and one of the women on the committee, Nola Dillard."

"Ah, well, I won't be able to do it then."

"I...what?"

"I'll take you and Mr. Macelli and his wife. The doctor."

"Olivia?"

"Yes. Olivia. The young lady who brought magazines here a few weeks ago. Just the three of you."

"Uh, Mrs. Poor, I don't understand. Olivia really has no need to be there, and I believe she has to work tomorrow. Nola, on the other hand, has been a very active member of the committee from..."

"No," Mary said. "Nola is not invited. I'll take you and Mr. Macelli and his wife and that's it. Otherwise there's no tour."

"But if she's working..."

"Then we'll pick a day for the tour when she's not working."

Alec was quiet for a moment. "Well," he said, "all right. I'll see what I can do."

"Good. I'll see you in the morning, then."

Alec hung up the phone, frowning. That was weird. Mary Poor must finally be losing it. He sat at his office desk for a few minutes, debating his options. Then he picked up the phone again and called Olivia.

"This puts you in an awkward position, I know, but could you do it, please? One last favor?"

"Paul's going to be there?"

"He needs to be there. You, on the other hand... I guess you made an impression on the old woman."

"Well," she said, "I suppose it's good in a way. It'll force me to see Paul. I'll finally have to tell him about the baby."

"You still haven't done that?"

"I haven't talked to him at all. He's left messages for me to call him, but I've been avoiding the situation."

"Olivia." He wished she would get this over with. "What are you waiting for?"

She didn't answer.

"It's none of my business, right?" he said. "Well, would you please call Paul to let him know the change in plans? I have to call Nola and uninvite her."

CHAPTER FIFTY-ONE

"There is no earthly reason for you to go on that tour, Olivia," Paul said.

She held the receiver between her chin and shoulder as she opened a can of cat food for Sylvie. "I'm aware of that," she said, "but apparently Mary Poor refuses to do it if I don't go."

Paul groaned. "Christ. She's so damn...controlling. How does she even know you exist?"

Olivia tensed. "I met her one time when I dropped Tom's old magazines off at the retirement home."

Paul was quiet for a moment. "Was that something else Annie used to do?" he asked.

"Yes." She didn't offer him any more information than that. She didn't like him just then.

"Why haven't you returned my phone calls?" he asked.

"I haven't wanted to talk to you."

"That's not what your good friend Alec told me. He said there's something important you need to talk to me about."

Olivia set Sylvie's bowl on the floor. "Well, actually, I do have a lot to tell you—to straighten out with you. Could we go out for an early lunch somewhere after the tour tomorrow?"

"All right," he said. "You're not going to show up for the tour with your hair dyed red or anything, are you?"

She gritted her teeth. "You can be very cruel."

He hesitated again. "I'm sorry," he said. "I just feel as though you've become a stranger all of a sudden. You've been living a life I know nothing about."

"You're the one who wanted it that way."

"I know." He drew in a weary-sounding breath. "I'll see you in the morning."

Olivia pulled into the small parking lot near the keeper's house at nine the following morning. Paul and Alec were already there, leaning against Alec's Bronco. She felt their eyes on her as she parked next to Paul's car, and she took a deep, steadying breath. Could there be a more awkward group than the three of them? She smoothed her blue jersey over her new white drawstring pants and got out of the car.

Seeing Paul and Alec side by side was unnerving. Two very attractive men. As she walked toward them, she felt a little of the sleaziness Alec had spoken of the other night. She had slept with both of them.

Alec looked a little tired. He smiled his greeting at her, holding her eyes a moment too long. There was a camera around his neck, a camera case over his shoulder, and he wore jeans and a blue short-sleeved shirt, the dark hair on his chest clearly visible at the open collar. She quickly moved her eyes to the relative safety of her husband.

"Good morning, Paul," she said.

He nodded stiffly. She didn't think she had ever seen him look quite so uncomfortable.

She was relieved when the van from the retirement home

pulled into the parking lot. Alec helped Mary down from the passenger seat, his hand on the old woman's elbow. Mary was wearing a white-and-blue-striped dress and white sneakers.

A young blond woman jumped out of the driver's seat, a paperback book in her hand. "I asked Mary if I could do the tour with y'all, but she said no way." She grinned. "When Mary says no, you don't argue. So I'll be out on the beach."

Mary watched her young driver strike out for the beach before turning to her uneasy guests. "Good morning, Mr. Macelli. Mrs. Macelli," she said.

"Hello, Mrs. Poor," Olivia said, and Paul grunted a barely audible greeting.

Mary turned her gaze to the house. "It's been a good long time since I've set eyes on this place," she said. "I thought for sure I'd never see it again." She looked toward one of the bulldozers near the edge of the dune and shook her head. "Well, let's take a look inside."

They followed Mary slowly to the front door of the house. She walked with the aid of a cane. She was taller than Olivia had expected her to be, and she looked very old, much older than she'd seemed at the home.

Alec walked next to Mary, with Olivia a few steps behind them, and Paul behind her. Olivia glanced back at her husband once, encouraging him to keep pace with her, but he looked straight through her. He seemed very unhappy about this entire outing, and she figured that her presence was the cause of his dismay.

They walked into the spacious, airy living room of the house. There was a large brick fireplace, faced by two wicker rockers and a wing chair. Paul clicked on his tape recorder, while Mary turned around in a circle in the middle of the room.

"Needs a paint job in here," she said, lifting her cane

toward one of the dingy walls. "I never would have let it get this gray."

Alec took a few pictures while Paul stood rigidly in the center of the room, holding the recorder in his outstretched palm.

"Well, let's see. What can I tell you about this room?" Mary asked herself. "It was, of course, the hub of the household. When Elizabeth was young, she and Caleb and I would play games in here at night, and I remember a few nights when this room would be filled with survivors of one wreck or another. We'd keep them for a few nights or so, till they could get back to the mainland." She looked down at the wicker rocker. "I did many a crosswords in that chair, I can tell you that," she said.

It was, if anything, slightly cool in the living room, yet Olivia could see that Paul was perspiring. He pulled his handkerchief from his pocket and wiped his forehead. She couldn't imagine that her presence alone was enough to have drained all color from his face. She wanted to ask him if he was ill, but it was too quiet in the room. He wouldn't want the attention drawn to himself.

They walked into the kitchen. "The damn room I fell and broke my hip in." Mary touched Alec's arm. "If it weren't for that wife of yours, I'd still be lying there on that floor."

Alec smiled at her.

Mary told them about the hand pump that used to stand in one corner of the kitchen, and the cisterns that collected rainwater to be used in the house. She showed them the pantry and the large downstairs bedroom, along with the tiny bathroom that had been added on in the sixties.

"Upstairs now," the old woman said, lifting her cane toward the narrow stairway.

Alec and Paul practically carried Mary up the stairs, each

of them taking an elbow and nearly lifting her off her feet as they climbed to the second story. They stopped at the first room on the right, a large bedroom with rustic furniture and a quilt on the bed.

"Caleb's mother made that," Mary said, pointing her cane at the quilt. She began talking about the room. It had been the bedroom of her daughter Elizabeth, she said, whose boyfriend had set a ladder against her south window one night, and carried her away with him to escape the isolation of Kiss River.

Paul was not well. He closed his eyes as Mary spoke, and his breathing was fast and shallow. Olivia could actually see the staccato beating of his heart in the collar of his shirt. She leaned toward him. "Are you ill?" she whispered.

He shook his head without looking at her, and she took a step away from him. Mary spoke about Elizabeth's bedroom a few minutes longer, and Alec took some pictures before they moved on to the next room, another bedroom, this one much smaller than the first. Olivia saw the white spire of the lighthouse through the window.

"And this one was Annie's room," Mary said. They stood in the hallway, peering inside.

"*Annie's* room," Alec said. "You mean...*my* Annie?"

"Yes indeed," Mary said. "The room where Annie brought her young men."

"Where she...?" Alec frowned. "What are you talking about?"

Mary turned to look squarely at Paul. "*You* know what I mean, don't you, Mr. Macelli?"

The Adam's apple bobbed in Paul's throat. His face had gone gray, and his fingers shook as he turned off the recorder and hung it on his belt. "I have no idea," he said.

"Oh, I think you have a very good idea," the old woman

said. "An *excellent* idea. She loved the way you looked when you'd come over in your costume. You know, from the *Lost Colony* play."

Alec turned to face Paul. "What is she talking about?"

Paul shook his head. "God only knows." He looked at Mary and spoke loudly. "You have me confused with someone else," he said.

Olivia could barely breathe. She wished she could do something to break the tension crackling in this hallway. She wished she could stop Mary Poor from saying another word, but the old woman was already opening her mouth, already pointing her cane toward the double bed.

"How many afternoons did the two of you spend in that bed?" she asked Paul.

"I've had enough." Paul turned toward the stairs, but Alec caught his arm.

"What's going on, Paul?" he asked. "I think you'd better tell me."

Paul faced them again, but he shut his eyes. He took off his glasses, rubbing the reddened patches of skin where they had rested on either side of his nose. He looked miserably at Mary. "Why are you doing this?" he asked the old woman, his voice very soft. "What possible good can it do?"

Mary shrugged. "I guess that's up to you."

He hesitated a moment before putting his glasses on again and shifting his eyes to Alec. "I *did* know Annie at Boston College," he said.

"*Paul,*" Olivia said, stunned.

"The truth is," Paul said to Alec, "I knew her long before you did. We had a relationship. A very *serious* relationship. We were together for two years before you ever met her, before you even had a clue she existed." There was a weird sort of pride in his voice. "She was mine long before she was yours. That blue cloisonné horse in your kitchen? I gave it to her. She loved it. She *treasured* it." Paul looked at the floor for a moment, as if collecting himself, as if trying to decide what to say next. Olivia didn't dare look at Alec, but she could hear the raw sound of his breathing.

"We talked about getting married," Paul said. "About raising a family." A slight smile played with the corners of his lips. "We even had names picked out for our kids, but then the summer after our sophomore year she met you and broke it off with me. The problem was, I could never get her out of my mind." He looked pleadingly at Alec, as though surely Alec could understand. "How could anyone know Annie and just forget about her?"

Alec shook his head, almost imperceptibly. "No," he said. "Please don't tell me you..." His voice trailed off and Olivia rested her hand on his back. She wanted to hold him, to slip her hands over his ears so he would not hear whatever Paul had left to say.

"Paul," she said. "Maybe that's enough."

He didn't seem to hear her. "I came down here one summer, years ago." Paul folded his arms across his chest, then unfolded them. He slipped his hands into his pants pockets, took them out again. "I got an apartment and a part in the *Lost Colony* play." He was no longer looking directly at Alec. Rather, his eyes were focused on the floor of the small bedroom. "I saw Annie and realized there were feelings left—on both sides. We...a few times we met here." He glanced up at Alec and nodded toward the bedroom.

"Annie wouldn't..." Alec looked at Mary. "Is this true?"

Mary nodded solemnly, and for the first time Olivia realized that she was behind this confession. She had orchestrated it.

Alec glowered at Paul, but when he spoke, his voice was little more than a whisper. *"Bastard,"* he said.

"I think..." Paul blinked rapidly and returned his gaze to the floor. "I've always thought that Annie might have been pregnant when I left the Outer Banks. She was very upset, and when I interviewed her for the article in *Seascape,* she lied to me about Lacey's age." He looked up at Alec, patches of crimson on his cheeks. "I'm truly sorry, Alec, but I think Lacey may be my daughter."

Mary made a sudden sound of annoyance. "Lacey's no more your child than I am," she said. "Annie got rid of your child."

Alec's eyes widened. "Got rid of...?" The anger was beginning to boil up in his voice. "That's impossible. Annie would never have had an abortion."

Mary looked at Alec, and Olivia did not miss the compassion in the old woman's eyes. The sympathy. "She did," she said, "and it wasn't easy on her either. She got rid of Paul's child and one other later on."

Alec took a step toward Mary. "What the hell are you..."

"Alec." Olivia closed her hands around Alec's arm and pulled him tightly against her.

"Lacey is the child of that young man she did stained glass with," Mary said. "Tom what's-his-name?"

"What?" Paul exclaimed.

"Oh my God, no." Alec closed his eyes and leaned against the door frame as though he could no longer hold himself up. He looked at Mary again. "How can you possibly know that? How can you possibly be sure?"

"Annie was sure," Mary said. "I'd seen her upset more times than one but never like when she realized she had Tom's baby inside her. She couldn't have another abortion, she said, though later on she changed her tune about that.

But this one was just too close to the first time. It was still too fresh in her memory. So she had the baby. She never told Tom it was his, and I think by the time the little girl— Lacey—was born she'd almost convinced herself it was yours, Alec."

Mary narrowed her eyes at Paul. "Did you think you were the only one?" she asked. "Did you think you were something special Annie couldn't possibly resist? Well, let me set you straight then. You were just one of many Annie brought to this bed. She had tourists in the summer, fishermen in the fall, construction workers in the spring. It wasn't just the PTA or the Red Cross Annie couldn't say no to. It was anyone who wanted a little part of her spirit."

Paul looked as though he was about to get sick. He turned on his heel, and they listened to the clattering of his shoes on the stairs. Olivia still clung to Alec's arm, but he'd turned his head away from her as he leaned against the doorjamb, his hand to his eyes.

Olivia looked at Mary. Every year suddenly showed in the old woman's face. She looked as though she might collapse there on the landing, as though it was only the slim reed of her cane that was keeping her upright. Olivia let go of Alec and walked into the bedroom, bringing out a straight-back chair. She set it behind Mary, who lowered herself into it with a sigh. Then Mary reached out to take Alec's hand. His eyes were rimmed with red when he looked down at her.

"Listen to me, Alec," Mary said. "Listen good, all right? Annie had a need she just couldn't get taken care of. It was too big for any one man to ever make a dent in, but I know for a fact you were the only one she loved. She hated herself for what she was doing, and I hated myself for the way I helped her. In the last few years, she was winning the battle, not seeing anyone, not bringing anyone over here. It was hard for her. She was fighting her own nature and it was uphill all the way. She was winning too, and proud of herself, until *he* came back." Mary nodded toward the stairs where Paul had disappeared.

Olivia rested her hand on Alec's back again. He gazed numbly at Mary, and she was not certain he could hear the old woman's words. He was glassy-eyed; the muscles in his back were rigid beneath her hand.

"It was just the one time with Tom, as far as I know, Alec," Mary continued. "Not an ongoing sort of thing. Annie felt bad about it. Terrible. And she always wanted you to know the truth about Lacey, but she just didn't know how to tell you." Mary licked her lips. "Remember when she had that marrow surgery? She nearly told you then, because she was so afraid she'd die without you knowing, which is just what happened in the end, I guess. She didn't want to hurt you. She never wanted you to suffer because of her weakness."

Alec extracted his hand from Mary's grasp. He walked past Olivia and headed down the stairs. Olivia watched him go, as Mary sat back in the chair with a long sigh. She seemed to crumble, her body folding in on itself until she sat several inches lower in the chair than she had a moment ago. Then she looked up at Olivia.

"Did I do a terrible thing just now?" she asked.

Olivia knelt at her side, resting her own hand on Mary's. "I think you've done all of us a tremendous favor," she said.

CHAPTER FIFTY-TWO

Olivia had to get Sandy, the young woman from the retirement home, to help her walk Mary down the stairs of the keeper's house and out to the van. Both Paul's Honda and Alec's Bronco were gone by the time she crossed the parking lot on her way to the beach, and a half dozen or so workmen had appeared, milling around the bulldozer and the lighthouse.

Mary didn't say a word to either of them as they descended the stairs, and the old woman winced each time she took a step with her left leg. She was quiet out in the parking lot as well, and quiet as she climbed into the van. But once the door was closed and Sandy had helped her with the seat belt, she turned to speak to Olivia through the open window.

"You see to it that Alec's all right," she said, and Olivia nodded. That had already been her plan.

It was after eleven when she got home from Kiss River, and she walked directly into the study to call Alec. His phone rang for a long time, and she was trying to figure out what message she could possibly leave on his machine when he answered.

"Alec," she said, "I'm so sorry."

He didn't respond for a moment, and when he did, the

weariness in his voice was palpable. "I don't think I can talk right now, Olivia," he said.

She closed her eyes. "I just want you to know I'm thinking of you."

She got off the phone and walked into the kitchen. She should eat something; she had to be at the ER in less than an hour, and she wouldn't have another chance to eat until quite late. The thought of food, though, was nearly revolting. She made herself a cup of tea instead and was carrying it into the living room when Paul's car pulled into the driveway. She set the tea down and met him at the front door.

He stood on the deck, looking pale and beaten. "May I come in?" he asked.

She stepped back to let him into the living room. He lowered himself onto the rattan chair with a sigh, and Sylvie jumped onto his lap and began purring loudly. Olivia sat down on the couch, across the room from him, and lifted the cup of tea to her lips. She felt an easy, almost druglike calm settling over her.

He smiled weakly. "Well, I got my eyes opened in one fell swoop, didn't I?"

"I guess we all did."

"I piled up the rest of her stained glass and dropped it off at the studio on my way over here," he said, "with the understanding that Tom Nestor will donate it for me." He shook his head. "Tom Nestor. I never would have guessed... I never..."

"Saint Anne," Olivia said quietly.

Paul groaned. "I destroyed the tapes of the interviews, Olivia. I bashed them in with a hammer."

"How very dramatic, Paul."

He looked hurt, and she didn't bother to apologize.

"I burned her pictures, too, although I have to admit it wasn't easy."

"You didn't save a single one?"

"Nothing. There's nothing left of her."

"Good," she said. "You need to be done with her, or you're never going to be able to get on with your life."

He looked at her. "It's all been so ugly. What's happened between us, I mean. *I've* been so ugly."

She said nothing. She could hardly disagree.

"Do you still want anything to do with me?" he asked. "Do you still want to be a part of my life?"

She shook her head, slowly, as if trying out the motion to see how it felt, and he dropped his eyes quickly to the floor.

"Maybe you're just reacting to what happened this morning," he said.

She set her cup on the coffee table and leaned toward him. "I'm reacting to everything that's happened over the last year, and to all those things that happened in your past that I knew nothing about. I'm reacting to your lack of respect for your own marriage, as well as for Annie's and Alec's. Even if I could forgive you for all of that, I could never trust you again. You lied to me throughout our entire marriage."

"I *didn't,* Liv. I told you I'd had a serious relationship years ago, and you said, 'Let's put the past behind us,' remember? I would have told you all about Annie if you'd wanted to hear it."

"You never even mentioned you'd spent a summer here."

"I was trying to pretend that summer never happened."

"You should have told me Annie was here before I took the job."

"I tried to talk you out of taking it."

"If you had really wanted to dissuade me, all you had to do was tell me your former lover lived here. But you intentionally avoided mentioning that fact."

"I was wrong, Liv. I've been wrong about a lot of things. I'm sorry." He looked down at his hand, at his wedding band. "Do you still want to go out to lunch?"

The question seemed so ludicrous she laughed. "*No,* I don't want to go out to lunch."

He set Sylvie on the floor and stood up. "Well." He looked

unsure of his next move. "Is it all right if I use your bathroom before I go?"

"Of course."

He left the room, and it was a full minute before she realized he had to pass the nursery to reach the bathroom. She went rigid on the couch, listening, trying to remember if she had left the nursery door open or closed. She stood up slowly and walked into the hall, where she could clearly see that the door was wide open. She steeled herself and walked into the room.

Paul stood next to the crib, his hands on the rail. He looked over at her when she stepped into the room, and dropped his eyes to her stomach.

"Are you...?"

"Yes."

"Is it mine?"

"Of course," she said. "That night you stopped by in April. That night you pretended I was Annie."

"Oh, my God." He turned away from her, leaning heavily on the crib.

She didn't want to watch him wallow in his guilt. She walked through the house and out to the back deck, intentionally sitting in one of the chairs rather than on the settee so he would not be able to sit next to her if he came out. She watched a windsurfer gliding across the sound. He was blond. Tan. She could not guess his age from this distance, but he was good. Maybe as good as Alec.

It was a while before Paul joined her on the deck. He turned one of the chairs around so he was facing her, and very close.

"You're nearly five months?"

"Twenty-one weeks, yes."

"How are you feeling? Is everything going all right?"

"I'm fine," she said. "I'm healthy. I had an amniocentesis done, and it's a boy."

"A boy." He smiled, and she wished she'd kept that fact from him. She was irritated by the pleasure on his face.

"You should have told me," he chided. "It would have made a difference. It would have brought me back to reality."

"I wanted you to want me because I was *me,*" she said, "not because I was carrying your child."

He nodded, reaching a tentative hand out to touch her belly. She gritted her teeth, turning her head away from him so she would not have to see the emotion in his face.

"Annie made a fool of me," he said.

She snapped her head back to him, brushing his hand away. "You made a fool of yourself."

"All right," he conceded, "all right." He sat back in the chair. "Is there any way we can work things out?" he asked. "Shouldn't we try, for the sake of our son if for no other reason? You know as well as I do that we had something genuinely good for a long time."

She folded her arms across her chest. "It's over, Paul. I don't want you anymore. That's the bottom line."

He looked out at the sound, and when he spoke again, his voice was thick. "But what about the baby? I want to be involved in his life."

"Well, perhaps you should speak to that lawyer of yours about your options."

He winced, his eyes reddening behind his glasses. Then he stood up, very slowly, as if some invisible force was holding him down. She said nothing to stop him as he walked across the deck to the house. In another moment, she heard the front door open, then close.

Out on the sound, the windsurfer skimmed gracefully across the surface of the water. Olivia watched him as she lowered her hands to her lap, as she pulled the ring from her finger, slipped it into her pocket. She watched him until it was time to leave for work.

CHAPTER FIFTY-THREE

Alec dug out the old box of photographs from the closet in the den and sat down on the living room sofa to sift through them. He had not looked at these old pictures in years, and he had intentionally avoided them since Annie's death. The box was full of her. Looking through the pictures now, he could actually see in the lines of her face, or in the uncertainty of her smile, when she was going under, when she was giving in to her dark side. All those times she'd slipped into those seemingly inexplicable periods of withdrawal made sense to him now. *I'm going to die as punishment for all the bad things I've done.*

Two abortions. All the nights she'd visited Mary. Alec had been grateful to the old woman for the company she'd given Annie on those nights he'd had to work on the mainland.

Fishermen. Tourists. She would take them into that little bedroom, the one that would fill every few seconds with the light he had thought of as his and Annie's.

Alec heard the back door slam. Lacey was home. *Damn.* He'd wanted this time for himself. He *needed* it. In a moment she appeared at the door of the living room.

"I'm home," she said, proudly, "and it's only nine-fifteen." She looked at the box next to him on the sofa. "Why do you have those old pictures out?"

He stared at the girl who, quite suddenly, was not his daughter. "I just felt like looking at them," he said.

To his dismay, she came into the room and plunked herself down next to him. She smelled of tobacco. She smelled, he thought, a little like Tom Nestor.

"I really like this one," she said, reaching across him to pluck a photograph from the box. It was of her and Annie sitting side by side on the beach, taken just last summer. "Mom looks so happy," she said.

I've never been happier than I've been this last year.

Alec started to cry. He turned his head away from Lacey, but it was no use trying to hide the tears. He wouldn't be able to this time. They were going to take over. He would never be able to stop them.

"Please don't cry," Lacey said, alarm in her voice. "I can't *stand* it, Daddy, *please*." She stood up. "Do you want me to put these away?" She reached for the box, and he caught her hands.

"No," he said. "I want to look through them."

She frowned down at him. "Why are you doing it? It just gets you upset."

He struggled to smile. "I'm all right, Lacey."

She shoved her hands in the pockets of her shorts and stared at him, unconvinced. "Do you want me to look through them with you?" she asked.

He shook his head. "No," he said. "Not tonight."

She left the room, reluctantly, and Alec dug through the pictures until he found the few he had taken of Annie when she was pregnant with Lacey. She'd been constantly sick during that pregnancy. She could keep almost nothing down, and she put on so little weight that her obstetrician came close to hospitalizing her. She'd had weird pains, which a slew of doctors were unable to diagnose, and she'd spent most of those nine months in bed, while Nola helped Alec take care of Clay.

Annie's labor with Lacey had been frightening. Neverending. Alec stayed with her, holding her hand and helping her breathe, until he thought his own body would give out. He didn't know how one woman—how one *human being*—could tolerate so much pain.

Just before Lacey was born, just in those few minutes when Annie must have felt the baby's head crowning, she began screaming for Alec to leave the delivery room. At first he thought he'd misunderstood her. She was hysterical, and he tried to pretend she did not actually say what he thought she was saying. But the doctor understood her words, and, the nurses looked at each other, perplexed.

"You'd better leave, Dr. O'Neill," one of them said. "She's so distraught. She's not going to be able to concentrate on what she has to do unless you go."

He left the room, enormously hurt. He stood in the hallway of the obstetric unit rather than go to the waiting room, where Nola and Tom and a few other friends had gathered. He wouldn't have known how to explain his presence to them.

Later, he asked Annie why she had made him go, and she wept and apologized and told him she'd been confused, she didn't know what she was saying.

How scared she must have been to have sent him away when she needed him most. How terrified that, somehow, with just one look at that newborn baby, he would know. Had she watched him carefully after that, studying *his* face every time he studied his daughter's? Had she looked for his suspicions? Had she tried to tell him the truth once or twice or dozens of times? Or did she know that never, never would he have believed her capable of anything less than complete fidelity?

He stayed up until nearly midnight, tormenting himself with picture after picture, until he was so drained he could barely climb the stairs to his room. Still, he couldn't sleep. Too many memories. Too many clues he'd missed. They'd argued about sterilization. She'd insisted she have her tubes tied rather than Alec have a vasectomy because, she said, she couldn't bear to have him go through the pain and discomfort. Coming from Annie, that explanation had sounded perfectly rational. And what about all those times she'd tried to keep Tom Nestor sober and closedmouthed around him? And all the times he'd catch her crying for no apparent reason? *Oh, Annie.*

His mind was churning. There was a coiled tightness in his muscles he had not felt in months. He needed to *do* something. *Go* somewhere. He needed to see the ligthhouse.

He got up long before sunrise and left a note for Lacey on the kitchen table. Then he drove through the dense, early-morning fog to Kiss River.

He was nearly to the lighthouse when he spotted the horses at the side of the road, and he pulled over to watch them. They looked ethereal in the fog—clearly visible one minute, mere shadows the next. He could make out the colt who had been hit by the Mercedes. He was grazing close to the side of the road; apparently he had learned nothing from his experience. Alec could see the faint scar on the colt's hindquarters where he had stitched the wound closed. With Paul's help. *The cloisonné horse. She'd treasured it.* Had she?

Alec growled at himself. He wished he could turn his thinking off. Shut it down.

He drove on to the lighthouse. The white brick blended into the fog and he could barely see it from the parking lot. He let himself in and began climbing the steel steps of the eerie, echoey tower, and he didn't stop until he reached the top. He stepped out onto the gallery. He was above the fog here, and the lantern must have shut off only minutes earlier in anticipation of daylight. The sun was rising over the sea, a breathtaking spectacle of pink and gold, lighting up the sky and spilling into the water.

Alec walked around to the other side of the gallery and looked toward the keeper's house. Through the fog, he could just make out a second bulldozer and a backhoe tucked into the bushes near the side of the house.

He sat down on the cool iron floor of the gallery, facing the ocean and the sunrise. He closed his eyes and leaned back against the black gallery wall, waiting for the lighthouse to work its usual magic on his nerves.

Had she come up here with any of them? Did she ever make love with them up here? On the beach below?

Stop it!

He opened his eyes again, drumming his fingers next to him on the floor of the gallery. He sat forward and peered over the edge of the gallery. Below him, the ocean crept ever closer to the base of the lighthouse. Through the thinning fog, he could see the white-tipped waves nibbling at the few feet of sand remaining between the water and the brick. Damn, it was close.

...we should just let it go.

Alec sat back again, slowly, a small smile on his lips. For the first time, Annie's words elicited no fear in him. None at all.

He left Kiss River and drove down the island. No one would ever guess it had been foggy an hour or so earlier.

The sun was already blazing across the Banks, and as Alec drove over the bridge into Manteo, it lit up the boats on the sound.

He parked in front of the retirement home, but that was not his destination. Instead, he walked across the street to the quaint little gray and white antique store, frowning when he noticed the *closed* sign in the front window. It had not occurred to him that it was too early for the shop to be open.

There was a car in the driveway, though. He peered through the front door and could see light coming from a room at the back of the shop. He knocked, and in a moment a woman came to the door.

She opened it a few inches. "Can I help you?" she asked. She was sixty or so, Alec guessed. Gray-haired and grandmotherly.

"I know you're not open yet, but this is important," he said. "I'm looking for an antique doll for my daughter. I think my wife used to buy them here for her."

"Annie O'Neill?"

"That's right."

She opened the door wide. "You must be Alec." She smiled. "Come in, dear. I'm Helen."

He shook the hand she offered.

"I'm so pleased to meet you," she said. "Annie bought the dolls for her daughter's birthday, right?"

"That's right. I'm a little late with it this year."

"Better late than never." Helen leaned against a glass counter filled with old jewelry. "Annie was such a good customer. Such a lovely person. She gave me that." She pointed to a stained glass panel hanging in the front window. The little gray antique shop stood against a background of grass and trees. Yet another creation of Annie's he had never seen.

"It's nice," he said.

"I was so sorry to hear about...everything," Helen said, as she led him into a small back room, where dolls sat here and there on pieces of antique furniture. One of them—an imp with red hair—caught his eye immediately.

"Oh, that one." He pointed toward the doll. "Without a doubt."

"I had a feeling you'd pick her. It's the first one with red hair I've seen, and when I got it in a month or so ago, I thought to myself, wouldn't Saint Anne have loved this one? Her face is a very high-quality pearly bisque, and she has her original human hair. That all makes her quite expensive, though." A small white tag was attached to the doll's arm, and Helen turned it over so Alec could see the price written on it.

"Wow." He smiled. "Doesn't matter."

Helen picked up the doll and carried it to the front of the store. She stuffed some tissue paper into the bottom of a large box and placed the doll inside. "Annie used to like to wrap them up herself," she said. "I think she made the paper. But I suppose...would you like me to wrap it for you?"

"Please."

She cut a length of blue and white striped wrapping paper from a roll and began taping it around the box. "Annie came in here all the time," she said, cutting off a piece of tape. "She just lit up the store. We still talk about her." She attached a premade bow to the top of the box and slid it to him across the counter. "Everyone misses her so much."

"She'd like that," Alec said, handing her a check. "I think being forgotten was one of her biggest fears."

He could hear Lacey's music blasting from upstairs when he got home, but he stopped in the den first to call Nola.

"I have some news," he said, "and you're not going to like it. Brace yourself, okay?"

"What's that, hon?"

"I'm resigning from the lighthouse committee."

There were two beats of silence before Nola spoke again. "You're joking," she said.

"No."

"Alec, *why* in God's name would you...?"

"I couldn't begin to explain it to you, Nola. I nominate you as the new chair, and I wish all of you great luck with your endeavors."

"Wait! Don't you dare hang up. You owe us an explanation, Alec. I mean, really, don't you think? What am I supposed to tell the others?"

He ran his fingers over the silky blue on Lacey's present. "Tell them I've had an epiphany," he said. "Tell them I've been set free."

He carried the box upstairs and knocked on Lacey's door. She let out a little scream. "Don't come in yet, Dad," she said.

"What's the matter?"

"Nothing. I'm not dressed. Just a second."

He heard her frantically rooting around in her room, and he wondered what he would find when he was finally allowed in.

She opened the door after a minute or two. She was dressed in her usual shorts and T-shirt, with her hair tucked under a wide-brimmed straw hat.

"What's with the hat?" he asked.

"Nothing." She was a little winded. She looked at the box in his hands. "What's that?"

"A very belated birthday gift."

She took the box from him and sat down on her bed, and he leaned against the door frame to watch her. She bit her lip as she raised the lid.

"Oh." She gasped. "She's *incredible,* Dad." She lifted the doll from the tissue paper and touched its hair. "A redhead." She looked up at him. "Where did you ever find one with red hair?"

He shrugged and looked secretive.

Lacey stood up and placed the doll in the center of the shelf above her dresser, just below the poster of a leather-vested, long-haired thug.

"Well," she said, sounding suddenly timid. "I have something to show you too, but you're gonna freak, Dad."

Alec smiled and folded his arms across his chest. "You know what, Lacey? I think I'm just about unfreakable right now. What is it?"

She kept her eyes on him as she slowly lifted the hat from her head, revealing exceedingly short red curls. She had cut off every speck of black, leaving herself with very little hair at all, but all that was there was red.

"Oh, Lace," he said. "It's beautiful." He pulled her against him, and she stayed easily in his arms. He held her close, pressing his cheek against the damp curls and breathing in the sweet, clean scent of her hair.

Someday he would have to tell her the truth about her parentage. Someday he would have to tell Tom. But not now. Right now, she was his.

CHAPTER FIFTY-FOUR

Was it this painless to end a marriage?

Olivia got out of bed with the realization that she had not once thought of Paul since he left the house the afternoon before. Of course, she had worked late last night, later than she had to, letting the patients absorb her time and attention. She'd worked until she was so exhausted that she knew sleep would be immediate and dreamless once she got in bed.

Now, as she showered, as she dried her hair, she had the feeling she was carefully holding thoughts of Paul at bay, as if letting them in, letting them get a grip on her, might be more than she could manage.

She *was* thinking of Alec, though. She had the day off, and as she busied herself with housework, she listened for the phone to ring, willing him to call. She would not call him again. He needed to work this out in his own good time.

Around noon, she reluctantly left the house to go to the store. She had two bags of groceries with her when she turned onto her street an hour later, and she spotted Alec standing on the pier behind her house. Although she was three or four houses away, her view of him was nearly unbroken, and she stopped her car to watch him. He was leaning against one of the pilings, shading his eyes to look out at the sound. An aching tenderness filled her. What a horrendous day he must have had yesterday. As stunned as she had been by what she'd learned about her husband, it could not compare to what he'd learned about his wife.

She drove on, and he must have heard her pull into the driveway, because by the time she started unloading the groceries, he was helping her.

"I'm glad to see you," she said, looking at him over the top of the car. "I wasn't sure if you'd call, and I didn't want to disturb you."

"I thought I was taking a risk coming over here." He lifted a bag of groceries into his arms. "I figured maybe Paul would be here, and I'm not ready to meet up with him yet." He stopped midway to her front door. "He's not here, is he?"

"No." She unlocked the door. "Come in."

He followed her into the kitchen and set his bag next to hers on the table. "So—" he glanced up at her as they began unloading the groceries "—have you spoken to him?"

She put a quart of milk in the refrigerator, then leaned back against the counter. "He stopped over yesterday afternoon," she said. "He was very apologetic, very distraught. Absolutely dripping with remorse." She heard the mockery in her voice and wondered if she sounded as hard to Alec as she did to herself. "He'd been a fool, he said, and he destroyed the taped interviews he'd made of Annie and burned all her pictures." She shook her head. "I guess he never did lose his flair for drama. I told him about the baby, and if guilt could kill, I would have had a dead man on my hands." She smiled ruefully. "He said he wants us to get back together, that we should try to work things out for the baby's sake, but I just..."

Her voice caught suddenly, surprising her, and she turned her face away from Alec.

"It's all right, Olivia," he said quietly. "Let it out."

She shook her head. "But I'm not *sad.*" Tears filled her eyes and she wiped at them with her fingers. "Really, I'm not."

Alec reached his arm toward her. His fingers slipped around the nape of her neck, and she let him pull her to him, shutting her eyes as his arms closed around her.

He held her, letting her cry for a long time. He offered no platitudes, no words of false comfort, as though he knew that her only chance for healing lay in her tears.

"I'm through with him." She spoke into his shoulder. "It's over. I don't love him anymore. I don't think I have for a long time." She was quiet for a moment, relishing the closeness of Alec's body, knowing this was where she wanted to be. She flattened her hand against the small of his back. "Yesterday must have been terrible for you," she said.

"Yes."

"Do you want to talk about it?"

"Sometime," he said. "But not right now."

"Mary Poor knew exactly what she was doing, didn't she?"

"Yes." Alec pulled gently away from her. "That she did." He picked up the yogurt and cottage cheese from the table and carried them over to the refrigerator. He bent down to put them on the bottom shelf, and she noticed he was not wearing his wedding ring. It had left a band of light-colored skin on his tanned finger.

When he stood up again, his eyes went to the window above the sink. "Where's Annie's peacock feather?" he asked.

"Oh," she said. "I broke it the night Paul told me that he

and Annie had..." She caught herself and looked away from him, out the window, trying to think of some way to finish the sentence without saying too much.

Alec finished it for her. "The night he told you that he and Annie had made love."

She looked up at him, stunned. "How did you know?"

"Was it just once since you've been here?"

"As far as I know."

"Just before Christmas, right?"

"Yes. But how..."

"I figured it out last night. I spent the night putting clues together. She gave me plenty, and I missed them all because it never occurred to me to look for them." He leaned back against the refrigerator. "One night, just before Christmas, she came home late from the studio and she was extremely upset. She had a sliver of glass in her hand, and she couldn't get it out herself. I took it out for her, and she cried the whole time. Then she wanted to take a bath before she came to bed. She said it would help her relax, but I guess she just wanted to wash away any evidence of Paul before she got into bed with me."

He lowered his eyes to the floor, and Olivia bit her lip.

"When I was thinking about this last night, when I was putting the clues together, I realized something must have happened between her and Paul that night, but I was hoping that maybe they didn't actually..." He looked up at Olivia. "But they did, huh? I mean," he smiled wistfully, "it wasn't just that he tried to coerce her and she steadfastly refused him?"

She returned his sad smile. "Paul said it was...a mutual thing."

He shook his head. "I didn't think you knew, Olivia. I figured that if you did, you would have thrown it up in my face when I accused you of being a less honest person than Annie."

"I considered it," she said, "but I didn't want to hurt you."

He took a step toward her and cupped her head in his palms, kissing her softly on her forehead. "Thanks," he said. "I don't think I could have handled hearing it from you just then." He rested his hands on her waist and sighed. "Now I have to figure out when and how to tell my little girl that Tom is her father."

"Oh," she said. "I hadn't thought of that. I suppose it's something she needs to know. Medical history and all of that."

He nodded. "I have to wait, though, until I can accept it myself before I can expect her to. I want to tell her in a way that won't make her think less of Annie—that will make her feel *compassion* for her. I don't think I can do that quite yet."

"You're a good father, Alec."

"I thought you had some doubts about that."

She shook her head. "About some of your methods, perhaps. But I never doubted your intentions or your love for Lacey." She touched his cheek. "Are you glad you know the truth?"

He nodded. "Yes," he said. He raised his hands until his thumbs grazed the sides of her breasts. "It's eased my guilt about loving you."

"You took off your ring," she said.

"So did you."

She smiled, pressing her forehead to his chin. "Alec...?"

"Hmm?"

"Could we go to bed?"

He laughed, his breath warm against her cheek. "Yes," he said.

They made love at a more leisurely pace than the last time. The sun outside her window poured warm, thick, honey-like air into her room and slowed them down, made them take their time. She was straddling Alec as he came, and she watched his body strain and arch in the golden light, as he must have watched hers only seconds earlier.

When his breathing had settled down, he opened his eyes and looked at her. "You look beautiful up there," he said. He stroked his fingers along the gold chain resting against her breasts. "I love you, Olivia."

She was aware of her nakedness, something that had not concerned her at all only a few minutes ago. But now she felt as though she was all stomach, the rest of her body small and inconsequential.

"It scares me to love you," she said.

"Why?"

"I just finished loving a man who wished I was Annie. I'm afraid that loving you might end up being the same thing."

He shook his head against the pillow. "I want *you*, Olivia," he said, his hands tightening on her thighs. "I want you just the way you are, with your organized mind, and your craving for structure, and your driving ambition, and your ability to put yourself first." He touched her lightly where her body was joined to his, and she shivered. "And with your genuine, and thoroughly unsubtle, carnal needs."

"And with my pregnancy?"

He slid his hands to the firm golden orb of her belly. "I've already raised and loved another man's child," he said. "I can do it again."

CHAPTER FIFTY-FIVE

September 1991

The electricity went out in the Manteo Retirement Home at about eight-thirty in the evening, and the portable radio grew scratchy and unintelligible. The residents, along with some of the staff, huddled together in the candlelit living room, taking turns playing with the knobs on the radio, fighting the dying batteries.

Mary sat off in a corner, the folded newspaper with its finished crossword puzzle resting on her knee. She didn't need the radio to know what was happening outside. She could feel the devastation in her bones.

She'd opened the window in her room a few hours earlier and let the air blow over her skin. She'd sniffed it, tasted it, and she knew the storm was very close. *It's time,* she thought. For days she'd had a feeling about this one. Even before the residents of the Outer Banks were told to evacuate, she knew this storm would be like no other. It would hit head-on, with a sudden punch at the defenseless coastline, the mere preamble to a beating that would last hours.

Trudy tried to talk her into joining a game of canasta.

"If anyone should be used to storms, it'd be you, Mary," she said when Mary declined. "Look at you, sitting there like a scared little girl."

She wasn't scared, but she didn't bother to defend herself to Trudy. She wasn't afraid at all.

She went to bed far later than usual, but still she could not sleep. The wind was ferocious. It howled eerily through the big house, and every once in a while she could hear the crackling sound of a tree snapping in two. One of the windows in Jane's room blew out during the night, and her screams brought everyone out into the hall. Jane spent the rest of the night on the pull-out sofa in the living room.

Mary finally slept a little toward morning. When she woke up, the sky was overcast and foggy, and the little circle of stained glass hanging in her window cast weak, muted colors on the walls of her room.

She joined the others downstairs in the dining room, but she couldn't eat. After breakfast, when everyone else went out on the porch to look at the downed trees and the broken windows in the neighboring houses, Mary walked into the kitchen, where Gale and Sandy, the only two members of staff who had made it in this morning, were loading the dishwasher. They looked up at her when she walked into the room.

"What is it, Mary?" Gale asked.

"I need one of you to take me to Kiss River," she said.

Sandy laughed. "You're nuts, Mary. The Outer Banks flooded last night and they said on the radio a lot of the roads are still under water. We probably couldn't get there if we wanted to."

"Please," she said. She hated this. She hated having to beg, having to depend on these young girls for everything. "I'll pay you."

Gale laughed. "With what, honey? Do you have some money tucked away we don't know about?"

Mary leaned heavily on her cane. Her hip was throbbing this morning. "If you don't take me, I'll find another way to get there."

Sandy and Gale looked at each other, finally taking her seriously. A few weeks ago, someone had gotten to Mary's puzzle before she did, and when they refused to drive her to the store for another paper, she'd walked the mile there and back herself.

Sandy slipped a plate into the dishwasher and wiped her hands on a paper towel. "All right, Mary," she said. "I'll take you. But don't expect us to get very far."

Mary rode in the front seat of the van, while Sandy drove. Sandy tried to get her to talk, but finally gave up. Mary had little to say today. She tapped her finger on the top of her cane, straining her eyes through the milky fog, trying to make out where they were.

The main road up the island was clear of water, but the storm had taken its toll on the buildings. Each time the fog thinned, just for a second or two, Mary could see glassless windows in the houses, boards and brush littering the sand. The street was peppered with shingles blown off the roofs.

They turned onto the road that ran through Southern Shores and she wondered how Annie's family had fared. Had they evacuated? Had Olivia gone with them or stayed here to doctor anyone hurt in the storm? She was head of that emergency room now. Most likely she had to stay.

Alec had invited Mary to dinner last week, and she had been surprised by the invitation, surprised that Alec held no grudge against her for her role in Annie's betrayal. Olivia had been there—obviously pregnant, a complication Mary had not even guessed at—and she and Lacey and Alec cooked while Mary sat at the kitchen table, observing the outcome of her revelations in the keeper's house. They were happy people, those three. Survivors of her last, and most likely final, rescue.

Paul Macelli had moved back to Washington, they told her, where he was working once again for the *Post* and writing poetry, reading it on the weekends to his faithful covey of followers.

"Here we go," Sandy said, as the van approached a long stretch of road that was under water. Gamely, she put the van into four-wheel drive and plunged in, and in a few minutes they were on dry road again. Sandy patted the steering wheel.

"Good girl," she said.

Mary looked out toward the sea, but the fog hugged the beach, and there was little she could make out. They hit a few more patches of flooded road before finally reaching Kiss River.

Sandy pulled onto the narrow road that led down to the lighthouse. "Wow," she said. "Lot of trees down."

Mary didn't care about the trees. She barely took note of them. Sandy stopped the car at the edge of the parking lot, and Mary managed to pull the van door open before her young driver had a chance to get out.

"Stay here," Mary said.

"No way. I'm coming out there with you."

"I don't want you with me." Mary got out of the van and slammed the door shut, surprised at her own strength.

Something in her voice must have convinced Sandy. "If you're not back in fifteen minutes, I'm coming to find you," she called out the window as Mary began walking away from the van.

Mary stepped from the paved lot to the wet sand, testing her legs, and began walking in the direction of the lighthouse. A dagger of pain cut into her left hip with each step, and her cane sank into the sand as she walked, but after a minute or two, the pain lessened and she thought no more about it.

She was nearly on top of the bayberry bushes before she saw them. The fog clung to the ground, to Kiss River, as it had many times in the past, and she had to rely on some inner sense of direction to keep herself on course. She found the path through the bushes, and once on the other side of them, could make out a couple of bulldozers and a truck laden with long, steel beams. They rested idly next to the keeper's house. She walked a bit closer to the house, squinting, looking for damage. There was a bald spot on the roof where it had lost a few shingles, but the house itself was still standing, still in one piece, as far as she could see. A few windows were blown out, though. And right next to the cistern, a backhoe was tipped precariously onto its side.

The sea must have been all the way up here, she thought. And if it had been high enough to reach the house, it had been plenty high enough to...

She turned around and squinted up into the sky for the white tower, the black iron gallery. Maybe it was just too foggy to make it out. She walked in the direction of the lighthouse, barely using her cane now at all. She kept her eyes skyward. Had she gotten confused? Was she walking in the wrong direction? In her heart, though, she knew that wasn't the answer. She'd known since last night, when she'd listened to the rain spiking against the roof of the retirement home and the wind snapping trees in half as though they were kindling. She'd known then what she would find out here today.

She took a few more steps. Quite suddenly, a gust of wind swept the fog out into the ocean, and she could see the scene in front of her as clearly as if she were looking at a painting in a museum. The sea hissed and swirled around the jagged remains of the Kiss River Lighthouse. The tower was one-third as tall as it had been, the cylinder of white bricks chewed off at an angle, and a few dozen feet of the circular stairs jutting into the thinning fog. The ground was littered with huge chunks of brick, the scene so startlingly clear that she wondered how she had missed it a few minutes earlier. The lens itself was nowhere to be seen, and she pictured it lying on the floor of the ocean, an enormous, prism-studded shell.

She glanced over at the bulldozers again, and the truck, waiting and ready to build a track that would not be needed. She shook her head, remembering the time she and Annie had sat up on the gallery and she'd told the younger woman, "If it's time for the sea to take the lighthouse, we should just let it go."

Mary could not resist a bittersweet smile at the memory. She began walking slowly back to the parking lot, the pain in her hip kicking to life once again as she shuffled through the wet sand. When she had nearly reached the row of bayberry bushes, she turned around for one last look at her lighthouse. "The time has come, Annie," she said. "It's finally come."

★ ★ ★ ★ ★

ACKNOWLEDGMENTS

I'm indebted to Cher Johnson, Mary Kirk, Arlene Lieberman, Suzanne Schmidt, Laura and Pete Schmitz and Joann Scanlon for reading various drafts of *Keeper* with enthusiasm and insight.

Veterinarian Holly Gill, emergency room physician Martha Gramlich, Outer Banks nurse Betsy McCarthy, Outer Banks artist Chris Haltigan, stained glass artist Jimmy Powers, lighthouse enthusiasts David Fischetti, Hugh Morton and John Wilson and National Park Ranger Warren Wrenn all shared their expertise with me and graciously endured my endless questions. Also, *The Keeper's Log*, issued by the United States Lighthouse Society, proved to be an invaluable source of inspiration.

I'm grateful to Peter Porosky for altering my vision and to my former editor, Karen Solem, for her faith, patience and wisdom.

Award-winning author
DIANE CHAMBERLAIN

Joelle D'Angelo's best friend, Mara, is left with brain damage after she suffers an aneurysm giving birth to her son. Alone and grieving, Joelle turns to the only other person who understands her pain: her colleague—and Mara's husband—Liam. What starts out as comfort between friends gradually becomes something more, something undeniable.

Torn by guilt and the impossibility of her feelings for Liam, Joelle goes in search of help for Mara. She is led to a healer in Monterey, California, who is keeping her own shocking secrets. But Joelle soon discovers that while some love is doomed, some love is destined to survive anything.

The Shadow Wife

Available wherever books are sold.